BOOKS BY

Cecelia Holland

Until the Sun Falls   (*1969*)

The Kings in Winter   (*1968*)

Rakóssy   (*1967*)

The Firedrake   (*1966*)

UNTIL THE SUN FALLS

UNTIL THE SUN FALLS

Cecelia Holland

AN AUTHORS GUILD BACKINPRINT.COM EDITION

Until the Sun Falls

All Rights Reserved © 1969, 2000 by Cecelia Holland

No part of this book may be reproduced or transmitted in any form
or by any means, graphic, electronic, or mechanical, including photocopying,
recording, taping, or by any information storage or retrieval system,
without the permission in writing from the publisher.

AN AUTHORS GUILD BACKINPRINT.COM EDITION

Published by iUniverse.com, Inc.

For information address:

iUniverse.com, Inc.

620 North 48th Street, Suite 201

Lincoln, NE 68504-3467

www.iuniverse.com

Originally published by Atheneum

ISBN: 0-595-00799-6

Printed in the United States of America

FOR EDWARD CRANZ,
WILLIAM MEREDITH
AND PETER SENG
All for different reasons

If Heaven grants a way, you will embark on wars beyond the sea. . . . Beyond the mountain rocks you will launch campaigns. . . . Send back news on wings.

TEMUJIN, GENGHIS KHAN

Hence fear and trembling have risen among us, owing to the fury of these impetuous invaders.

THE EMPEROR FREDERICK II

Note

Temujin, Genghis Khan, died in 1227, and his empire, which stretched from the Volga to the Yellow Sea, was divided among his heirs. According to the custom of the Mongols, Tuli, the youngest of Temujin's four sons by his first wife Bortai, received the hearthlands of the Mongol people: the territory around the Onan and Kerulan rivers; this was the core of the empire, the Mongols' home graze, the stronghold of the tribe. To the third son, Ogodai, fell the land immediately west of Tuli's portion, and the Great Kuriltai, the assembly of all the notables of the Mongols, elected Ogodai the Kha-Khan—overlord of all the world. This was according to Temujin's wish. The second son, Jagatai, received the Transoxiana—modern Uzbek and Kazakh.

The eldest of the four sons, Juji, was dead. Bortai had spent the nine months preceding his birth as a prisoner in an enemy camp, so his paternity was in dispute, and although Temujin officially acknowledged him as his son, relations between them had been strained at best. Yet his heir, his second son Batu, got a full share of the inheritance: the land from the Aral Sea to the Volga "and as far as Mongol horsemen had trod."

Although each khan was master within his own domain, the Kha-Khan was supreme over them all in what we would call foreign policy. When Batu struck west across the Volga, he did so as the servant of Ogodai Kha-Khan, and the Kha-Khan sent his great general Sabotai to serve as Batu's chief aide. Mongol tradition had awarded to Tuli the great majority of the Mongol army, and Batu recruited his troops mainly from conquered peoples. To swell their numbers, and probably to raise the general standard of discipline and talent, Batu appealed to all his relatives to come and bring their personal troops.

At this time the Mongol armies were without peer. Not for twenty years was Mongol cavalry to suffer a major defeat anywhere in the world. They were nomads, bred to the natural violence of the steppes, trained since babyhood to shoot and ride, and they considered war the chief occupation of man. They used compound bows with a pull of around one hundred sixty pounds and a killing range of up to three hundred yards. Their horses were as hardy as the men themselves, and just as highly trained. The basic unit of the army was the tuman, or ten thousand man column, subdivided into thousands, hundreds and tens. Each man was equipped with two bows and a string of led horses that he could switch to when his own mount tired.

They were tremendously mobile; often armies unused to fighting Mongols thought that they were battling several columns, when actually they were faced with only one, operating at great speed. In the European war, one Mongol tuman covered two hundred and seventy miles in three days. Speed is a hallmark of the nomad army; discipline is not. The Mongols were disciplined to drill-like precision. In an age when most commanders thought it a feat of organization if a majority of their troops arrived on the battlefield in time to fight, the Mongol generals consistently co-ordinated the movements of separated columns down to the last detail. Just how widely separated the columns could be Sabotai proved when he managed the European invasion with an army in Poland and another in Hungary communicating almost flawlessly across a rugged mountain range, in the winter. Nor were their communications with the Kha-Khan, six thousand miles away in Karakorum, less good. Mongol couriers, riding from waystation to waystation, sometimes averaged two hundred miles a day.

The army that stood poised on the Volga River in our year 1237 contained a full fifteen tumans of the finest Mongol horsemen—one hundred and fifty thousand men. In Sabotai it possessed the greatest living Mongol general, veteran of the two Khwaresm wars, of the Chinese wars, co-leader with Jebe Noyon of the great raid across the Caucasus in 1221. It also contained a number of the Altun Uruk, the

Golden Clan, descended of Temujin and bred to the World-Empire.

Their first task was to subjugate the tribes north of the Caspian—the Kipchaks, the Alans, the Old Bulgars and the Old Magyars. This they accomplished in the year before this story opens. In the attack on Russia and the invasion of Europe, I've followed the accepted timetable as closely as possible; the most important exception is that I've skipped the year between the fall of Kozelsk and the attack on South Russia, during which the Mongols rested and chased rebellious Kipchaks.

Psin and his family are my invention. The other major characters are taken from history. The only one of the Altun Uruk to whom I may have done a great disservice is Mongke, who was ten years older and probably a good deal more like his father Tuli than I've made him.

With some misgivings, I've used modern place-names almost exclusively: the references run from Korea to Vienna and sometimes it's better to be understood than right. I've tried to use the most familiar forms of the various Mongol words and proper names: thus the Turkish "Yasa" instead of the more correct "Jasagh" and "Genghis" instead of "Chingis," which I am informed is the *only* way to spell it in English.

Finally, the quotations, with the exception of the one from the letters of Frederick II, are from the *Secret History of the Mongols*. An official history of the dynasty begun during the reign of Kubulai Khan, in the 13th century, it was translated from the original Mongol into Chinese, from the Chinese into Russian, from the Russian into French, and from the French into English.

Cecelia Holland

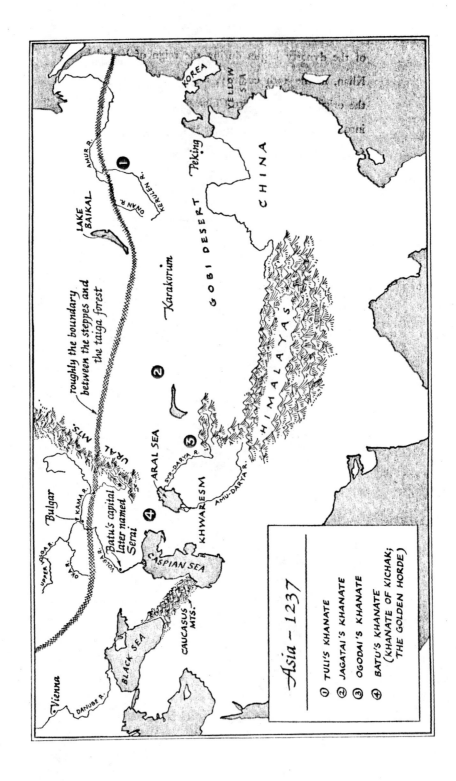

Asia – 1237

① TULI'S KHANATE
② JAGATAI'S KHANATE
③ OGODAI'S KHANATE
④ BATU'S KHANATE
   (KHANATE OF KICHAK;
   THE GOLDEN HORDE)

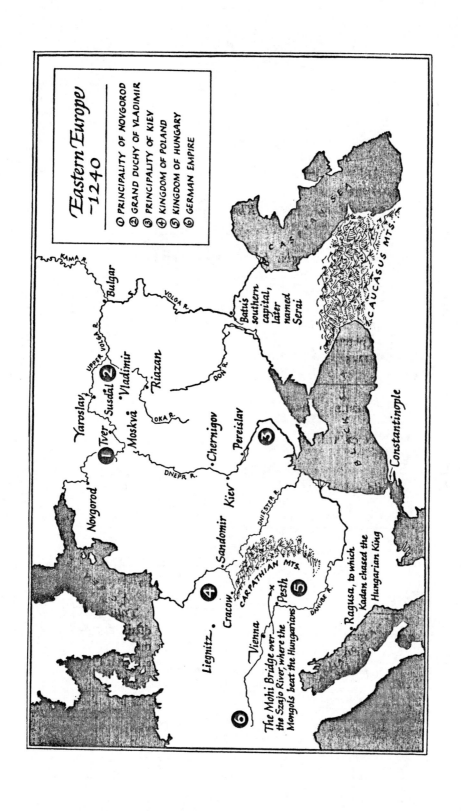

Eastern Europe
~1240

① PRINCIPALITY OF NOVGOROD
② GRAND DUCHY OF VLADIMIR
③ PRINCIPALITY OF KIEV
④ KINGDOM OF POLAND
⑤ KINGDOM OF HUNGARY
⑥ GERMAN EMPIRE

KAMA R.
Bulgar
VOLGA R.
CASPIAN SEA
UPPER VOLGA R.
Yaroslav
Tver • Susdal ② • Vladimir
Moskva • Riazan
OKA R.
DON R.
Batu's southern capital, later named Serai
CAUCASUS MTS.
Novgorod ①
• Chernigov
Pereislav ③
Kiev • Sandomir
DNEPR. R.
DNIESTER R.
BLACK SEA
Constantinople
Cracow ④
Liegnitz •
CARPATHIAN MTS.
Vienna
Pesth ⑤
DANUBE R.
• Ragusa, to which Kadan chased the Hungarian King
⑥
The Mohi Bridge over the Szajo River, where the Mongols beat the Hungarians

The Children of Genghis Khan

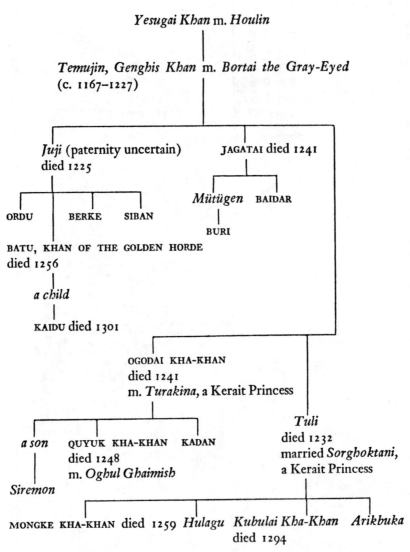

Yesugai Khan m. Houlin

Temujin, Genghis Khan m. Bortai the Gray-Eyed
(c. 1167–1227)

Juji (paternity uncertain)
died 1225

JAGATAI died 1241

ORDU   BERKE   SIBAN

Mütügen   BAIDAR

BURI

BATU, KHAN OF THE GOLDEN HORDE
died 1256

a child

KAIDU died 1301

OGODAI KHA-KHAN
died 1241
m. Turakina, a Kerait Princess

a son   QUYUK KHA-KHAN   KADAN
died 1248
m. Oghul Ghaimish

Siremon

Tuli
died 1232
married Sorghoktani,
a Kerait Princess

MONGKE KHA-KHAN died 1259   Hulagu   Kubulai Kha-Khan   Arikbuka
died 1294

Names in SMALL CAPITALS are characters in the story

Part One

QUYUK

Temujin said, "It would be seemly to get drunk only three times a month. It would be preferable, clearly, to make it only twice or even only once. It would be perfect never to get drunk at all. But where is the man who could observe such a rule of conduct?"

YE LUI HIMSELF MET PSIN AT THE DOOR AND WALKED BEHIND HIM into the anteroom. Psin looked around at the shimmer of the silk hangings and the gold filigree and sat down. "I'm hungry."

"As the Khan wishes." Ye Lui snapped his fingers at the slaves prostrated behind him. "Would the Khan prefer rice wine or kumiss?"

"Kumiss." Rice wine was a drink for effeminate Chinese. Psin glared at Ye Lui for suggesting it. The slaves pattered away, keeping their eyes averted. Psin undid the laces of his coat and threw it off. He thought of asking Ye Lui why he had been summoned, but Ye Lui would only say that he didn't know. He probably did know. The slaves returned with a dish of meat, and Psin took it and dipped his fingers into it.

"Did you ride far?" Ye Lui said.

Psin chewed and swallowed. "I came by post horse—three days riding." Let him figure out for himself how far Psin had come. He fixed Ye Lui with another glare and stuffed his mouth with meat.

The door from the corridor opened and a great hulk of a man walked in. Psin's hand paused halfway to his mouth, and he stared.

"Sabotai." He looked at the meat in his fingers and put it in his mouth.

Sabotai settled himself down on cushions. He wore silk clothes, and his hair and thin grey beard were neatly combed. "I came as soon as I heard you were here," he said.

Psin tossed the empty bowl to one side. A slave scurried after it. "Everyone knows why I am summoned but me." Sabotai had been with Batu Khan, fighting Alans and Bulgars and other, nameless tribes. "How does the fighting go, in the west?"

Sabotai smiled. "We have some Kipchaks yet to run down."

Ye Lui poured kumiss into two bowls. Slaves brought one to Psin and the other to Sabotai. Sabotai looked into his as if he expected to find a bug swimming there.

"I suppose they mean to send me on campaign," Psin said.

Sabotai smiled at his kumiss. "I shall leave the pleasure of telling you to the Kha-Khan."

"I have been the Khan of my clan for more than thirty years. In all that while I've taken my people to winter pasture only four times. This was the fifth. Would have been the fifth. You could have let an old man—"

Sabotai smiled. "You know the Yasa—if your clan needed you you could have refused to come."

Psin hissed through his clenched teeth.

"As for being an old man," Sabotai said; he stroked his grey beard. "Have more kumiss."

"On your father's grave," Psin said. He lifted the cup. While he drank he did not look at Sabotai.

When he set the cup down Sabotai said, "Insulting me won't get you out of this. Whom did you leave with your people?"

"Tshant." Psin wiped his mustaches on the back of his hand. "He's been the true Khan since he was old enough to walk around a yurt—his father always off on the Kha-Khan's errands."

"Well. You'll have to send for him, the Kha-Khan wants him, too."

Psin squinted at him, thinking. It had to be the western campaign. He wondered how Tshant would like that. "Where am I going?"

Sabotai shrugged.

"Why?"

"Who are we to question the Kha-Khan?"

"Khans ourselves."

"You are." Sabotai smiled. "I am not. You tried that argument with this one's father; do you think it will work any better with the son?"

"Ogodai is no Temujin." He watched a slave pouring him more kumiss. He had run foul of Temujin more than any other man who survived it; he suspected that he had amused Temujin. "You have a minor horde of the Altun with you, don't you?"

Sabotai leaned back. The silk coat rustled over his chest, and against it his vast, gnarled hands seemed rough as old wood. "Several, yes. Quyuk, Kadan, Buri, Baidar, Mongke—"

Psin winced.

"And two or three others."

"Your councils must be the awe of the west."

Ye Lui came in from the inner chamber. Sabotai glanced at him, turned back to Psin, and said, "I spend most of my time keeping them from killing one another." He rose.

"The Universal Khan awaits you," Ye Lui said, and bowed. Sabotai bowed; Psin only nodded. Ye Lui led them in.

The Kha-Khan's chamber was huge and round, cushioned in silk and hung with cloth-of-gold, carpeted to muffle all sound. Psin refused to be impressed, but it was hard work. In the middle of it, beneath a yellow canopy, the Kha-Khan sat on his gilt-trimmed dais. Jagatai sat behind him and to one side. They wore the fancy blue coats of the Yek Mongols and the gold collars of the children of Temujin; they both had their father's green eyes.

Music filtered dimly into the chamber, but Psin could see no musicians. When he and Sabotai bowed the gold of the dais reflected their feet. When they prostrated themselves the gold reflected their faces. Sabotai rose, but Psin only rocked back to sit on his heels.

Beside the Kha-Khan stood a table carved of alabaster, so thin the shadow of Ogodai's hand showed through when he reached for the cup there. He lifted the cup and drank, unsteadily.

"Psin Khan looks rebellious," he said to his brother.

Jagatai nodded. "So he does. Rebellion is foul, especially when the rebel is a miserable Merkit. What was it that my father used to say when Psin Khan grew rebellious?"

Ogodai laughed, hiccoughed, and reached for the cup again. "He said, 'Psin Khan, once they called you Psin the Honest. Now they call you Psin the Stubborn. Dead Psin, they may call you, soon enough.' "

Jagatai nodded. "That was it. That was it exactly. What would be an amusing way of—"

"Enough," Sabotai said. "You break the Yasa, growing drunken."

Jagatai blushed vividly. He turned his face away. Ogodai blinked a few times, rapidly, and said, "The Yasa is mine. I can do what—"

"The Yasa is ours," Psin said. "It belongs to your people. You are the Kha-Khan. It's not right for you to act before us like an upland chief on a drunk." He looked at Jagatai. "Nor you."

Jagatai's head turned. Of all Temujin's children he looked the most like his father. His green eyes were dull; he held his chin too high, so that he seemed to look into the ceiling. "I am the greatest of my father's drunken sons. So great am I that I even know when a subchief of the sniveling unhappy Merkits is telling me the truth."

Psin made a gesture with his right hand; his wrist rested on his knee and he did not move it. He smiled. Jagatai saw and swiftly made another gesture.

Sabotai was furious. He said, "Stop casting spells on each other. We're getting farther and farther from the reason for all this. All the way from the Volga River I came, just to sit and listen to you behave like drunken oxen."

Ogodai and Jagatai stared at him, making their eyes round in mock surprise. Sabotai drew himself up very straight, frowning. Ogodai shrieked with laughter and fell over backward. Grinning, Jagatai glanced at him and said, "Sabotai. You amuse your Kha-Khan greatly."

"I am sick over it," Sabotai said, with massive dignity.

Ogodai sat up again. "You sit in the wrong place to see how funny the world is. Yes, I know. Psin Khan, we instruct you to ride with Sabotai to the camp of our nephew Batu and there to serve in the campaign against—" He waved a hand. "Whatever lies west. Wherever you find rebels."

Jagatai nudged him, and Ogodai shouted, "I remember." He glared at Jagatai and swung back to Psin. "You are to take Tshant Bahadur with you."

Psin shrugged one shoulder. "You know that Mongke Khan is with Batu, my Khan."

Jagatai reached across Ogodai's lap for the silver jug of wine. Over his brother's arm Ogodai said, "Mongke and Tshant were both with you in Korea, Merkit. You handled them there. Do it again." He took a deep breath, and his face darkened. "In the name of God, why do you all whine so much about tending to a pack of brats? Are you not both married and fathers?"

Psin pretended to wipe his mustaches so that he could hide his smile. "Why did you send them all to Batu, my Khan?"

"I have better things to do," Ogodai said. "I am the Lord of the Earth and childish pranks and quarrels only annoy me."

Jagatai said, "Do you have someone to rule over your clan while you are gone, Psin Khan?"

Psin nodded. "My son Sidacai."

Ogodai was contemplating the ceiling. Jagatai said, "Sidacai is in the Kha-Khan's guard. He will be released from duty."

"You will serve Batu as you would serve us," Ogodai said to the ceiling.

"As you would have served my father," Jagatai said. He smiled faintly, his eyes on Psin. "As you did serve him will suffice."

Ogodai stared upward. For a while no one said anything, until Sabotai asked, "Are we dismissed?"

"Oh. Yes. Go." Ogodai never looked from the ceiling.

Psin and Sabotai prostrated themselves again, got up, and walked out. In the antechamber, Sabotai heaved an enormous sigh.

"Things are not as they were."

Psin laughed. "No. Things are somewhat better, I think."

"Wretched."

"Oh? Even drunk they are both cleverer than Temujin was. Not so fierce, maybe. Not so haughty."

"Temujin was—"

"Less subtle than these."

Sabotai swelled up. Psin gathered his hat and gloves. "When he lived you said as much, often enough—you and Jebe. Does dying improve a man's mind?" He put one hand on Sabotai's shoulder and pushed. "Come along. I must find Sidacai and see how much he remembers of his own people."

Sabotai preceded him out the door. "Batu at least is—"

Psin waited for him to finish, but Sabotai did not, and at last Psin said, "What do you wish of me, in the west?"

"Reconnaissance."

They walked along the wide corridor that led to the courtyard. Two men in Turkish clothes passed them; Sabotai glanced after them disinterestedly. The smooth boards of the floor resounded under Psin's boots. Carrying bowls of fruit buried in snow, two slaves ran by, bowing in midstep. At the door, Sabotai stepped to one side and let Psin go first. They passed into the bright sunlight of the courtyard. Psin blinked; it was cold, and he hooked up his coat.

"Batu must have made some reconnaissance."

The courtyard was half-empty. Three camels lay beside the gate. Sabotai stared at them. "Batu doesn't understand such things. I'm suspicious of his findings."

"You flatter me."

Sabotai started down the wide, shallow steps. He glanced over his shoulder at Psin. "You are the master of reconnaissance. No one ever admits it because you are a Merkit, but everybody knows it."

"They don't trust me."

Sabotai lifted one arm, and across the courtyard a groom answered with a wave. "They trusted you enough to send you to Korea. You came by post horse?"

"Yes."

"Was it bothersome?"

"Better than under Temujin." The groom was bringing two horses on leadropes. "I don't want to fight in this war, Sabotai."

Sabotai laughed; the sound heaved out of his chest like great bubbles in water. He spun to face Psin. "I might have thought so, had you not just said so. I know you well enough, Psin. When you complain you are happy." He swung back to watch the horses coming. "It will be a good war."

The camp of the Kha-Khan's guards lay outside Karakorum, on the west. Psin rode around beneath the walls. Yellow pennants streamed from each tower and cast their shadows rippling over the uneven ground. For the Gobi, the wind was light. Two or three herds grazed south of the city, scattered across the plain: one was the band of white mares who provided the Kha-Khan with his kumiss.

Cities to take. An interesting problem, taking a city. Psin remembered the raid over the Caucasus, more than ten years before. If Sabotai had already beaten the Alans and Bulgars, the Christians were the next target. Psin had seen some Frankish knights in Outremer, when the Mongols fought the great war against the Muslims. The Franks were big, limber men who rode exceptionally strong horses. They fought with swords rather than bows. He wished he'd been more interested, back when they were fighting in the west. Heavy cavalry, the Franks would try to ram into an enemy line. Interesting.

"Hold up," a sentry called. "Declare yourself."

"Psin of the Black Merkits. Let me by."

The sentry jogged his horse over. "Psin Khan. Our camp is honored." The sentry bowed.

"I am honored," Psin said. He rode by. The camp stretched on across the plain toward the mountains, ten thousand yurts, all in rows neat as Chinese writing. The officers' yurts were on wooden platforms, with steps leading up. Men lounged on the platforms before their doors. Psin rode down the central street, trying to remember where Sidacai would be, and immediately got lost. He turned down a side street. A troop of dogs yapped at him. He passed four young children playing in the dust, and they turned to watch him, their eyes narrowed. The smell of meat simmering brushed his nose and he sniffed.

Finally he asked directions from a man loitering at the corner of a street. Sidacai was all the way across the camp. He lifted his horse into a canter. Two great wagons rumbled past, drawn by oxen; they were full of grain. Ahead, he saw his own dark red banner. That would be Sidacai's post, and he galloped up to the yurt beneath the flying banner.

The yurt was of honest felt, at least; some of the others were silk. On the platform, Sidacai lay half naked in spite of the cold. A Hindi slave girl played the sitar in a corner beside the door.

Psin stepped onto the platform from his saddle and walked over to Sidacai, who ignored him. He rolled Sidacai over with his foot. Sidacai sprang up, his hand leaping toward his dagger.

"Forgotten me already?" Psin said. "Your doddering old father, soon meat for the vultures?"

"I didn't know it was you," Sidacai said. He put one hand to his head and groaned. "You might have called out."

Psin grabbed him by his long hair, led him to the edge of the platform, and threw him off. Sidacai howled in midair, landed on his back, and bounced up, his face red with rage.

"You can't—"

"Drunken child," Psin said. The Hindi girl was still playing. "Come back up here and see whether I can."

Sidacai spat into the dust. A crowd gathered in the street, laughing and calling to Sidacai. He vaulted up onto the platform again, and Psin caught him before he could steady himself and tipped him

off. Sidacai landed rolling easily on his shoulders. The crowd hissed
and booed. Sidacai got up and sprang. He landed in the middle of
the platform, scattering bowls and a jug across the planks; he dove
at Psin before he was on his feet. Psin sidestepped him, kicked him
in the thigh, caught his wrist, and whipped him off into the street.
The crowd ducked, and Sidacai this time lay still a moment, flat on
his back in the coarse sand.

"Well?" Psin said. He pulled his belt up over his belly.

Sidacai rose. The crowd screamed advice and pelted him with
handfuls of sand. His shoulders were slick with sweat, and the sand
clung to him. He whirled, glared the crowd into silence, and paced
up and down a little, thinking it out. Psin put his hands on his hips
and grinned. They were about the same height, but Psin was much
heavier through the chest and shoulders.

Sidacai prowled around to the other side of the platform, near
Psin's horse. Psin followed him. The Hindi girl got up quietly and
crossed to the other side of the door; she went on playing. Sidacai
feinted, and Psin dodged to one side. Lunging, Sidacai caught him
by the ankle.

Psin sat down hard on the platform. Before he could get up,
Sidacai was beside him; Sidacai planted one foot in the small of
Psin's back and shoved. Psin flew off into the midst of the mob. He
scrambled up and whirled.

"Beloved sire," Sidacai said. "How you've aged."

Psin charged. He hauled himself up onto the edge of the platform, although Sidacai tried to kick him away, and straightened.
Sidacai rammed into him shoulder first, and Psin wrapped both
arms around his son's chest. He could feel the edge of the platform
under the balls of his feet. Sidacai elbowed him, shoved, kicked, and
butted him in the jaw, but Psin hung on, throwing his weight forward slightly to balance himself.

"Give up," Sidacai whispered. "These are my underlings, do you
want them to see me beaten by a toothless grandfather?"

Psin ducked his head and bit him on the shoulder. Sidacai yelled.
His hands flew up, and Psin with a thrust of his elbows knocked
him back and away. Blood ran down Sidacai's chest. Psin wiped his
mustaches.

"Not yet toothless, colt."

Sidacai threw his head back and laughed. All around the crowd cheered, beating their hands together. A crust of bread struck Sidacai accurately in the mouth. Psin glared at the crowd and waved them quiet. Sidacai said, "Come inside, I'm thirsty."

"Drunk."

"Old pig. I only counted one tooth."

They went into the yurt. The Hindi girl followed them. Sidacai gestured toward her. "Do you like her? I thought I'd send her to you—the music's relaxing."

"Ayuh. And when your mother saw her we'd need relaxation." Psin sat down with a grunt. "You're strong, for such a stick. You hurt your old father."

"Against you nobody's strong. Like fighting a mountain." Sidacai poured kumiss into bowls and gave one to Psin. "What are you doing here? It's early for the clan to be on winter pasture."

"The Kha-Khan summoned me."

Sidacai sat on his heels. Reaching behind him, he dragged a fur cloak from the couch and arranged it over his shoulders. "If I go mad from being bitten I shall curse you always. Why do they want you? For the China war?"

"I'm to go with Sabotai to Batu. I suspect he's having difficulty with the Altun."

"Hunh. The Russians, then. Dull fighting. But you've always liked new places."

"I've been there before. You're going up to the Lake and play Khan. Tshant comes with me."

Sidacai only stared a moment. Finally he lifted his cup and drained it. "I am no khan."

"You'll learn."

"I know nothing of it."

"My brothers will help you. And Malekai."

"I'd rather stay here."

"Jagatai will order you back."

"Why you?"

"Sabotai requested me, I think."

"Have you seen the Kha-Khan?"

"Yes."

Sidacai turned his head and bellowed for a slave. He poured more kumiss into his cup. "They don't trust you. They hate you. Don't go."

"Why not?"

"Maybe they want to kill you. Far away where no one will care."

"These Khans don't hate me, and they trust me or I wouldn't have commanded six tumans in Korea. If Temujin never had me killed Ogodai won't. And it was Sabotai who asked for me. I'm sure of that."

"Are you taking Mother?"

Psin nodded. "And Artai."

"You are so trusting."

Psin shrugged. He pulled at his mustache, his eyes on Sidacai. "Well, I'll keep it in mind. Now I've got to go. Sabotai wants to leave quickly. You ride post horse to the Lake and when you find the clan send Tshant straight to the Volga—Batu has a main camp there. Tell him to take his mother and your mother and two yurts and the necessary slaves and my dun horse."

Sidacai nodded. "Will he go?"

"He'll go or face me for it." Psin scowled. "What do you mean, will he go?"

"You know how he is."

"You tell him that I sent for him on the Kha-Khan's order." He stood up. "You might say I have no desire whatsoever to command over him again, after Korea."

Sidacai's head bobbed. "Do you want her?" He jabbed an elbow at the Hindi girl.

"No. I have all the women I can handle right now. And you know how I hate music."

Psin had fought two campaigns in Korea. The first, a reconnaissance raid, had been the kind of fighting he liked best: very fast, very hard, and more dangerous than usual. On the second campaign he had taken Tshant, his eldest living son, and two of Temujin's grandsons, the Altun Mongke and Kubulai, as tuman commanders. Tshant and Mongke were deadly enemies.

"Fighting Koreans was a relief," he said to Sabotai. "Do you remember how Jebe and Mukali fought?"

Sabotai grinned quickly between swallows. They were eating in a waystation on the road to the Volga camp, and the food was so bad that they gulped it to keep from tasting it.

"Once I went into my yurt and Tshant had Mongke down and was strangling him," Psin said. He had finished eating. A bit of limp cheese lay before him on the table; he pressed one forefinger into it and studied the fingerprint. "A couple of days later Mongke knocked Tshant off his horse and tried to trample him."

"How did you get them apart?" Sabotai said. He set his bowl down and wiped his chin. Particles of meat clung to his beard.

"I? A lowly Merkit, a subchief, nothing more than the father-in-law of one of the Altun women, come between the woman's husband and her cousin in a friendly argument? I kept them riding in opposite directions."

Sabotai laughed and yawned. "This campaign should be interesting."

"How much trouble do the Altun give you?"

Sabotai leaned back. Slaves moved around them, clearing the table and fetching kumiss. The waystation was all but empty; a balding captain dozed beside the door, and the smoke settled just over Sabotai's head.

"Buri and Quyuk are closer than two out of the same womb. They hate Batu. In a council Batu's brothers will support him on any issue. Anywhere else they quarrel among themselves. Baidar and Kaidu are the brightest and steadiest of the lot, if you want my opinion. Kaidu is a pleasant youngster, you'll like him. Kadan is a damned drunk and keeps to himself. He hates Quyuk more than anything else in the world, and he rather likes Batu because of it. You'd never know he and Quyuk are brothers. Mongke hates everybody."

"Even you?"

"Me he likes. Is that a compliment or the worst sort of insult?"

Psin undid the laces of his tunic. "A compliment. Mongke I know, of course. I fought under Batu once, against the Muslims, and I know his brothers well enough to say they're nothing. But the others—are they good commanders?"

Sabotai shrugged one shoulder. "They're all young, except Batu and Baidar. They are brave. They've brought their personal armies, thank God, so that we have Mongols for troops instead of Kipchaks who won't learn or can't."

"Mongke's men don't follow him well enough for my liking."

The night wind dragged at the yurt. Sabotai stretched his arms over his head, glanced at the captain snoring by the door, and dropped his hands to the table top. "What's wrong with Mongke?"

"Nothing much. He can't command three crippled oxen and a shaman's cart in a pitched battle, but he'll raid as well as any of us."

Sabotai's chest swelled up. He held his breath a moment and let it out with a sigh. "You must know what I mean. He's not trustworthy."

"He has a vivid imagination. He can see just what an enemy should do to crush him into little bits. So he runs before they can."

"He's a coward."

"Say that to his face." Psin yawned until the bones in his jaw cracked. Sabotai's lips quivered; obviously he was resisting a yawn himself.

A slave came in and prostrated himself on the floor. "My lords, your horses wait."

Sabotai groaned. "I'm dying for some sleep."

"Wait until the next station," Psin said. "Come along."

They rode steadily west, through desert bordered by blue mountains. Twice a day they reached waystations, changed horses, and rode on. They got little sleep. Psin thought Sabotai was worried about what was happening in the Volga camp and the city called Bulgar while he was gone. Sometimes, when they reached the second waystation of the day early in the evening, they rode all night, dozing in the saddle, a rope tied between their horses.

Twice they met caravans going west—the camels, swaying on their great feet over the stony ground, reminded Psin of the Muslims who had spoken of the Franks of Outremer. He spent half the night in a waystation talking to the men of one caravan in his rusty Arabic. The cameldrivers, from Damascus, mentioned the Franks even before Psin could ask.

"How do they fight?" Psin said.

"By the Compassionate God," the head driver said. He raised his hands and eyes toward the ceiling. "When they are on ground of their own choosing, there is nothing that can meet their charges. There was one, now long gone from Outremer, who stood head and shoulders taller than you, lord."

Psin glanced at Sabotai, who was listening. Sabotai said, "Taller than you?" He sounded shocked.

"And as broad," the Damascene said. "He was a Norman. The stories are still told of him. He was king of Antioch."

"They use swords," Psin said.

"Lances also. They don't throw them, they hold them, thus." The Damascene locked his elbow against his side and held his hand palm up before him, the fingers curled around an unseen lance haft. "Their charge is terrible."

Psin smiled, so that his eyes narrowed. "Mongols don't usually wait to be charged."

One of the other Arabs laughed softly. The head driver said, "All the world knows that Mongols are the greatest fighters."

"Someday we'll fight Franks, maybe, and see." Psin looked at Sabotai.

"I can't understand more than a few words," Sabotai said. "My Arabic's gone bad, and I'm sleepy."

Psin glanced around at the Arabs. In the low firelight their faces shone; their dark eyes were full of unease and soft fear. Sabotai lay back and pulled his coat over him. Psin finished his kumiss.

"Your God be compassionate," he said to the Arabs. They smiled, quick to try to please him, and he laughed in their faces. "Take my regards to your khan, whoever he is."

He lay down, his face away from the fire, and slept with the faint scent of Arab in his nostrils.

They left long before dawn, crossed the river there, and headed on west. Psin was beginning to feel that his legs fit the saddle better than the ground. Sabotai was older than he was, and he watched for signs of failing strength, but Sabotai only grumbled more and walked very stiffly when they dismounted.

On the twenty-first day they came to the place where they had to leave the main road and travel north. The waystation lay in a bowl of valley, shockingly green after the desert; wells bubbled up out of the ground all around the site of an old city. Only a few huts stood, scattered through the valley, and the hillside they rode over was white with old bones. The flat ground of the valley was covered with apricot trees, so that the air was full of the smell of over-ripe fruit.

"We burnt this city when we fought the Kara-Khitai," Sabotai said.

Psin reined in and looked. Far across the valley he could see the snowy tops of high mountains, but the dusty haze hid the slopes. "Yes, I remember—there was a mosque—it stood there. And the wall had spikes over it. When we came down here, it was just after a rainstorm, and we could see the mountains. You can't see them now, only the tops."

Sabotai frowned. "I don't remember that."

"I do. I stormed the wall." Psin recalled something else of that battle and hunched his shoulders. "There were four gates to the city, and their banners were white with green markings."

"Ayuh. I remember. You're right. God above, you were young then."

"Younger than Mongke." He kicked his horse up; the memory made him nervous.

"Long ago," Sabotai said. "Ah, well." He reined his horse around a knot of low bushes. "That was Temujin's first great campaign—he made no mistakes in it. Before then he was sometimes wrong."

"He learned," Psin said. He slipped his feet out of the stirrups and let them dangle. The soles of his feet were numb from pressing against the stirrup bars. "No man could say anything greater of him—he learned."

"Oh, he had some other virtues," Sabotai said.

Psin grunted. The campaign against the Kara-Khitai had been his third under Temujin, and the first in which he had commanded his own tuman. Before then he had seen Temujin only from great distances, riding through the camp, with his aides like hawks swooping around him, and the glitter of his name fencing him off from the unworthy.

"You were not ordered to storm the city," Temujin had said.

No, my Khan.

"You were ordered to encircle and wait for the rest of the army to join you."

Yes, my Khan.

"You disobeyed me, child. I won't tolerate that. Look at me, child. If you face my enemies, you can face me."

No, my Khan.

Temujin's soft voice, so quiet, had told him for half the day what the penalties were for disobedience, had told him how lucky he was that he had succeeded. Psin remembered quivering under that gentle voice.

"If you had failed, child, there would now be so little left of you that a jackal would starve over your bones."

Who would save me if he wished me dead? For years afterward when he heard Temujin's voice his stomach contracted and his mouth dried up.

Now he and Sabotai picked their way through the ruins of the city wall; the grass had grown up over the stones. No stone stood high enough to be seen above the grass. Greener grass in rectangles showed where houses had stood; weeds and wild herbs sprouted in the streets and seeded into the wind that no wall broke. The light was strange, as if the haze diluted it.

Temujin's power had lain banked in his eyes: green like this new grass they glowed sometimes in Psin's dreams and when he woke he spent the day following uncertain and haunted. Even Jebe had flinched before Temujin's gaze.

"What are you thinking about?" Sabotai said.

They had been standing for some time in front of a yurt. Psin mumbled something and dismounted. Sabotai showed the station captain their credentials; he talked to him in a firm cold voice, arranging for a change of horses. Psin walked over to a bush and made water. When he was through he saw that the bush grew up out of a matrix of dry bones.

THE BLACK MERKITS WINTERED AT THE SOUTHERN END OF LAKE Baikal, on the choice pasture and the teeming forest along the river there. Sidacai had no trouble finding the head camp. Before Temujin had come, the Black Merkits had fought over this pasturage with a clan of Uirats, more numerous and richer; the Merkits had grazed the land for generations, and only that had kept them coming back, year after year, to pay for it in blood. Temujin had given them this land for all time, and now they could stretch their camp along the river basin for three days' ride.

Tshant's yurts stood in a horseshoe bend in the river. Sidacai found them in the middle of the day. Some women were washing; his mother of course wasn't with them. He rode on past, hearing their laughter and gossiping voices while they sloshed the laundry in the big tubs by the river. Dogs and children and a little flock of piebald goats sprinkled the high grass in the horseshoe. The yurts made an orderly curve along the bank.

Tshant was always orderly. Sidacai thought of that and wrinkled his nose. He reined in before the biggest of the four yurts and called, "Brother? Will no one welcome the returning warrior?"

The yurt door was open, and when he dismounted he could see Tshant's wife, Kerulu, inside sewing felt. She looked over at him. Her bright hair, the hair of Temujin's family, gleamed in the light from the fire.

"Tshant," she called. "Sidacai's come back."

"Ah?"

Deep inside the yurt something heavy and careless rolled over, grunted, and made its way to the door. Tshant walked stooped out into the sunlight and straightened. He stared at Sidacai.

"What are you doing here?"

"Brother mine, your welcome is so loving."

Tshant snorted. He looked all around the camp and shaded his eyes with his hand to look south. "He didn't come back with you?"

A troop of ponies, each carrying a whooping boy, hurtled through the camp, wheeled at the riverside, and swept out again. Sidacai dismounted. "No, he didn't. The Kha-Khan has sent him to the west."

"Oh." Tshant grimaced. "He was thinking that this winter maybe he could play at being old and unwell." He turned, cupped his hands around his mouth, and shouted, "Mother?"

Sidacai stripped the saddle from his horse. Artai came out of the yurt next to Tshant's, and Tshant bawled, "The Kha-Khan has sent him to Russia."

There was a long pause. Sidacai looked over, across his horse's back. Artai was standing before her own door, her arms folded over her breast. She was small and her dark hair was stippled with grey; when she was angry her nostrils flared.

"They use him like an ox," she said finally. "When will they leave him alone?" She saw Sidacai and her face softened. "Sidacai. At least we got you back in exchange."

Tshant had called a slave to take Sidacai's horse. He called, "Mother, we need salt," and went back inside his yurt. Sidacai went over to Artai.

"Now," she said, "tell me why you've come."

"The Kha-Khan has ordered Tshant to Russia, too."

For a moment her face didn't change. Abruptly all the fine wrinkles and the deep lines around her mouth creased into a smile. "He can take me, then."

"Psin said that he should. And my mother."

"Good." She patted his hand, rising. "Go see her." She walked back into her own yurt.

A very young boy on a spotted pony galloped up and skidded to a halt in front of Sidacai. "Who are you?"

Sidacai looked him up and down. The boy had flamboyant hair and hazel eyes. He wore a brocade coat with gold hooks. "I'm your uncle Sidacai."

"How do you know who I am?"

"You're Djela."

"Yes." The boy grinned. "I know all about you. You're in the Kha-Khan's guard and you drink too much. And you've not married because my grandfather won't let you marry anybody but a princess and nobody's offered him a good enough princess yet for you. I fell off my pony last summer and knocked all my front teeth out."

"That's good." Sidacai started toward the next yurt, and Djela trotted along beside him.

"My father says when he goes fighting again he'll take me with him. When I grow up I'll speak as many different languages as my grandfather does, maybe even more. I already know how to say horse in Chinese."

"Useful." Sidacai bent to crawl into his mother's yurt.

"I have a friend named Dekko, but nobody can see him except me. Muko had twin kids and I was the first one to find them, they have spots and they were awfully little. They're grown up now, almost."

"Good."

Sidacai stood up inside his mother's yurt; Djela had come with him. On the other side of the front room two slaves were fixing a broken chair. One looked up and spoke softly into the back room. Sidacai looked around and sat. The silks and brocades here were as rich as any in Karakorum, including those in the Kha-Khan's ante-chamber. The fire burnt in a big iron pot so that no coals or soot got onto the carpet.

The veil across the door into the front room trembled, and Sidacai's mother moved into the room. She bowed to Djela, put her cheek gently against Sidacai's, and settled herself next to him. Her robe was so stiff with gold thread that it bent in sharp angles. Her black hair hung over one shoulder, and the clasp at the nape of her neck held a jewel the size of Sidacai's thumb. She smelled of regal lilies, Sidacai had never seen a regal lily, but he knew what they smelled like because she had told him. Her hands like ivory leaves lay in her lap before her, soft as a newborn's, the nails faintly pink. Djela had stopped talking and was staring meekly at her.

"You come unexpectedly," Chan said.

"My father sent me."

She nodded, lowering her eyes. Sidacai was always astonished, seeing her after long absences, that she had borne him. She seemed younger than he. "He is well, your father?"

"Yes. The Kha-Khan has sent him to the west—to Russia."

The long eyes regarded him, expressionlessly, before she turned to call one of the slaves. "Bring rice wine for my son."

The slave crept out. Chan turned back to Sidacai. "You must be in disfavor, to be sent back here."

At the base of her long throat another jewel flashed. Sidacai stared at it. He could not believe that she would cross the northern route to Russia in the winter, that she could endure the snow and the cold. Her wrist was so slender he could have snapped it between thumb and forefinger. "No," he said. "I am to play khan. Tshant is going to Russia too."

The slave returned with the wine. Sidacai hated it but drank it for her sake. She took the jug and the cup and poured it for him.

"Artai will go, then," she said, handing him the cup.

"Yes."

"Tell me of Karakorum."

"Oh, the winds blow, the sands bite."

Djela's mouth was slightly open; he was staring at Chan. Sidacai glanced at him, amused. Chan said, "Djela, surely there are more interesting things outside?"

"Can't I—"

"No. You talk too much."

Djela's shoulders sagged. He left the yurt.

"He's a very annoying child," Chan said. "They treat him as if he were the son of a god."

"He doesn't seem spoiled to me."

"Tshant worships him." Her teeth pressed against her lower lip. "Did he say anything of me?"

"He wants you to go to Russia with Artai."

She scowled. "That will be tedious."

"Where is Malekai?"

"Up the river. He has a new child. I wish you would marry."

"My nephew tells me my father wants me to marry a princess, but they're in short supply."

"Your brother married no princess."

Sidacai laughed. Malekai had married a Mangghut. "Perhaps I'll find a Chinese wife."

"No. Would you bring another woman to suffer in this barbaric captivity?" She put her hands to her hair, smoothing it down. "I don't want to go to Russia."

"He said—"

"I know what he said. He said I am to be packed up like a chest and carted off across the steppes and when I get there all my clothes will be filthy and wrinkled." She undid the clasp in her hair, pulled a long black hair out of the hinge, and did her hair up again.

"Sidacai." Tshant thrust his head and shoulders through the door. "Coward."

Sidacai jumped. Tshant crawled all the way in and stood up. "I think he built that door small so that no one could come in here without bowing to her." He jerked his chin at Chan. "You couldn't tell me to my face that I have to go to Russia. You had to get it to me roundabout."

"I never had the chance."

Tshant was taller than Psin, taller than Sidacai, but while Psin was massive Tshant was lanky, with ropy muscles and long flat bones. He sat on his heels and glared. Chan ignored him as if he had never come in.

"And besides all that I am to escort a troop of women and slaves," Tshant said. "Still, it may be worth the trouble to see what knots you can tie yourself into, trying to be khan."

"You stink," Chan said. "Get out." She snapped her fingers at one of the slaves, who handed her a mirror. She turned her level eyes on Tshant until he flushed, looked at herself in the mirror, and ran one forefinger over her cheekbone.

"I ask your pardon," Tshant said. "I'm angry."

"I dislike you. You remind me of your father. Leave."

Tshant backed out, jerking his head at Sidacai to follow him. Sidacai did so. Outside, Tshant said, "I wish I reminded her even more of the old ox."

"I shouldn't try to."

"No. Come to my yurt. Between him and Kerulu I don't dare look at Chan twice in one day. What do you know of the western campaigns?"

"Mongke's there."

Tshant halted in midstep, settled back slowly onto both feet, and smiled. "Mongke. How enjoyable. Of course. The Kha-Khan's sent them all to Batu, hasn't he? To keep them from tearing Kara-korum up by the roots. Psin will be gnawing his mustaches."

He swung around to look back at Chan's yurt. Every time he moved, Sidacai jumped, alert to the strength in Tshant's arms and shoulders. It was like standing next to a stallion. Tshant said, "I'm

taking Djela. We'll ride on ahead. Malekai can escort the women
and their baggage. Come inside. I can't remember much about Russia."

He started off again, and Sidacai hopped to catch up. Tshant
swore pleasantly under his breath and said, "Mongke. How interesting."

Psin cursed steadily. They had ridden all day long under lowering skies, and in the early evening the first storm of the steppes
autumn had broken over them. Sleet lay crusted on his horse's
mane, and his mustaches were frozen so that they crackled. He
could barely see Sabotai through the driving rain and snow. But the
horses were walking quickly, their heads high. Psin shivered. When
they had left the last waystation the captain had told them that the
Volga camp was only a day's ride north.

"Stop out there—stand still!"

The voice swooped up on the wind. Psin jerked his horse down.
Sabotai sidled closer and leaned forward; wet snow caked his coat
front.

"It's Sabotai and Psin of the Merkits. Who's there?"

For a moment the rain lashed at their faces and they heard nothing. Sabotai took a breath to shout again, but before he could a man
on foot staggered toward them. He walked up to Psin's horse and
laid one hand on the thick neck.

"Sabotai?"

"Here."

The man lifted his head. He was not a Mongol; all Psin could see
of him was his shape.

"You've reached the Volga camp—we never expected you so
soon. Go straight on."

"Thank you," Sabotai said.

They whipped their horses into a trot. Despite the wind and sleet
in their faces, the horses were eager and almost broke into a canter.
They had gone hardly a dozen strides before Sabotai's horse
swerved off to avoid running into the stockade wall.

"I'm freezing," Psin said. "Which way?"

"I don't know," Sabotai said. He reined back and looked up

through the dark. "They hadn't built the wall when I was here last." He shouted, but in the wind no one heard.

"We could die in this damned storm before we found the gate." Psin wheeled his horse. "Which way does the wind blow on this steppe?"

"From the north."

"No help in that. Come on." Psin rode off along the wall, headed east.

The wall made a lee, and the sloppy snow was light on the ground directly under it. Psin's horse lengthened its stride. They could be going in exactly the wrong direction. But perhaps the wall had more than one gate. Psin ducked his chin in against his chest and pulled his hat down hard over both ears. He could hear Sabotai galloping along just behind him.

They were veering north again, not in a sharp turn like a good corner but gradually. They'd built the damned wall in a circle. Psin opened his mouth to call to Sabotai, but suddenly his horse dove to the left and stopped dead.

"What?" Sabotai said, running his horse up alongside Psin's.

"Gate." Psin pointed. The gate was shut; it rose up twice as high as his head. He shouted, "Open this gate," but there was no answer. Furious, he stood in his stirrups and hammered on the gate with his fist.

"Who's there?"

A shutter clapped open, and a head thrust out through a window in the wall. Psin scraped the ice and snow off his horse's mane, balled it up, and hurled the ball into the man's face.

"Let us in, you fools. Did we come all from Karakorum to die of cold here? Open this dung-eating gate."

The gate had begun to open before he finished shouting. Behind it were half a dozen men with lances and bows. Sabotai rode in among them and they recognized him and began to cheer. None of them was Mongol. A torch bloomed and the light spread across their faces—Psin decided that they were Kipchaks or Bulgars, and he almost grinned at the thought that they should cheer Sabotai. His horse jammed its shoulders in between Sabotai's horse and the gate, so that they could not close it and Sabotai had to move.

"It's a foul night," the sentry said. "You didn't have to come far, did you?"

"I'm cold," Psin said.

Sabotai kicked his horse. "Yes. Take us to the Khan's yurt."

The gateman started off, trotting on foot down a street that ran due north. Psin could tell the sleet was changing to pure snow from the way it rasped on his cheeks. Sabotai gestured, and he rode over closer to him.

"This is new-built," Sabotai said, "but much better in the planning than Karakorum, don't you think?"

"I can't see anything of it. Cities are for burning, not for living in."

"There's a Merkit speaking."

The gateman had stopped, up ahead, in front of a smaller gate. This stood open. The wall was man-high and enclosed other buildings. Psin stopped to let Sabotai ride through in front of him, dismissed the gateman, and turned when he had entered to shut the gate.

No slaves waited in the courtyard. Psin dismounted and held Sabotai's horse, looking around. "Everyone's gone to bed."

"I doubt that."

Psin did also. Lights showed through the slits of windows in the great building before them. "I'll take the horses. You go in and tell them to put the pots over the fire."

"Do you know where the stables are?"

"I'll find them." Psin knotted up his horse's reins and slapped it on the rump. Sabotai smiled and stamped up the stair to the front door. Psin went off after the trotting horse, leading the other.

The horse jogged straight to a low barn full of horses. Psin caught him at the door and took both inside. The warmth and the dank rich smell engulfed him. He tugged off his gloves and thrust them into his belt. The horses nuzzled at him, jingling their bits. He unsaddled them, threw the gear under the mangers, and tied each horse to the pole that ran at waist height along the wall.

All around him the horses stamped and rustled the straw. He rubbed down his two with a wisp of straw, working over them until they were dry. Outside the wind rattled doors and loose shingle; he could hear the snow hissing on the roof. He forked hay from a great heap of it onto the floor in front of his horse and turned to get some for Sabotai's.

The door opened, and Mongke, gorgeous in red satin, walked in.

He stared at Psin, latching the door behind him with one hand.

"So my uncle sent you, did he?"

Psin looked him over. Mongke was smaller than he by a full head, and Mongke hated to look up at anybody. Psin went to the hay pile and thrust in the fork.

"Answer me," Mongke said.

The cold still lingered in Psin's hands. He blew on them, lifted the fork with its mat of hay, and walked back to Sabotai's horse.

"Answer me."

"Why should I?" Psin dumped the hay and went back for another forkful. The young man in the center of the barn stood rigid, trembling. Psin leered at him. He got more hay; when he threw it in, the horse swished its tail across Psin's knee.

"If my father were alive—"

Psin turned suddenly. The fork's two tines flashed right under Mongke's nose. Mongke bounded back. He looked from the fork to Psin and back to the fork. Psin held it by the throat, watching Mongke.

"Your father's dead, boy. Is there something you want of me?"

Mongke said nothing. He didn't seem to be angry, only waiting. One of his small lean hands rested against his dagger's sheath. Psin laughed. He tossed the fork into the hay pile, walked over to stand next to Mongke, and looked down at Mongke over his shoulder. Mongke swore and backed up quickly. Psin laughed again. He went to the door and let himself out and slammed the door shut behind him.

The next morning, Psin rode out to look at the Volga camp. The storm had passed over and the sun burnt down on glittering snow. All the roofs were covered with it. Children bounded screaming through the street, hurling snowballs at one another. Swathed to the ears in heavy clothes, they looked like bundles of old fur.

The city was laid out on a grid pattern. Psin, used to the concentric circles of Karakorum and the great ordus, got lost twice before he realized what was wrong. Outside the Khan's compound there were only a few wooden houses; the streets were lined with yurts. Across the low round roofs he could see a spire, like a Christian church. Riding back, he saw two of the wooden houses burnt to shells. The stench of smoke hung in the air and made him cough. The sunlight was warm, and when he finally returned to the compound his cloak lay before him across the withers of his horse.

A slave ran out to meet him and said that Sabotai and Batu had been hunting him all morning.

"Where are they?"

"In the council room, Khan."

"Where is Mongke?"

"In his house in the city, I suspect, Khan."

"The others—Quyuk, Kadan?"

"In Bulgar, Khan."

"Oh. That's right." Psin went inside. Bulgar was the great city in the north, where the Kama River met the Volga; when Batu conquered the Bulgars he had left their city standing.

Batu was sitting in a carved chair, one leg across the arm of it, the foot idly swinging. Psin bowed and Batu said, "Psin Khan. I've not seen you since the kuriltai."

"Nine years. I hear you've found some good game up here."

"I have to make something of my patrimony." Batu jabbed one hand at a table loaded with hot and cold meat and jugs. "Eat. Where have you been all morning?"

"Looking at your city." Psin went to the table. He could smell meat pies all the way across the room. The pies were under a linen napkin in a dish, and he tucked the napkin back, sat down on the floor beside the table, and began to devour pies.

Sabotai uncorked a jug and poured himself kumiss. Batu said, "What do you think, Psin? The Russians take generations to build churches. We built one in a single summer. It took a lot of slaves, and we had to bring the wood down from the north. That's why I like being near the river."

Psin finished his fourth pie. "Why in God's name did you make all the streets straight?"

"To confuse good Mongols." Batu helped himself to a piece of fruit. "If an enemy ever gets inside my walls, he'll have to charge down streets so wide and straight I can riddle him with arrows without leaving my palace."

"Clever," Sabotai said. He stretched. He wore clean, neat

clothes, and he had bathed; Psin could smell soap on him. "Are your brothers in Bulgar?"

"All but Siban," Batu said. "He and Sinkur are off harrying Mordvins." Batu rolled an apple in his palms. To Psin, he said, "The Mordvins live between Bulgar and the Russian cities. I want them frightened before we ride."

"When do the rivers freeze?" Psin said.

"Within the month. I have scouts out, and they're to report it."

Sabotai frowned. He looked over at Psin. "When will Tshant get here?"

Psin wiped up the crumbs on the pie platter. All the pies were eaten. "If he comes with my women, in the spring. I think he'll come on ahead."

"If he does, when will he arrive?"

"Within ten days."

"You're bringing your women?" Batu said, one eyebrow cocked.

Psin nodded. He poured out kumiss into a silver cup. "I enjoy being waited on."

Batu glanced at Sabotai and back to Psin. "Your Chinese wife as well?"

"I'll kill any man who looks at her, Batu. With my own aged hands." Psin drank and wiped his upper lip on his sleeve.

"Oh, my interest is purely aesthetic." Batu turned to Sabotai. "Have you seen her? She is magnificent."

"Sometimes I think only the Muslims dress their women properly," Psin said.

"You don't trust us," Batu said.

"You're very astute. How many tumans do you have?"

"Fifteen, full strength. Plus an engineer corps and a fair supply of baggage wagons. Each of my illustrious kin brought his own tuman. Some of them are overstrength. Quyuk's, for example."

"I saw Mongke last night."

"He came down when he heard you were here. He doesn't like you."

"I need half a tuman for reconnaissance," Psin said. "Give me an apple."

"God above," Batu said. He threw an apple, left-handed but still accurately. "I can see that we're going to do this properly. Half a tuman? The best of the troops are in Bulgar. We'll start all campaigns from there in any case."

Psin took a bite of the apple. The taut skin broke under his teeth and juice filled his mouth. "If I were you, Batu, I would keep Mongke and Tshant posted in different places."

"I want Tshant with me. He's the only man of you who plays intelligent chess."

"Do you want a Russian slave?" Sabotai said.

Psin nodded. "A man, my age if possible, and fairly intelligent. And co-operative."

"Why not a woman?" Batu said. "They're comforting."

"I don't want comfort, I want to learn Russian."

Batu's face furrowed. "I thought you already spoke it. I thought you spoke all the languages in the world." He laughed. "Legends grow, so far from home."

"And I'll need a good horse," Psin said. "That brute I'm riding now is too small for me. A string of good horses."

"Look through my barns."

Sabotai rose. "Psin, come with me, and I'll explain what the country's like, west of here."

Batu said, "When are you going to Bulgar, Psin?"

"Tomorrow."

"That should be pleasant. My kin are going wild up there. If we don't fight soon they'll be uncontrollable."

"We'll fight," Sabotai said. He looked at Psin and smiled maliciously. "And if they aren't in condition to fight, they'll have very little leisure to worry about it in, if I have anything to say."

They all dined that night in Batu's chambers. Batu kept half a dozen small housecats, and Mongke ate with one on his lap. Nobody said anything until the food was gone and the slaves were removing dishes and wiping off the table. Sinkur, Batu's second-in-command, and Batu's brother Siban had come in unexpectedly from the Mordvins' country, but they left the room at once to play chess. Mongke put one foot up on the table and stroked the grey cat's long soft fur.

"Have you spoken with the Russian slave yet?" Sabotai said.

Psin nodded. "I spent the afternoon with him. He'll serve. Mongke, if you want sport until the winter, I'd be honored if you'd join me raiding."

Mongke's fingers burrowed into the cat's fur. "What help could I give to the great Psin?"

Psin spat. "Don't bother."

Sabotai leaned forward. "What will you do?"

"I was going to let Mongke raid through the cities between the Volga and the Oka—you said you want to take them this winter. If Tshant gets here soon enough, he'll raid across the steppe to that river you told me about—" He snapped his fingers. "The Dnepr. I'll ride through whatever lies north of the Oka to Novgorod."

Batu said, "I've had spies and sympathizers in the cities between the two rivers for months now."

"Who besides Mongke can raid there?"

Mongke said, abruptly, "I'll go, Psin."

"Good." Psin heard the cat drop to the floor, and Mongke stood up. Mongke's arm shot into Psin's sight, caught up bowls and pieces of fruit, and arranged them on the table top. "Riazan is here. Yaroslav, Tver, Vladimir, Susdal. Moskva, Kolomna—"

"You know it well," Psin said, surprised.

Mongke nodded. "I'm the best man you could send."

"Do you speak Russian?"

Mongke laughed, settled back into his chair, and gathered up the cat again. "Russian? Why should I speak Russian? I have Russian slaves."

Psin grimaced. "Don't trust them. Half a tuman. You take one thousand. Scout the roads, the cities, the estates, the herds, the fields. Tshant will take two thousand to the Dnepr. I'll take the rest."

Sabotai glanced at Batu, who beamed and leaned forward. "Psin. If you wouldn't mind—"

"Take the Altun with you," Sabotai said. "They need the exercise."

"They won't want to go," Mongke said. "They're having too good a time in Bulgar."

Softly, Sabotai murmured, "Psin shall make them go."

Psin met his eyes. Sabotai slouched back into his chair and nod-

ded three times, slowly and purposefully. Psin couldn't help grinning. He looked at Mongke, who was puzzled, and back to Sabotai.

"Oh. Shall I. Well, now."

"I had a bad dream," Djela said. He pulled Tshant's arm around
his waist. He rode in front of Tshant on the post-horse; the cloak
was belted around them both.

"I heard you," Tshant said. He veered the horse around a snow-
covered clump of shrubs and let it pick its own way down the
slope. With one arm he held his son. "What kind of dream?"

"I dreamt we rode down a long road with cliffs on both sides.
The cliffs made shadows on the road. And in front of us ran black
dogs, black bulls and black horses, in and out of the places where
the sun was bright."

Tshant pressed his arm against Djela. "It was only a dream." The
horse wallowed through a drift and started up the other side of this
little ravine. Its hoofs skidded on rock or ice, and it stumbled.
Tshant reined in.

"But they were ghosts, Ada. The black dogs and horses and
bulls."

Tshant unwrapped the sash around the cloak. "You were only
dreaming. I have to clear this rat-eaten nag's hoofs out again."

Djela wiggled out from under the cloak, and Tshant dismounted.
The slopes and the low shrubs were covered with snow, blinding
white under the sky so blue it hurt Tshant's eyes. Djela's green coat
made a great patch in the midst of it. The boy slid down from the
horse and began to leap through the drifts, splashing the snow with
his hands and shouting. Tshant picked up one of the horse's fore-
feet. The ice had balled up in the hoof so that the horse stood not
on its own feet but on a pad of rock-hard snow.

"Ada, can you see me?"

Tshant glanced around. "No. Where are you?"

"In the snow."

Tshant dug out the ice with his knife. "Come back."

"I'm here."

"Don't run around like that. If you sweat you'll freeze."

"I know. But I'm tired of riding."

"We'll be there soon." Tshant tended to the horse's hind hoofs and straightened up. He picked up Djela and set him in the saddle, mounted behind him, and draped his cloak around them again. Djela snatched up the reins. "Let me do it."

"Good. I'll sleep."

He put his arms around the boy and shut his eyes. The glare of the sun on the snow made his eyelids red-gold. They bumped up the slope and along a level stretch. The waystation captain had said that they were within a day's ride of the Volga camp, if the snow didn't slow them down too much.

"There are no more stations," the man had called after them. "Take another horse."

Tshant dozed. The vigorous warmth of the child pressed against his chest. He dreamt of the winter pasture by the Lake, of Kerulu murmuring in the twilight; he saw Djela riding a black bull down a wide sunlit road.

The horse lurched, and Tshant jerked awake. Djela said, "He stumbled again."

Tshant looked around. They were on a plain that stretched limitless to the sky. Here and there a low shrub had thrown off the snow and stood stark against it. The wind stirred, and long streamers of snow rose from the ground and marched across their track. Behind them their trail was already filling. The snow rose into the sky and the blue vanished behind a thin mist. The sun shrank to a silver disk.

"It's going to storm."

"I'm hungry."

Tshant took dried meat from the pouch under the pommel of his saddle and gave it to him. Djela gnawed at it, growling. He had taken up pretending he was a dog before they left the Lake. They lumbered on, the horse's breath like smoke.

"Will we be there tonight?"

"I don't know." Tshant frowned. The plain up ahead, where it dipped, was covered with irregular lumps. He reined in.

"Is it a camp?" Djela said. "Are they men sleeping?"

"It looks like that," Tshant said. But men would not lie so, covered with snow, not in the middle of the day. He reached behind him and took his bow from the case. "Hold the horse."

Djela bounced a little, eagerly. Tshant strung his bow and pulled the top off his quiver. "Now, slowly, ride in among them."

The horse started forward willingly enough but when they were close stopped and would not go farther. Tshant muttered. He dismounted, holding his bow with an arrow nocked, and walked to the nearest lump. The snow was crusted over it. He kicked it, and the snow burst, and the frozen body of a man tumbled over the snow. Djela yelled, surprised.

The horse reared, whirling, trying to bolt. Djela wrestled with it, sawed on the reins, and the horse backed up in a rush. Tshant caught the rein. "Mordvins. We must be near the Volga camp." He led the horse through the lumps of frozen men, mounted up behind Djela, and kicked the horse into a trot.

PSIN AND MONGKE REACHED BULGAR IN THE FORENOON, THREE days after they left the Volga camp, and in the midafternoon Psin had all the troops camped around the city turned out for inspection. Quyuk, the Kha-Khan's eldest living son, was in command of Bulgar; he rode beside Psin along the lines of the five tumans drawn up before the walls.

"They're badly mounted," Psin said. The Mongols rode native stock, smaller than Psin was used to, and very long in the back. The tumans in their rows stretched out across the plain, countless heads bobbing, countless eyes turned on him and Quyuk. Behind them the iron-blue shoulders of the hills rose against the unclouded sky.

"I think you'll find them adequate," Quyuk said carelessly. He pointed to three rows of horsemen grouped around a banner with a two-headed dragon. "Those served under you in Korea, I think."

"Mongke's honor guard. Yes."

The wind was right in Psin's face, cold and edged with coming snow. A horse neighed and a thousand others answered. "What kind of condition are they in?"

Quyuk shrugged one shoulder. His horse skittered sideways and he clubbed it over the ears with his fist. "They've done little fighting since the spring. But they race their horses, and they patrol along the river. That's where the other two tumans are now."

Psin glanced at him. Quyuk rode a much better horse than any of the troops'. Psin decided it was a crossbred, half native and half Mongol. He kicked up his horse and cantered along the line, returning the salutes. At the end of the line he wheeled his horse, so that when Quyuk caught up with him they were facing each other, their horses shoulder to shoulder.

"Any of the Altun who wish it may come with me," Psin said. "When I ride to Novgorod."

"We are all honored by the invitation, of course," Quyuk said. He reached for the jug on his saddle.

"Perhaps I'm not making myself clear," Psin said. "If I take it upon myself to nursemaid a pack of well-bred savages, I expect rather more than being told they are honored."

Quyuk's great brows flew together. "No. Perhaps you aren't

making yourself clear, Merkit."

Psin smiled at him. "You are coming with me, Quyuk. You and your brother and your cousins. All but Batu's brothers. Is that clear enough?"

"I don't wish to. Is that also clear?"

"It's irrelevant, Quyuk."

"You can't give me orders."

"Oh? I think I can. I think I will."

Quyuk's hand darted toward his belt, but Psin, expecting it, clamped his fingers around Quyuk's wrist. Quyuk's face was bright red and his eyes glittered. He shot a quick glance at the watching army and twisted his arm, but Psin only squeezed harder. He didn't think Quyuk would cry out. Looking over his shoulder, Psin saw that the men around them noticed nothing. Quyuk strained, and Psin tightened his fingers. He heard a rasp, like a bone grating on another bone, and Quyuk's lips trembled with pain.

"Do I make myself clear, Quyuk?"

Quyuk's eyes looked slippery. He blinked at the tears. "Let me go."

Psin twisted his wrist. Quyuk's mouth jerked open and he gasped.

"Do I make myself clear?"

"Yes."

Psin let him go. "Good. I look forward to this raid." He saluted the armies, and their arms flew up in answer, all across the plain, five tumans of arms. Reining his horse he galloped back toward the city. Temujin was probably shaking in Heaven over this treatment of his grandchildren. But while he rode through the gate he changed his mind. Temujin was probably laughing.

He rode straight to the house that Quyuk had set aside for him and Mongke, put up his horse and went inside. Mongke was in the main room, sprawled naked on a couch, red wine at his elbow and fluffy cakes in a dish on the floor beside him. Kaidu in a silk tunic painted with flowers paced up and down, talking about the fighting against the Kipchaks. Psin recognized him by his resemblance to Batu, who was Kaidu's grandfather. Psin stopped in the doorway and listened. Kaidu hadn't heard or seen him, but Mongke's eyes flickered in Psin's direction and he smiled.

"Have you met Psin yet?" Mongke asked Kaidu.

"No. But I saw him when he rode out with Quyuk. He's fat."

Mongke laughed. "No. Unfortunately. He's just very big. My father told me once that Psin Khan is the worst general and the best soldier in our armies. Come inside, Psin, and have something to drink."

Kaidu whirled. Psin went into the room and sat down with his back to the fire. "Tuli always mixed things up. I'm a terrible soldier, but I make a passable general."

Mongke laughed genially. His eyes were bleary with malice. "How did you find the society of my dear cousin?"

"I cracked his wrist for him, I think." Psin studied Kaidu. The boy was lanky, but he moved without awkwardness. "All the Altun are to ride out with me to Novgorod."

"Oh?" Kaidu said. He turned his head toward Mongke. "What does Quyuk say about that?"

Psin pulled off his felt socks. "He's overcome with joy."

"With a cracked wrist." Kaidu laughed. "I'd love to have seen that."

"I heard you talking about the Kipchaks. Have you fought them recently?"

"No. And I'm sick of being caged up here. Quyuk won't let me do any of the things the others do to pass the days."

Psin smiled. Kaidu reminded him of himself at that age. He did like him. "They don't have their women here, I noticed."

Mongke shook his head. "We all left our wives in Karakorum to keep watch on Ogodai and Jagatai, and who would bring concubines out here, when there are so many ready to hand? My wife at least is better equipped to handle my uncles than I am, and I know Quyuk's is."

"My wife is in the Volga camp," Kaidu said.

"You live here," Mongke said. "How do you like that wine, Psin?"

"I'm an old man and my tastes take a while to change." The wine was strong and sweet. "I think I can learn to enjoy it." He finished off his third cup.

Mongke smiled. "Well, then. It comes from the land west of Kiev—Hungary. A good reason to go fighting there."

"Who needs reasons?" Kaidu said.

Psin laughed and got up. "You'll excuse me—I'm learning Russian this afternoon."

"Are you going to Quyuk's house for dinner?" Mongke said.
"Yes."

Mongke grinned. "Excellent."

Psin spent all afternoon repeating Russian sentences. Dmitri, his slave, took great pleasure in his new employment; he was rapidly acquiring the mannerisms of the teachers Psin remembered from his childhood. When Psin couldn't hear the difference between two sounds, Dmitri scowled and clucked his tongue, paced up and down a few strides, and with an air of great patience settled down again to repeat the words, over and over.

"The horse is in the field," Psin said. "The horse was in the field. The horse will be in the—what is it?"

The slave at the door bowed. "The kumiss, Khan."

"Bring it in."

"The horse . . ." Dmitri said softly.

"The horse gallops on the plain." The slave set a jug of kumiss on the table. Psin pointed to Dmitri and to the jug, and Dmitri took a cup from a shelf and poured the kumiss. "The horse galloped on the plain. The horse will gallop on the—" Psin took the cup and drained it. "Plain."

Dmitri muttered something in Russian, and Psin said, "What?"

"I said, Heaven help the Christians before a man who learns so fast."

"Christians."

"Yes." Dmitri put the word through its paces. Psin repeated it after him. Dmitri growled the *r* in his throat, insistently, and Psin growled back.

"All Merkits talk that way," Psin said. He rattled off the various forms of the word again, forcing out the *r*'s. "I have to go. Make yourself useful. Quyuk should have provided me with more slaves. Tomorrow maybe we can talk about something other than horses?"

Dmitri bowed. "The Khan wishes."

* * *

The dinner in Quyuk's house began with a crash; Quyuk's brother Kadan walked in so blind drunk that he tripped over a chair and fell into a table loaded with hot meat. When they had covered his burns with grease and slapped him almost sober, and two slaves had mopped up the mess on the floor, they all sat down at the great round table and gorged themselves. Quyuk began to bait Kadan, who could barely focus his eyes on his plate. Mongke, sitting beside Kadan, laughed softly with each new jibe, until Kadan in his bear-like rage swung back and forth between them, his mouth working.

Quyuk was keeping his right arm in his lap. Psin lifted his head and called, "Quyuk, does your wrist hurt?"

Mongke howled gaily. "He says he's sprained it—show them all your strapped wrist, cousin."

Quyuk used his knife deftly with his left hand. "I've tied it to my belt. Now, listen to me, all of you, before you get too drunk. Psin Khan, the Great Merkit, says that we are all to go raiding with him to Novgorod."

"I'm staying here," Buri shouted. "Who wants to gallop around in the snow?"

"According to Psin, you do," Mongke said. "And you're going to enjoy it just tremendously." He leered at Psin.

Buri drew one arm back and smashed the elbow into Mongke's chest. "Be quiet, rat's meat." He wheeled on Psin. "Take all the others, but I stay here."

Mongke was gasping for breath. He reached toward his dagger where it lay on the table. Baidar, who had said nothing at all since coming in, put his hand lightly on Mongke's shoulder and restrained him.

Kadan struggled his head up. "I'm n-not going either."

Quyuk's eyes narrowed. "If I have to go, brother, you go with me."

Buri looked startled. "You're going?"

"Yes," Quyuk said. "Listen to me, all of you."

They were all snarling at each other; they ignored him. Quyuk leapt up.

"Be quiet when your next Kha-Khan speaks."

Psin busied himself with bread and gravy. The rising murmur of voices had stopped; nobody said anything, until Kaidu in his high voice began, "They say my grandfather may—"

"Your grandfather is in the Volga camp," Quyuk said. "My mother is in Karakorum. When my father dies, which please God may be soon—"

Psin said, "Don't talk so much, Quyuk."

Kadan and Baidar murmured under their breath. Psin took an apple from the bowl in the middle of the table; he turned slightly, three-quartered away from Quyuk, and cut the apple in half.

"To speak of the death of a Kha-Khan," Psin said gently, "this is a crime you could die for."

"What does the Yasa say about men who attack their betters?"

Psin smiled down at the apple and halved one of the pieces in his hand. "A question with some fine points to it."

"The blood of the Altun may not be spilled," Baidar said, raising his voice above the mumble of comment around the table. "So says the Yasa."

"Oh," Psin said. "I never spilled his blood." He put a piece of apple in his mouth. The sweetness flowed over his tongue. "The Yasa says that any who disobeys his commander shall die. Is that not so?"

Quyuk said, "You are not our commander."

"Am I not?"

The muttering had died out. Psin did not look at Quyuk. He could feel the uncertainty around him. Baidar said, "What were the Kha-Khan's orders to you?"

Psin peeled one of the pieces of his apple. "That I am to fight rebels. All rebels. I am the Kha-Khan's servant, not a piece of silk to stroke your hands with." He looked up.

Their faces were all turned toward him. Quyuk and Buri were furious, Mongke sleekly amused, Kaidu and Baidar uneasy; Kadan had passed out. Baidar, leaning his forearms on the table, looked a moment at Quyuk and swung back to Psin.

"You shame us. I'll go to Novgorod with you."

"And I," Kaidu said.

A smile slipped across Mongke's face, like a cloud over the moon.

Buri shrugged and settled back. Psin watched him from the tail of his eye. Jagatai's grandson, Buri had by rumor inherited Jagatai's temper. But Buri was watching Quyuk, expectantly.

Quyuk said, "And if I still refuse?"

Psin shrugged. "I'll deal with you however I have to."

Quyuk looked at Buri. Buri hunched his shoulders and looked down at his hands in his lap. Psin stood up and put his dagger on the table. Still looking at Buri, Quyuk grimaced. He said, "Have I any choice? I'll go with you, Merkit."

Psin bowed. "You honor me, noyon."

Quyuk sat down. His flat stare held Psin's a moment, before he smiled. "Baidar is right. You shame us. I really think you are honored."

Mongke laughed. "You'll never learn, Quyuk."

"Mongke, shut up," Psin said.

Kaidu was watching him with awe on his face, his mouth half-open. Psin grinned at him. "Eat something, boy. You'll blow away in the steppe wind if you don't."

Buri was slapping Kadan and shaking him, trying to wake him up. Mongke leaned forward. "Throw water over his head. Burn his feet. Hurry up, or we'll have no good fighting."

Psin sat down again, and Mongke wheeled toward him. "We wrestle, after dinner. It helps settle the blood."

"You don't wrestle," Psin said.

Mongke grinned. "I watch."

Buri swore and swung away from Kadan. "He's out. Psin, do you wrestle?"

"I'm an old man, Buri."

Mongke, Kaidu and Buri all booed him. Quyuk beamed, delighted. "Still, they say you're in good condition."

"I'd make very poor sport. I'm a bad wrestler. Why don't you shoot?"

"Shoot?" Quyuk looked around. "Where?"

"Out in the compound yard. In the horse pens."

"But it's dark out," Kaidu said.

Psin shrugged one shoulder. "So it is. Haven't you ever fought in the dark?"

"No,"

"You will. As long as Kadan can't wrestle—"

"Yes," Quyuk said, smoothly. "Let's shoot. Buri, go have some of the slaves put up targets. Use the horse pens. Psin is right. We've been neglecting our education." Quyuk grinned. "Of course, Psin, you'll shoot with us."

"Of course."

Psin had sent a slave into the city to bring him his bow. While they waited for the targets to be set up, Mongke came over to him and said, "Quyuk doesn't give up."

"I didn't think he had." Psin glanced around. Slaves were tying torches to the walls and lighting them; at the far end of the horse pen the targets showed dimly. "Would he shoot me in the back?"

"No. Why?"

"He was . . . very happy when I suggested this."

"No. But Quyuk is the best shot of the Altun." Mongke seated himself neatly on a fence rail. "He probably thinks he can beat you."

Psin took his bow from a panting slave and strung it.

"He's never seen you shoot," Mongke said. "I have."

Kaidu was dragging the tip of an arrow over the ground, to make a shooting line. Buri drifted over, stared at Psin's bow, and held out his hands. "May I see it?"

Psin gave it to him. Buri brought it under the torchlight. "This is one of Arghun's."

"The next to last he made. I have six of his."

"My grandfather has fifty-two." Buri set his fingers to the empty string.

"Your grandfather is Jagatai and can afford them."

"By the Name." Buri flexed the bow; his hand on the grip wobbled. "I can barely—hey, Quyuk."

Psin took back the bow. Buri looked at it again, frowning. Mongke laughed and kicked Buri gently in the side. "He's a Black Merkit; he's an ox. Let's go."

"Kaidu first," Quyuk shouted. "He's the youngest and weakest."

Kaidu blushed, grabbed his bow, and stepped to the line. The targets were staggered, some farther away than others; the farthest was at the limit of accurate range. Kaidu drew and shot, and down by the targets a slave called out, "White in the third."

Baidar slapped Kaidu on the back, but Quyuk and Buri jeered. Buri shouted, "Which were you trying for? We should make him specify his target."

"You try it," Kaidu said. "The light's terrible."

"What light?" Baidar stepped up to the line. "I can't see the target."

But he shot well enough; the slave called, "Gold in the fifth."

"No sport," Quyuk said. "If Baidar can hit the farthest target— make another line, Buri. Twenty paces. Maybe we should take down a few of the torches."

"Can you hit something you can't see?" Mongke said, in Psin's ear. "Quyuk can."

Buri paced off to the new line, marked it, and took his bow. Psin glanced at Mongke. In the weak light Mongke's eyes were only shadows, but the curve of his wide smiling mouth showed.

"Shoot," Quyuk said.

Buri shot. Psin could hear the arrow and see it for most of its flight. The slave shouted, "Red in the fourth."

Kaidu laughed, and Buri shoved him angrily away. "You try it, Psin. You've got the strongest bow."

"Take down the last four torches," Psin said. He stood at the line, picked out the last target, and frowned. Slaves ran off to douse the torches around the targets.

Quyuk said, "That's my trick, Psin." He sounded amused.

"Give me an arrow."

With the torches out the targets were only blurs. Psin glanced at Quyuk. There was no sense in it if he couldn't beat Quyuk. He took the arrow from Mongke and said, "Go down and put out another four torches and move that target."

Buri said, "Put its back to him, Mongke." He laughed.

"You have to see it at least once," Quyuk said. "Or shall we give you three arrows?"

Mongke was already gone. Psin looked at the arrow in his hand, nocked it, and shot it at the ground by his feet. The string shattered the arrow in half lengthwise. "My quiver is over there. Get me one of my own." He kicked the ruined arrow away. "Your arrows lack spline, Buri."

"It wasn't mine. Mongke gave it to you."

"Who gave it to Mongke?" Buri knew how strong Psin's bow was. "Mongke, are you ready?"

Far down the shooting range, full of amusement, Mongke's voice called, "Ready, Khan."

Buri handed Psin one of his own arrows, and Psin nocked it. "Throw a torch."

Something hurtled through the air and hit the ground. Mongke had figured out what Psin wanted. Psin bawled, "A lit torch, Mongke."

Mongke laughed. A light showed on the sidelines, and the torch hurtled through the air over the targets. Before it fell and a slave covered it, Psin saw the switched target. Mongke had moved it up and turned it sideways. It was no wider than a man's hand.

"Damn him," Quyuk said. "He's too full of tricks."

Psin shot. He heard the arrow hit something; he hoped it was Mongke, but he knew it was the target. Immediately torches bloomed. Mongke himself ran over, looked, and wheeled.

"Solid hit."

Kaidu crowed, and Baidar grinned almost triumphantly. Quyuk pursed his lips. "Now. A good shot. I'll try it. Mongke, move the target again."

Psin stepped back. It was cold, and he had proved nothing. A slave came over to him with a bowl of kumiss.

"Throw the torch, Mongke."

Quyuk's shout echoed off the high wall. The torch swung up, lighting the shooting range, and Buri swore under his breath. Mongke had set the target back where it had been, face forward. There was no problem to it. Quyuk shot twice, swiftly; the first arrow hit the target, and the second went off to the side. Mongke came darting up into their midst.

"Quyuk, you missed me." Mongke hitched himself back up on the fence rail.

"You'll insult me once too often," Quyuk said. "By God, I'll—"

"Let him alone," Psin said. "He's jealous; he can't shoot." He gave the kumiss back to the slave. "Now let's put up the torches again and do this properly."

* * *

"When do we start on these great raids?" Mongke said. "Incidentally, Quyuk's sent us a present."

Psin watched the slaves pouring hot water into his tub. His head throbbed, and it irritated him that Mongke was apparently suffering nothing from the kumiss and wine and overeating of the night before. "When Tshant gets here."

"Oh. Well." Mongke hitched himself up onto a window ledge. The cold air seeped through the shutters, and Psin shivered. "Don't you want to know about the present?"

The slaves stood back, respectfully. Psin climbed up onto the stool and stepped cautiously into the water. He yelped. The hot water cut through layers of grease and dirt; the surface of the water turned scummy. He settled into it, wincing. One slave held out soap.

"Six slave girls," Mongke said. He sounded miffed. "All rather enchanting."

"Enjoy them while you're here," Psin said. He felt parboiled. He was sure his face was bright red. The soap lacerated his arms and chest. He ducked his head under the water and re-emerged, water streaming into his eyes.

"That must be why you're such a great fighter," Mongke said. He crossed his legs. "You divert all your sexual energies into fighting and giving orders. Unless of course you have no sexual energies?"

Psin sputtered at him. Mongke cocked his head.

"I've heard old men grow tired of girls. After all, you haven't paid any attention at all to any of the slaves here."

Psin scrubbed vigorously. He hated bathing. Quyuk and Mongke last night had forced him into a bet; if he couldn't make a certain shot he had to bathe. "You stink," Quyuk had said. "Honest Mongol dirt, I'm sure. We need some honest Mongol dirt here— what a shame if you were to carry it all back with you to the Gobi." Psin had not made the shot.

"And we've provided you with a marvelous new wardrobe," Mongke said. "Roupen, the Khan's clothes."

The slave bowed and left the room. Psin let another slave comb out his hair. "What kind of women?"

"Two Kipchaks, two Russians, one Alan—Heavenly Name. They are savage, the Alans. Quyuk and I . . . And a girl from the west, from Poland. She's the tamest of the lot."

"Poland."

Psin stood up in the tub. The water swirled and splashed around his knees. A slave threw a robe around his shoulders, and two more slaves rubbed him down briskly with squares of linen. His skin tingled; he hated admitting it was pleasant. Roupen came in with an armful of silk and satin. Psin opened his mouth to order him out again, but Mongke was grinning, and Psin kept quiet. The slaves dried him thoroughly, even between the toes and behind his ears, and dressed him with light, deft hands. The unfamiliar textures caressed him.

"You've worn silk underwear half your life," Mongke said. "This isn't so different. Those mustaches are very unbecoming. Why don't you cut them off?"

"No!"

The slaves draped a gold collar around his neck; Roupen smoothed out the medallions. Psin blushed. He could hear Mongke laughing under his breath. The slaves stood back, and Psin waved them away. His belt lay across the table beside Mongke's knee. When he went to it the rustle of the silks deafened him.

"How can you live dressed like this?"

"It's possible to learn. You can't wear that belt, the buckle will wear through your tunic."

"Not since I started walking have I gone unarmed." Psin took the dagger in its sheath from the old belt and rammed it through the sash on his new coat.

"Now that you're fit for noble company," Mongke said, "come look over these girls. The Alan intrigues me, but I'll need help."

"If you need help, you shouldn't—Yes?"

"Tshant Bahadur has arrived," the messenger said, from the door. "He's up at Quyuk Noyon's house."

Mongke leapt down from the windowsill. "I'll go—"

"No." Psin snatched up his sable cloak and started toward the door. "You are to go inspect your men. They need remounts. That's a command, Mongke."

"I—"

"If you break a command, I can order you back to Karakorum. Go on."

Mongke's mouth twitched sulkily. Psin went out of the room.

When he left the house the harsh cold struck him. The grease he'd just washed off had protected him against it before. His horse waited, and he mounted and galloped off to Quyuk's house. The wind was bitter. In the streets of Bulgar, conquered Bulgars worked and talked and skittered out of his way. His horse spun a rock out from underhoof and it smashed against the wall of a mud hut. He cantered through Quyuk's gate.

A slave rushed out to take his horse, and the sentry held the door open for him. He went through the empty room where they had dined the night before and into another, smaller room. Quyuk and Buri were talking in low voices at the far end; they looked up when Psin walked in.

"Here he comes," Quyuk said. "But so splendid."

"I don't need comments," Psin said. He draped his cloak over his arm. "I was told my son is here."

"And your grandson. I've summoned them."

Buri sat down and thrust his legs out in front of him. "We have a good reason why you can't take us all raiding. Someone has to command in Bulgar."

"Oh? Why?"

Buri's face grew dark red. "Because—who will send out patrols? Keep the peace? Collect taxes?"

"Your underlings will probably go on conducting your business as well without you as they do now." Psin shook out his sleeves. "However, I doubt they'll have to suffer through leaderless. Sabotai should be here within a few days."

Quyuk wandered aimless around the room, running his hand over the wall. He paused at a window. "You're enjoying being older, wiser, and tougher than the rest of us, aren't you, Psin?"

"Very much. Buri, you go down and help Mongke find remounts for my troops."

Buri said, "I want to go drinking."

"I'm giving you a command."

Buri stared at him, turned his head to look at Quyuk, and said, "Do you have any orders for me, Quyuk?"

Quyuk smiled. "Go help Mongke."

"With your permission." Buri swept his gaze across Psin and started out.

The door opened, and a Mongol servant came into the room. "Noyon, Tshant Bahadur is outside."

Quyuk turned. Psin nodded to the servant. "Send him in." He took a chair from the wall and moved it closer to the center of the room. Quyuk frowned thoughtfully. Buri lingered by the door.

Dressed in leather armor and sheepskin boots, his face smeared with grease against the cold, Tshant strode in, closely followed by a small boy. He bowed to Quyuk and nodded to Psin. The small boy emitted a cry of delight, ran over to Psin, and wrapped both arms around Psin's left leg.

"You came quickly enough," Quyuk said. Buri was staring at Tshant.

"I was ordered here or I wouldn't have come at all," Tshant said. He sat down. "Djela."

Djela trotted back to Tshant, who picked him up and held him in his lap. Tshant said, "Djela Noyon. Jagatai's grandson."

"And mine," Psin said. "But that's just an accident. Buri, I thought you were leaving."

Buri turned and left.

Quyuk said, "Does Mongke know you're here?"

"He will." Tshant was unhooking Djela's coat. He set the boy on the floor and peeled the coat off.

"What have you done with my women?" Psin said.

"They're coming, with carts. Malekai is escorting them. Since you decided that Sidacai could rule the clan." Tshant was straightening Djela's clothes. "I sent Kerulu to Karakorum."

Quyuk scowled.

Psin watched Djela. He had come well through the long hard trip. Freed from his father's attentions, he wandered around the room, curious. "You should have sent Djela with her."

"No," Tshant said. "Sabotai said you had orders for me."

"I've got two thousand men picked out for you. Take them and ride the steppe west. The steppe starts considerably south of here. In the west there is a river called the Dnepr. Ride it, raid, take prisoners, and come back with useful information."

Tshant hawked. "I'm to go off into the middle of a country I know nothing about with two thousand men I've never seen."

"Exactly. But it's a bit of a ride to the steppe, and you'll have time to get to know your men."

"I want to rest."

"You'll leave either tomorrow or the day after."

Tshant's face clenched. "No."

"I'm not going to argue with you. If you don't want to go I'll put Mongke in command and take you with me to Novgorod." Psin with an effort kept from grimacing.

"No," Tshant said. "I'm not going to ride reconnaissance while these—" he stabbed his hand at Quyuk—"cattle sit around—"

Quyuk lunged forward, and Tshant whirled, crouched. Djela watched with shining eyes. Psin got up and walked between Tshant and Quyuk.

"They aren't going to sit around. They're coming with me. You are going to the Dnepr." He held out a hand to Djela, and the boy ran over, beaming. Psin led him to the door. At it, he said, "Tshant, if you fight me, I'll make you beg to be let go on long rides through hostile territory."

Abruptly relaxed and even mild, Tshant was sitting down again. "No need to flex your muscles. I'll go." He paused a moment, unsmiling. "What a pleasure to see you again, Father."

"Of course," Psin said. He took Djela out.

Tshant listened to the door shut and raised his arms over his head and stretched. Quyuk was looking out the window; he said, "Your relations with him aren't exactly cordial, are they?"

"We worship one another, but Father blushes so when he has to be affectionate."

Quyuk snorted.

"Your relations with your father aren't ideal, I've heard."

"The Kha-Khan hates me. He's afraid of me." Quyuk moved back across the room. His loose houseshoes scuffed on the plank floor. "I don't like him either."

"Don't look to me for help. Jagatai and Ogodai are teaching your nephew to be Khan. I'm committed to that."

"He's a handsome boy, your son."

"My father says he looks like your grandfather. You know I'm feuding with Mongke."

Quyuk nodded.

"I don't want fights with all my wife's cousins. While I'm with this army, I'll support you against my father if you keep the others out of my quarrel with Mongke."

Quyuk's eyes rested on him. He crossed his arms over his chest; one hand moved nervously up and down the other arm. His right wrist wore a bandage. He said, "You're blunt."

Tshant nodded.

"Very well. I'll agree to it. But you might not kill Mongke, you know."

"I won't." Tshant smiled. "I only mean to hurt him a little."

Quyuk's mouth twisted. "You remind me of your father."

"Oh?" Tshant looked at the bandage, and Quyuk nodded.

Tshant rose; he thought of what he would have to do before he could leave on his raid. "Where has my father taken my son?"

"He's living in the city. Take the street before the gate here, ride down three streets, and turn north. Fifth house from the end. Mongke is there, too."

"How convenient." Tshant gathered up Djela's things and went to the door.

Quyuk said, "Tshant. From what I just saw, against your father you'll be very little help."

Tshant smiled. "That's right." He opened the door and went out.

Psin found Mongke still in the house, only half-dressed, and eating fruit steeped in wine. He put Djela to one side and said, "I told you to go to the camp."

"I know. But my horses are all lame. A pity."

"Take one of mine."

"Oh, well." Mongke got up and strolled leisurely around, dressing. "You don't mind if I—"

"Yes. I do. Move."

Mongke drew his dagger and looked at the blade. Djela said, "Is that the man my father hates?"

"I am," Mongke said. He put up the dagger and went to the door, just fast enough so that Psin could not shout at him. Psin's palms were sweating. He wanted to throw Mongke out bodily. He sent a slave to saddle a horse; Mongke pretended to have lost a boot and poked around looking for it.

"Djela," Psin said. "Go down the corridor to the room at the end. Ask for Dmitri. He'll take you around the city."

"But I want to stay here. I want to tell you about our ride. It was snowy and we found—"

"Later." Psin ruffled the boy's hair. "I have to talk to your father. We'll have plenty of talking later. I have some things to tell you, too."

"Good."

"Say the name again."

"Dmitri. I remember." Djela ran out.

Mongke looked disconsolate; he was fully dressed and there had been no sound of a horse in the courtyard. He picked up his bow and left. Psin sat down, rubbing his chin. A slave girl came in with red wine and poured it for him.

A horse clattered in the courtyard. Psin bounded up, but it was only Mongke leaving. He turned away from the window, surprised that he was so tense. The girl smiled at him, and he gestured to her to leave.

Through the window he could see all but one corner of the courtyard. The snow, swept off by slaves, lay in a dirty heap against the southern wall. Dmitri and Djela came out of a door down the wall and walked toward the stable; Djela was talking, his bright face lifted toward the slave's. Psin heard something about snow and frozen men.

Tshant rode through the gate, dismounted, and gave Djela his coat. Djela tried to push it away; he said it was warm, too warm for a coat, he would run to keep warm, did he have to wear it? He had to wear it. Tshant said something to Dmitri, who bowed, and gave his reins to another slave. Psin pushed away from the window. He could feel the tension growing in his back and shoulders, the resistance and the strength to fight Tshant. Tshant, like them all, would have him down and beaten if he stopped shoving long enough for them to draw a free breath. He settled himself in a chair, his wine cup on the floor beside him.

Tshant came in. "Good morning, Father. We had a lovely trip out from the Lake."

"Was the snow bad?"

"Terrible."

"I suppose everyone's all right, or you would have told me. I wish you'd brought my dun horse with you."

"Malekai will bring him. He would have slowed me down." Tshant stripped off coat, gloves, hat, belt. "Tell me about Russia."

"I wish I knew. I'm here to do reconnaissance. All I know is that the steppe runs west at least as far as the river I told you about. The steppe begins a day's ride south of here, and the forest stretches on way north of where we'll be going."

"Where is Mongke?"

"He's not here. You can fight with him when I'm done with you."

"Who are our enemies? Cities or tribes?"

"Cities. I suppose many of them are like Bulgar. Did you look at the Volga camp? Batu built it on a Russian plan, in part."

"I spent the night, no more."

"You came faster than we did. I think Sabotai has had more trouble with the Altun than with enemies."

"But you love making men do what they don't want," Tshant said softly. "I told Quyuk I'd support him against you if he stays out of my fight with Mongke."

"Your loyalty makes me weep with pride."

"What use am I against you?"

"None. How is Artai?"

"Very well. Happy. She's glad you sent for her."

"And Chan?"

"Furious. She's done nothing but complain about the whole trip. Now that she's sure nothing she says will change things."

Psin grunted. He could hear Chan's voice in his mind, light and pure as porcelain, full of careless reproach. He shifted in the chair; even thinking about her kindled him.

"She'll cause you trouble," Tshant said. "My cousins like women, I'm told."

"I'll tend to Chan."

Tshant scratched his nose, smiling. "I'm sure you will."

"Your men are camped in the point of land where the rivers meet. You'll have trouble finding remounts."

"I'll need a Russian-speaking slave."

"Your thousand-commanders will get you one."

"Good. I'm taking Djela."

"I think you're a fool."

"Nonetheless. You took me fighting when I was his age."

Psin stood up. "I think I was a fool. I took Tulugai and Kinsit along with me to Khwaresm. Where are they now?"

"They did not die in Khwaresm."

"Still." Psin turned his back on Tshant. He hadn't thought of Tulugai and Kinsit for some while. They had died in China. "They learned too young not to be afraid. Fear keeps a man alive, I think. In ways."

"The ways aren't worthy of us. They were in the Kha-Khan's service. They could expect to die."

Psin clenched his teeth. Heat in waves flowed over him. He kept still, staring, waiting for Tshant to say one thing more. It occurred to him that he mightn't be so angry if he had thought more often of his dead sons. "When you lose one, you'll know better than that."

Tshant's chair scraped against the floor. Psin could hear him stand up.

"I lost a son and a daughter before they could draw breath," Tshant said. His voice came from near the door. "I don't mean to lose this one. Djela is mine, and I'll do what I think I should with him."

The door slammed. Psin whirled. He was alone in the room. His blood heated, and he took a step toward the door. Through the window he heard a horse's hoofs pounding frantically in the court-yard.

Tulugai and Kinsit had looked like him: big, stocky, awkward in their youth. When they had talked to him their respect had filled him up with satisfaction. They had never fought him. He turned and kicked the chair across the room.

He kept Tshant and Mongke away from each other easily enough; their troops were camped on opposite sides of the city. Mongke reported that he would be able to leave the next morning. Tshant's men had trouble getting horses and Psin didn't think they would leave Bulgar before he himself did.

Djela and Psin spent most of the afternoon with Dmitri, learning Russian. Djela was full of excited stories about his ride. He said, "And I'm going raiding with Ada, too. He said so."

Dmitri frowned. "You're young, noyon."

"Not so young. Am I, Grandfather?"

"Young enough."

"Can Dmitri go with me?"

"No. Dmitri's going with me to Novgorod."

From the tail of his eye Psin saw Dmitri's small start and smiled. "Where are you from, Dmitri?"

Dmitri said, "Riazan, my Khan."

Psin looked away from him and pretended to listen to Djela. Dmitri was from the north, somewhere, but from what city he had never said. Riazan wasn't in the north.

That night Mongke of his own accord ate with his troops. Djela, Tshant, Kaidu and Psin ate in Psin's house.

"They will know me before we reach the Dnepr," Tshant said, when Psin asked about his men. "They're good enough, but they need a strong hand."

"Take Kaidu with you," Psin said. "You might find him useful."

Kaidu exhaled hard, as if his breath had been pent up. His eyes burnt. "Thank you. I want to go."

Djela looked tired; he leaned his head on Tshant's chest and shut his eyes. Tshant put one arm around him. Psin thought of saying something, but Tshant's heavy eyes looked too much as if he expected it. "You know what I want you to do," Psin said. He signed to Dmitri, who was pouring the wine.

"Yes," Tshant said. "You want to know the country as well as a man born to it, and all without stepping your horse's hoof on it yourself." He reached for his cup. "I'll do it. I may have trouble, with the horses in the condition they're in."

"Are they unsound, or just—"

Tshant snorted. "Unsound? A horse we'd slaughter for meat would look good next to these. Foundered. Windbroken. Bad backs. I saw one horse out in the remount herd urinate pure blood —bad kidneys. Mange. I could have pulled the winter coat off one of those nags with my hands. Bowed tendons, active splints, running sores. Half of them are so underweight I'd give them two years on pasture before I tried to ride one."

Psin chewed his mustaches. Of all the armies, Tshant's had the farthest to ride. "The Altun have private herds, off near the hills. Take them. They're crossbreds and they're bigger than these."

Kaidu said, "But those are our horses."

"They'll carry your men. Tshant, take them."

"Quyuk won't like it."

Tshant laughed. "Quyuk hasn't liked anything much for the past few days, I understand." He dragged Djela into his lap, and the child murmured in his sleep. "I'll take his horses first."

Psin had intended the Altun herds for his own remounts. The next day, after Mongke left Bulgar with a great thundering of drums, he rode out and told his thousand-commanders to see that each of the men he would take to Novgorod had at least one sound horse to ride. Both thousand-commanders looked skeptical.

"We'll steal others on the way, if we can," Psin said. "Have you seen Quyuk Noyon?"

One of them grinned. "The word is that he's drunk. Kadan Noyon is over across the camp."

"Ah?" Psin turned his horse and rode over east.

Kadan was talking to the commander of his personal tuman. When Psin rode up they both rose. Psin dismounted. He could hardly believe that Kadan was sober; he'd never seen him less than stumbling drunk. Kadan said, "What do you think of our camp, Khan?"

"Don't remind me." The camp was filthy and ill-kept. "We're leaving tomorrow, you know."

"I know."

Psin looked around, at the camp. "When Sabotai gets here he'll tend to this. He'll probably burn it and start out fresh."

"It was bad when we got here, Khan." Kadan smiled apologetically.

"You should have cleaned it up, instead of letting it get worse."

"Quyuk said it was too much trouble."

"Quyuk had better learn that taking trouble is easier than taking Sabotai or me." Psin sat down and pulled off his hat. Meat was cooking in a covered pot, and his mouth watered at the scent.

"Aren't you going to remark that I'm sober?" Kadan said.

"It's the most extraordinary thing I've ever seen. Why?"

Kadan grinned. "Because I'm not as clever as Quyuk. For me, it's easier to do things properly the first time. I'll be no hindrance to you, Khan. In fact, I intend to enjoy seeing my brother take orders for once."

"I don't need help from you."

Kadan huffed; it was a way of laughing without opening his mouth. "You'll get none. I'm like Mongke. I'll sit back and watch and in the end . . . well. Quyuk has a long unsettled debt with me."

Psin spat and turned to his horse. Kadan was staring into the cookfire, smiling. Psin put one foot in his stirrup and swung up. "Kadan."

Kadan looked up.

"While I command, nobody quarrels. If you fight Quyuk, you fight me. Understand?"

He turned his horse and cantered off without an answer.

THEY WON'T COME TO US, NOT SO MANY OF US," BAIDAR SAID. "The Mordvins are natural cowards." He stood in his stirrups to ease his back. Quyuk, beside him, was paring his nails, his rein on his horse's neck. Psin looked all around; the snowfields stretched on a little way before they met the black forest. Behind him two thousand men rested their horses.

"Kadan," Psin said. He disliked the emptiness of the fields. They were two days from Bulgar and they had seen no hoofprint, no trace of the Mordvins.

Kadan trotted up. Psin pointed ahead of them. "Take five hundred men and ride advance guard. Push them. I want you half a day's ride ahead of us. And stay sober."

"Yes, Khan." Kadan whirled and galloped back to the line, shouting names. Men jogged out of the uneven mass of riders, forming up in a separate army alongside. Psin turned, running his eyes over the Altun.

"Buri. Take two hundred men and ride our southern flank. Stretch out, but keep in contact with us." He squinted, judging men and distance. "Don't overextend. That forest will break up our formation."

Buri stared at him, swung his head, and said, "Quyuk?"

Quyuk apparently nodded. Psin did not look at him. Buri spun his horse and loped into the army, his right hand gesturing. Psin waited until Buri's hand moved toward a man of Mongke's honor guard, and Psin shouted, "None from Mongke's banner. Take others."

Buri skidded his horse to a standstill and turned toward Quyuk. Psin slashed his whip down on his horse's shoulder; his horse leapt forward, between Buri and Quyuk, and Psin said, "Take others, Buri."

Quyuk, behind him, said softly. "Take others, Buri." Psin could hear his amusement. He looked over his shoulder and back toward the thousand-commanders. "Orta, five hundred men, ride rearguard. Arcut—no. Kalai, two hundred, in the same formation as Buri but to the north."

The thousand-commander and the commander of Mongke's honor guard swung out and started collecting men. Buri cantered off, and his men in a string followed, every other leading a riderless horse, their remounts. Kadan and his men were already well ahead. Baidar trotted up to Psin and said, "The customary banners, I suppose."

Psin nodded. "Or have you forgotten them, too?"

Baidar reddened. Psin kicked up his horse and the six hundred men still with him trotted forward. The shadow of the banner over Psin's head flashed across the snow in front of him. Horses surged around him. He waited, amazed at his own calm, until the remaining thousand-commander remembered to organize the column, turned, and looked back. The column was disorderly, but at least they weren't getting in each other's way. Quyuk, beside him, looked bored.

The road traveled along the bank of the river, and the trees had been cut back, for a comfortable margin on either side. They could follow it for a few days at least, until the army had fallen back into discipline. The snow glared under the sun, and Psin narrowed his eyes against it, smiling. In a few days the Altun would be almost worth working with.

The Mordvins did not attack. Psin camped early that day, to rest the horses and to let Kadan get far enough out in front. Couriers dashed madly back and forth from either flank and to the rear-guard, and the center column milled unhappily through the trees, trying to trample out a campground. Psin spent half the night making sure that the horses were getting enough to eat; where the snow was thin they pawed through to reach the grass, and elsewhere they ate the leaves and bark of the trees. He went to sleep satisfied that they could forage well enough. There was no moon that night, and the rising wind rustled the leaves in the forest.

The next day they camped somewhat later, and the day after that, after dark. With the camp routine fixed now they had the horses turned out and the gruel pots over the low fires before Psin had walked the stiffness out of his knees. Quyuk had said nothing all that day. Psin passed him, sitting beside a fire, and saw Quyuk's face slack with fatigue. Baidar sat opposite him, shoveling half-cooked gruel into his mouth. Psin stood just outside the circle of the firelight until they noticed he was there.

Baidar only nodded. Quyuk lifted his head, and his eyes were murderous.

"If I can take it, boy, you can," Psin said. "At your age you should be riding me into a ruin." He went off.

At his fire one of Buri's men waited, sitting cross-legged on a saddlecloth. He struggled to his feet when Psin came up.

"Lord," he said. "My commander sent me to tell you that he will not ride this pace."

Psin frowned. "Did you come all the way from his camp?"

The man laughed raggedly. "No—his messenger met me halfway there."

"Tell Buri that, if he wishes, he may quit. I can always use extra horses."

The messenger sank down again. Psin went to the pot over the fire and dipped out the steaming gruel. Dmitri and Arcut, the other thousand-commander, shared his fire; they were collapsed beside it.

"What does that mean?" the messenger said, finally.

"It means," Psin said, "that any man who can't keep up with us can go back to Bulgar. On foot."

Arcut jacked himself up on one elbow. Psin tasted the gruel and swore when it burnt his tongue. The messenger licked his lips, and Psin reached for the dipper. "Have you eaten?"

"No."

"Here. You can ride out tomorrow."

"Thank you."

The messenger snatched up a bowl. Psin blew on his to cool it. Arcut said, "Can you enforce that, Khan?"

Psin shifted, trying to get the weight off his rump bones. He consoled himself that he was hardly as sore as Quyuk and Buri. "I can. I will. Is that answer enough?"

Arcut smiled; Psin could hear it in his voice. "Yes, Khan."

That night, before he slept, Psin walked around the camp; he dug up the snow to find grass, tasted it, walked to the river to see how much the ground sloped toward it, and went back by another route, studying the way the wind blew the snow into drifts.

The moon rose over the tops of the trees, and the snow lay blue under it, broken by hoofprints and the dark shapes of the horses. To the north, the forest was like a cliff beneath the sky.

Standing on the plain so far from his campfire, he had to brace himself against weariness. The wind sighed in his ears. He trudged back, following as much as he could the trails the horses had broken, and rolled himself up in his cloak and slept.

He woke up shivering. It was far colder in this dawn than the night before. Some of his men were already up, stamping and slapping their arms against their sides to get warm. Their breath smoked in the air. Psin sat up. Snow had drifted over him during the night, melted from the heat of his body, and frozen into a crust. He rose crackling, shedding ice. The cold struck him in the face and he gasped, surprised.

"Eat and let's go," Quyuk shouted, off to Psin's left. "Wake up, you sandpigs. Get up."

Dmitri was heating gruel; Arcut trotted up, riding one horse bareback and leading the other two. Psin lifted one hand and caught the ropes when Arcut threw them. The horses were wild with the cold. Psin thrust the doubled end of one rope through his belt and rammed his bridle under his coat so that the bit could warm up. Arcut, dismounted, slung his saddle onto his horse's back.

Psin bent to pick up his saddle. Suddenly the horse hitched to his belt reared up and almost dragged him off his feet. He lurched and grabbed for a tree. The horse plunged, throwing itself back on its haunches. Its forelegs thrashed above Psin's head. He wrapped one arm around the tree and caught the end of the rope, bracing both feet wide apart. Arcut whirled; when the horse reared again Arcut caught one foreleg at the fetlock and threw his weight against its shoulder. The horse crashed down on its side, and Psin leapt across its flailing hindlegs to sit down on its head.

Somebody was laughing. Psin looked up and saw Quyuk, already mounted, tossing a snowball from one hand to the other. Psin glanced at the fallen horse's rump; a white splash of snow marked it. Psin leapt up.

Quyuk cocked his arm to hurl the second snowball. Baidar, from nowhere, surged up behind him and flung him off his horse. Quyuk bounced, and the horse bolted.

"Catch your mount, cousin," Baidar said. His voice rang in the cold air. Quyuk, sprawled on his back, looked too stunned to hear.

Psin's horse had gotten to its feet. Arcut was holding it by the head. Psin took the rope and waved Arcut away; he saddled up as quickly as he could, swore when the horse fought the bit, and mounted. Baidar had gotten Quyuk's horse for him, and they were both riding off to the head of the line. Arcut was waving the yellow banner high over his head.

"Move out," Psin called. "Slow trot."

Arcut nodded and pulled the yellow banner off the staff; he had the white one ready over his saddlebows. Psin moved up beside him.

"Next time, saddle your horse before you bring him in."

Arcut nodded. He swung the white banner up. They started off at a jog. Psin could see Quyuk, far ahead, but he made no effort to catch up with him, and Quyuk stayed well in the lead all that day.

Two days later, still following the road beside the river, Psin's column passed beneath the walls of a city. The gates were barred tight, and swarms of people gathered on the walls; they blackened the ramparts around the main gate. Psin drew his men off a little to circle around the city. They plunged through the heavy snow under the trees, and the column struggled to keep its shape. Under the city walls Psin could see even rows in the snow—plowed ground, he thought. A new trail toward the gate showed where a herd of cattle had run for cover when Kadan and the vanguard passed that morning. The people on the walls yelled insults and threw garbage and offal at the Mongols. The trash skidded over the snow crust, far short of the army.

"What's that they keep shouting?" Psin said to Dmitri.

"Tartar," Dmitri said. "That's what Russians call Mongols."

"Tatar?" Quyuk said. "They're calling us Tatars. We should skin them."

"There are no more Tatars," Psin told Dmitri. "All the Tatars are Mongols now."

They circled back to the cleared ground, toward the river. Dmitri said, "I think it comes from the Latin word for Hell—Tartars are people from Hell."

He had switched to Russian. Psin made him repeat some of the words and nodded. "Well, we're not Tatars, and they shouldn't call us that. We beat the Tatars a long time ago."

"But they don't mean—"

"They do. It's an insult." Psin kicked his horse into a faster trot. "Arcut, keep moving."

He swung back to look the city over. The walls were twice as high as the one around the Volga camp; they were built of logs, the ends cut to dovetail. There were a few fresh trunks in the wall, and the logs lying on the ground were painted black. He started off again, and the townspeople hooted and called him a coward.

Baidar was reining off from the column, looking ahead, and Psin galloped to catch up. Baidar swung around and pointed. "Kadan started to lope, up there."

"Hunh." Psin nodded. He stood in his stirrups, looking down toward the river ice. "Go down to the river and see if there are tracks on it."

Baidar charged off. Snow flew over Psin's hands. He rode up to join Quyuk and Arcut and said, "Fast trot. Arcut, spread them out on either side of the river."

"What's wrong?" Quyuk said.

"I'm not sure." Baidar was coming back. "Dmitri, what do you put on the trees in the stockade walls? To keep them from rotting from the damp in the ground."

Dmitri frowned. "I don't know."

"You lie."

Quyuk moved, reaching for Dmitri, but Psin stopped him. He shoved his horse against Dmitri's. The Russian's broad pale face was unafraid.

"I don't like you lying to me," Psin said. "If you don't want to answer, say nothing. Coal tar, I think. It makes no—"

Baidar plunged in among them. "A large number of horsemen rode along the river this morning. Not Mongol."

"Good."

Arcut's banners had the men changing formation; already over a hundred were across the river and riding up that bank. Dmitri said, "How does he know they're not Mongols?"

"Their horses are shod," Psin said. "Baidar, take the north flank. Quyuk, go south. Let's move. Arcut, lope."

The horses broke into a slow canter. Of his own accord, Arcut had sent out two scouts, Psin kept right by Dmitri. "Don't try to run, and I won't tie you. If I have to you'll ride face-down all the way to Novgorod and back." He saw Dmitri's muscles loosen.

"Signal to Buri," Psin said to Arcut. "Keep him even with us."

Arcut hauled his red banner from his saddlebags. The open road ahead was narrowing. The forest wall closed in on it and pinched it, and the road ran up a low hill just ahead. The scouts disappeared over it. Psin got out his bow and pulled the top off his quiver. "Arcut. Watch Dmitri."

The red banner snapped overhead. Somewhere, across the river, Buri's column would see it and quicken their pace. Psin's horse stumbled, caught itself, and started up the gentle slope of the hill.

A scout appeared on the crest, waving his arms. He turned his horse broadside to the oncoming column and pointed back the way he had come. Psin shouted, "Full gallop," and whipped his horse. He hated charging up a slope. All around him the horses gathered speed. Even over the pounding of the hoofs he could hear the whine of the wind in the pine trees close to them. The scout whirled off the crest of the hill and plunged down out of sight.

Psin's horse leapt up to the height, collected himself, and charged down the other side. Before them, Russians fought and shouted, their backs to Psin. He nocked an arrow. Kadan had turned back and attacked the Russians pursuing him. Psin dropped his rein and drew his bow. He saw his arrow streak up into the sky, alone, but before he could see it start to drop the sky turned black with arrows. The Russians never even wheeled. Their ranks slid down into the snow like water. Psin's horse veered sharply to the left, crashed into Baidar's, and nearly fell. Psin shot one more arrow. He saw a body lurch up and fall back in a spray of snow; his horse carried him past the Russians and into the midst of Kadan's men.

"Eeeeeeeyyyaaaaah!"

The yell carried over the uproar, and the uproar died and let the yell wail away into nothing. They sat on their horses, suddenly motionless, around a vast circle packed with crumpled bodies and melting, bloody snow. Half a dozen horses stood in the tangle, and while Psin watched stupidly another horse kicked out and heaved itself up onto its feet. Nothing else moved but the Mongols.

Quyuk said, "If all Russians fight like that, we'll be building ships on the ocean shore before the summer's out."

"I think we surprised them," Baidar said.

Quyuk laughed. Psin shook himself and looked around. "Well, go collect your arrows. Arcut, I want a column again. Where's Kadan?"

Kadan was coming toward him. Dmitri sat in his saddle, looking stonily at the forest across the field. Psin gave him a hard look and rode up to meet Kadan.

"What happened?"

Kadan shrugged. "They chased us—there were at least five hundred of them, and I didn't know what you wanted me to do. So I ran on ahead of them. But they stopped or something."

"They probably couldn't keep up."

"Maybe. I turned around and came back after them, and my scouts told me you were coming, so I rushed them and held them here until you could take them from behind."

"Good. We're too close to the city, though. You might have sent a messenger to me and had me ride faster. There weren't five hundred of them, either."

Kadan shrugged. "They covered so much ground—"

"They charge in looser ranks then we do." Psin looked back. "Move out. They may have more men in the city. Our rearguard is coming after us and I don't want them to run up on our backs. Push your horses."

"I've been pushing my horses since we left Bulgar."

Psin laughed. "Oh, well, if you think so you don't know what pushing means. Arcut, white banner."

Dmitri said, "You gave them no warning."

"If they hadn't been shouting so much they would have heard us," Psin said. "Why should we give them warning?"

"It's not . . ."

After a pause Dmitri used a Russian word, although they had been speaking Mongol. Psin said, "What does that mean?"

"It means to give your enemies a reasonable chance."

"Hunh." Psin lay back. They had camped early, to let Kadan get out ahead of them again. The road had tapered off to a narrow trail, and their camp sprawled through the trees around a knob of a hill. "To give them a chance to kill more Mongols than necessary? Dmitri. Consider this. The essence of war is to kill your enemy and not get killed yourself. We are not a numerous people, we Mongols, especially so far from home as this."

Dmitri glanced all around. His wide brow was deeply wrinkled. Psin drank some kumiss and put the bowl down again, near the fire.

"Why are the Christians your enemies?"

"Because they are not our friends."

"You never asked us—"

"Oh, we asked. We sent ambassadors to each city west of the Volga. If the ambassadors were lucky they came back alive. How long have you lived in Mongol camps?"

"Since . . . last spring."

"Then you should know better than to ask me such questions. Talk Russian. I'm not learning it as well as I want to."

Tshant cupped his hands behind his head, put his back against his saddle, and said, "I know even now what my father will say. We can't lay siege to these towns." He poked around his upper jaw with his tongue and spat out a pine needle. "Tell that pig's rectum not to put the cooking pots under the trees."

"Why not?" Kaidu said.

In the banked firelight Tshant's face turned a mottled purple. "Because the needles get into the gruel."

"I mean, why can't we siege these towns?"

"Oh, we can. For a few days. Enough to soften them up. We can't starve them out. We can't live so long off this country, not in winter. We'd starve first."

Djela ran into the shelter beneath the tree, singing a song

Tshant's Russian slave had taught him. Tshant caught his coat and
pulled him down, rolling him over and over in the soft pine needles.
Djela whooped with laughter. The branches overhead swayed, and
the Russian slave ambled in.

"How far to this obscene river?" Tshant said.

"For a Russian, many days," the slave said. Kaidu could never
remember if he was Alexei or Gregor. "For a Mongol, who
knows?" The Russian thrust out his thick lips and shrugged heavily.

"Aaaah." Tshant lay back, Djela hooked securely under one arm.
"My father will be halfway to Novgorod by now."

"I like your father." Kaidu smiled.

Tshant's face lay in shadow; his voice came muffledly out of it.
"That's because you haven't caused him trouble. If he decides
you're difficult he'll go at you like salt in a wound."

"Nevertheless—"

"If your great-grandfather had died at birth my father would be
a clan chief who thought the trip from Lake Baikal to Karakorum a
long ride."

Kaidu could think of nothing to say to that. He looked down at
the stirrup leather on his knee and, taking the knife from the fire,
began to bore a new hole in it. They'd left Bulgar ten days before;
every time he mentioned Psin, Tshant bristled. Kaidu had liked his
own father, who was dead, and he thought his grandfather even
finer. It bothered him when Tshant talked about Psin that way.

"We'll never see Mongke now," Tshant said. "We're too far out
of his way."

Kaidu glanced over and grinned. They had followed a river most
of the way out, until Tshant decided that its twists and turns were
delaying them too much. But when they passed a Russian city—
Murom, the Russian slaves thought, or Riazan—Tshant had lingered half a day, hoping to sight Mongke's army. Now after crossing featureless steppe they were riding along a river Tshant
thought emptied into the Dnepr.

"Many days," Tshant said, abruptly. "How many days,
Gregor?"

"Many," the Russian said.

"Ten? A hundred?"

"Ten, maybe."

"Or maybe a hundred?"

The Russian grinned. "Maybe."

"Go to sleep."

The Russians were unbelievably stupid. Kaidu had mentioned it to Tshant, and Tshant had burst out laughing. That had surprised Kaidu more than anything else. Tshant had shouted, "You be so stupid, boy, if you're ever captured and asked questions." And had galloped off, with Djela right behind.

Kaidu studied the Russian's pleasantly broad face. The man was stupid. Tshant gave them too much credit. If he were Tshant he would start by burning the Russian's feet off and ask the questions afterward.

Two days later, the northern flank of Tshant's army passed another city. Kaidu, riding point, sent a message down the line, but Tshant declined to come see.

"It's big," Kaidu said to the Russian riding beside him.

"Not as big as Novgorod."

With rising panic Kaidu realized he should be remembering everything he saw. Smoke rose from the southeastern corner of the compound and trailed off toward them. He supposed they were signaling. Maybe they had a warcamp outside the city. If they were signaling they meant to attack. He passed the word down, his heart thundering in his throat. He could hear his men shouting to one another, commenting on the great walls opposite them. The ice gleamed under the light snow that covered the river, gleamed and went dull. Kaidu looked up at the sky. Clouds were thrusting up from the west, roiling and black. The wind had torn their undersides to shreds that hung down almost to the steppe.

"Noyon," the Russain said patiently.

Kaidu whirled. The man next to him in line said, "Noyon, the commander says the smoke is from burning garbage."

Hot blood rushed into Kaidu's ears. The faces of the men around him were politely blank. He jerked his eyes toward the city.

He could see people on the walls, pointing. The wall looked monstrous. It was made of wood; stumps covered a field alongside the river. The snow blurred everything.

Burning garbage.

That afternoon, unexpectedly, they came to a stretch of river too turbulent to freeze. When they first approached, Kaidu took the low booming ahead for thunder; the clouds overhead were ferocious. But when they moved closer he saw the foam and the spray over rocks in the riverbed, and saw the rapids charging wildly off across the plain.

"Noyon," the Russian said. "We are to camp here. The commander—"

Kaidu gestured that he heard. He wheeled his men around to make a campsite; before the steamy odor of gruel had risen Tshant was there, riding around looking. Kaidu went to his fire and watched his Russian stir the pot.

"It's going to snow," Tshant said.

Kaidu sprang up. In the constant howling of the rapids he hadn't heard Tshant behind him. He looked west; under the clouds, the sky was a dirty pink. "Yes, I think so."

"Tell me about that city."

Tshant dismounted and stripped his saddle off his horse. Djela appeared behind him, on a rangy black.

"Well," Kaidu said. "My Russian says it's not as big as Novgorod."

"Your Russian's name is Alexei. And he's probably never been to Novgorod."

"It wasn't very big. It's got a wooden wall—"

"What kind of wood?"

"I wasn't close enough to see."

"Oak, probably."

"The wall looks about five times man height."

Tshant nodded. He dumped his saddle on top of the saddlecloths, dug a rag from his saddlepouch, and scrubbed vigorously at his horse's back. The horse sighed and its head sank.

"There must be ramparts. I saw people standing on the walls."

"That makes sense."

"I saw only one gate."

"You saw only one side."

"They'd cut down the trees all around it. I saw the stumps."

"Any boats?"

"I didn't see any."

"How fast is the current in the river?"

"How fast is the . . ."

"Was the ice smooth or rough? These rapids are part of that river. It's obviously steeper here than there. How much more?"

"The ice was smooth."

Tshant ducked under his horse's neck and scrubbed from the far side. Kaidu could see no sign of approval on his face—no expression at all.

"What do they grow in their fields?"

"The fields were covered with snow."

"Any herds?"

"I didn't see any."

"Any people outside the walls?"

"No."

"What were they burning?"

"I . . . don't know."

Across the horse's back Tshant's stare was too even. "Wood? Vegetables? Grain? Old clothes, dead Mongols?"

"I don't know."

"Use your nose. Was there a road?"

"I didn't see one."

Djela in his gold-hooked coat came by, tugged at Kaidu's sleeve, said, "Gregor is teaching me more Russian," and ran off.

"Gregor," Tshant bawled. "Keep watch on him." His eyes followed his son's progress through the camp. Gregor plunged off in pursuit, and Tshant walked to the horse's head and wiped out its nostrils.

"I'm sorry about the smoke," Kaidu said.

"The Russians don't signal with smoke. They don't camp their fighting men outside the walls, either." Tshant turned the horse loose and let it find its own way to the grass. He shook the snow out of his saddlecloths and stretched them over a frame near the fire to dry. "My father's first campaign under the Genghis Khan was in China. He told me the first time they attacked a Chinese city, the Chinese set off rockets and burning lights. He says if he'd been in command the army wouldn't have stopped running until the Gobi turned to pure water."

Kaidu laughed, thinking of Psin, solid, immovable, running from burning lights. "He must have been young."

"He was younger than you."

Djela ran back, shouting Russian words at the top of his lungs. Behind him, carrying a skin of kumiss, Gregor strode. Djela rushed up to Tshant and hugged him, thrusting his head under Tshant's arm. "I'm happy."

"Good. Gregor—"

Tshant sat down with a thump; Djela had tripped him. Djela danced out of reach, dodged a snowball, and caught another square in the mouth. Tshant pointed to the ground. "Sit, will you? If you don't behave, I'm sending you to the Volga camp."

Gregor came over with bowls of kumiss and handed one to Tshant. Kaidu opened his mouth to ask Tshant what he thought of the city they had passed, but before he could speak a white flake dribbled down onto his chin. He looked up; the sky was darker, and snow floated down toward his face.

"Rough going tomorrow," Tshant said. "Sleep."

Psin and his column plowed through the forest, headed northwest. The road was off to their right, but it was so narrow that only half a dozen men could ride abreast down it, and Psin wanted to stretch out. He was sure there were other roads.

"It's getting hilly," Baidar said.

"And rocky." Psin took his feet out of the stirrups and worked them to get the blood back into his toes. Immediately his feet warmed up. In Russian, he said, "Novgorod is on a lake in the middle of hills. Isn't that right, Dmitri?"

Dmitri looked around, startled; he said, "I've never been to Novgorod."

"Why do I speak Russian with a Novgorod accent, then?"

"How do you know you do?"

Psin laughed. His progress in the language amused him. It wasn't as easy as Chinese, but it wasn't as hard as Arabic. "When you know the language a man speaks, you can think like him. I am from Novgorod."

"God help us."

Baidar and Quyuk beside them couldn't understand, and rode staring straight ahead, affronted. Quyuk's right cheekbone was bruised. In the darkness the night before he had tried to shove Psin under a horse, and Psin had clubbed him across the side of the head with a convenient rock.

"Khan," Arcut shouted. "Message coming."

Psin turned and looked back. Through the trees he could see men riding together. The message was coming up from the southwestern flank, from man to man. Finally one rode into the center and said, "There is another road, parallel to the one north of us."

"Tell Buri to send a scouting party along it. Twenty men."

The man trotted off through the trees with his message. Psin and the others rode up a steep slope and angled down the other side.

"Are we going to keep on like this?" Quyuk said.

"No," Psin said. "We'll make a camp before tomorrow night and use that as a base."

"Where?"

"Up ahead."

"Where up ahead?"

"I don't know yet."

Quyuk reeled in false dismay. "Is there something Psin Khan doesn't know? Can it be?"

"Shut your mouth," Baidar said.

At noon of the next day they found the place where the two roads met; three others met there too. It was a wide stretch of open ground, large enough to pasture their horses, high enough not to get sloppy when the snow melted around their fires. Psin ordered the flanks to make a camp.

"You knew this was here," Dmitri said.

Psin nodded, glancing around. He saw a good place to make a fire against a tilted rock and started for it, but Quyuk and Baidar got there first. Arcut was holding a spot almost as good.

"How did you know?" Dmitri said.

"Because I'm a general of reconnaissance." Psin jogged toward Arcut. He had known that the two roads probably met, but he hadn't expected anything as fine as this. If Dmitri was overawed, the others would be too, he hoped. He dismounted.

Arcut said, "Kadan isn't back yet."

"He'll come in before dark. Cook something, I'm hungry. And watch him." He nodded to Dmitri. All around, the men were milling their horses to trample down the snow. Two men riding bareback galloped past with almost forty horses on a string. Quyuk and Baidar were building their fire. Slaves dashed about around them, laden with baskets of dung for fuel.

Dmitri was struggling with the girths on Psin's saddle, and Psin pushed him away. "I have to ride this camp yet. Stay here. If Kadan comes in while I'm gone, Arcut, tell him to camp to the north a little and keep us supplied with meat."

He rode over to Quyuk's fire, shoving his way through the packed horses and men fighting over good camp spots. Quyuk was walking his horse back and forth to cool it out. He looked over at Psin.

"How long are we going to stay here?"

"Until I find Novgorod." Psin looked at the bruise on Quyuk's face. "Did you hit something in the dark, noyon?"

"Yes. But whatever it was will suffer for it." Quyuk smiled, so that his eyeteeth showed.

"Hunh." Psin brought his whip down on his horse's shoulder, careful to let the thongs snap in front of Quyuk's face. His horse bounded away. Two strides later the horse shied violently. Psin wrestled with it. Something struck him hard in the back of the head. He knew it was a snowball. He whipped the horse out of range.

WHEN PSIN GOT BACK BURI AND KADAN WERE BOTH AT QUYUK'S fire. He summoned Arcut and the other thousand-commander over and gave them standing orders. "When you ride out, keep extended, so that you can see what there is to see out here. If you are attacked, retreat back here. Send me news so that I can arrange an ambush. If you don't think your courier will reach me soon enough, send him straight back and retreat on a curve. Don't engage any Russians on your own."

Quyuk cleared his throat. "May we perhaps kill a deer if we could find one, Khan?"

Buri laughed. Psin glared at him. "If you think so dangerous a beast safe for you to handle."

Now Baidar laughed.

"I want sentries out in rings centered on the camp. Kadan, that's yours to do. The outermost ring will be at least half a day's ride from the camp. Buri, I want you to ride south, following the road you crossed yesterday. Kadan, take the road leading west out of this camp and follow it until it turns north."

"Will it?" Kadan said.

"Yes." Psin looked around at their faces. They were tired, but not so tired as they had been after the first few days' riding. "In my absence, Baidar will command the camp."

Quyuk roared and sprang to his feet. Psin said, "In my absence Quyuk will be gone too. I won't be here much."

Buri said, "Where Quyuk goes I go."

"I told you once before, Buri. I can always use extra horses."

Quyuk thrust his head forward. The firelight turned his eyes deep red.

"Merkit, you talk a lot. Too much. You talked us out here and you've talked us gentle so far. I'm sick of talk. What else do you have, Merkit?"

Psin looked at Buri and saw the sinews standing up in his throat and his mouth trembling with eagerness. "Baidar. Watch him for me." He got up.

"Come on, old man," Quyuk said. His voice hissed across the fire. "Come and fight me."

Psin unbuckled his belt. "I should think a boy of your good mind would have learned by now. I don't go to you, Quyuk. You come to me."

Quyuk snatched out his dagger and plunged around the fire. His arms were longer than Psin's. He held the dagger low, aimed at Psin's belly, and Psin sucked in his breath. He stood still, watching Quyuk prowl toward him. The belt dangled from his hand.

He glanced at Buri again and saw Buri's hot glittering eyes and Baidar's, behind him, doubtful. He pulled the belt through his fingers, so that he held it by the tongue end.

"Yaaah!"

Quyuk came in from one side like a leopard. The dagger flashed in the firelight. Psin jumped backward and slashed the belt at Quyuk's face. The lean brown face jerked back out of range, and Psin rushed forward. Quick, he thought. Make it quick. The dagger's ruddy blade streaked up between his chest and Quyuk's, and Psin caught it on his forearm and brought the belt down like a whip. He felt, together, the slice of the dagger across his arm and the belt buckle striking bone.

Somebody shouted. Psin wrapped his bad arm around Quyuk's waist and threw him hard, away from the fire. Quyuk rolled, his arms crossed in front of his face. Psin with the belt pursued him. He remembered just before he struck to grab the buckle end and swing the other. Quyuk lashed out with his legs and Psin dodged, flogging Quyuk across the arms and head with the belt. He could hear Quyuk's gasping breath and the flat thudding of the leather on flesh. Quyuk kicked him in the shin, and he grunted, but he brought the belt down so hard that blood popped from the edge of the welt on Quyuk's hand.

"Stop," Buri cried.

Psin leapt back, away from Quyuk's legs, and turned. Buri was on his feet, and his face was taut.

"Quyuk?"

Quyuk had rolled almost into the fire. He pressed his hands against his face. The backs of his hands were ridged with welts. He lurched up onto his knees. Psin stood still, the belt buckle clenched in his fist. Across Quyuk's forehead a cut oozed blood. Kadan whispered something.

"Get up," Psin said, quietly.

Lowering his hands, Quyuk rose. Welts streaked his face. He touched his forehead and looked at the blood on his fingers.

"What punishment?" Buri shouted. "What punishment for the man who spilled the blood of the son of the Kha-Khan?"

Baidar thrust at him, spat away from the fire, and went back to his place. Uncertainly, Arcut said, "The Yasa——"

Quyuk straightened. "The Yasa says that the blood of no highborn man shall be spilled." He reached out and caught Psin by the left arm and held it toward the fire. Psin's sleeve was sodden with blood from the dagger slash. Quyuk flung down Psin's hand. "No price against either of us." More softly, he said, "I'll get you my own way, Merkit."

He strode off from the fire. Baidar came up by Psin and looked at the wound. "You could have killed him with that belt buckle."

"I know."

Arcut and Baidar led him off to his own camp, and Dmitri without a word brought a long strip of linen for a bandage. Arcut pulled up Psin's sleeve and wrapped the bandage around his forearm. The blood seeped through at once. Dmitri put a handful of dirty snow on it.

"Buri never tried to help him," Arcut said softly.

"If he had, Quyuk would have killed him." Psin tugged his sleeve down. "I won't die of that. Dmitri, bring me some kumiss. I'm riding out tomorrow, Arcut. Go tell Quyuk that he's coming with me."

"You're out of your head. He'll kill you as soon as you're alone with him."

"Don't be stupid. He'll try, but he won't kill me. Go on, go tell him." Psin grinned. "And come back and tell me what he says."

Quyuk rode in absolute silence. His eyes flickered from side to side. Psin's opinion of him began to rise; very few men could sustain a cold rage for five days solid. Since they'd left the camp, Quyuk had said not one word to him and had looked him in the face only twice.

The welts were subsiding; the cut on his forehead would be

healed before Psin's arm stopped giving him trouble. Psin wished he knew what Quyuk was thinking.

The forest around them shivered in the chilly winter stillness. They heard owls at night, and wolves, and they saw the tracks of huge elk during the day. Every night one or two of the twenty men around them would bring in game, and they would eat it for dinner and sleep under the pine trees, all without more than a few words.

Psin hated the forest. Traveling in a loose pack they covered less ground than he wanted. A man riding within calling distance of his companions could grow absent-minded and realize only after a long while that he'd drifted off and was lost, and no shouting would raise his friends. He could only ride back across the track, his horse plunging and stumbling in the snowdrifts under the trees, until he found a trail to follow. The black boughs that swayed over their heads shut out the sun, and the sky looked much farther away, seen through the trees.

Dmitri, on Psin's left, sneezed and snuffled. His horse stumbled, and Dmitri jerked him up again. The horse, with all four legs braced, skidded a length across a patch of open snow. Through the gouges in the snow Psin saw a rock face.

"There's the river again," a man called; his voice came from Psin's left, but the trees hid him from view.

"Stay away from it."

If there were people around, they would be near the river. Dmitri sneezed and Psin looked hard at him. Dmitri had been acting like a man with a cold for three days, but his nose never ran. Psin thought he was preparing a way to warn any Russians they might try to ambush. He whipped his horse up a little incline and reined in. Dismounting, he threw Dmitri his rein and scraped away the snow. On an incline the snow should have been shallow. It was not. He swore, poked at the frozen earth, and mounted again.

Quyuk put one hand to his face and shook his head.

They rode on, crossed a little stream, and floundered through immense drifts on the far side. Looking up, Psin caught a glimpse of one of his men, well ahead, angling his horse across a steeper slope. The trees were thinning out. His horse snorted and backed up, refusing the hill, and Psin had to whip him into taking it. The footing was solid rock and ice. Psin's horse went to its knees over a fallen log. When Psin got off to let it regain its feet, he glanced at Quyuk.

Quyuk's eyes looked strange. His horse heaved its way up toward Psin's, and Psin reached out to catch the rein. "Are you all right?"

Quyuk pressed one hand against his forehead. "No." His voice was so low Psin could barely hear it.

"What's wrong?"

"My head hurts. I can't see."

He swayed in the saddle. Psin whirled. Dmitri was waiting, sharp-eyed. Psin took two steps away, suspicious suddenly, and shouted up the slope.

"Dai. Come get my Russian. Tie him into the saddle. Keep on going north and leave me sign. I'll catch up with you by tomorrow night."

Dmitri said, "Khan, I—"

"Too close to home, Dmitri. Go up to Dai."

Dmitri's horse staggered up the rest of the slope. Psin took Quyuk's rein and his own and led the horses down toward the stream they had just crossed. Where they had crossed, the ground was level but on either side the stream ran through a gorge. Psin led the horses into the gorge heading east and followed it back until the walls straightened up and the sunlight vanished. Quyuk had his eyes shut; he was hanging onto the pommel of his saddle with both hands.

The gorge widened a little, and Psin stopped the horses. He drew Quyuk down out of his saddle. Quyuk groaned and twitched feebly. Psin let him sag onto the ground and got their cloaks from behind their saddles.

"Oh, God," Quyuk mumbled. Under his tan his skin was pale green. He put his head down, his cheek against the snow, and shut his eyes.

Psin spread out one cloak and helped Quyuk move onto it. Quyuk said, "I'm going to be sick."

"Go ahead." Psin got a bowl out of his saddlepouch and scooped snow into it.

Quyuk braced himself up on one elbow and vomited into the snow. His hair hung across his cheeks. Psin knelt beside him, wrapped the bowl of snow in the other cloak, and threw one arm around Quyuk's chest to hold him. Quyuk was trembling. His body strained to retch. They had eaten little that morning and he had nothing to throw up. Psin's arm began to ache, down along the wound. Quyuk hung there, almost sobbing.

"Are you all right?" Psin said.

Quyuk gasped something that sounded like yes. Psin laid him back against the cloak, unwrapped the bowl of snow, and threw the other cloak over Quyuk. The snow was melting. He went to his horse for a piece of cloth. When he came back Quyuk's eyes were shut tight and his breath came in whimpers, but his color was better. Psin dampened the cloth in the melted snow and washed Quyuk's face.

"Good," Quyuk whispered. "The cold."

Psin soaked the cloth and put it over Quyuk's forehead. "Lie still. Go to sleep. I can't stay down here. If anybody catches us here we're ended. I'm going up to the top of the bank. If you want something, don't yell. Whistle."

"Hunh."

Psin loosened the girths on the horses, slipped the bits out of their mouths, and tied the reins up over the pommels of their saddles. There was no grass, but the horses started gnawing at the bark of some stunted shrubs that grew out of the gorge wall. He took his bow and quiver and climbed up the wall. The rocks were slippery and when he tried to use the shrubs for handholds, they pulled loose and he nearly fell. He took off his gloves, and the cold struck at his hands like a snake. When he finally flung himself over the edge and lay on the top of the bank his hands were bleeding. He walked along to a place where a pine grew close to the ravine, crawled into the low branches, and sat still, his bow across his knees, watching north.

Tshant cursed steadily. His men were scattered all along the riverbank, galloping flat out over ground as rough and broken as the worst stretches of the Gobi. Behind them and finally falling back, a huge army of Russians was screaming insults and daring them to turn and face them.

The ground opened up right under his horse's hoofs. The horse bunched and leapt. Tshant clung to the mane. The horse landed and somersaulted completely over, and Tshant sailed off and crashed into the far bank of the little stream. He lay still a moment, everything white before his eyes, and staggered up. His horse was hobbling toward the bank. One foreleg hung. A white shard of bone thrust out just above the fetlock.

Russian voices howled, growing nearer. Tshant had been in the last rank of his column. He scrambled up the bank; his men were racing away, and the Russians, spread out, their armor flashing in the sun, saw him and whooped and threw lances.

"Father!"

Djela was galloping toward him, beating his horse with his bow. A lance rattled across the crusted snow between him and Tshant. Djela crouched over his horse's withers. Far down the river, the Mongols were swinging to charge back. Djela's horse sat down right before Tshant, and he caught mane in one hand and his son's belt with the other and swung up behind him.

"They're too close," Djela cried. His hair whipped Tshant across the face.

Tshant swung around. The Russians were streaking up toward them, their lances raised. One man raced well before the others. Djela's little chestnut horse ran madly across the plain but the knights were swooping down on them. Tshant pried Djela's bow out of his hand, grabbed an arrow, and shot back over the horse's rump. The leading Russian fell off his horse.

"Here come our men," Djela called. He raised his voice. "Come on! Come on!"

The air overhead hummed with arrows. Tshant reached in front of Djela to take the rein out of his hand. Wrapping one arm around Djela's waist, he spun the chestnut around and charged the Russians.

The Russians wavered. Their cries rose less triumphantly; on the flank away from the river many circled off to go home. Tshant thought they outnumbered the Mongols easily two to one. He filled his lungs and howled.

"Eeeeeeeyyyyaaaah!"

Arrows like narrow birds hurtled into the Russian line. Tshant nocked another of Djela's child's arrows to the child's bow and shot. The chestnut swerved to avoid a corpse and thundered on. Dead men and horses sprawled across the snow. A wounded horse galloped straight for them, and Tshant slowed the chestnut; the riderless horse charged past, bugling, two arrows thrusting from its side and the blood like a banner across the snow in its track. Tshant looked over his shoulder. His men were strung out behind him in a great arc, and the arrows poured like a moving wall into the Russians. Djela squealed happily.

The Russians were forming up again. The first storm of arrows had riddled them but they were swinging shields up, spurring their great horses forward. They bunched together like a club and drove straight for Tshant.

With Djela before him hopping madly up and down, Tshant could not shoot. He dragged the chestnut down to a trot and his own line swept up alongside him. The stream opened up before him again. The chestnut almost fell down the bank. Djela screamed. Tshant dropped the rein, ready to jump free, but the chestnut recovered and plunged out over the ice.

Six Russians in a wild charge bore down on them. A horse shrilled. The ground seemed to heave up under them. Tshant let go of Djela. Russian horses surrounded him. An axe flew past his ear and a salt spray wet his face. The chestnut ran into a Russian horse and staggered. Its mouth gaping, a black-bearded face swam up before Tshant, the eyes filmed over with fighting rage. Tshant drew his dagger and jumped. He caught the Russian around the neck and plunged the dagger in through one armpit. His impact carried the Russian and himself off the horse, and somehow they twisted and the Russian landed hard on top of him on the ice.

The ice cracked. Cold water spilled over him. He thrust and kicked at the dead man, and his head went under water. The cold wrapped itself around his chest and throat. At last the Russian slid away from him. He thrust his hands over his head, toward the air, and his fingers scratched against ice.

In his terror he almost opened his mouth and breathed water. He scrabbled at the ice over him, clawing at it. He saw nothing but blinding light and a flash of brilliant colors. His legs, milling frantically, struck the bed of the stream and he thrust himself up. His head struck the ice hard enough to daze him but one arm, outstretched, shot through the water and into the air. Ice water trickled into his lungs. He scrambled up after the arm and dragged himself over the split and bouncing ice.

There was nobody there but Mongols, and few of them. Far away he heard shouts and a roar like a huge fire. The air against his face felt hot. He began to shiver. Suddenly he was shuddering down to his bones. His teeth rang together so hard they hurt.

Somebody flung a cloak around him and he clutched at it with hands that would not work. The men around him were shouting about a fire and dry clothes and hot food.

He said, "Where is my son?"

The man before him stared a moment and shrugged helplessly.

Tshant snatched at him. "My son. Where is my son? Damn you—"

They caught his arms and held him still and dragged him downstream toward a fire. Their voices flowed over him like the icy river. He struggled, snarling, but they only clutched him tighter. Finally, exhausted, he let them bring him to the fire.

They stripped off his soaked clothes and rubbed him with snow and dried him off. He submitted. He could see the stream, the ice smashed into blocks, the gaping dark holes that gurgled and sucked at the ice. Horses and dead men strewed the ice and either bank. A head bobbed face down in one of the gaps, dark water lapping at its hair. His mind was frozen. Somebody put a bowl of warm kumiss in his hands and he drank, gulping. Somebody else pulled a woolen tunic over his head, made him stand up, and dressed him.

"You're lucky you aren't dead," Gregor said. "People who fall into Russian rivers in the winter usually die."

Tshant locked both hands in Gregor's shirt front and shook him. "Where is Djela?"

"I'm right here," Djela said. "Ada, are you all right?"

Tshant shut his eyes. He turned around very slowly and looked down. Djela was standing there, his red coat covered with dirt and dirty snow, chewing on a piece of dried meat. He beamed at Tshant.

"He went after the army," Gregor said. "The chestnut horse ran away with him, I suspect."

"It was fun," Djela said.

"Fun?" Tshant was having trouble speaking. The words forced themselves up through something thick in his throat. "When we fight, boy, you stay by me. Do you hear me?"

"I couldn't—"

Tshant slapped him twice, as hard as he could. Djela fell on his back. Gregor reached out and put his hand on Tshant's arm, and Tshant whirled. "Keep your hands off me, Russian."

Djela got up and stood, very stiffly, his hands at his sides. "I couldn't stop the horse," he said. He was trying not to cry. The mark of Tshant's hand like a ritual scar stood out on either cheek. "I would have stayed. But you'd thrown the reins over his head and I couldn't reach them."

He turned and walked away. Tshant called, "Djela."

Djela ignored him. He went to a fire and sat down with a group of men, and one of them handed him a bowl full of kumiss.

Tshant's thousand-commander came up toward him. He said, "Collect all the horses you can and we can leave. Did we wipe out the Russians?"

"No. Half of them got back to the city."

Tshant thought of Kaidu, riding with half the men the other way of the river, and how angry Kaidu would be at missing a good fight. It had to be a great city to hold so many men. He looked at Gregor.

"What's the name of that town, Gregor?"

Gregor hesitated a moment, but the look on Tshant's face apparently warned him. "Kiev."

"Someday I'll burn it. Come on."

When they started off again, Djela would not ride near Tshant. He sent Gregor after the boy to keep watch on him. They camped in a bend of the river, early so that the men could rest; Djela did not come to Tshant's fire. At nightfall, Tshant went hunting him. Some of the men Djela had ridden with in the end of the fighting had wrapped him in a cloak and put him to sleep beside their fire. He didn't wake when Tshant picked him up and carried him back.

In the morning, Djela refused to say anything. Tshant ate between giving orders to his thousand-commander and packing up his gear. When they were ready to leave, he rode over to Djela's horse and said, "I'm sorry. I thought you'd been killed."

"When I tell Ama—"

"I don't think you'll see her for a few years."

"I'll tell Grandfather."

"Go right ahead. If I'd hit you as often as he hit me when I—"

He stopped abruptly, remembering, and laughed. Djela turned with a frown.

"What's funny?"

"I ran off from Psin once in the middle of a battle and he beat me. I suppose your sons will ride away in the middle of battles. If they do and you beat them for it, just remember that I only hit you twice."

Quyuk said, "I still hate you."

"I don't like you either." Psin kicked at the roots and frozen black earth at his feet. "This damned forest is half swamp."

"What you did makes no difference."

"What made you think it would?"

Quyuk scowled. Psin threw his reins back over his horse's head and mounted. He grinned at Quyuk. "If I lost you, child, your father would string me up by the toes over a slow fire. If I lose any of my men without good reason, my reputation suffers. When do you suppose it thaws in these woods?"

"How should I know?"

Quyuk kicked his horse on past Psin. Psin followed him down a trail that led between two rounded hills. They had seen tracks of hunters in the forest. He wanted a prisoner from Novgorod and from the way Dmitri acted he knew they were close. He trotted his horse past Quyuk's and to the man leading Dmitri's horse.

"How is your cold?"

Dmitri snuffled, grinning. "Please, Khan, I won't try to run away. These ropes hurt."

"They aren't tight enough." Psin looked across the ridges to their west. His men were scattered throughout this part of the forest; he saw one ride silently through a patch of cedars. Beyond him, the lake glittered. Psin tried to remember whether cedars grew only where there had been a fire or never where there had been a fire. Someone had told him. . . . He shrugged and rode on.

Ahead, somebody yelled. Quyuk, directly behind him, called, "That wasn't Mongol."

"No."

The men near Psin galloped down the slope before him toward the shouting. Horses crashed through the brush just beyond the next ridge. The yelling broke out all across their path. A horse whinnied—the high, inquisitive call of a horse near strangers. Hoofs beat on the ground, and four Mongols sailed up the slope before them, ducking the swinging pine boughs.

"Woodcutters," one shouted. "Lots of them—hurry, we need help."

"Come on." Psin whipped up his horse.

Once they left the top of the ridge the forest closed in around them. He heard an axe ring on a tree. Mongol voices rose, yipping; they were trying to keep in contact with each other. The forest must be thick. Psin's horse leapt a windfall and staggered through drifted snow. A Russian voice howled angrily. Now, between trees, Psin could see them, the Russians on the ground striking with their axes and the Mongols still on horseback trying to capture them without getting killed. The interlaced branches of the trees trapped the axes and blinded the Mongols. One Russian fell heavily.

"Quyuk, over there."

Quyuk plunged past him; his face was scratched from the pine branches. Psin grabbed the reins of Dmitri's horse and held it next to his.

In Russian, Dmitri shouted, "Run—go tell Novgorod—"

Psin glanced at him. All the woodcutters were overpowered. Two were sprawled unconscious in the snow, and the Mongols were trussing up the others. Dmitri sighed.

"Shall I gag you?" Psin said.

Dmitri did not look at him. "No, Khan. Please."

"Then don't shout." Mixed in with the false humility in Dmitri's voice was exasperation. Psin turned toward the woodcutters. "Tie them and let's go. Quyuk, take charge of the prisoners."

Quyuk waved in answer and rode over to watch two Mongols

hoist a huge Russian up into the saddle of a Mongol horse. Psin called over a man doing nothing and gave him Dmitri's reins. "Don't let him out of your sight."

"Yes, Khan."

There were six woodcutters, and they were already packed up neatly on the column's spare horses. Psin rode over to Quyuk. "Take them back to our camp. Move fast."

"Where are you going?"

"To see this city."

"Let me go with you."

"No. We're too close. I should have known—" His horse jerked up its head. "Anyway, I'll go alone. You know how to—" His horse plunged around suddenly and pricked its ears, looking north. "Go!"

On the heel of the word a Russian voice roared in the woods to the north. Quyuk flung up his head and called to the Mongols. He held a saddleless horse on a leadline, and he threw the rope to Psin. More Russian voices were calling out, all around them. The Mongols yipped and clattered south along the slopes.

Psin whirled his horse and plunged into the depths of the forest, away from the lake, where the cover grew thickest. He heard Russians shouting and a clash of heavy metal, and hoofs pounded by. He wondered if the woodcutters had been bait in a trap, doubted it, and reeled in his led horse to wrap a rag over its nose.

"Yip yip yip—"

That was far away, and the sound of horses dimmed. Ahead of Psin the slope fell away steeply into a ravine. He forced his horse down it. Here the snow lay like a light frost; the branches above and the looming cliff walls kept the ground clear. Pale green moss covered the trunks of the few trees near the top of the ravine. The darkness grew deeper and thicker. Psin's horse ducked its head and crept on down the trail into the ravine. Holding the leadrope up high, Psin maneuvered the horse behind his. The trail was so narrow the two horses couldn't walk side by side.

He heard a distant cry and the sound of something heavy charging through brush. He heard a call that ended in a question. His horse moved one hoof at a time and slid a little with each step. When Psin looked back the way they had come he saw the edge of the bank above them stark against a patch of clear sky. The trail down grew steeper, and he held onto his saddle with one hand.

The horse stepped cautiously out on flat ground. Psin reined him down until the led horse could gain the level bottom of the ravine and started at a walk north. Under the overhanging cliff, a thin stream lay, frozen to the mud of its bed. Psin's horse stretched out into a fast walk, and he let his reins slack.

Novgorod was vast. Pennants floated from the peaks of its towers, and the sun glinted on the sloping roofs. Psin, shy in his patch of forest, could see people on the cleared ground outside the city. It was the first time he had ever seen Russians peacefully beyond their walls. A few carts stood in the snowfields.

He dismounted, his bow close to his hand on the cantle of his saddle, melted snow and drank it in slow sips. A whiff of smoke from a wood fire reached his nostrils. He wished he could go nearer so that he could tell what they were cooking. That kind of information could be got from merchants and captives but he never trusted their answers.

They would have a short growing season, whatever they grew in their fields. More likely they were merchants and hunters. The wind was rising, and it smelled of the town—dry wood, a lot of people, smoke, and vaguely of rot.

Something clattered in the distance, and he rose. Whatever it was was coming up along the lake. He thought he knew. Settling down again, he studied the town and the people outside the walls.

One of the men in the fields straightened and pointed, and another man, between the first and the town, shouted something. Psin caught the Russian word for horse. A troop of horsemen jogged out of the forest beside the lake, yelled, and waved their arms. He saw no prisoners with them, no Mongol horses.

The gate was opening. It swung out, a useful thing to know, perhaps. Psin checked his horses, who were watching the Russians. He could tell by the way the Russians rode that they thought they had won a great victory. He watched them ride into the town, and the men in the fields rushed after them, excitedly.

When it was dark he meant to go up closer and look at the structure of the walls. He made himself comfortable. The sun hovered in its winter zenith, barely out of the treetops; he wouldn't have long to wait.

Going back, he rode almost constantly, cursing the forest and hunting while he rode. At sundown he slept, his belly half full of badly cooked meat. He didn't dare make a proper fire for fear the heat would melt the snow off the upper branches of the trees near him and show, a great dark splash, that he was there. He slept with his face toward the sky, so that the rising moon woke him, and rode on until the moonset and slept again until sunrise. The sun was so little in the sky, with the shortest of days coming, that he had barely warmed himself up before it set again. Long before he reached the camp he was weary down to his marrow.

Nobody looked surprised to see him. When he tramped up to his fire and threw his gear down, Quyuk looked up and said, "What took you so long? We've been back nearly a full day."

"I stayed the night in Novgorod." He sighed and sank down on his heels. "Oh, God. I thought my legs would be permanently crooked."

"They are." Quyuk turned his head and yelled, "Tunkut, bring the Khan his dinner."

"I'm too tired to eat."

Baidar came over, a halter swinging from his hand. He nodded to Psin and sat down next to Quyuk. "And how was Novgorod?"

"Go look for yourself."

Tunkut thrust a bowl into his hands. The scent of stewed meat made his stomach thrash. He dipped his fingers into it and the gravy burnt him and he swore.

"I thought some few days alone might improve his temper," Quyuk said. "But he's as surly as ever."

Psin blew on his meat. "Did Buri follow that road?"

"Yes." Baidar took an awl and began mending the halter. "It stretches on south. There are signs it's often used, even in the winter."

"What about Kadan?"

"The road to the west turns north five days' ride from here."

Baidar thrust the awl through the leather. "How did you know it would turn?"

"I guessed. Is it well-used?"

"Ask me," Kadan said. He grinned down at Psin. Buri was right behind him. "The road is not used anymore. It was once, long ago, but the ruts are very old. It dwindles down to a goat track before it turns north."

Psin nodded. "Did you find the city?"

Kadan's mouth dropped open. The others murmured softly and looked at each other. Psin forced even more meat into his mouth and tried to chew and nearly choked.

"Yes," Kadan said. "It was deserted—I think within ten years."

Psin gulped down a piece of meat and coughed. Immediately all four of them leapt on him and pounded him on the back. He shouted and waved his arms, and one of them whacked him so hard his face hit the ground in front of his feet.

"I'll fry the lot of you!"

They subsided. "Did you hear Psin say anything?" Quyuk asked Buri. "I thought I heard a voice."

Psin brushed dirt off his nose. "I was asking you to desist."

Kadan laughed. "Oh, Khan." He sprawled out on his back. "Yes, I found the city. Why did they leave it?"

"I don't know. Was it burned at all?"

"No."

"I thought maybe Novgorod had driven them out. Maybe . . . How is the hunting?"

"Good. The forest is full of deer, elk, wolves, bear—"

Baidar said, "Buri killed a bear with one arrow."

"It was this big," Buri said. He stood on his toes and held his hand at arm's length over his head.

"A bear, in this season?"

Buri shrugged. "Sometimes they roam in the winter."

"Not often. How is the grazing? I passed some racks of bones, coming in, that looked like horses—"

"Not that bad," Quyuk said. He grinned. "But the horses are starting to wander. The grass is gone, and the trees don't have much bark left."

Psin lay back. "Tell me everything tomorrow."

Quyuk snorted. "Old man. Go sleep in the sun. What about the prisoners?"

"I'll talk to them tomorrow." He shut his eyes.

Kadan said, "What could they tell him he doesn't already know? Buri, go fetch his slave over here."

Psin yawned. "No, I'll go to my own fire. Is anybody still out hunting?"

"No. Why, where do we go now?"

"Home."

Part Two

—◆—

TSHANT

—◆—

Temujin said, "In everyday life like a fawn, at feasts and celebrations carefree as a colt, but on the day of battle swooping like a falcon to the attack. In daylight alert as a wolf, in the night vigilant as a black crow."

SABOTAI STOOD IN THE MIDDLE OF THE FLOOR AND LET HIS SLAVES peel off his winter clothes. His face, seamed and pouched beneath the eyes, looked far older now that Psin had spent two months with young men.

"We took Riazan with no trouble, aside from what my tumans gave me. You were right. They are inexperienced and badly disciplined, and the remounts are enough to strike a man blind."

"Has Tshant come back yet?" Psin said.

"No. And will you kindly take your muddy boots off my carpet. Thank you. Batu and his brothers are enthusiastic and they know their work."

"You were thorough. I passed Riazan coming back."

Sabotai shrugged. "You said cities are for burning. The sack of it was a crime against war. They were looting before they'd taken half the city, and burning before the buildings were properly looted. Have you seen Mongke yet?"

"I talked to him this morning. How heavy were your casualties?"

"More than I expected. Many of them were accidents." Sabotai pulled a chair around to face Psin's and sat in it. "They got caught in burning houses, or trampled by men behind them. Most of the dead weren't Mongol. I have one tuman of Kanglis, or I had, and I've combined them with the tuman I used to have of Bulgarians. Together they come barely to full strength."

Psin grimaced. A slave poured out wine for him, and he drank some of it. The warmth of the room and the bright, shaped colors relaxed him.

"It was worth taking," Sabotai said. "Ogodai will be pleased. I've sent off a train of plunder to Karakorum seventy-five carts long."

"Just the Kha-Khan's tenth, or your own as well?"

"The tenth. Not since Reyy fell have we taken a city quite so rich. Although in different things. Furs. The sables are excellent. Gold, silver, pearls and jewels—an emerald to rival the one your Chinese wife wears. We have grain enough to feed us through the winter, and lumber enough to build Batu another Volga camp. The slaves are of very high quality."

"They're merchants. There should be good plunder."

"Yes. Riazan was the first step. Now for the major problem. Tell me things."

Psin stretched his legs out. "The chief noyon is the Grand Duke Yuri. He winters in Vladimir, the largest city. Mongke says he is summoning his knights, and I suspect he'll raise an army of at least three or four tumans, at least one quarter mounted. You know the way the towns lie between those rivers. If he is pushed he'll probably retreat toward the southwest, where the food is."

"What if he goes north?"

"It would be a great help to the Kha-Khan."

"Good. If I take the cities west of Vladimir—Moskva, Susdal, Kolomna—what will I accomplish?"

"You'll outflank him. He'll have to go north."

"I thought so. I have two tumans camped in the area around Riazan, and another patrolling the stretch of forest between Vladimir and Moskva. Within the month I'll cross the rest of the army over the Volga—by then, I hope, we'll have adequate remounts. Do I have to take Novgorod this year to protect what we conquer in the south?"

"No. But it would be useful. They can't give us serious trouble from the north, but they can do us some damage if they want."

"I'll leave it for last."

"What else?"

"Nothing but details. For example, you might want to go to the Volga camp before we attack."

"Why?"

"Your wives are there."

"So soon?" Psin rose. He hadn't expected them before the spring. Chan's face and Artai's floated into his mind.

"Don't leave immediately, please." Sabotai smiled, and Psin plunked down again. "I sent an escort for them. They should be here fairly soon."

"Then why did you—"

"I wanted to see what you'd do. Naturally I don't want you running off to the Volga camp. How much do you trust Mongke?"

"Absolutely."

Sabotai grimaced. "I don't."

"I'll take responsibility for him. He says that we can't siege the Russian cities, and I agree with him, but they can be stormed easily enough. Are you going to split the army?"

"Yes. But you're not commanding either branch. I'll let Batu enjoy himself. We'll divide after we take Moskva. How is your relationship with Quyuk?"

"He hates me like a father."

"I thought he would. You brought them all back in one piece, though, and from what I've seen of your men they're in better shape than mine."

"They should be. I had them working."

"Do they obey you?"

"Sabotai, you're offensive. They'll fight anything I point them at."

"I meant no offense. Quyuk is sometimes . . . Anyway. When your women get here, enjoy them. You are going to ride vanguard for me when we move out."

Psin groaned. "How kind you are."

Sabotai grinned.

To accommodate Psin's wives and slaves, Sabotai had provided him with a larger house near the north gate of Bulgar. Mongke had moved all their gear into it before Psin came back. The house had two storeys and an enclosed garden. Mongke took over the second storey for himself and a growing retinue of slaves, free servants, women and some friends from his new command; Psin discovered shortly after moving in himself that Mongke's entourage consisted mostly of the women.

"What a joy to have you back," Mongke said, sliding into a chair. He draped one leg across the table in front of him. Psin, hanging up his coat and baldric, noticed a new scar on Mongke's face and more muscle on his slender body. "We had such fun while you were gone," Mongke said. "I'm rather proud of my reconnaissance."

"So am I." Mongke had reported to him in full the day previous, before Psin went to see Sabotai. "Did you fight against Riazan?"

"No. How was Novgorod?"

"Worth seeing."

"None but you saw it, Quyuk tells me. What did you do to him? He hates you even worse than when you left."

"Unfortunately, I was around when he got sick."

Mongke's head jerked up. "The headache."

"Yes. Does he get them often?"

"Not . . . often. Did he let you near him? He killed a slave who tried to help him once, when he couldn't see because of it."

"Your father used to get headaches like that."

"He drank too much."

"So does Quyuk."

"That's so." Mongke rose. "Well, I'm going into the city. About Quyuk, watch Buri. Buri shows what Quyuk's thinking."

"Thank you. I've already noticed that."

"You would have."

"Mongke, wait."

Mongke paused in the doorway. Psin chewed on his mustaches, spat them out, and said, "When my son comes back, don't fight with him. Put him off any way you care to. I'll deal with him."

"No."

Psin's teeth clicked together. The new weight in Mongke's voice unsettled him. "I don't want either of you killed."

"I never started this," Mongke said. "He did. I won't push it to him, but when he comes at me, Khan, I'll do all I can to kill him."

Tshant fresh from a long raid would be hard to kill. "Don't push. I can't ask for much more than that."

"Ask." Mongke smiled. "That's a pleasant word to hear from you, Khan." He turned and went out the door.

Psin snorted. He heard a slave call out, and the gate into the courtyard boomed open. A woman's voice, upstairs, said something questioningly. He shut his eyes, enjoying the emptiness of the day before him. Cartwheels rolled over the paving stones in the court-yard, and a drover's whip cracked.

"Psin."

His eyes flew open. Artai stood in the doorway, swathed in a great cloak, her gloves in her hand. He rose and held out his hands, and she rushed into his arms. He hugged her, his cheek against her hair, and sighed, overcome.

"Did you grow wings? How did you get here so quickly?" The smell of her hair stirred every memory in him.

"Oh, we brought carts." She stood back and smiled at him. "Are you glad to see me?"

"Yes." He pulled her close again. She was warm and gentle in his arms, and the familiar touch of her hands was like balm. "How is the clan? Did you have any trouble getting here?"

"Everyone's fine. Oh, Psin."

He shut his eyes. She always made him feel safe; wherever she was the ground seemed steadier to walk on. "Ask the question."

"You man. Did you miss me?"

"No." He laughed into the collar of her cloak. "But if you hadn't come I'd have died of loneliness."

"You always say that same thing."

"It's always true. I didn't have the leisure to miss you. You're so light. Didn't you eat, coming out?"

"The food they cook at the waystations isn't fit. We ate. You're just stronger. You look well." She pushed herself away from him. "You look better than when you left us."

"I've been riding. Reconnaissance. Did you bring my dun horse?"

"Did we bring your dun horse?" She sat down. "Khan, if we'd had to drag that beast another day I think Malekai would have stabbed himself. He kicked. He bit. He bolted. He reared—" She lifted one hand and let it drop to her knee again. "I've never seen an animal so ill-behaved. When are you going to ask about Chan?"

He sat on his heels beside her. "I thought you'd mention her soon enough."

"She says the wind and the dryness have ruined her skin. She brought a chest full of cream and perfume and such things, though. I'm glad we gave her something new to complain about. She'd been fading for lack of variety."

Psin picked up her hand. "Ssssh. She's not like us. You'd be unhappy if you had to live in China."

"I'd be miserable. She's not. She's wild to see you." Her slow smile deepened the creases at the corners of her mouth. "You look so well. Where is Tshant?"

"Raiding. He'll be back soon."

"He took Djela, of course."

"Yes."

"I knew he meant to. You might tell him, sometime, that the way you raised him isn't the only way." She tugged her hand free and stood up. "Where are we to sleep?"

"How many slaves did you bring?"

"Sixteen," she said, and started toward the door.

Psin stood rooted. "Sixteen? In God's name, woman——"

"Well, you really didn't expect us to come unattended all the way out here, did you? I brought two women to cook, three to do campwork, four men to drive carts, and seven to keep guard."

"Sixteen slaves? I've already got five here."

"Good. We shall be carefully looked after. Are you going to show me where to put my things or not?"

He scowled at her, and she smiled. Her eyes shone. He tried to look furious, could not, and with a laugh led her by the hand into the corridor.

To Artai he gave the two small rooms in the southwest corner of the bottom floor; he sent Dmitri to take Chan's people to the big room on the northeast corner. Artai's male slaves packed in chests and bundles. The women began to arrange furniture and air out clothing. A warm scent of women filled the rooms. Psin sat down on the couch in the sleeping room and watched Artai direct the slaves.

"Where did you raid?" she said, and when he told her, listened as if she knew what he was talking about. Psin knew well enough that she didn't. "How are the supplies here? We had some bad meat in the Volga camp. I'm going to need cloth for winter trousers. Mine are falling apart."

"You'll find everything you need in the market."

"Who is here besides you and Sabotai?"

"The Altun, in force. Mongke lives upstairs. Quyuk and Kadan are in the center of the city. Buri——"

"Who is Buri?"

"Jagatai's grandson—Kerulu's nephew." That she did know. Psin slouched back on one elbow, amused. She was trying to keep him here, away from Chan. "Baidar also—Jagatai's son. And Kaidu, who is Batu's grandson. He's out with Tshant."

"Do they ever come here?"

"Some of them," He shifted his feet as if he meant to get up.

"Hold this a moment." She dropped a heap of linen on his lap. "Eya, that's not where I want those."

She reached into a chest and got a pile of little wooden boxes out and moved briskly across the room to stack them somewhere else. "Vortai, will you please come here and take out this chest?"

Psin watched her bustle around; she looked so furiously busy that he knew she wasn't busy at all. She came back, her cheeks ruddy, and plopped down beside him. "When does the fighting begin?"

"It has." Psin ran his thumb along the edge of the linen stacked up on his thighs. "Do you think perhaps I could get out from under this?"

"Oh. I forgot. Could you put it up there? On top of that cabinet? What kind of wood is this?"

"Maple. The Russians are good workers in wood."

"Look how the grain goes."

"Yes, I see it." He turned toward the door.

"What will you want for your dinner?" she said, sliding nimbly in front of him to block his way out.

"Anything you wish." He picked her up bodily and moved her, ducked the reach of her arms, and went to the door.

"But you will be eating here."

"Yes. I will." He patted her cheek and left. The dim calm of the corridor muted the racket inside the room. He shook his head and went across the house to Chan's rooms.

Here there was only silence. Two slaves he recognized from Artai's yurt by Lake Baikal padded by, their heads bowed and eyes averted. He opened a door and went into a large room hung with tapestries and smelling of lilies. The floor had been bare wood before, but now a Bokhara carpet covered it, each fringe splayed carefully over the dark wood. He crossed it to the little side door.

In the tiny room Chan sat with her back to him, combing her long black hair. On the wall in front of her hung a sheet of gold polished into a mirror. She wore a dark blue robe—silk—never sturdy Mongol trousers. She heard him come in; he saw her eyes in the mirror looking at him. But she didn't stop combing her hair.

He paused just behind her and sat down on his heels. In the mirror their eyes met, his face looking over her shoulder. He could smell regal lilies as if they blossomed in the room; he could smell the scent of her long hair. Her cheek made the silk look rough.

She drew the comb once more through her hair and put it down and laid her hands in her lap. He could read nothing in her eyes. Her image in the mirror seemed cast around with a net of beaten gold. He put one arm around her waist and dragged her against him. She stiffened, as if to resist him, and in the mirror he saw her look away. Her hands touched his, cool, like raindrops. He buried his face in her hair.

But that night he ate and slept with Artai. To disturb the order of such things would only wreck the peace of his house.

Tshant left his army in the fields across the river from Bulgar and with Djela and Kaidu rode into the city. Djela carried their standard, glowing. On their way back from the Dnepr they had met an army of Russian knights and harried them into a bloody ruin. Heads decorated the standard.

"Sabotai must be getting ready to leave again," Kaidu said. "Look." He pointed to carts, heaped with sacks of grain, rumbling across the marketplace. Beside each cart rode four armed men, and the sides of the carts carried the mark for army goods. "Psin's back; there's Quyuk."

Tshant swung around, saw Quyuk jogging down a sidestreet, and bellowed. Quyuk spun his horse and cantered over. Kaidu said happily, "We finished off a herd of Russians, and we've been to the Dnepr and back—how was your raiding?"

"Instructive," Quyuk said. "I heard the horns blowing when you came into sight. Where are you camped?"

"Across the river." Tshant lifted his reins. He wanted to get to the palace and report to Sabotai before he had to face Psin. He had lost over five hundred men. "Djela, come back here."

Kaidu had let his reins fall and was gesturing broadly with both hands. "The city is on a tremendous bluff right over the river, on the western bank. I hear you took Riazan."

"Not us. Sabotai. They stormed it." Quyuk moved his horse to block Tshant's. "You don't seem to want to talk, Tshant."

"We have to go," Tshant said. "I—"

He caught sight of a bright blue litter swaying into the market-place and stared at it, standing up in his stirrups. A slave held the curtain so that the woman inside could step down. Tshant caught a glimpse of her face.

Quyuk drew in his breath harshly. "Ah, now. There's a sweet little thing for a man to get into."

Tshant glanced at him. Quyuk was watching Chan with bright eyes. "Don't try. That's my father's second wife."

Kaidu muttered something. Quyuk swore. "Oh. Damn him. Everything good I see, I find, belongs to Psin Khan. Where did he get her?"

"At the sack of Kinsai." Tshant edged his horse away.

Quyuk was staring after Chan again. She was buying cloth; her hand stroked a bolt of red wool. One of her slaves carried a parasol to shade her from the sun. Her head turned and she gave Quyuk back a stare as cold as solid rock.

"Stay away from her, Quyuk," Tshant said. Quyuk's hand was clenched around his rein.

"Grandfather," Djela called.

Tshant whipped around. Psin on his big dun horse was jogging through the crowded street behind them. The dun looked meaner than usual. Foam flecked his shoulders and neck and splashed down from his mouth, and he gnawed on the bit. Psin kicked him up between Tshant's horse and Kaidu's.

"I heard the horns," he said softly, "and I saw your camp. You seem to have mislaid some of your men."

"We met trouble," Tshant said. He glared at Kaidu to keep him quiet.

"Oh? Nothing you could have run from? Your information had better be very good to be worth five hundred Mongols."

"If we counted the Russians we killed, I think you'd say they came cheaply enough."

"You weren't sent to kill Russians," Psin said. "You were sent to—"

He looked past Tshant and Quyuk and his mouth twitched. "That woman."

"If you don't want her, Khan," Quyuk said, "I might take her in."

The dun horse started to fight, and Psin jerked him in the mouth. "You'd regret it, Quyuk." Tshant saw him measure Quyuk from the tail of his eye. To Tshant he said, "Go up to the palace. I'll hear your report there."

"Grandfather," Djela said. "I almost got killed."

Psin leaned out to ruffle the boy's hair. "You look alive, though. Your grandmothers are here. Artai will want to talk to you."

He forced the dun away from the other horses; his whip lashed down on the dun's barrel. The horse bolted, and Psin caught him up on the bit and fought him over to Chan. He said something to her and galloped off. The dun's neck curved like a round of stone, and his ears pressed flat back into the flying black mane. Chan looked after him expressionlessly.

"That's my grandfather's best horse," Djela told Kaidu.

"He might have broken him a little better."

"Come on," Tshant said. "We'd better get up to the palace. Quyuk, are you coming?"

"No. I know where your father lives. I'll take your son there."

Quyuk was still watching Chan. Tshant said, "Stay away from her. I've seen him go wild twice in my life, and both times it was over her. You don't know what he's like when he's wild."

"I can guess." Quyuk relaxed suddenly. "There are thousands of beautiful women in the world."

Tshant grinned at him and started off. It amused him to think that even Quyuk was afraid of Psin.

"When do we move?" Tshant said.

Sabotai opened one eye to look at him and closed it again. "In five days," Psin said. Tshant had just finished reporting, and Psin had decided not to fight with him over the high losses he'd sustained. "Moskva goes first."

"Go away," Sabotai said. "I'm thinking. Or else keep quiet."

Tshant's mouth twisted. Psin got up and went into the next room, and Tshant followed him. "What's wrong with Sabotai?"

"He's planning a campaign, that's all. He's like that when he thinks."

"I thought you had the campaign all worked out."

"Yes, but now he's attacking Kiev—that city you mentioned." Psin collected his hat and cloak.

"Am I staying with you?"

"Unless you don't want to." He thought of the house packed with people. "We have slaves until they run after you begging for something to do. Your mother—"

He broke off, remembering. "Did Quyuk say anything about Chan?"

"He was taken with her."

"I'll kill him if he touches her."

"I told him so. He looked as if he believed me." Tshant looked as if he were thinking of laughing. "Come on. I'm hungry."

They went out toward the courtyard. "Djela said something about nearly being killed."

"He wasn't. I thought he had been for a while."

"You got separated?"

"Yes." Tshant glanced over at Psin, and Psin grinned.

"Now you see what I mean. Actually, the problem's not with losing the child, it's dying of anxiety before you find him again."

"So I found out." They stopped at the door, and a sentry opened it. "Was the ice solid on the rivers you crossed?"

"Down to the stones. Why?"

"I was fighting on a frozen stream and it broke, and I went in."

Psin's chest tightened. The sunlight was strong, out on the step, but he felt cold. "You were lucky."

"Very. I came up under the ice."

The pit of Psin's stomach contracted. They walked on a few strides, Tshant looking straight ahead. When they were at the foot of the steps into the courtyard Tshant said, "God. I was scared."

"You were lucky."

"Uh-huh. You went to Novgorod?"

"All the way."

The bright sunlight dissolved the lingering chill. They went on toward their horses. Psin's dun was slick with sweat and pawing the ground.

"That horse and Chan may change the Altun's opinion of you," Tshant said.

"Oh," Psin said, and laughed. "The Altun hold a very high opinion of me."

He mounted and the dun bucked. Psin talked him quiet again and rode beside Tshant; together, they trotted out into the city.

"Don't fight with Mongke," Psin said.

Tshant barked a laugh. "Tell me not to breathe."

"Don't breathe."

Tshant was lying in the sun. He had slept until noon, eaten half an ox for breakfast, and was drinking red wine as if it guaranteed his youth. He had answered Psin's questions until Psin suspected he was making up the answers. Tshant had never been so careful about detail. Tshant arched his back, folded his arms behind his head, and admired the sky. Psin grunted.

"If you have to fight, don't do it with knives, bows or horses. Don't kill him. I need him."

"What for?"

Djela ran into the garden, chattering contentedly to someone not yet in sight. He waved to Psin, and Psin waved back. Dmitri came out of another door with a tray of cups and wine. Psin caught his eye and nodded, and Dmitri poured wine into one of the cups and handed it to him.

"I asked what good Mongke is to you."

"He scouted the Russian cities."

"Along with one thousand other men, all probably better than he."

Chan came into the garden behind Djela. Psin frowned; Chan hated Djela and never went anywhere near him except for a good reason.

"Tshant, for once, listen to your old father."

Tshant snorted.

"Your poor old father who has grown bent and grey in the service of the Kha-Khan—"

"Give me room to weep. You might drown for the tears."

"Damn you. I said, don't fight with Mongke."

"And I say I will."

Chan came over to Psin and said, "Spread your cloak for me that I may sit."

Psin got up and took his cloak off the stone bench he'd been sitting on and put it on the ground for her. Djela was gone. Chan had probably bribed him to lead her innocently in here.

"Have you ever heard of a place called Rome?" Psin said.

"Never." Tshant squirmed around to look at Chan. She turned her face away with an expression of intense disgust.

"The people from Novgorod think it's the chief city of the land west of the Dnepr. Europe." Psin frowned. The captives' description of Rome and of the Khans and noyons who ruled from it confused him. "There is a great khan there, and a priest, like the Nestorians, only very great." He looked at Chan's head, beside his knee, and laid his hand on her hair. Against the smoothness of her hair he could feel how rough and calloused his hand was.

"Don't ," she said. "You hurt me."

Tshant snorted.

Chan opened her eyes. The tiny room was pitch dark. There were no windows in it, and no light shone under the door. The little nightlight beside the couch had gone out long since.

She could feel Psin beside her; she could feel how asleep he was, even though they didn't touch at all. She thought there was at least a handspan of space between them, shoulder and shoulder, hip and hip, knee and knee, space their bodies warmed, where the warmth of their bodies mixed like the subtle oils of perfumes in a bowl.

He was so warm. He was so big. The other men she couldn't remember at all. Their faces swam sadly like melted wax and their bodies had moldered away from her memory as they had from the earth. She had been raised for a concubine, to be a receptacle for men to come in, and before she had been fully grown there had been plenty of them.

He didn't care about that. She had never understood why. He never let other men even look at her for longer than a glance, but

that she had had three masters before he got her didn't seem to
matter. It made her angry, sometimes, almost enough to see what
would happen if she ever looked back at the men who looked at
her.

She moved her hand, pretending she was asleep and dreaming,
and touched his side. Immediately he stirred. "What's the matter?"

"Hmmm?"

"You woke me up."

"No," she said. "You woke me up."

He rolled over and put his arms around her. "We can argue
about it later."

She wedged her elbows inside his and pushed him away from her.
"I'm tired. Go to sleep." But with her ankle she stroked his calf. He
liked that.

"I'm tired too." He grabbed her again. "Let's wear each other to
ruins."

She tangled her fingers in his hair and pulled his head back.
"Would you have taken me with you from Kinsai if I had had lotus
feet?"

She could feel the surprise run through him. "What?"

"Would you have—"

"Why are you speaking Chinese?"

"Because I am." Tears stung her eyes, and she blinked them back.

He twisted his head sharply, so that she lost her grip in his hair,
but he didn't put his head down. He hitched himself up on his elbows, and his fingers brushed her cheek. She struck his hand aside.

"I'm not crying."

"No. I wouldn't have. What good are lotus feet to a Mongol?"

Despondency overwhelmed her. She didn't understand why
sometimes she could do nothing but cry. She let her hands slide
lifelessly down his back, like dead leaves. His great bulk above her
seemed more distant than stars.

In Mongol, he said, "If you cry, I'll beat you."

She jerked herself back together, as if her limbs had been on
strings in far corners of the room. She hit him in the back as hard as
she could and lunged up to bite him. His weight pressed her down;
his flat stomach lay against hers, and when he breathed it drove the
breath from her lungs. His mustaches tickled her throat. He pene-

trated her, and she gave an undignified yelp and wrapped her legs
around him. She remembered Kinsai burning and the sound of the
horse in the garden where she had hid, she remembered the time
they broke the bed in Karakorum and the way he had told the Emperor Temujin that he could not have her. The triumph coursed
through her body like a dream of wings, and she shut her eyes and
stopped thinking at all.

How much help can we expect from inside the cities?" Psin asked.

Sabotai studied the board before him. Batu, who was playing against him, rested both forearms on the table and grinned, delighted. "Very little," Sabotai said. "I had to use Turks, of course. When I sent out the agents. Besides, the Russians certainly will keep a watch on anybody at all related to us."

Batu moved a pawn and settled back again; his eyes darted from Sabotai's face to the board to Sabotai's face.

"At any rate," Psin said, "large groups of the peasants are fleeing from the fields to the cities. We'll have no trouble taking the individual holdings of the noyons once we hold the towns."

"No." Sabotai moved his elephant. "I've brought in forty thousand head of horses from the south. That should solve the remount problem."

"Temporarily."

Batu leaned back and stared at the board, one hand to his chin. With the other hand he shifted two pieces. "Check."

"As long as they can forage," Sabotai said, "we should have no difficulty. In the summer we can rest and let them graze all they wish." He picked up a piece between the first two fingers of his hand and carried it across the board. "We have certain other problems. Kadan and Buri have been stupid drunk since you came back from Novgorod. We'll have to pack them out on litters. You did a good job with them, Psin. But it should have lasted a little longer."

"They'll dry out when we ride," Batu said cheerfully. "Check."

Sabotai glanced at the board and without hesitation moved, and Batu pounced on him. "Checkmate."

Sabotai had been wheeling to talk to Psin. He jerked his gaze back to the board. Psin rose and went over to look; he saw that Batu had built a perfect fence of pawns around Sabotai's overlord. Sabotai glared at the board and with a growl swept the pieces aside.

"Another."

"No," Batu said. "You don't pay attention. You're a decent player when you concentrate but when you don't there's no excitement in it. The game wants blood, Sabotai. It wants sweat." Batu gritted his teeth as if he were heaving at a great boulder.

"How can I concentrate on a game when we're—"

Kaidu burst into the room. "Psin—Sabotai. Mongke and Tshant are fighting in Quyuk's room."

Psin swore. "Let them fight—beat each other's brains out."

Kaidu's voice cracked. "But they have knives."

Psin and Sabotai bolted for the door. Kaidu ran ahead of them down the corridor. A crowd was gathered at the far end, in front of the door into Quyuk's room. Psin heard somebody yelling and Quyuk's voice rose up over it: "Give way—give them room!"

"Let me through," Psin shouted. He forced his way into the pack of slaves and guards and elbowed Baidar savagely to one side. He heard Djela's voice, thin with fright, inside the room. Abruptly someone was thrusting the boy into Psin's arms. Psin threw him to Baidar and squeezed into the room.

Quyuk stood pressed into a corner, a table overturned at his feet. Mongke and Tshant were prowling around each other, crouched. The carpet beneath their feet was rucked up so that they had to be careful of their footing. Kadan sprawled on the couch under the window. Mongke held a knife, but Tshant had none, and Psin noticed it lying on the carpet near the fallen table. Tshant was trying to edge over to it, and Mongke was keeping him off.

"Come on, big man," Mongke said softly. His fingers clutched the knife hilt so hard his knuckles were yellow. "Come on. Show me how strong you are."

Next to Psin, Sabotai murmured, "Let them fight—we can keep them from killing each other."

Mongke glanced over at the sound of his voice, and Tshant lunged behind him, fingers splayed, for the knife on the floor. Quyuk bounded over the table into a safer corner. Mongke's knife flashed. He kicked Tshant hard and knocked him rolling. Tshant had missed the knife. Mongke bent and picked it up in his left hand. Tshant rose, his eyes on the two blades. One side of his tunic hung down, slashed through just below the armpit.

Psin started. Immediately Sabotai on his left and Baidar on his right wound their arms through his and held him still. Tshant was circling against Mongke's left hand. Mongke hissed something Psin could not understand.

"Let me go," he said.

"No," Sabotai said. "Baidar, hold him."

Tshant feinted to the left, swung back, and plunged left again. His right hand caught Mongke's left wrist and twisted. Mongke grimaced. He drew the other dagger across Tshant's body, just lightly. Psin sucked in his breath. Tshant backed away. His tunic hung in rags, and he tore it off, and the mob in the doorway murmured at the two long stripes on his body. Blood trickled down over his ribs.

"You can do better than that, Tshant," Mongke said. "Come kill me, Tshant."

Tshant shook his hair out of his eyes. He circled again, this time to Mongke's right. Mongke turned, following him, and led with his left shoulder. Tshant bulled in. He got Mongke by the belt, but Mongke gashed him twice across the chest and Tshant dodged, letting go. He put one hand to his chest.

"You're playing dangerous, skinny," Tshant said. "I'll kill you before you can cut me to pieces."

"Try," Mongke said. He moved, sliding his feet over the bunched carpet, toward the couch Kadan lay on. Kadan was stone blind with drink. Mongke maneuvered Tshant toward the door, glanced over Tshant's shoulder, and met Psin's eyes. Psin wrenched at the arms pinning his, but Sabotai and Baidar only tightened their grip until he couldn't move at all.

Tshant had finished attacking the knives. With each step he drew his hands over the furniture behind him, hunting another weapon. Mongke glanced toward Psin again. Psin's lungs burned, and he realized he was holding his breath.

Mongke lunged in toward Tshant, who tried to grapple with him. The knives flickered. Blood spilled over Tshant's back and sides. He flung Mongke against the wall and sank down on one knee, panting.

Baidar said, "He's slicing him up, Sabotai."

Quyuk was right next to the door. "We can stop it when we have to."

Mongke snapped at him. "Try." He bounded in, both knives low and out. Tshant straightened—on the carpet where he had knelt a pool of blood glittered. He stepped back off the carpet and brought it up after him in both hands. Mongke lost his footing and fell hard into a cabinet. Tshant took two long strides toward him and caught the top of the cabinet and rocked it forward with a crash on top of Mongke. The doors sprang open and heaps of clothing spilled out. Only Mongke's leg showed, motionless.

"Clever," Baidar said.

Tshant stood still a moment, swaying. His leggings were soaked through with blood. Finally, he turned his head, looking for the knives, and saw one where Mongke, falling, had dropped it. He started toward it.

Abruptly Sabotai turned Psin loose. He cocked one finger at Quyuk and pointed to Tshant. Quyuk picked up a chair, smashed it against the wall, and with one of its legs stretched Tshant out cold on the floor. Psin knelt beside him and rolled him over.

"Heave," Baidar said. He and Sabotai shoved the cabinet up onto its base again. Psin glanced at Mongke. His fingers, pressing gently against the back of Tshant's head where Quyuk had hit him, found no breaks, and he sighed.

"How is he?" Baidar said.

"He has to be bandaged," Quyuk said. "We can take him in the carpet."

He and Psin rolled Tshant up in the carpet and lifted him. Kaidu forced his way in through the door and came over to help. Quyuk with Tshant's feet went first. When Psin passed Sabotai, he said, "If he dies, Sabotai—"

Sabotai looked up from Mongke. "He didn't, and he won't." He put his hand on Psin's shoulder. "I'm sorry. But I think it was necessary."

"The next time you play chess, don't use my blood."

They carried Tshant just down the corridor. Two women with warm water and ointment followed them there from the crowd around Quyuk's door. Psin stood by the bed, watching them wash and staunch Tshant's wounds. Each of the slashes was over two hands long, but none was deeper than the skin.

"He's strong," the younger of the two women said. "He'll be roaring to get up tomorrow morning."

"Keep him here until he's healed."

The woman smiled. She was Russian; her skin was white as cream and her round eyes were bright blue. She said, "I'll care for him."

The way she handled him led Psin to think that she had cared for Tshant before. He turned away, snorting.

Kaidu said, "You'd better find Djela, Khan."

"Where is he?"

"Baidar gave him to me but he got away and ran."

Psin started down the corridor. "He's probably gone back to our house." He went past the dispersing crowd, around a corner, and through the high main door into the courtyard.

The sentry there saluted. Psin looked around, saw no sign of Djela, and said, "Did my grandson come through here?"

"He went toward the stables, Khan."

Psin trotted down the steps and strode across the yard, headed for the low barn. Sabotai was probably right to let them fight everything out. His arms hurt where they had held him. He swung open the stable door and called, "Djela?"

There was no answer, and the stable was almost empty. His dun horse stood munching hay at one of the ricks; he'd broken the rope that tied him to the pole. Psin went over to him and led him back to the saddle racks, feeding him hay with each step to keep him quiet. He tied him fast with new rope and started saddling him.

"Grandfather?"

"Oh. There you are."

Djela crawled out from under the hayrick. Straw covered his coat and his face was filthy with tears and dust. "I was talking to Dekko."

"To—oh." Dekko was a little boy who showed up in Djela's conversations sometimes. "What did he have to say?"

"He said—" Djela burst into tears. "Is my father dead?"

Psin scooped him up. "No. Your father's fine. He tipped a cabinet over on Mongke. I don't think he hurt him, but a man can hope. Stop crying."

"I thought he was dead. Mongke cut him. I saw him cut him."

Psin hugged him. "It's all right. Everything's fine. I wouldn't have let Mongke hurt him badly."

"Baidar and Sabotai were holding you. I saw them. They wanted him to get killed."

Psin laid his cheek against the boy's hair. Djela's arms around his neck almost choked him. "No, they don't. They just wanted to teach him not to fight with Mongke."

"They wanted him to die."

"You remember when I told you not to pat Malekai's dog, don't you? And you did."

Djela sobbed. His chin jabbed Psin in the shoulder.

"The dog bit you, didn't he?"

The chin jabbed him again.

"And you didn't pat him anymore, did you?"

"No."

"Why? Because I told you not to, or because he bit you?"

"I want to go home."

"We will. Right now."

"I mean back to the Lake. I want to go back to the Lake."

"We can't, Djela. Not for a long time."

"I want to go home. I want my mother."

The child began crying again, more softly but more terribly as well. Psin rocked him. The dun horse looked toward them, his ears pricked up. Psin sat down with Djela in his lap and listened to him cry. He thought, This is all the fault of Temujin. Like everything else in the world.

Artai said, "Be careful."

"I will."

"Watch out for Djela, when he reaches you."

"I will."

"Watch out for Tshant."

"Tshant's big enough to watch out for himself. You make sure he stays on his back until he heals. He'll try to ride out after us when he wakes up."

She looked back into the house, thoughtfully, and said, "He won't wake up for a while. Mongke stuffed him full of bhang last night."

"Mongke?"

"Oh." She threw one hand up. "The two of them sat in there cursing at each other so loudly none of us could sleep. When they heard you ride in, Mongke went upstairs. I would have told you but you needed sleep."

"Unh." Psin turned to the dun and mounted. Mongke had gone earlier. The first light crept into the courtyard. The dun pawed the stones, and Psin's three remounts shifted nervously away from him. Artai moved back out of the wind.

"Come back," she said.

Psin lifted his hand to her and started toward the gate. He turned, just outside it, and looked back; at the side door, not the one Artai stood in, he saw something move. Dead leaves skittered across the paving stones. It was going to snow. He waved to Artai again, grinned at Chan hiding in the other doorway, and galloped his horses down the street toward the main gate.

THE STORM STRUCK THEM WHEN THEY CROSSED THE VOLGA. PSIN, riding beside Sabotai, pulled up the collar of his cloak and rammed his hat down over his ears. Before he could get his gloves back on, the snow had blotted out everything. Sabotai threw up one arm and pulled his horse down to a walk.

"Mongke."

Mongke galloped up out of the army behind them.

"Can you guide us to Moskva in this weather?"

Psin dug a length of wool out of his saddlepouch and wrapped it around his face. Mongke was thinking. He glanced at Psin and said, "I think so."

"Choose your scouts."

Mongke trotted off again. Sabotai wheeled around and called to Baidar to get colored lanterns out of the baggage train. He said something to Psin, and Psin shook his head.

"I can't hear you."

The wind was screaming past him toward Sabotai. Sabotai nudged his horse closer to Psin's, leaned out, and shouted, "Look behind you."

Psin twisted around to look at the army. Aside from himself, Sabotai, and his and Sabotai's remounts, he could see three other riders. The rest of the five tumans behind them were lost in the driving snow.

He could hear noises—horses neighing, the clank of metal—even above the wind. He could see nothing but a dark grey cloud, full of whirling snow, and the dim shapes of the other three horsemen. They were roping themselves together. Slowly they faded out entirely.

Sabotai cupped his hands around his mouth and bellowed for Baidar. There was no answer. Psin's horses all wheeled at once to put their tails to the wind. Sabotai roared again.

Through the noisy twilight lights moved: red, blue, yellow and green. They bobbed toward them, at first only hazy splotches. The wind swung around, hurling snow into Psin's face, and he heard the plopping of a galloping horse's hoofs. Baidar with lanterns hung from his saddle cantered up to them.

"Every hundred-commander is to see that his men are roped together," Sabotai said. "And he is to carry a lantern on his saddle—yellow. Hang all four of those on a staff so that we can carry it high."

Mongke trotted up. He came so suddenly Psin reached for his bow. "All my scouts carry red lanterns. I'll drop back whenever I can to make sure you're following me."

Sabotai nodded, and Mongke whipped his horse into a gallop and vanished into the storm. Psin squinted, trying to see him. Abruptly a red light glowed ahead, so faint he could barely pick it out: Mongke had unshuttered his lantern. The red light bounced a little and disappeared.

"Do you have a rope?" Sabotai called to Psin.

Psin took rope from his saddle and threw the coiled end to Sabotai. Batu charged up and roped himself to Sabotai's horse on the other side. Baidar with the lanterns mounted on a staff rode directly in front of them, and with Sabotai slightly ahead they started off again.

The dun horse hated moving into anything wet and kept his head down around his knees. Snow drifted across the pommel of Psin's saddle. After every few strides he scraped packed snow off the saddle and his shoulders. Sabotai was slouched down, his face working thoughtfully, and Psin swerved the dun over to him.

They leaned together, standing in their inside stirrups, and shouted in each other's ears to be heard. Psin said, "Do you think we'll be able to signal in this light?"

"If the hundred-commanders pay attention."

"This storm is luck for us."

"How?"

"No Russian will expect us in this weather."

Sabotai laughed. Psin settled back into his saddle and cleared out the snow. His remounts were jogging along directly behind the dun, letting him break the snow for them. When the wind veered or dropped, he could hear men calling and horses trotting behind him, but he knew if he turned he would see nothing.

He thought of the Kipchaks behind them, who made up half of two separate tumans, and of how they must feel going to fight under Mongol commanders sworn to kill them if they hesitated one step, surrounded by Mongols whose attitudes toward the snow and the Kipchaks would be similar. He decided he would not like to be a Kipchak.

Ahead, a red light grew steadily from a rosy haze to a lantern, and Mongke developed out of the flying snow. He lifted one arm and waved it violently north.

"Baidar," Sabotai said. "Shutter all lanterns but the green."

Baidar swayed down the staff, latched the shutters, and swung them up again. Sabotai held up one hand. He meant that they should move west until the hundred-commanders had a chance to see and interpret the change. Psin could see him counting to himself, marking off strides. His hand fell, and Psin reined the dun around. A tree loomed before him and he circled it.

The wind dropped, and he could hear the yells and whistles of the thousand-commanders directing their columns. He looked over his shoulder; he could see not a man, not a horse, only the flicker of a yellow lantern. The snow slapped him in the face and the wind blew his hat off. He caught it by the string and put it on again.

When he turned forward again he saw Mongke's red lantern wobbling away in the snow. Mongke had come back to make sure they had all turned. Psin glanced at Sabotai and nodded.

Sabotai opened his mouth but said nothing, waiting for the wind to lull. When it did, he howled, "How long will this last?"

Psin shrugged and held up one finger, closed his fist, and held up four fingers. He shrugged again. Sabotai looked annoyed, and his lips moved steadily. Psin let his weight slump into the saddle. He trusted Mongke: he went to sleep.

The storm was still raging when he woke up. He thought it was evening. The grey was much darker, and the wind was rising from a scream to a deafening roar. He was sitting in a block of snow, and it was so cold the snow hadn't melted at all. He smashed it with his fist and brushed the chunks off his saddle. The dun's mane hung down in icicles.

Sabotai tugged on the rope that tied them together, and Psin rode over there. Sabotai shouted, "Batu says we should camp."

Psin looked up at the sky; snowflakes pounded his face. His

mustaches crackled.

"Here comes Mongke," Batu screamed.

Mongke cantered up, dragging his remounts behind him. "Camp," he shouted. "Up ahead. Good foraging."

Psin nodded. Sabotai called signals to Baidar. He was solid white, the snow clinging in shelves to his shoulders. When Mongke signaled that they could camp, Psin could see Sabotai counting off strides. They began to turn, and they kept turning, swinging steadily around to trample out a camp among the trees. When they turned straight into the wind it nearly tore Psin out of his saddle. The rope between him and Sabotai was stiff with ice. At last they caught up with the tail end of the army. Sabotai waved toward the center, and he, Psin and Batu galloped into the middle of the great circle. Passing the Kipchaks, Psin caught a glimpse of faces dulled from cold and misery.

Sabotai said, "How far did we come?"

"Far enough." Psin dismounted and flexed his legs. His knees hurt.

"My toes are frozen," Sabotai said. "My rump is asleep."

Batu snorted and slid down, to beat at his sides with his arms. His eyes darted cheerfully around them and he smiled.

"Where's that baggage train?" Sabotai said.

"Coming." Baidar trotted into their midst. "Mongke's found a meadow up ahead where the horses can graze."

Sabotai nodded. The baggage train lumbered into the camp. Slaves dropped off while it rolled and ran to find their masters. One of Sabotai's, swathed in fur, stripped the saddles from their mounts, linked them together with lead ropes, and jumped up on Baidar's horse to pony them over to the pasture.

With the horses gone the cold was suddenly penetrating. Sabotai crawled into the nearest cart. The baggage masters were breaking up the train, sending carts here and there; inside the one Sabotai huddled in, Dmitri and two of Psin's women slaves were already cooking gruel and warming kumiss. Psin leaned against the tailgate and blew on his mustaches to thaw them out.

"Half a day's ride in good weather?" Sabotai said.

Psin shook his head. "Less. Enough. If the Russians have sentries posted along the river, they won't have seen us. If this snow keeps up we'll be under their walls before they know we're coming."

Dmitri handed Sabotai kumiss and he gulped it down. Dmitri took the bowl to fill it up again. Sabotai said, "If this snow keeps up you'll be carting a frozen general back home with you."

Batu had collected his brothers and was talking to them. All but Batu himself looked exhausted. Batu was trying to talk them into playing chess with him. His cart pulled up alongside Sabotai's and Psin's, and Batu's brothers all lunged for it, scrabbling at the tailgate with their frozen hands.

"Is Batu never tired?" Sabotai said.

"Batu is an old woman." Quyuk hitched himself up into the cart beside Sabotai. "My brother has thrown me out into the snow."

"Why?"

"I tipped the pot into the fire."

"Are you drunk?" Psin sniffed.

"Very." Quyuk flopped back and lay still.

"They're probably all drunk," Sabotai said. "Except Kadan. Kadan never drinks on campaign."

Dmitri brought Psin a dry tunic and helped him put it on. Psin crawled into the corner opposite Sabotai's. Kaidu was trying to get into Batu's cart; Batu and Berke were shoving him back. "Sleep in the snow," Batu shouted. "Be good for you. Toughen you up."

"Let me in," Kaidu wailed. "I'm cold."

Psin drank his third bowl of kumiss. Quyuk was snoring. Two slaves heaved their saddles into the cart, and Psin's bowcase narrowly missed Quyuk's head.

"Eat," Sabotai said. He thrust a bowl of gruel into Psin's hands.

They ate as much as they wanted; Moskva wasn't so far away they had to worry about food. Mongke had said the city could be stormed. Finished, Sabotai crawled back past Quyuk and curled up under a mountain of fur robes. "Come in and put the tailgate up."

Psin climbed up and pulled the gate after him. The camp was quiet, and the snow was drifting up already over the wheels of the carts. He dragged his sable cloak over his shoulders and lay down, suddenly tired.

The storm battered at them all the next day, and that night again everyone who could crawled into or under a cart to sleep. Psin woke up halfway through the night from a dream in which he had been drowning in quicksand; his face was crushed against Sabotai's back. When he moved, somebody behind him groaned and kicked out—Quyuk. The two women slaves were curled up at Quyuk's feet, and Dmitri and Sabotai's slave huddled together across Psin's legs. He twisted his head to get some air and inhaled the stink of the banked fire, the garbage, the wet fur, wet wool and closely packed people. Quyuk and Sabotai had him wedged in between them so tight he could hardly move his arms.

Gradually he drifted back to sleep. The sound of the snow needling the roof and walls of the cart filled his dreams.

By noon of the next day, the snow had stopped. The sky was jumbled with massive clouds scurrying south. Sabotai ordered the lanterns put up and the banners broken out. They jogged through a thick stretch of oak forest, where the snow lay up to the horses' bellies. The wind strengthened and grew steady out of the north, colder than before. Psin smeared bear grease over his face to keep out the chill. When Mongke cantered up to them to report, his lips were blue and his teeth chattered so hard they couldn't understand what he said. He clenched his jaws and started again.

"River ahead—frozen down to the bottom, but the b-b-banks are steep. I'll leave sign—"

Psin tossed him a jug of kumiss, and Mongke struggled the plug out and drank, his throat working hard. Done, he nodded to Psin and plugged it up again.

"The snow is level. There's no sign that the bank drops off there."

"You've lost a horse," Baidar said mildly.

"I broke its leg going over the bank."

They rode on. At the river Mongke had smashed down a great wide trail all along the bank. Psin's horse refused it the first time and he whipped it down. The dun, on the leading string, leapt snorting to the ice and slid three lengths. When they reached the far bank the dun bounded up it and almost dragged Psin out of the saddle.

"He needs to be ridden," Sabotai said.

Psin shook his head.

That night the camp was more comfortable, since the scramble to sleep in the carts was over.

* * *

Tshant stood in his stirrups and looked all around. The glittering snow lay unbroken under the trees. The forest looked dead; only a few leaves clung to the branches, and in the bitter cold nothing moved or sounded. Behind them, their trail wound back along the meadow. Their remounts dug vigorously at the snow, trying to get at grass.

Djela said, "Is that it, up ahead?"

"I think so." Between Djela's hat and the collar of his cloak only the tip of his nose showed, bright red. They started off again, toward the strip of beaten ground ahead of them. The horses smashed through the thickening crust on the snow. When they reached the army's trail Tshant reined in again. He couldn't see the other side of the trail, which stretched on and on beneath the trees, a ghost of itself. The wind had blown the snow almost even again before the crust froze, so that only great round dimples marked where one hundred and fifty thousand horses had trotted past. The wind was right in their faces.

They turned and rode along the edge of the trail. Twice now they'd had to veer off because the army had eaten up all the fodder for the horses. Most of the trees they passed were missing branches, and the bark was stripped off as if by knives. It was getting colder. The sun hung over the horizon, dim through the trees.

Tshant's back hurt. He said to himself, I am all right. The cuts along his ribs still burned when he moved too quickly. He made his horse lope; Djela fell behind him to use the trail he broke. He was hungry but he didn't want to eat. He couldn't think of anything that would taste good.

At sundown he stopped and switched his harness to another horse and helped Djela with his. Djela said, "Maybe Dekko is following us the way—"

"Dekko doesn't exist. You made Dekko up."

Djela threaded the end of his girth through the ring on the saddle and hung from it to get it tight. "Dekko does so exist. You can't see him because he won't let you."

"Dekko isn't real."

"Lash my girth, Ada."

Tshant lashed his girth. Djela scampered around to hook his sad-dlepouch and bowcases to the cantle on the other side. "If you liked Dekko, he'd—"

"Don't talk to me about Dekko."

"Grandfather knows about Dekko."

Tshant hitched the other horses together on the leadline and mounted. "I'm sure he does. If there's anything in this world Psin doesn't know about, it would surprise me."

"Me too." Djela jumped, grabbed the pommel, and scrambled into the saddle.

Tshant snorted. His heart was thumping strangely. He pressed one elbow against his side, to feel if the cuts had opened up again. He didn't think they had. He started off again, fixing his eyes on a particular tree so that he wouldn't get dizzy, and Djela dropped behind again to follow him. Tshant whipped the horse into a fast trot, following the fading trail of the army.

When the army reached the Oka River, Sabotai broke it into four columns, sent one under Kadan up for a vanguard, and let one camp on the river for half a day as a rearguard. Mongke's scouts would report to Kadan now, and Kadan would send couriers back if Mongke's news warranted it.

Sabotai and Psin rode in the center column; the other, under Quyuk and Baidar, rode on the south flank of the vanguard. Psin could tell that Sabotai was worried about something.

"The snow held us up," Sabotai said.

Psin shrugged. He got dried meat from his saddlebag and chewed on it, letting the juice make broth of his saliva.

"We should have crossed their outpost line by now."

"Do they have one?" Psin said.

"Maybe not. We haven't seen a trace of any Russians."

They parted to ride around a tree and met again on the other side. Psin's horse stumbled over something and he jerked him up. The snow here lay more shallow than across the river, and they were beginning to make some speed.

"The patrols out here should have reported to us by now," Sa-botai said.

"Wait. They were scattered. They'll come."

"I want to know where the Grand Duke is."

Ahead, a yellow banner fluttered, taut in the wind, and Sabotai reined up. The horses on his leadline almost crashed into him.

"Scouts," Psin said. He twisted around and looked for Kaidu, who was carrying their bannerstaff. Kaidu had already dipped his banner in reply.

They cantered across the meadow just ahead. A horseman appeared among the birch trees on the crest of the next ridge, lifted one arm in salute, and galloped down toward them. His horse left a swath of shadow behind him in the snow.

"Mongke's," Psin said.

The scout dragged his horse to a stop before them, saluted, and said, "We've sighted Russians, up ahead. Outriders. We shot three but two got away."

"Where were they going?" Psin said.

"Southwest, Khan."

"To Moskva," Sabotai said.

"Or Vladimir."

Sabotai nodded. He tugged at his beard, which he seemed to have laced up with his coat that morning. "Don't kill any you see," he said to the scout. "Let them go back and say we're coming."

Psin choked. The scout whirled and dashed his horse back up the ridge, and Sabotai told Kaidu to send up the white banner.

"If they know we're coming," Sabotai said, "they'll run to the cities. The more we beat when we take the cities, the fewer we have to run down later."

"They might lay ambushes."

"No. They'll run. Let them get into the habit of running from us, and when we have it all they'll come back begging to be let in again."

"If you think so, it must be true."

"Delicately phrased."

Just before they camped that evening, a courier galloped up from Buri, commanding the rearguard. Tshant and Djela had ridden up to them that morning, and Tshant wanted to know Sabotai's orders.

Psin growled. "Is he well?"

"I didn't see him, Khan."

"He shouldn't have left Bulgar so soon."

Sabotai made a motion with one hand. "He's here, we can't send him back. What shall we do with him?"

"Do whatever you want."

"Good." To the courier, he said, "Ride back tomorrow and tell Tshant he is to stay with your column and share Buri's command."

Psin squawked. Sabotai looked over, his eyebrows cocked in exaggerated surprise. Psin said, "You don't know my son, if you think he'll split a command."

"Does he command well?"

"He's inexperienced. Otherwise, yes."

Sabotai waved the courier off.

"He'll tear Buri to scraps," Psin said.

"Buri can take care of himself."

The column was trampling out a campground. Psin rode along beside Sabotai, thinking about Tshant. Finally, he said, "What do you want of them, Sabotai?"

"I want them to be generals," Sabotai said. "No man can rule a khanate unless he is a good general. The Kha-Khan cannot command the world unless he has good generals."

Psin didn't bother to ask how pitching two hotheads together would make either of them another Sabotai. He reeled in his remounts on the leadline and called over a slave from the baggage train to take them into the center of the camp.

"All the Altun are good fighters," Sabotai said. "But they aren't flexible enough in command. They need experience more than anything."

"At killing one another?"

Sabotai grinned. he flung one leg across the pommel of his saddle and slid to the ground. "Ah. My ankles are broken."

"You sound like Jebe." Jebe at Psin's age had complained constantly, mainly of his arthritis. Until the day he died Jebe had handled a bow or a horse as well as any young man; the arthritis had mysteriously healed whenever he had to fight.

"Still, I never used to be tired."

Mongke galloped up to them and jammed his horse to a halt. Snow flew across Sabotai. Psin said, "What are you doing back here?"

"The vanguard is within half a day's march of Moskva. Kadan won't keep riding without Sabotai's command."

Sabotai was drinking kumiss mixed with honey. He put the bowl down and climbed up on the tailgate. "You left your post."

Mongke spat. "My post is everywhere: I'm a scout. If we keep riding—"

Psin dismounted. Dmitri led off his horse. He reached up over the tailgate for the bowl the woman inside was filling; Mongke whipped his horse up and slammed in between Psin and the cart. Psin leapt back.

Mongke said, "I kill a horse getting here—"

"I'll send a messenger to Kadan," Sabatai said.

"I'll go. I—"

Psin reached up and hauled Mongke out of the saddle. "Don't you ever do that again." He shook Mongke hard, threw him into the snow, and slapped the horse's rump. The horse trotted off. Sabotai had sent a slave after Batu and his brothers.

"Don't you realize?" Mongke said. He stood up, covered with snow. "Moskva—"

"Just because we don't leap up and down doesn't mean we can't do what's necessary," Psin said. "Get something to eat and sleep."

"Berke," Sabotai called, to Batu's brother. "Take four horses and ride to Kadan; tell him to keep moving. Mongke, has he got a scout with him to take him there?"

Mongke nodded.

"Good. Berke. He's to throw his column around the city and seal it off. We'll storm it when we get there. Hurry. He's camped for the night."

Berke stamped off. Batu said, "How far is it?"

"Half a day's ride for the vanguard, Mongke says."

"Are we going to follow him?"

Sabotai looked over at Psin, and Psin shook his head. Sabotai walked around Mongke, took Psin by the shoulder, and drew him a little to one side, standing so that Psin's bulk hid him from Batu.

"I think we should. Kadan has a tuman only. If he stretches ten thousand men around a city wall he'll be open to a strike from inside."

"If it were Mongke I'd say yes," Psin said. "But Kadan has sense enough to keep his line secure."

"What good will it do us to hang back?"

"Give these columns some rest. They've fought the snow all the way from Bulgar. Kadan doesn't need support to invest a city of that size—only to take it."

"Unless the Grand Duke's army is there."

"He wouldn't take his army from Vladimir to Moskva."

"I wish I knew where they were."

"We'll find out. Camp here the night. Tomorrow evening we should reach Moskva. If we ride all night we won't get there until tomorrow morning anyhow."

Sabotai pursed his lips. "The moon is full."

Psin nodded.

"We'll camp here until moonset and leave then."

Psin closed his eyes. "In the pitch dark."

"Oh, well. They won't see us coming." Sabotai slapped him on the shoulder and strode off to talk to Batu.

WAKE UP," BATU SHOUTED.

Psin bolted upright. Batu laughed in his ear. The darkness was smothering; through the cart walls Psin could hear horses neighing and the high voices of the men. He threw his robe off and crawled down to the tailgate.

"Eat something," Dmitri said. "Something hot."

"Later." He dragged on one boot and reached for a sock to put on over it.

Sabotai was struggling to get his arms into his coat sleeves and shouting orders that no one seemed to hear. A loose horse galloped by, shrilling. Psin hunted through the cart for his left boot, swearing under his breath. Torchlight flickered weakly in over the tailgate. He found the boot and thrust his foot into it. The two women went on serenely cooking gruel. Dmitri held out his coat.

"I hate gruel," Psin said. "Can't we have something else to eat?"

"I've put honey in it, Khan." The Kipchak woman handed him a bowl.

"Eat it," Batu said. He spooned the stuff into his mouth. "Good for you."

"Tepid, weak, stomach-turning—I hear you, Sabotai."

"Then why don't you come out?"

"I'm not dressed yet." He poured the gruel down his throat and laced up his boot. Something struck the cart so hard it rocked. Dmitri dodged the flood of gruel when the pot tipped over; hot coals skittered across the floor. The women danced about, scooping them up with horn spoons.

"Tshant and Buri will bring the baggage train," Batu said. "We have to ride like Mongols now." He walked hunched over to the end of the cart and jumped out. Psin followed on hands and knees.

"Psin, come catch this brute of a horse."

Psin dragged his saddle out from under the cart. "Why, can't a bunch of Mongols handle a Merkit horse?"

The horse whistled and kicked out. Its hindhoofs cracked on the side of the cart, which swayed violently. Psin plunged through the men trying to hold the horse; the dun saw him coming and spun around, legs braced.

"Calm down, lambkin. Easy, sweeting." Psin took the rope and went quietly to the horse's head. "You cock-eyed spittle of a perverted dragon."

The dun licked his hand. Sabotai was mounted and giving yet more orders. Two couriers flashed through the torchlight. Beyond the light lay only a vast and noisy darkness, full of horses.

A drover's whip cracked. They were linking up the baggage train again. Psin forced the bit between the dun's teeth and jerked his girth tight. The dun would not stand still to be mounted. Psin swung up, and the dun tried to bolt.

"Ride on the north wing," Sabotai said. "Carry a green lantern and watch for my signals."

Psin nodded. He wheeled the horse over to the nearest cart and took down one of the lanterns hanging from the side. The army was moving. The center of the column was already out of the camp. His remounts jogged up, and he hooked the leadline to his saddle. The last of the column cantered past his cart. He swung out to ride around them and come up on the north side.

The beech trees on the next ridge crawled with horsemen. Out of the racket and confusion of breaking camp had come the single motion of an army riding. The rumble of the horses' hoofs drowned out the wind. Lanterns glowed, red, green, blue, white and yellow, and the tossing manes of the horses were like pine branches in the wind. For a while, cantering around to take up his post, he was separate from the great mass of the army. The dark swarm in the middle of the dark night did not seem like many riders, but one great creature that bounded over the ground and spilled through the stiff and naked trees.

The dun horse bucked. Psin whipped him and maneuvered him around a clump of rocks that lumped up the snow. The horse lengthened its stride to pass the mob alongside them. Psin gave him his head.

In the darkness the riding was treacherous. The column spread out far more than in the daylight, because if a horse stumbled or a rider fell the men behind would ride right over him before they saw. Sabotai's lanterns flashed busily, directing the sides of the column this way and that. Psin acknowledged the orders under his sign by swinging his own lantern. The stars were out, shivering cold, and the wind rose steadily. North of Psin a wolf howled.

Ahead the green lantern flashed three times. Psin waved his red lantern and bellowed, "Swing out, north wing." He dropped back a little, yelling, and the north wing spread out toward him. He looked up toward Sabotai and saw the green lantern flashing more complexly.

"Move up—come up level with the front of the column." He rode around to the end of the extended wing and galloped forward, and as if he were linked to the line they all burst into a gallop and hurtled along through the total darkness beside him. They swept up a slope and charged down the other side, gaining ground swiftly on the head of the column. Sabotai was turning toward them a little, and Psin corrected his course.

Light glowed up ahead—watchfires, leaping against the trees. Russians. He pulled his bow out of the case, leaving his rein draped over the dun's withers, but before he could nock an arrow lanterns winked on and off in the midst of the fires. Mongke's scouts must have lit them to guide Sabotai in toward the river.

They plunged down toward the fires. Psin's remounts loped freely beside the dun; whenever the wind changed a little he could hear them pounding over the snow, the breath whumping out of their nostrils. The lanterns ahead flashed an order and Psin shouted to his wing to slow down.

They swept in between fires. Men dodged wildly out of their way. Psin, expecting the riverbank, checked the dun hard just before they slid down it. The ice rang like stone beneath the horse's hoofs. The leadline strained, and a horse ran into the dun from behind. The dun kicked back. Psin's remounts got tangled up, bit and clawed at each other, and straightened themselves out before they had to scramble up the far bank.

The column was veering south, and Sabotai's green lantern flashed again: Psin and his wing held back hard to take up the rear of the swerving column. Faint light streaked across the snow, and the watchfires seemed paler. The eastern sky bristled with the dawn. Psin relaxed a little. He leaned out to whip his remounts into line again. The snow was blue, the air itself was blue, and the watchfires they passed on the far bank shrank down to puddles of weak light. The wind shrieked around his ears.

Some of the men around him were changing horses already—
leaping onto the bare backs of their nearest remounts and leaving
the saddled horse to gallop along beside them. They hadn't been
riding long enough to change horses, and Psin started to yell at
them. But the green lantern started to wink and he had to charge
out of the midst of the rearguard to see.

The lantern winked four times quickly and twice slowly. Psin
swore. He shuttered his lantern to show that he didn't understand.
The green lantern flashed off entirely. Sabotai was definitely getting old if he couldn't even send signals anymore. Now the yellow
lantern was winking, and the center of the column slackened speed.

They were coming up to a thick stretch of trees. The column
thinned down to pass between it and the river, along the bare space
there. Psin swore again and swung the dun horse into the thick of
his men; he flung his leadrope to one and dashed off again. He galloped the dun straight through the thick trees. The horse leapt like
a deer over a windfall, smashed Psin's knee against a tree, and
plowed through a clump of birches. Psin held his hat on with one
hand. The dun thrashed out of the wood and Psin lashed him once
to keep him settled. The horse flattened out, racing at top speed
toward Sabotai.

The snow, still glittering blue in the dawn light, flew past under
the horse's reaching hoofs. The main column fell behind as if they
weren't moving at all. Sabotai was playing with the green lantern
again. Psin could see him clearly, his features unnaturally distinct in
the fresh light. He charged the dun up to him and slowed the horse
to Sabotai's pace.

"What in God's name do you want me to do?"

Sabotai shouted, "I was warning you about the trees ahead."

"Four short and two long? Did you just make it up?"

"Three long to slow down."

"I read four short and two long, Sabotai. It may be fun to invent
new signals but—"

The dun collected himself and jumped a small stream. Psin
rocked back in his saddle.

"I told him three long."

Sabotai sounded angry. Psin shouted, "I definitely saw six
flashes." A tree branch might have gotten in the way, so that a long

flash seemed two short ones. He spun the horse around and galloped back along the line of the column. The green lantern flashed two long.

"Sabotai. This is no time for lantern drill."

He fell back to his own wing and collected his remounts; they picked up speed, obeying the order. But Sabotai had forgotten to tell the center of the column to move out, and Psin's wing began to run up on the center's heels.

"Batu," Psin roared. "Move up."

Batu was galloping along beside the center, a little apart from the main group. He waved. "Sabotai gave me no signal."

"Damn Sabotai. He's a—"

The white lantern flashed, and Batu answered it with his own. The center plunged on, finally drawing ahead of the rearguard. It was full day, and the lanterns were getting hard to see. Psin thought perhaps Sabotai had signaled and Batu hadn't caught it.

He rode in close to the nearest of his remounts, kicked his feet out of the stirrups, and jumped. The horse shied away from him and he landed off center, his arms around the horse's neck. The horse staggered. Psin hauled himself up onto the heaving back and steered over closer to the dun. The dun reached out to nip Psin's new mount, and he grabbed his rein, whipped his horse up ahead of the dun so that he could kick the dun in the nose, and settled down. Ahead, Sabotai was raising the banners, and in the east the first long rays of the sun shot across the horizon.

They rode down on Moskva well before noon. Kadan was already camped around the city, on the frozen swamp at the foot of its low hill. The main army washed in like a flood, split exactly down the middle, and swung around to embrace everything, Kadan, hill, city and all. They crashed through the heavy woods opposite one gate and spilled out over the narrow strip of fields, and the two wings came together precisely before the tall stone main gate into the city. Psin's wing, charging around the east side, packed the river from bank to bank with racing horses.

The Mongols already there cheered, and the Mongols coming in cheered, and the people on the city wall screamed insults; the horses neighed, the wind howled, and the pine around the hill moaned. In the uproar Psin halted his column and posted them into camps, two on the city's side of the river, one in the middle on the far bank. The ice between the city and the far camp was trampled free of snow and blazed under the high sun. Psin jogged across it to find Sabotai.

From the peaks of the city's towers pennants flew. People crowded the walls and the roofs of the buildings near the gate. The snow at the foot of the hill was flecked with arrows. Just below a gate lay half a dozen dead and frozen knights and two horses with their guts strung over the ground. Psin's horse shied, and he realized that he was still riding bareback, with only a halter and leadrope for bridle.

"Psin."

Kadan jogged up. His face glowed, and he smiled.

"Have you lost that strange horse of yours? I could have taken this pile six times by now. Did you see the bodies? They tried to beat us off. Sabotai's over there."

Psin looked up at the city. "It doesn't look like any problem, does it?"

"No. They shoot stones at us with catapults, now and then, and all night they were popping fire arrows over the wall. Odd people. They d-don't seem to know that snow won't burn."

"They're frightened," Psin said.

"They should be. I have some Kipchaks, you know. And they're going to take Moskva or die, so they're quite definitely going t-to take it."

"We had a ride getting here. Oh. Sabotai's invented a whole new signal. Four short and two long mean 'trees ahead, bear south.' Remember that, it might prove useful."

Kadan frowned. "I didn't know—"

"I'm joking. I have to go find him."

"Where is my brother?"

"Sabotai sent him off hunting for the Russian field army."

"Good. I'd hate to have to share a siege with him."

"We won't siege it."

He turned his horse and jogged over to Sabotai's camp. Three men were busy rigging up a sort of tent, using lances and a bearskin. Sabotai sat before a fire warming his feet. His boots stood beside him, the laces dangling.

"I'm sorry about the signal," he called, when Psin rode in. "Esugai heard me to say four long. Something must have cut up the first two long flashes."

"Trees." Psin dismounted and a man took his horse. "This looks like a village."

"It's not an important city." Sabotai curled his toes. "Except to me."

"Which way did you send Quyuk?"

Sabotai grinned. "I thought you'd figure out about that. I sent him over toward Tver. If the Grand Duke is there he could be troublesome. If he's not he won't bother us."

"Tver is . . . west of here?"

"West and north. Here. Drink."

"God. You've put honey on it. How can you ruin kumiss like that?"

"Because I'm an old man."

"Tell me when you get arthritis."

"We can storm it this afternoon, I think. Look at them up there. They're gawking at us."

Psin finished the bowl of kumiss. "It's not going to be so easy. That's a steep ride to the main gate."

"I have men cutting battering rams, and when the baggage train gets here we'll have catapults. We can scale the wall with ropes."

"Kipchaks first, of course."

Sabotai nodded happily. "Batu's brothers are out looking for the best places on the wall."

"I'm sure you're going to create a diversion. What?"

"You."

"You're very funny, Sabotai. Do I dance?"

"If you'd like to. You should take half a tuman and set fire to the wall at some point opposite the one we're trying to storm."

"Better than climbing up a rope. Can I choose my men?"

"Yes, if you want."

"I'll take Mongke's honor guard and Arcut Bökö, the thousand-commander who went with me to Novgorod. That's three hundred men. I don't need half a tuman."

"If the wall collapses—"

"I doubt it will, but if it does three hundred men can hold a breach."

A courier was picking his way through the camp toward them.

Psin stood up. The man trotted his horse over and saluted.

"I come from Quyuk Noyon. He has good information that the Russian army is gathering on the Volga due north of Vladimir."

Sabotai jerked his head toward Psin. "Find Mongke." To the courier, he said, "How reliable is this?"

"Very. We met some of the tuman that's scattered over this country and they say they had to run from the army only six days ago."

Psin had sent a slave to Mongke's camp. He swung around. "They won't stay on the Volga, they'll go north, toward Novgorod. If they stay on the Volga they run the risk of being encircled."

"Do they know that?" Sabotai said.

"I should think so."

"Well, then." Mongke was coming; Sabotai nodded to the courier. "Go back to Quyuk and tell him to maintain contact with the army and harass them if possible. Mongke, assign one of your scouts to take Baidar and his tuman to Kolomna."

Mongke nodded. His coat was thrown loosely over his shoulders, and he thrust one arm through the sleeve. "I'll go."

"No. We need you. Let Baidar command alone."

Psin said, "Sabotai, maybe—"

A roar went up from the walls of the city above them. The gate had swung open. Psin shaded his eyes with his hand. A company of knights was riding out down the road, pennants flapping over their heads, and they had a truce flag hitched to one bannerstaff. Sabotai muttered something under his breath.

"Psin, go find out what they want."

Psin took the courier's lathered horse. This whole side of the Mongol camp was on its feet, watching. Most of the men held their bows ready. The knights proceeded solemnly down the steep road toward them. The city's ramparts swarmed with people watching.

"What is it?" Batu shouted.

Psin waved at him and shrugged. He rode at a canter to meet the oncoming Russians.

They stopped and waited for him; there were twenty of them, all glistening in their armor, their full beards lying on their breasts. The banners crackled in the stiff wind.

"Do you speak Russian?" one of them bawled, when Psin was

within talking range.

Psin reined up. "Passably. What do you want?"

Their leader stepped his horse forward. "I would speak with Batu Khan."

"Batu is indisposed."

"Sabotai, then."

"Sabotai as well."

The man laid one gloved hand on his yellow beard. His eyes darted over the camp. "To whom do I speak?"

"I am Sabotai's chief aide."

The men behind the leader cried out. They wanted to talk to Batu, not to a subordinate. Sabotai himself would not do. The leader swung and silenced them and turned stiffly back to Psin, his armor creaking.

"What is your name?"

"Psin Khan. They call me Psin the Stubborn."

"We come to warn you that your doom is at hand. While your puny army lingers here the Grand Duke Yuri marches against you with five hundred thousand men."

Psin's mouth twitched. "Even if that were so our doom would rest in God's hands and not the Grand Duke's. But Yuri is on the Volga and he hasn't gathered up all his men yet. We shall have Moskva by nightfall."

A young man behind the leader called, "Come and try, pagan." The others rumbled angrily and nodded. Their hands tightened around their lances. Psin looked them over, still smiling, and lifted his reins.

"If you've nothing more to do than tell us about ghost armies, I'll go."

The leader raised one hand to keep his men quiet. "Do you have the power to make terms?"

The young man shouted, "Never."

Psin nodded. "Sabotai speaks through me."

"And Batu?"

These people obviously thought Batu was the commander. Psin dropped his reins on his horse's neck. "Batu as well."

"What terms for the peaceful surrender of Moskva?"

"No," the young man cried.

"Complete surrender," Psin said. "We will sack the city and burn it. The people will be slaves."

For once the company was silent, their eyes filled with shock. The leader said, "Is there no mercy in you?"

"Mercy enough. You will live. If you don't surrender, you'll die."

"And many of you as well."

Psin shrugged. "Everybody dies. I've said what the terms are."

The leader looked away, toward the river. Behind him the young man dropped the point of his lance. "We shall never surrender," he shouted. His horse bolted forward. The leader whirled, throwing one hand out to stop him, but the young man only brushed past. The lance was aimed at Psin's chest.

Psin whipped his horse around. The young man tried to follow but his horse, bigger and more burdened, couldn't turn so fast. The lance wavered past Psin, close enough that he could have caught it. His horse reared, and the young man fought his own horse around to bring the lance to bear.

Six arrows impaled him, all at once. They thrust up from his chest, his side, his throat, and out of the Mongol camp rose a deep snarl like a bear's inside a cave. The young man pitched out of his saddle and lay on the frozen ground, face up.

Psin flung his arm up to stop the charge he knew was coming. To the leader he said, "Get back inside your wall."

"We are not truce-breakers," the Russian said. "He was mad—"

"He was a Russian—you all lie. Get inside before I let them kill you all."

He galloped off down the slope. The Mongols strained, waiting for the single order to charge. When he cantered into the camp a cheer ripped out of them. The thousand-commanders, riding bareback, raced up and down the lines to keep order. Psin jogged back to Sabotai's camp.

"What did they want?" Sabotai said. "Other than your blood."

"Terms. I told them."

The courier from Quyuk was gone. Mongke and Batu were stringing meat on an iron spit. One of Mongke's hands was red with raw juice, and his sleeve was soaked. Psin dismounted. "What happened to you?"

"Oh," Mongke said, laughing. "When that Russian charged you I had a chunk of meat in my hand, and I squeezed it too hard."

"Will they take the terms?" Sabotai asked.

"No."

Sabotai looked relieved.

"Fire," Psin called.

Mongke's guard drew their bows and shot. The fire-arrows hurtled up into the blue sky, trailing smoke, and slipped down into the wall. The defenders on the ramparts screeched something. Psin trotted back and forth behind his line, watching the arrows burn down. "Light them."

The defenders leaned off the wall to beat at the flames with sacks and coats. Psin lifted one hand, dropped it to his side, and shouted. Another volley of arrows streaked across the slope. On the wall a man took one through the chest and fell, tumbling, into the snow at the foot of the wall.

Dim under the roar of the fires burning at intervals along his line, the screams and cheers of the fighting on the far side of the city reached Psin's ears. The defenders scurrying back and forth on the walls would sometimes throw up their arms, pointing back across the city's roofs. When the arrows flew again, they whirled back and began to pour cauldrons of water down the wall.

"Fire at will," Psin called. He reined the dun horse down and laid both hands on the saddle pommel.

The wall was burning, down near the foot. Heavy black smoke rolled up, blotting the wall out of their sight. Psin kicked the dun into a jog again. "Can't you shoot any faster than that? Are you Mongols or Chinese? Arcut, your half of the line start firing at the top of the wall."

"We can't see it, Khan."

Off near the main gate something crashed; horses began to whinney and a lot of people shouted all at once.

"What do you mean, you can't see it? You know it's there, don't you? Shoot faster, you fumble-fingered crossbred pack oxen."

The air between the line and the wall was a constant bridge of arrows. Smoke rolled thickly across the wall. The wind changed, and the smoke blew suddenly away. This whole section of the wall streamed flames. No Russian stood on the rampart behind it. Arcut bellowed, "Remember where—" The smoke swept back across the wall, and Arcut cursed it.

A plume of smoke rose from the far side of the city, the color and shape of a tornado. Psin stood in his stirrups. He was sure the smoke came from inside the wall.

"Arcut. Mount up your half of the line. Get your ropes out, and let's pull that wall down."

Half the line broke and ran for their grazing mounts. Arcut ran past Psin, slowed just enough to say, "Are you out of your mind?" and caught his horse. Psin unhitched his rope from the cantle of his saddle and galloped in toward the flaming wall.

He could feel the heat long before he was halfway there, even through his leather armor. The smoke was filthy with embers. The dun slackened, and Psin talked him on. He charged into the smoke, coughed, choked, and held his breath. The wall rose up before him, at the top of a small cliff—high as a pine tree, blazing, the wall leaned inward already. Psin beat his way through the smoke. He could hear people screaming on the far side of the wall. His lungs ached from not breathing.

The smoke blew away, and he gulped the delicious air. The roar of the flames and the heat made the dun flinch back. Arcut and his men were close behind him. Arrows thudded into the burning wall.

"You didn't tell them to stop firing," Arcut yelled.

Psin tied a great knot in the end of his rope and flung it up. The knot caught between two of the logs in the wall just at the edge of the blaze, but the wind bellied it out and it swayed across the flames. Before Psin could pull it taut it fell back, burned in half.

"Stay upwind of it."

Some Russians still clung to the wall, just to windward of the burning; they hurled rocks and pots at the Mongols. A shard bounced off the dun's shoulder. Psin swung around and waved his arms at the rest of his bowmen, still firing grimly into the wall. He pointed straight up and over toward the unburnt section, and they shifted their aim. A rock struck him in the small of the back and he gasped.

The stretch of wall windward of the blaze was smoking, and the Russians were retreating back along it, away from the heat. A great splintering roar burst up from the smoke and flame, and the wall caved in of itself. Arcut and three other men had gotten ropes over the wall where it was smoking and were urging their horses away from it.

"Get in there or you won't get to plunder," Psin shouted. "Sabotai is in the city. Hurry up."

"We're hurrying," Arcut shouted. "This damned—" A chunk of paving stone smashed into the side of his face. He reeled; Psin caught the reins of his horse and kept it pulling while Arcut recovered. Blood streamed down the side of his face.

The wall swayed, and the men tugging at it cheered. Smoke drifted over them. The wind was changing again. Psin threw Arcut his reins, twisted around, and waved the rest of his men in. They whirled after their horses. The wall split and cracked and with a high crash pitched forward toward them.

"In. In. Go on, you idiots, you'll lose your plunder."

They charged up the steep slope; their horses clawed their way across the fallen wall and into the city. A group of Russians on foot waited for them, hayforks and spades in their hands. When Psin's men swung toward them the Russians turned and screaming fled down a street toward the center of the city. Psin pulled his bow out of the case and followed them.

"Eeeeyyyyyiiiiiaaaah!"

The dun horse never faltered; when he reached the last of the fleeing Russians he ran right over him. Psin heard the man whine under the great hoofs. The street forked, and he reined the dun to the left. A shower of stones and household goods met him. Something heavy thudded off his shoulder. He swayed, and the horse lost its footing and skidded, shrilling, halfway across the street. Psin raised his bow, saw a face in a window two floors above the street, and shot. The arrow struck the scroll work but the face dropped out of sight. The dun heaved himself up on his feet and charged on.

"Burn them—"

That was Arcut. Psin glanced back and saw him racing along behind him, the first of a stream of Mongols coming at a full gallop with torches in their hands. Arcut wheeled his horse straight for a doorway that stood half open on the right side of the street. The horse clattered up the step and into the house. The door caromed off something inside and slammed shut. The men behind him were all plunging into the buildings nearest them, screaming and waving their torches. Most of them left their horses in the street.

Flames shot out of an upper-storey window, and a woman shrieked. Something large and squirming sailed out of the window between the flames—a man, wrapped up in a carpet. The rain of stones and furniture halted entirely. Four Mongols staggered out of the house nearest to Psin. One carried a girl over his shoulder. The others were heaving rugs full of plunder along behind them. The girl was screaming with each step.

Psin turned the dun and galloped off down the street. The houses he passed were empty, the alleys deserted. Ahead, he could hear fighting, and behind him the swelling crackle of flames. The dun stretched out into a pounding run. Cinders floated down into the street before him. The street curved, and the dun on the wrong lead sailed around the corner and into the midst of a mob.

Men shouted, the dun reared, and Psin reversed his grip on the bow. All around him were blond heads. He stabbed at them with the sharpened tips of his bow. A man lunged up toward him, and he gashed open his face. The dun began to kick and rear. The Russian mob shoved by him, wailing. Many of them were women. Psin shouted at them in Russian to surrender and, when they did not, thrust at them with his bow, aiming for eyes. They didn't even try to attack him; all they wanted was to get by him.

He rode through them to the edge of the great square and saw why. The square was packed with people. At the far end, against the brown buildings, banners were spread out and waving: the yellow, the red, the black. An ocean of heads washed around him. He turned the dun broadside to block the street.

The mob stopped moving. Mongols were crushing through them, to encircle the square. There were hundreds of people here, and all the ways out were blocked. The Russians milled, dazed, their stained and haggard faces turned upward toward the riders. The noise swelled, hysterical. Psin could see that some of them had been trampled in the press.

Batu's voice rose, from across the square. "Surrender or we'll kill you all."

Psin took a deep breath and translated it at the top of his lungs.

The people gave one last outcry and fell silent. All around the sound of weeping began. Batu pushed his horse forward, the yellow banner behind him. He called to Kaidu to organize the horde of prisoners. His brothers were shouting to their men. Sabotai sat back in his saddle, one foot up on the pommel, watching expressionlessly. Above the weeping of the Russian women the harsh voices of the Mongols resounded like the cries of triumphant birds. Psin looked up into the smoky sky. It was just sundown.

Now, VLADIMIR."

Kolomna had fallen right after Moskva. Both cities lay in ashes behind them. Kaidu with four hundred men stayed to see to the captives. The rest of the army drove on in two columns to Vladimir. Batu took one branch and swung around to attack the Grand Duchy from the southeast, and Psin and Sabotai led the others in from the west.

"The Russian field army is on the Sit' River," Sabotai said. "Halfway to Novgorod. They aren't coming to meet us."

"I know where they are," Psin said. "I camped there while I scouted Novgorod. He'll be waiting for an army from the north."

Tshant and Buri had caught up with them the day after they left Moskva. Buri's face carried bruises on each cheek, and Tshant had a broken nose, but neither of them would talk about what had happened.

"Let me go support Quyuk," Buri said. "Maybe we can—"

"No." Sabotai glanced at Psin, who nodded. "No. First we have to take Vladimir."

"Cut him off from his supply base," Tshant growled. He rode on Sabotai's left; Buri rode on his right. "Are you stupid, whelp?"

Buri spat at him, and Sabotai jerked back. "If you must fight, don't do it across me."

The Kipchaks grumbled at the pace Sabotai was forcing. They thought they had done well enough at Moskva to earn a rest. Buri thought that Sabotai should ease the drive enough so that the baggage train could keep up. Psin and Tshant shouted him down, and they left the baggage train behind with half a tuman to guard it.

"We'll lose all our plunder," Buri said.

"We can always steal it back again."

Tshant and Buri fought without pause. They argued over the cooking fires, they taunted each other in the dark while sensible people were trying to sleep, and they rammed into each other during the day's riding. Three days after they'd left Moskva, Buri lost his temper completely and started to flog Tshant with his riding whip, and Tshant yanked out his bow and flogged back, and they galloped the length of the army beating one another while the soldiers hooted and jeered them.

"Let them fight," Sabotai said. "It sharpens their wits."

Psin sat twisted in his saddle, one hand on the horse's rump, and watched the two racing back and forth. The snow in their tracks was flecked with lather and blood. "Somehow I think your reasoning rather too fine."

Buri's horse, wheeling, slipped and somersaulted, sending Buri headfirst into a snowdrift.

"Think what the army will say about their commanders," Baidar said.

Buri clawed himself out of the snow, ran to his horse, and without missing a stride hurled himself into the saddle. He set out again after Tshant.

"They'll say that the Altun ride like leopards," Sabotai said mildly. "Superb co-ordination."

Tshant drove his horse square into Buri's. Both horses fell.

"Rough on the mounts," Baidar said.

Psin cupped his hands around his mouth and yelled, "Scouts coming."

Tshant froze, halfway into the saddle, and looked ahead of the army. Four men were galloping down. Buri mounted and cantered back to his place in line, casing his bow, and Tshant following didn't try to catch up.

"Can you keep discipline if they fight like that?" Baidar said.

"Some men are not to be disciplined," Sabotai said.

"The Ancestor—"

"Those were the Ancestor's words," Sabotai said. "Temujin said that to me thirty years ago."

Psin rode out a little to meet the scouts. He heard Baidar say, "He must have been speaking of slaves."

"Vladimir is just ahead," the first scout said, and Psin nodded. He turned to call Mongke.

Sabotai said, "He was speaking of a young man who sometimes disobeyed orders, but always for the better."

"Mongke," Psin shouted.

The army stopped talking and tensed, eager; they knew when the commanders sent for Mongke they were about to fight.

"Who was it?" Baidar said.

Mongke galloped up the line.

Sabotai said, "It was Psin."

Psin jerked around to face him. Sabotai lifted his head and smiled. Psin's gaze dropped to the snow at his horse's feet. In his memory he saw Temujin's fierce eyes.

Dead Psin, they might call you, soon enough.

Mongke said, "Vladimir is just over the horizon."

"Yes," Psin said.

Sabotai crowded his horse in between them. "Then let's go take it," he said.

Tshant jogged through the camp, looking for his father. Djela had wandered off and Tshant knew he would be with Psin. He glanced up once at Vladimir's great wall. Sabotai had offered the city terms: if they surrendered outright, no one would be killed, but if they resisted, the whole of the people would die. Vladimir was resisting.

"Ada."

Djela was waving to him from beside a fire near a snow wall. Tshant trotted over and dismounted. "Don't run off without telling me where you're going, will you?"

"You were asleep." Djela sat down. "Grandfather's gone to talk to Sabotai. When are we going to take the city?"

"Pretty soon."

"Can I—"

"No." Tshant picked up a leather jug, shook it, and heard the kumiss sloshing. "I've told you. You can't go into a city until you're old enough for a man's bow. Fighting in the open is different. You can always run."

He drank some of the kumiss and retched; it had honey in it.

"My cousin Buri was here, he was looking for you, and I told him—"

"Buri?"

"Yes. He's my cousin. I didn't know that. He says that Mongke is my cousin, too. Mongke taught me a new game."

"You've forgiven him for cutting me up, have you?"

"You hit him on the head and almost broke his skull, Grandfather says. Anyhow, Grandfather says you wouldn't get into so much trouble if you didn't hunt it out. Grandfather—"

"Damn your grandfather. What new game?"

"You play it with string." Djela pulled a clot of string out of his coat. He untangled it carefully.

"Everybody knows that one."

"This isn't the same one."

Djela wound the string between his fingers. "Now. You do this, and this—" He dropped loops and picked them up again, and the string made a star. "See?"

"That's very—"

"Tshant."

Tshant whirled. Buri climbed over the snow wall. He looked around and sat down quickly beside Djela.

"What do you want?"

"I think we should call a truce between us," Buri said.

Tshant relaxed. "Why?"

"Because it does nobody any good when we fight. You know I'm not afraid of you." Buri thrust his jaw out.

"I'm not afraid of you either."

They stared at each other. Djela began to hum a song. Tshant gathered himself to leap on Buri, and Buri hunched his shoulders, ready to meet him. Tshant's eyes began to itch. Abruptly they looked away simultaneously.

"All right," Tshant said. "Truce."

"Good." Buri leaned forward. "You know they're fighting, on the other side of the city."

"Yes." Vladimir stood on a crossroads, and the gigantic main gate opened up across the city from Psin's camp. The garrison had been trying to foray out ever since the Grand Duchess declined Sabotai's terms, but each time the Mongols had beaten them back.

"And you heard what your father did at Moskva."

"He burnt out part of the wall and rode through it."

"I say we ought to try that here. Not to ride through it. But if we burn out a part of their wall, they'll have to post more men at the breach to hold it, and they may weaken the guard on the main gate enough to let us in."

"Hunh." Tshant looked toward the city. They'd been here now for four days, waiting for something to happen—for Sabotai to think of something. "We could try it."

"If I mention it in the council, will you support me?"

"Yes." Tshant moved closer to him. "We'd better work out the details first, though. Where do you think we should start?"

"I thought of it," Psin said. "But they've soaked the wall with water. It won't burn, it's too wet."

Buri leaned forward. His hands opened and closed. "Tshant and I talked about that. We think we can dry out the wall if we light bonfires under it."

Psin glanced at Tshant, startled. Tshant was listening intently. Sabotai shifted a little and said, "And what are we to use for fuel, children? Bonfires won't burn on nothing."

Tshant said, "The baggage train came up yesterday. Use the carts. Fill them with old clothes, firewood, anything. Smash them up, stack them under the walls—"

"We need the carts," Sabotai said. He flushed dark red. "This plan of yours is profligate in the extreme."

"We'll find other carts in the city," Batu said. "I like the idea."

"You would," Sabotai said. "Kadan?"

"We have some prisoners," Kadan said. His gaze was unsteady. Psin thought he got confused about sieges: never drunk on campaign, always drunk in his leisure, he'd been half-drunk for two days. "We could use the prisoners to move up the carts."

Mongke said, "Their water supply is close to the wall. If we burn it out we can cut off their water, maybe."

Sabotai caught Psin's eye, and Psin nodded to him. Sabotai leaned back. "Ordu, what do you think?"

Ordu glanced at the rest of Batu's brothers, and they all nodded in unison. Berke said, "We can't maintain a siege much longer, Sabotai. We've very nearly grazed off the forage."

"We needn't use prisoners," Psin said. "The garrison would kill them as soon as they would us. The catapults could throw bundles of dry wood against the wall, and we could shoot fire arrows into the bundles."

"I think it's a good idea," Batu said.

Mongke elbowed him roughly in the ribs. "We've agreed on the idea. We're looking for a way to handle it."

"Don't shove me, you—"

Kadan reached out and tore Mongke away from Batu. "Sit down and quipe—and keep quiet."

Mongke snarled at him. Psin caught his eye and scowled, and Mongke leered back sullenly.

"Stop making faces," Sabotai said. "I agree with Psin. The catapults are no use to us now."

Psin looked up at the sky. Just that morning Sabotai had talked of the catapults as if they were the totem of his clan. The black sky was full of stars, and the wind cried over it; the moon was just rising.

He refused to believe that Tshant and Buri were sudden friends. But Djela had said something of it, in his casual way, when Psin came back to his camp in the early afternoon. Maybe Sabotai was right. He sneaked a look at the two of them, sitting side by side; Buri was expounding the advantages of burning down various specific parts of the wall. Tshant, watching Sabotai's face, murmured something, and Buri slipped in a smooth appeal to Sabotai's vanity. Sabotai snorted, unflattered.

Mongke said, "The well they get most of their water from is here." He jabbed a thumb at the sketch of the wall in the dirt before them. "It's very close to this angle. If we can collapse the wall in upon it—"

"How can we do that?" Kadan said, and slapped at him. Mongke slid easily out of Kadan's reach.

"We can catapult stones into the wall while it burns."

"Oh." Sabotai looked at Psin. Amusement danced in his eyes, and Psin wrinkled his nose at him.

"At any rate," Batu said, "we can't linger. We have to take Vladimir and go catch the Grand Duke's army before their reinforcements get to them from Novgorod."

"We'll try this tomorrow," Sabotai said. "Mongke's suggestion of the wall near the well satisfies me. We can break up six or seven carts and tie them into bundles. We'll have to arrange for a continuous volley of arrows to rake the top of the wall so the garrison can't wet down the carts before they get burning well enough. Buri can see to that."

Buri nodded and started to get up.

"Sit down. I'm not through. To hold the defenders off the wall, we'll need to shift many of the men now grouped before the main gate over to Buri's command. Tshant will be in charge of holding the main gate while we try this trick. Batu and I will supervise the use of the catapults, and Psin and Kadan will organize some effective diversion elsewhere along the wall."

Kadan lurched upright. "What kind of diversion?"

"You and Psin may decide that."

Psin said, "We'll take the battering ram over to the north gate."

"I need it," Tshant said.

"Do without it."

"You cut your own. The ram is there, and it stays there."

Psin stared at him. "*You* cut your own. You wouldn't have remembered about the ram if I hadn't mentioned it first."

"Of course I would have."

Sabotai said, "Psin, take the ram. Tshant's men can cut down one of the trees at the foot of the hill. Are there any questions?"

Tshant's teeth clicked shut. Psin looked off, past Mongke's right ear. Mongke seemed interested in something; he was thinking hard, and slowly he turned his head to look straight at Psin.

"No questions," Sabotai said. "It's late. Let's get some sleep. We'll start before dawn tomorrow."

"Keep moving, you oxen!" With his bow Psin beat at the men jamming the street. He could see nothing. The shouts and yells of the men drowned out his voice. He took a deep breath to shout again and tasted the smoke in the air. The roof of a house just across the way from him was smoldering—falling embers must have started it. "Great God—move!"

The mob shuffled forward, the horses fought, the men howled and shot useless arrows at nothing. Psin looked over his shoulder. The main gate lay hardly six lengths behind him, and through the shattered uprights hundreds of horsemen poured, to collide with the men already crushed together in the street.

"Father."

Tshant was on the roof above his head, clinging with one hand to the coping. "They've thrown up barricades ahead—get them shoving. That's the only way we'll—"

"I've been," Psin roared. "What's happening?"

"Fires all through the quarter where we burnt the wall." Tshant looked out over the city. "They're looting in this section and we've not even taken the citadel yet."

Psin kicked his horse, and the dun surged forward, nipping, driving the horses in front of him. Abruptly the dun shied back. In the narrow opening he left in the pack Psin could see two dead men in the street, trampled to gore. He whipped the dun across them.

"Look out," Tshant cried. He swung himself up onto the roof and ran easily along the edge toward the alley. A flight of arrows thumped into the roof where he had been. He leapt down into the alley.

"Russians," Psin shouted. "Blue flank—"

Some twenty Russians dashed up over the roofs across the street, knelt, and raised their bows. Psin nocked an arrow and shot, and one man plummeted down into the heaving pack of Mongols. Psin laid another arrow to the string. They were caught like— He shot. The Russians had shields, and the man he'd aimed at jerked his up, but the arrow pierced through it and the man screamed and fell.

Ahead wood crashed and splintered, and the Mongols cheered. Other men in this pack were shooting at the Russians on the roofs, but the Russian arrows rained down. The man in front of Psin swayed in his saddle. A tuft of arrow feathers jutted from his side. Psin shot again, missed, and felt the crush loosening around him. The man before him slid out of his saddle and the dun jumped his body. Psin heard the man's thin wail. An arrow thunked into Psin's thigh, just below the skirt of his body armor. He swung his bow up again and shot a Russian jumping from one roof to another—the roof he left was flaming. The dun began to trot.

The whole great mob was trotting. The men around him began to yell. The arrow hurt; its head was lodged in his saddle and when the dun trotted the shaft wobbled up and down in the wound.

"Keep moving, you—"

They broke into a canter. The shattered remains of a barricade flashed by. Ahead, Russian voices called out, and a fountain of blood leapt into the air and sprayed across the onrushing Mongols, but the horses never hesitated. The dun's hoofs struck something soft and pounded again on the hard earth.

Looters swarmed through the houses they passed. Some of the men in Psin's column swerved off to break into the houses. More Russians raced over the roofs and shot arrows or threw furniture and stones down into the street. The dun horse shuddered and swept on. Another horse ran into it, and Psin's wounded leg smashed into the horse's side. The two horses galloped together, shoulder to shoulder, bouncing off each other with every stride. Psin reeled from the agony in his thigh. Abruptly the horse beside him slipped and fell. The arrow had broken off inside the wound.

They charged into the marketplace. The citadel threw its shadow over them, and arrows and stones hurtled down all around them. Mongke, his face streaming blood, galloped past at the head of ten men and raced down a sidestreet. A woman screamed, very close; a wounded and riderless horse staggered out of the alley beside the citadel. Psin dodged the dun horse into the lee of the citadel's door and stopped.

"Yip-yip-yip-yip—"

That came from a sidestreet. Psin pulled his thigh off the stump of the arrow, slung his leg up in front of the saddle on the horse's shoulder, and worked the arrowhead out of the leather. The square was packed full of Mongols, all milling, shooting down Russians on the rooftops and running down Russians on the ground. Another shower of arrows flew down from the citadel tower.

Buri with Mongke's honor guard driving behind him bolted into the square and forced a path through the mob. He looked around and cupped his hands around his mouth and yipped a dozen times. Psin drove the dun out of the citadel doorway and raced after him. Buri and his men veered down a sidestreet.

Barricades in this street, too: wagons, furniture, men behind them with bows and swords. Psin reined the dun over to the nearest building, spun the horse rump to the door, and sawed on the bit. The dun kicked out. His hoofs rang on the wood. He kicked again, throwing Psin up on his neck, and the wood splintered. Buri and his men were crouching in doorways across the street, shooting at the

Russians behind the barricade. Somebody whined in the building behind Psin. He wrenched the dun's mouth again, and the horse put both hindlegs through the door.

The dun neighed and fought clear, and Psin, jumping down, landed hard on his bad leg and fell. He lay still long enough to stick his finger against the wound. The blood was spilling out of it, and it felt big enough to see through. He staggered up, nocked an arrow, and held the bow in his left hand. With his right he knocked the shattered wood out of the doorframe. No arrow flew through the gaping hole to meet him, and he dove in. Again he fell, and heard his arrow snap under him. He got to his knees.

Two women were kneeling in front of a wooden frame against the far wall. They gasped but did not turn; their faces were bloodless and their eyes shut, their lips moving feverishly. Small oil lamps burned on the walls. Psin limped to one and pulled it down. He tore scraps off his tunic, dipped them in oil, and wrapped them around his arrowheads. The women began to pray out loud.

"Kill," somebody called, in Russian. "Kill the pagans."

Psin unbolted the door and threw it open. The dun horse was in an alley across the street, snorting. Its hindlegs were cut and blood flecked its shoulders and neck. Psin knelt in the doorway, set the lamp beside him, lit one arrow, and shot it into the barricade.

The other Mongols cheered. The Russians couldn't see yet what was going on, but from the roof over Psin's head a booming voice called, "They're firing the barricade, Andrei—"

"Buri," Psin shouted. Buri, in a doorway down the street, swung around and saw; he lifted his bow to shoot at the booming voice. Arrows plinked off the paving stones and the iron-bound doors opposite Psin. He shot three more burning arrows into the barricade, low, so that the men behind it couldn't reach them without exposing themselves to the Mongol bows.

Horses were coming, fast, down the street behind the barricade. Psin started up, heard iron shoes rattling on the street, and shrank back again. Russian knights. Flames were creeping over the barricade. The Russians behind it yelled to the knights. Buri was shouting orders; Psin couldn't hear the words. He nocked another arrow.

"If you shoot that, I will kill you," the woman behind him said.

He whirled, striking at her; his fist caught her in the throat and flung her against the wall. The knife dropped from her fingers. He drew his arrow back and shot her through the heart. Spinning, he grabbed another arrow and looked for a target.

The barricade was all fire, and the Russians were trapped behind it. The other woman wailed. More horses streamed down the street beyond the rising flames, and these were Mongols; Psin could hear their yipping and the rising hopelessness in the Russian voices. Buri and his men spilled out of their hiding places and caught their horses.

Psin turned back into the room. His leg throbbed and he felt his heart hammering in rhythm with it. The older woman, wailing, was bent over the one Psin had shot.

"She's dead. You've killed her."

The woman broke into wild weeping and put her hands to her face. Psin went over toward her to retrieve his arrow. "Never speak before you strike," he said. "It's bad luck."

The woman clawed at the dagger on the floor. He lunged to grab her, but his leg held him back, and she surged away, her fingers tight around the hilt. "On your head, pagan," she said, and stabbed herself.

She made a mess of it. The blade turned on a rib, and the blood leapt from her breast in dark spurts. He caught her before she fell, took the dagger, and said, "Not that way."

"I'm dying," she said, surprised.

"So you are."

He stretched her out on the floor, rammed the dagger into his belt, and shambled around the room looking for plunder.

"Pagan," she said, and sighed.

"Die, will you?" He took down the silver cross from the wall over the wooden frame. When he looked back she was dead.

Three Mongols burst in through the shattered door, and he whirled, almost collapsing on his bad leg. "Mine," he said. "Find your own house."

They backed out. He opened a cabinet and had to cling to it to keep his balance. A great haze swam before his eyes. He could see cups and gold plates, somewhere in front of him. His mouth filled up with water and he swallowed. His legs were going. He fell—

He swung over a void, rocking gently back and forth. He

couldn't open his eyes. They were open, but he couldn't see. He licked his lips so that he could speak.

"Lie still. You're bleeding all over me."

That was Tshant. He was very happy to lie still. He could feel arms under his shoulders and knees. Something hit him across the back, and he tried to gather his strength to fight it off. His head rested on something soft.

"Nothing broken. See how white he is."

"Go away," he said. "I'm sleepy."

Rocking him back and forth, the way Artai had rocked him once when he had been sick. He remembered being furious at her for it. "I'm no child." Now he was sick, and Artai was off by the Lake somewhere. . . . Nausea climbed up his throat. He lurched over on his side.

"Keep him quiet. He'll open it up again."

"He has. Look at the blood."

One of them was Tshant, but the other he didn't have a name for, although he recognized the voice.

Rocking again. He lay still. He couldn't remember if he had shut his eyes, but it didn't matter because he couldn't see anything anyway.

"Ada, he's so hot."

Djela. He struggled, trying to pull himself awake. Something was frightening Djela.

"Get away from him. When you go near him he moves."

It wasn't hot. It was cold, bitter cold, and a strong wind blew. I am in the forest. His father was gone. The Yek Mongols had taken his father and he'd had to run into the forest. Three of his six young brothers were with him. It was dark and they had no horses, only the dogs. The Yek Mongols were hunting them, and when they found them . . . Cold. Without coats they wouldn't live until the morning. Don't leave tracks. My brothers are so small. "I'm cold, Psin." We are hiding under a windfall and we all crowd together. Toki is cold. Toki is dead.

Cool woman's hands touched his cheek. They felt like Chan's hands, except that Chan never came near him unless she had to. Chan loathed him. He turned his face into the cushions and wept.

"What's wrong with him now?"

"He's fevered," Dmitri said. "Wash his face."

"He's crying."

He was, but he couldn't remember why. Because Toki was dead. He hung on, but the ropes around him dragged him off; his fingers scraped along the edge, and he fell and swung loose over the gap. Strange dreams plodded through his mind, but he knew they were dreams. He watched them pass. Somebody picked up his head and cradled it and put a bowl to his lips, and he opened his eyes and saw thin gruel.

"Damn you." He batted the bowl away. "Get me some meat."

The woman stood back, gruel splashed across her front. He'd never seen her before. She was Russian, round-eyed and white-skinned and tall. He hitched himself up on his elbows and his head wobbled uncontrollably on his neck. He didn't recognize the room, either.

"Where am I?" he said in Russian.

"In Susdal." She put the bowl down and washed her hands in a basin on the low table under the window.

"In Susdal." He lay back. "How long was I sick?"

"Fifteen days."

"And in that time we took Susdal."

She nodded. Turning from the basin, she called, in Mongol, "Djela, your grandfather is waked up."

"Grandfather." Djela ran across the room. He leapt up onto the couch and embraced Psin. His head burrowed into Psin's shoulder. "I was worried—you yelled so much."

"Ouch. Be careful, noyon. I'm in no shape to be mauled again."

The woman was moving around the room, straightening it up. When she passed through the light from the window he saw red glints in her hair. Djela said, "Ana took care of you. Isn't she nice?"

"Very. Where is your father?"

"Somewhere. He took Susdal all by himself. Everybody else is gone." Djela sat on the edge of the couch and beamed. "I'm glad you're well again."

"Where is Sabotai?"

"Coming back," Djela said. "They beat the grand noyon of the Russians. We heard yesterday."

The woman's eyes, patient and unhappy, avoided Psin. She stood still a moment, listening to the boy, and went on.

"Bring me some meat," Psin said to her.

"The fighting was terrible," Djela said. "When we took Susdal."

"Worse than Vladimir?"

"Much worse." He bounced a little. "We had to fight for two days here. But in Vladimir everything was burning. Ada saw your horse running loose and he galloped up and down asking everybody if he'd seen you, and finally somebody told him. And the house you were in was burning and you were lying there in a great pool of blood."

"Did they kill everybody?"

Djela nodded. "I could see the smoke all the next day." He curled up on the couch, his head on Psin's arm. "I was scared."

Psin hugged him. "I would have been if I'd had the sense."

Ana came back into the room with a bowl of meat. She said in Russian, "You couldn't keep anything down but gruel and kumiss. When you were sick."

He tried to sit up and could not. "I'm still sick. Feed me."

She sat beside him and spooned stewed meat into his mouth. The chewing hurt his jaw muscles. He swallowed one great chunk of meat and said, "I must have caught a fever in the wound."

"The wound was clean." She poured broth into his mouth. "It deserved to be. You bled more than any man I've ever seen who lived after."

"Russian arrows are poisonous."

The door opened and Tshant walked in. He stopped at the foot of the couch, his eyes blank, staring at Psin. "And I was so used to an undivided command."

"You can keep it a few more days. How did the battle go?"

Tshant shrugged one shoulder. "Sabotai caught the Russians on the Sit' River and surrounded them. They never even managed a counter-attack." He looked over at Ana and spoke slowly, carefully, so that she would follow the Mongol. "He'll get sick again if you feed him that."

Psin could see her trying to sort out words to answer; she gave up after a moment and said only, "No."

"It's you who has to clean up the floor, not I." He turned and stamped out.

She watched him go, brushed a wisp of her hair out of her eyes, and went off with the bowl. Psin lay still. He felt worn to nothing. Djela told him what Dekko had thought of Psin's being sick, and Psin closed his eyes and listened, drifting into sleep.

The next day he wasn't much stronger. He swore and clenched his muscles but he could barely lift his head. Ana fed him all day long, and Djela told him stories and played the string game with him. He grew tired too often, and after the least tiring things—eating made him tired.

Tshant came in during the afternoon and said, "Sabotai's scouts came in today. The army mustn't be far behind."

"What did they say?"

"We lost four hundred men." Tshant grinned. "And no Russian goes armed on the upper Volga."

Ana glanced at him quickly. She turned back to Psin. "What did he say?"

Psin translated it into Russian. Tshant sat down. "Bring me something to drink, girl." He gestured broadly, and she nodded that she understood; she left. He said, "Father, Sabotai has sent Quyuk back here."

"Oh? Is he here yet?"

"He came in with the scouts."

"Send him up to see me."

"Tomorrow. You look sleepy."

Ana handed him a cup. She had left a jug and a bowl beside Psin's bed, and Psin rolled over onto his stomach so that he could reach them and pour kumiss. When he was done his arms shook. He heaved himself over again, panting. The girl came over and packed cushions behind his head so that he could drink.

Djela said, "Ada, I made up a story."

"Good news." Tshant pulled the boy into his lap. "Ana, go away."

When the door had closed, he said, "I don't like to have her hear everything. She speaks better Mongol than she pretends to. Do you think we should take Novgorod this year?"

"What does Sabotai say?"

"I don't know. Quyuk thinks we need it to hold the northern

frontier. But if we don't start out soon—"

"I know. When the snow melts, the forest all around it will be swamp."

"So Quyuk says."

"I'm tired. I don't know. Maybe we should take it." He shut his eyes. "I can't think properly."

"It would be odd if you could," Tshant said. The fine shade of meaning in his voice made Psin open one eye. "I'll ask Quyuk to come up here tomorrow morning."

Psin nodded.

"Do you like the girl? Is she tending you well?"

"Yes."

Tshant rose; Psin heard the chair creak. Djela began to tell his story. The voices faded, and a door opened and shut. Psin slept.

When he woke it was full dark, and no lamp burned. The room was chilly. He lay still, more alert than he'd been that morning, and listened to the sounds of the house settling—the tiny groans and whispers of all that weight sinking down against the ground. The first time he had slept inside a wooden building, that had kept him awake and tense all night, but later he learned that all houses creaked.

Ana was there. He could smell the soft scents of her body, and he heard her breathing. He said her name, and she jumped, startled.

"Light a lamp," he said.

Clothes rustled, and she crossed the room. She had not been in the chair, but next to the window. The light glowed weakly in the lamp and she ran it up onto the wall.

"What's the matter?"

The lamplight washed her in pale colors. She wore a robe, she was barefoot, and her hair swung around her shoulders. "Why aren't you asleep?" she said.

"I'm not tired. I'm sick of sleeping. I'm sick of eating, too, and being told stories and having my son treat me like a . . . Who are you?"

She laughed nervously. "Ana Vasilievna."

"No. I mean . . . who owns you?"

"Your son." She sat down in the chair, half out of the light. Her eyes were impenetrable.

"Where did you come from? Susdal?"

"Yes. I lived in this house."

He laughed. "So. Ironic enough."

"I suppose so."

Her voice was soft, but there was an edge to it. He remembered the woman in Vladimir who had tried to stab him. He wondered if he could fight off a strong, healthy woman, when he was so weak.

"Were you alone here?" he said.

"No. I had . . . My family . . ."

She turned her face away a little. Her voice thickened. "What traitor taught you Russian?"

"Don't cry, woman. God's name." He dragged himself up almost sitting. She was trembling, and she put one hand to her averted face. "Don't cry," he said. "It won't do any good."

She wheeled on him. Her eyes were still only shadows. "No good. No. My father is dead, my grandmother is dead, and the little children are all gone, nobody knows where or will tell me, and I have to take care of a sick Mongol and sleep with a healthy one—"

Her lips clamped shut. He relaxed. In this mood she wouldn't attack him. He smiled, thinking he'd been wary of a woman. Her voice came again, low and heavy.

"You killed them all. All you could find. Everything burned, and the children were trampled, and the houses looted, and now there are horses stabled in the monastery and everyone must be indoors by sunset or they are killed too. The blood ran down the street. I saw it—it made waterfalls, little waterfalls."

"Not everyone died. You're alive."

"Because I'm a coward and when he came in the door I fainted. He broke down the door—he packed it, he seemed so huge." She laughed, and Psin's muscles jerked at the sound. "Now I find out he's shorter than I am."

"My son, this was."

She nodded. The lamplight shone on her tears.

"Tshant is tall for a Mongol."

"To me you're all small. Stunted, warped, like trees that grow in the wrong places. Ugly. Flat faces and little tilted eyes. When he brought me in here and I saw you I thought I should die—it was like being told to nurse a monster."

"Hunh." He thought of Chan, grinned, and reached for the jug.

"You sound as if that's funny."

"Very. One of my wives calls me a monster, now and then."

"Are you ugly even to Mongol women?"

"She is Chinese. To us, you know, you are not beautiful. You are too white, and your eyes too big, and your noses too long. Stop trying to make me angry. It's against our law to harm someone else's slave, and if I told Tshant what you'd said he would only laugh."

"Do brutes have laws?"

"I don't know. But we do."

"I hate you."

"Now you're losing your sense. Simple insult won't win you anything. You sound too desperate. Think a little."

"Don't laugh at me."

"You're very amusing." He sipped kumiss and put the bowl down again. He set it on the edge of the table, and it fell, splashing across the floor.

"Now you've made a mess," she said. "I think I shall scream."

She got a rag from a cabinet and knelt, mopping up the spilt kumiss. He lay on his side and watched her.

"Why aren't you with Tshant?"

"He's on watch. He always takes the first watch. He'll send Dmitri for me soon." Her hands with the rag stopped moving, and she braced herself up on her arms. "It's so horrible."

"Don't be silly." He took a tress of her hair between his fingers and pulled it gently. "You'll grow used to us—we aren't entirely vicious."

She began to mop again. The strands of her hair swung before her face. "No, you aren't. That's why it's horrible."

"If you enjoy feeling like that—"

The door opened soundlessly, and Tshant stepped just inside, a black shape against the light from the next room. He said, "Come along, girl." She rose, threw the wet rag into the bucket beside the cabinet, and walked out the door. He stood aside to let her pass. Reaching in, he gave Psin what Psin took to be a warning stare; the weak light from the lamp ruined it. Psin lay back, smiling, and tried to go to sleep.

* * *

Tshant said, "Did he wake up by himself?"

"Yes."

Her skirt rustled. She would not wear Mongol trousers. The skirt annoyed him. She walked very fast, so that he had to stretch his legs to keep up. Her hair swung, glowing in the light of each torch they passed, dark red.

"Does he talk Mongol to you?"

"Russian."

The sentry before his door straightened, saluted, and held the door open. Ana went through it. Tshant stopped to tell the sentry to wake him if a courier from the army should come. He could hear the girl undressing, just inside the door, and the sentry's ears reddened.

"Arcut will come in the morning with his report," Tshant said. "If Mudak and Ruyun come back, let me know as soon as they report."

"Yes, noyon."

He went into his room. All the lamps were lit. Djela was sprawled on the couch in the alcove, fast asleep, his mouth half-open. The girl in her shift picked up the trimmer and started dousing the lamps. Tshant went into the alcove and knelt beside Djela's bed. The boy did not wake up, and after a moment Tshant touched his hair and went out into the main room again.

She was lying on the couch, her face turned toward the ceiling. He sat down on his side of the couch to take off his boots. Her skin, so pale, was soft and sweet, and he liked the way she carried herself. At first he had thought she was stupid, with her silences and her brooding, but now he knew that she hated them all. He remembered the amusement in his father's voice, just before he'd opened the door.

"What did my father say?"

She understood him without his having to speak so slowly, and she knew more words now. But she still didn't talk unless she was spoken to.

"Nothing much," she said. "He told me I was silly."

"Why?"

"I said all Mongols are . . ."

She searched for a word, frowning, and he said, "Ugly or wicked?"

She actually looked at him. "What do they mean?"

He stood up and pulled off his tunic. "Ugly." He made a face.

"Yes," she said, and looked away again.

"Psin's ugly. So am I."

"Very."

"What do you think of him?"

She turned her head toward him. "I'm sorry, I didn't—"

He repeated it, slowly.

"Oh. He's . . . I like him. A little."

"More than you like me."

"Much more."

He lay down on his back and put his arms over his head. The silence stretched out. Abruptly, she said, "Will I have to have him, too, when he gets well?"

He rolled over on his side, startled, to look at her. She tried to meet his eyes and couldn't. She'd said that to shock him. He said, "You mean, sleep with him."

"Yes," she whispered.

He was tempted to say yes and see what she would do. He pulled the shift up around her waist, and she shivered and started to cover herself but did not.

"No," he said. "He doesn't believe in concubines." He made her sit up and pulled the shift off over her head. She grabbed for it.

"I don't like to sleep without—"

"That's too bad," he said.

THE KHAN IS AWAKE AND UP," DMITRI SAID. "YOU SHOULD GO IN there."

"Why?"

"Because he will injure himself." Dmitri was polishing brasses; he gave her only a glance. "He doesn't realize how weak he is."

"He spent all the afternoon playing with the little one. He's strong."

Dmitri dampened his cloth again. "You've never seen him strong. He's weak as a new child, now. At least send for Tshant Noyon."

"Holy Mother. You act as if they were your own people."

She sat down. Dmitri was only a free townsman, and she was of noble blood. She kept saying that to herself.

Dmitri swung his head toward her and frowned. "The Khan is well worth serving. If you're clever you'll—"

The door opened, and Psin came in. Ana leapt up. He had Djela on one shoulder. On his feet he seemed twice as big as when he'd been in the bed.

"You shouldn't be up," she said. "You're not well enough."

"I am. If I lie there one more day I'll go mad and chase everyone around the city, yelling at the top of my lungs and tearing my hair. Where is Tshant?"

"He's in his room, Khan," Dmitri said. "Quyuk—"

"Damn Quyuk." Psin swung Djela down to set him on the floor. "Dmitri, where is my horse stabled?"

Dmitri didn't even bother to look up. "He's turned out with the herds, Khan. And all the noyon's horses are lame or out."

Psin snorted. "If I'm strong enough to walk, I'm—"

Dmitri corrected a point of Russian grammar. Ana tried to keep from smiling. Psin got red in the face and Dmitri made him repeat the sentence ten times.

"All right," Psin said. "I won't ride. Someday, Dmitri, I'll teach you Chinese." He stamped out.

"I told you you should go watch him," Dmitri said.

* * *

Quyuk said, "Batu is an old woman."

"So you've said. Twice now." Psin leaned back. His heart was thumping against the base of his throat. Whenever he did anything at all his heart began to beat harder. "Sabotai is the man with the orders."

"But it's Batu who persuaded him. Batu says we can't hold our flank now if we strike at Novgorod." Quyuk clenched his fist and looked down at it. "If we take Novgorod and the cities on the Dnepr, we can hold Russia forever. If we leave Novgorod unburnt—"

"We have years for that."

Quyuk looked up quickly. His face was leaner and his bright eyes were shadowed, as if he were hiding something. He glanced over at the window. "Can anyone hear us?"

"No. What has Tshant done here?"

"He's taken the estates between the two rivers—everything but Tver and Yaroslav, which he's not manned well enough to attack. He's done a good job. We can keep Tver and Yaroslav penned up while we—"

"We can keep Novgorod penned up more easily. Besides, we're moving west next year, not north."

"What's west?"

"Europe. A spit into the sea, like Korea. Two years' fighting."

"And then what?"

"We will hold the world from sea to sea."

"All but Novgorod."

"Ah, don't be a fool."

"Talk to Sabotai. Please."

Psin thought, It's Batu, then, not Novgorod he's after. "I will. But it will do no good."

"He listens to you."

"He listens when he wants to. He's too clever to let me jabber at him when his mind's made up. From what you say, his mind's made up."

Ana came in, with meat and red wine on a tray. She set the bowl on the table in front of Psin, and Psin looking down said, "Serve the son of the Kha-Khan before you serve me, girl." He pushed the bowl over to Quyuk.

"What did you say?" Quyuk said. He took a spoon from Ana and began to eat.

Psin translated. Ana went out again, after another bowl.

"Someday," Quyuk said, "I will be the Kha-Khan."

"Not if I can help it."

Quyuk's eyes flashed. "Do you dare say that?"

"Did I not?" He smiled. "I said things to your Ancestor, Quyuk, that should have gotten me killed. Temujin let me live. A mistake, maybe. The habit's strong from overuse."

"If Temujin didn't kill you, I'd be less than he if I did."

"You could say so."

"Hunh."

Ana returned and served Psin, and he ate. Quyuk drank half the wine in the jug. At last, he said, "My father said when he exiled me here that I would learn to serve or die."

"Well," Psin said. "You've not learned to serve, and you're still alive. The Kha-Khan underestimates you."

Quyuk was pleased; his eyes narrowed to slits. "My wife and my mother will take care of the rest. All I need is to be alive and in Karakorum when my father dies."

"Siremon is alive, and your father's choice."

"Siremon is a child."

"Kaidu's age. He grows older, too—that seems to be the natural way of living. Your father might outlive your hopes." Ogodai was strong. The drink had riddled him through with small weaknesses, but he was strong. "And besides, child, you have us all to contend with. Every man who casts a vote."

"I can handle the Altun."

"Can you, now."

Quyuk's neck swelled. "I will deal with you all, when I am the Kha-Khan."

"Kill me," Psin said softly. "And kill Tshant and your brother and Mongke, and do what you can to kill Batu and his brothers. Kill the khans of all the clans from the Caspian to the China Sea. In the end you'll have nothing to be Kha-Khan of but black sand."

"Not all of you. Just . . . a few."

"You'd better learn to compromise with us now, Quyuk. If you kill one of us you'll have to kill us all. Do you think we would let you be Kha-Khan if we thought you'd break the Yasa?"

"I am—"

"No worth, until you start to make bargains."

The door opened, and Tshant came partway into the room. He stopped; Psin glanced at him. Quyuk had heard him enter. He said, "Psin, I'll bargain with you."

"With that look in your eyes, no. The Ancestor was a subtle man, Quyuk. He fenced the Khanate so that no one like you will ever come to it. Tshant, what do you want?"

Quyuk got up and charged out of the room. Tshant sank down into the chair he had left. "What were you talking about?"

Psin leaned back, surprised that he was almost dizzy. "His chances to be Kha-Khan."

Tshant was coiled up, set to spring, and his eyes burned. "Do you think he will?"

"Maybe."

"He's too dangerous." Tshant tried to loosen his muscles and could not. Psin saw the effort. "How can we protect ourselves?"

"We'll consider that when we come to it. I haven't been marrying off your sisters to half the tribes in the north to keep myself amused through the cold winter nights. He says you have Tver and Yaroslav invested but not taken."

"Tver is too far away, and Yaroslav is too strong. I have two tumans—understrength. I've been to Yaroslav. . . . But I have some captives, and if I could only make them talk, maybe we'd learn something worth knowing."

"Where are they?"

"Down in the basement. Do you want to see them?"

"Later. What does Yaroslav look like?"

Tshant shrugged. "It's on the Volga, where another river flows into it, and they've cut a ditch between the two, so that it's actually on an island. A wide ditch. The walls are of logs, like all the rest, but these have little houses built into the wall at each corner. There aren't many people there, but they're determined."

"All right. Now let me see the prisoners."

They went down the corridor to the stair. Psin's legs wobbled at the knees. He breathed deeply, and that made his heart beat in a broken rhythm. Going down the stair, he held onto the railing so tightly that he caught a splinter in the ball of his thumb.

"Most of them were in a party from Yaroslav that tried to get into Tver," Tshant said. He cocked his finger at a sentry, who followed them. They were in a damp stone hall stinking of cobwebs and rats. "We always let them out of the cities and try to ambush them when they're in the open."

Psin pulled the splinter out. "Good."

"The horses of the last party out of Yaroslav were gaunter than the ones before. But not ribby. They're not starving yet."

Two sentries saluted and Tshant nodded. "Open the door for us."

One of them said, "It's good to see the Khan well again."

"The air down here might make the Khan very ill very shortly."

They laughed. Tshant said, "The guard here changes eight times a day."

They walked into a lightless room. The air in the hall had been sweet compared to the stench in here. Psin wrinkled his nose. Something ran splashing across the floor. A light flowered, and Tshant waved the torch back and forth to spread the flame all around the head. In the light Psin could see almost all the room. Puddles of water covered the floor. Half a dozen Russians sat on a bench at the far end, their feet hobbled. Two had shaggy beards down to their belts, but the others were reasonably trim.

"He's from Yaroslav," Tshant said, and pointed to a blond man just out of youth.

The man stood up, throwing his head back defiantly. Psin said, "Come here."

"No."

One of the others murmured, "Mother of God, he speaks Russian."

Psin gestured to the sentry. "Drag him over here."

The sentry unbuckled his swordbelt and handed it out the door. The blond man set himself. Tshant said, "You see how they are. They won't talk."

"Have you tried to persuade them?"

"They die first. They won't talk. Whip, fire, iron—nothing opens their mouths."

The sentry grabbed the blond man by the shoulder and hurled

him down to the floor in front of Psin. The man groaned in rage.
Psin put a boot on his back to hold him down.

"I want a dry room, with a window," Psin said. "Sentries under
the window but out of sight."

"You were just sick," Tshant said. "Do you think you could stop
this one from killing you before the sentries came?"

Psin's teeth clenched. He caught Tshant by the wrist and
twisted. Tshant whirled around, his free hand jerking toward his
dagger. Psin let him go.

"See how weak I am?"

Tshant looked down at the Russian. "You'll squash him."

Psin backed away from him. "Go do as I say."

Tshant went by him. Psin looked at the other Russians. None of
them had tried to help the one at his feet. He kicked the man before
him lightly in the ribs, and they stiffened but said nothing and did
not move their hobbled feet.

"Such courage," Psin said, in Russian. He left the room.

Tshant was at the foot of the stair, talking to four Kipchaks.
They saluted and trotted up the stairs. Psin said, "Where are the
other prisoners from?"

"Places I've already taken." Tshant's mouth twitched. "You are
weaker. Before you were wounded I'd have dislocated my shoulder, turning like that against your hand."

Psin cuffed him hard. "Don't try my coat on quite yet."

Tshant looked as if he meant to cuff Psin back, but he only lifted
his wrist. The marks of Psin's fingers were fading like old bruises.
"I'm pleased to wear your badge, Khan." He bounded up the stair,
two steps at a time.

Psin swore at him. The stink of the basement made him gag. He
felt light-headed, and he waited a little before he tried the climb up
to the ground floor.

They brought the Russian in, still hobbled, and thrust him into
the chair across from Psin. The window behind Psin opened on the
little courtyard, brilliant with sunlight. While the sentries left, the
Russian blinked and winced away from the light, but he kept his
eyes turned toward the courtyard.

"You are from Yaroslav," Psin said.

The Russian said nothing. His face was set like iron.

"Everything will go much easier for you if you answer me."

The Russian's face contrived disdain.

Psin leaned back. He had put a cushion against the back of the chair. His dagger lay on the table next to the bowl of fruit the Russian was trying not to see. Psin took the dagger and pared his thumbnail.

"Mongols know little about tortures. I hear the captives we've tried to force to talk have died first. That's the trouble with tortures; they tend to kill people. The Chinese are more subtle at it. They have ways of loosening a man's resolve that don't kill. But they do tend to send a man mad. The Yasa says we may not kill madmen."

The Russian looked contemptuous. Psin picked up an apple and rolled it across the table to him. "Eat."

The Russian had caught the fruit before it fell off the table. He looked up, startled. His hands caressed the apple, stroking the tough, tight skin.

"Go ahead, eat it."

The Russian put the apple swiftly to his mouth and bit, watching Psin; he obviously thought Psin would try to swat it out of his mouth. He chewed. Before he had swallowed the first bite he was gnawing at the apple again. The fruit vanished faster than Psin had thought possible—the Russian even ate the core.

"I said that if you don't start talking, things will get harder."

The Russian shook his head. Psin took another apple from the dish and ate it, slowly, crunching it between his teeth. The Russian licked his lips.

"Horses like apples. Would you eat another?"

The Russian said nothing, but his eyes went back to the dish. Psin rolled an apple across the table, and this time the Russian caught it before it reached the edge. He tried to eat slowly but he couldn't keep from gobbling. This time he put the core on the table.

"As I said, horses like apples. I saw a horse eat meat once, in the middle of a bad winter."

The Russian wrinkled his nose.

"You don't believe me. Well. If you like apples, and horses like apples, maybe if a horse likes meat, you'd like meat. Unh?"

Suspicion flooded over the Russian's face.

"Maybe you'll talk better on a full stomach. Kuchuk."

The door opened at once, and Kuchuk looked in.

"Bring me two bowls of meat. Ask Oktana, she has some set aside for me."

"The Khan wishes."

Psin watched the door shut and pared his nails again. He did not look at the Russian. He didn't care whether the man tried to attack him or not, except that it would look odd to be feeding him afterward. He kept the dagger working. The Russian shifted a little in his chair, and Psin called, "Mulai."

The door popped open, and Mulai said, "Yes?"

"Nothing. I just wanted to make sure you were there."

Mulai shut the door again. The Russian relaxed.

The door swung open, and Kuchuk with two steaming dishes walked in. He put them down before Psin and laid spoons next to them. Psin pointed to the door. When the door had shut behind Kuchuk, he shoved one bowl over to the Russian's side of the table.

The Russian's nostrils flared. His tongue ran over his lips. The aroma of the meat seemed as visible as the steam. His hand moved toward the spoon.

"That horse," Psin said. "The one that ate meat. Do you know what it ate?"

The Russian paused, the spoon over the dish.

Psin picked up his own spoon. "He ate the frozen body of a man." He put a bite of meat in his mouth.

The Russian flinched. He looked down at his bowl. Psin spooned up some gravy and drank it. The meat was good, tender and only lightly cooked.

"Hah hah," the Russian said. "You make up stories." He began to eat.

"Sometimes." Psin finished his meat and pushed the bowl aside. The Russian was eating so fast gravy splashed over his clothes. He was done immediately.

"You are from Yaroslav," Psin said.

"You'll have to kill me," the Russian said.

"I've warned you twice. Twice you've not listened. Do you want to know what it was you just ate?"

"Beef."

"No. It didn't taste like beef, did it. It didn't taste like lamb, or goat, or even reindeer. It tasted a little different from—"

The Russian leapt up. "No. It was beef." The blood left his face. "It was beef."

"It was another Russian," Psin said.

"No."

"After all, a man must eat something, and if there's nothing else around—"

"No!" The Russian put his hands to his face. "Oh, God."

"I warned you before you ate it. You were greedy. You were hungry. You didn't want to believe me, so—"

The Russian leapt at him. Psin brought both feet up and kicked him in the chest. The Russian fell under the table. Psin shouted for Mulai.

Mulai and Kuchuk dashed in. They caught the Russian before he could rise and wrestled him up against the wall, one on each arm.

Psin put his feet on the table. "I think we shall take you to Yaroslav, boy. And we shall tell the people inside that you were so hungry you ate stew made of a fellow Russian. We can't kill you, of course. We aren't permitted to kill madmen, and you must be mad to do such a thing." Psin smiled. "I wonder what the people in Yaroslav would think of that. Or maybe we'll send you back to your friends in the basement—"

"No," the Russian said. He was sobbing. "I didn't mean to, I—"

"You seemed to enjoy it. You haven't even tried to throw it up."

The Russian tore at Mulai's grip on his arm, but Mulai only leaned harder against him. The Russian began to scream. While he was struggling Psin scratched the lip of his bowl with the dagger. Tears were rolling down the Russian's cheeks. Psin had expected him to vomit, especially after eating two apples. Tshant fed his prisoners better than Psin had thought.

"I think we'll throw you back with the—"

"You ate it too, you Tartar dog." The Russian's chest heaved.

Psin turned the bowl, so that the scratch was toward the Russian. "The bowls were marked. You're going back to your friends. Maybe—"

"No. No, don't. They'll tear me to pieces." The Russian's face worked. He had slobbered into his beard.

Psin wrinkled his nose. "I don't see any reason not to."

"Please don't put me in with them. They'll murder me."

Psin rubbed his cheek, scowling. He contrived to make his expression sneaky. "What will you give me?"

The Russian stared, and slowly his mouth grew firm and defiant. Psin let him work up his anger a little and said, "Do you have gold in Yaroslav? Jewels, maybe? After all, I can't give you something for nothing. What will you give me?"

"If I did," the Russian said, "how would you get at it, pig?"

"Oh. Well, I'm going to catapult flaming oil into the city and burn it out. If you tell me where your gold is, I'll—"

"The people—"

"They'll all die, of course, but it's easier to take a city with no people in it."

"You—you—"

Psin leaned back. "What reason has Yaroslav given me to be merciful?"

"You'd burn children?"

Psin made a face. "Unfortunate that you should mention that. I have a weakness for children." He paused, counting to himself. At five, he went on. "But these are Russian children, whose fathers refuse to surrender. They take their risks." He rose. "I have things to do. If you have gold inside the city, we can make a bargain."

The Russian was livid with righteous rage and self-sacrifice. He said, "I have no gold. But to save the children—if I told you a way into the city that required no killing, or very little—"

"What good would it do me? I'll lose very few men, doing it my way."

"But you'll lose plunder," the Russian said stiffly. "You'll lose all the cloth and much of the gold and jewels. And . . . the children . . . "

Psin sank back into his chair. "I'm not sure it's worth the effort."

"You said you had a weakness for children. Do you? Or were you playing at being human?"

"Hunh." Psin chewed on his mustaches. "Let me think about it. I might . . . Believe me, Russian. If I could take the city without killing more than necessary, I would. Mulai." He switched back to

Mongol. "Put him in a locked room, alone. And keep a sharp watch on him."

Mulai nodded. He and Kuchuk dragged out the Russian, who started yelling about ways to get into Yaroslav that would cost the Mongols no lives at all. Psin smiled at the shutting door and stretched his arms over his head.

Tshant climbed in over the windowsill. "You had him talking, at least. What was he saying? Or shouting, I should say."

"This afternoon he'll tell me how to get inside the wall around Yaroslav."

Tshant snorted. He sat down in the other chair. "How did you do it?"

Psin told him. Tshant blinked. "I'll admit it was efficient. But don't you think it a little extreme?"

"We'll take Yaroslav, won't we?" Psin cut an apple in half. He debated telling Tshant that the meat had been stewed mule, but he decided not to. He peeled the apple and ate it.

"Tell me what kind of meat it was," Tshant said.

"No."

"Hah," Tshant said. "So it wasn't human."

Psin blinked at him. "You're getting far too clever for your poor father's good. Get out. Let me think."

Tshant laughed.

LIKE THIS," ANA SAID. SHE STEPPED FORWARD, STEPPED BACK, AND kicked one leg across the other, her arms extended. Her hair swayed.

Djela said, "Let me. Grandfather, watch." He imitated Ana.

Psin stepped, stepped and kicked. "I feel like a fool."

"You look like one." Ana smiled. "You're too gross to dance, Khan."

Djela began to improvise, humming to himself. He spun around and with a screech jumped high into the air.

"Good Lord," Ana said. "Not like that."

"Mongols dance like that," Djela said. He ran in a small circle and jumped again. At the height of the jump he yelled.

Psin sat down on the bench. The sentries on the wall above them were pretending not to watch. Ana danced, her skirt rustling. The sunlight had warmed the bench and Psin took a deep breath, feeling better than he had all day.

"When—my—father—comes—back—" Djela roared, leaping with each word.

"When," Ana said. She stopped dancing and looked at Psin.

Psin stretched his arms out in front of him. He held her gaze a moment, and what he was thinking must have showed on his face, because she turned away suddenly and began to dance strenuously with Djela.

He could have her if he tried. She hadn't fought Tshant, not even when Mongols frightened her and she was still shuddering from the assault on Susdal. She wouldn't fight Psin now. That strong body, heavy-breasted, deep-hipped . . .

"Grandfather, come dance."

"Not I, noyon."

Djela was dancing furiously, his face bright red. Ana's back was taut, as if she could feel Psin's eyes on her. He thought of Chan, of Artai, and felt a little guilty.

Tshant would have taken Yaroslav by now, if the Russian hadn't lied. They would have heard if the tunnels weren't there. Tshant would have sent a messenger and they would have strung the Russian up over the gateway into Susdal with his guts dangling between his toes. Tshant could be dead. He would have gone first into the tunnels. The Russian had said they were sometimes patrolled.

He got up and went over to the warped little trees in the corner of the garden. Dead branches hung among the living, and he pulled them down and threw them against the wall.

Ana said, "Shall we go in?"

"If you want to."

Tshant had said, "I'll send a courier when we hold the city. Try not to get in trouble here." And dodged away from Psin's cuff. "Father. How slow you are."

I am too heavy to move fast. Tulugai and Kinsit had been heavy, too. He remembered Tulugai's slow voice saying, "We will come back when we come back, Father." And Kinsit quiet beside him, their horses side by side, big young images of him.

Tshant had been there, scarcely ten years old, but already long-boned and lean.

"Are we going too, Ada?" Tshant had said.

"No. They're just scouting."

China, flat and burning in the summer sun, tricked a man's eyes; when Tulugai and Kinsit rode away that day, they had seemed to vanish and reappear, dark specks on the dark golden plain.

He could not remember if Tshant had been sorry that they were dead.

He spent the rest of the day riding through the city. The people were sullen and stayed close to their houses. They refused to look at him when he rode past. Clusters of Mongols and Kipchaks off duty strolled or sat around, and the Russians avoided them. Psin saw an old woman going to the well walk across the street to keep from passing by two Kipchaks. Thinking about Tulugai and Kinsit, he drifted into the north section of the city, and rode into a street where there were no other Mongols or Kipchaks.

As soon as he appeared, the houses opened and Russians poured out. They stood on the streets, watching him; many of them were men and they all carried some weapon or another—clubs, a few

tools. He rode at a walk down the street and reined up in the middle. Looking back, he saw that they surrounded him.

He let his rein slide, set his hands on his thighs, and studied them.
He wanted them to jump him; he wanted the excuse to do something. But they only stood and watched, not threatening, not even
speaking.

"Well," he said. "Come along."

They stirred, and a woman called out, "Murderer."

He laughed and kicked the horse into a canter. The people scattered to let him through. If Tshant had died at Yaroslav, he would
show them murder.

When he got back to Tshant's house, Ana was in his room mending one of his coats.

"Where is Djela?"

"Asleep," he said. "He does sleep now and then, although it's
hard to believe."

She looked up quickly from her work. "Don't look at me like
that. Please."

"How am I looking at you?"

"Not now. Before. In the courtyard." She had been speaking
Mongol but she broke into Russian. "You know. Don't."

"I won't." He sat down and put his head back, his neck against
the back of the chair, so that he stared at the ceiling.

"Are you worried about Tshant?"

"Yes."

"He'll come back."

Her voice rang with false confidence. He shut his eyes. "I had
two sons older than Tshant. They didn't come back, once."

"Here? In Russia?"

"This was long ago."

"He'll come back."

"Are you in love with him?"

"Of course not."

If she'd been a virgin when Tshant took her she might have
fallen in love with him to give herself some reason for not commit-
ting suicide over being raped. He grinned at the ceiling. Of course
not. Hunh.

"My Mongol is getting better, isn't it?"

"Yes. It would help if you didn't speak Russian so much."

"Did Tshant say anything about me to you?"

"Tshant and I don't talk much."

"You didn't answer my question."

"No."

"No, you didn't answer my question, or no, he's never mentioned me to you?"

"Both."

A horse clattered into the courtyard below the open window. Psin turned his head. "See who that is."

She was already at the window. "It's a courier. He's coming into the house." She flew to the door. "I'll send him up here."

The door slammed after her. Psin looked up at the ceiling. The courier would come into the hall. He would talk to Kuchuk, perhaps. Now he should be on the stair, now in the room next to this one. But no feet sounded in the next room. His ears strained. The silence packed him in. A voice struck sharply through the quiet, down in the courtyard—a woman. Silence again.

Finally, the feet in the next room, coming quickly and with purpose. The door rattled and swung open. Kuchuk and the courier stepped inside and saluted, and Psin waved at them. Kuchuk said, "Khan, Yaroslav has fallen. The tunnels were there, unguarded. Two of them were above the level of the river ice. They had stakes set in them but we tore them out. The city is burning."

"Very good. How many men did we lose?"

"Two hundred," the courier said.

"Mongols?"

"Mostly Kipchaks. Tshant Bahadur is taking the army up to tighten the siege on Tver."

"Good. No news from Sabotai?"

"We expect a courier before sundown, Khan."

"Send him to me when he comes. And make up the baggage train. We'll leave for Tver within three days."

"What do we do with . . . Susdal?"

"Burn it."

Tshant stuffed meat into his mouth and tried to chew. His mouth was so full his jaws wouldn't close. The courier said, "Sabotai will be at Tver within four days. He wants the Khan, if the Khan is well."

"He is." Tshant gulped down the meat.

"From Tver we ride on Novgorod."

"Quyuk is in Susdal. Does Sabotai want Quyuk with us?"

"Yes. By all means."

"Good. Tell Sabotai that we hold everything between the Oka and the Volga, and we can take Tver at our leisure, provided . . . Never mind."

"He will be pleased to know that the Khan is well."

"The Khan's as strong as a horse." Tshant stood and walked around the yurt, looking out the door. He could see the party of Kipchaks he had sent to burn the villages along the river near Tver; they were making their camp at the edge of the great battered field.

"About Quyuk, noyon. He and Batu fought. It might be well to—"

"Let my—the Khan deal with Quyuk. Leave me alone."

"The noyon wishes."

Tshant laughed, and the courier looked at him, startled, and left. It was the first time the Tshant had ever had the formula applied to him. The noyon wishes. Noyons did not wish; they did the bidding of the khans. He picked over the remainder of his dinner.

Psin would be pleased at the taking of Yaroslav. Tshant tried out various possible replies to whatever Psin would say. Unfortunately, whenever he did this Psin said something Tshant hadn't thought of at all. He got up and went into the back of the yurt.

The girl was sleeping under several fur robes. He tapped her on the shoulder, and she sat up, blinking. He pointed out to the front of the yurt and said slowly, "Go out and clean up."

She didn't understand, but she was used to being talked to in Mongol. She smiled quickly to placate him and darted out past the hanging. When she saw the litter of bowls and spoons she nodded and began to gather the dirty dishes. Tshant watched her, wondering if it were worth the trouble to teach her more words. Sometime he would have to learn Russian.

His father would be completely well by the time he reached Tver, and he'd probably be in a bad temper. Psin was always in a bad temper when he'd seen no action. Almost always. He went to the door, sat on his heels, and looked toward the river.

I took it myself. He gave me no help, except with Yaroslav. All this I took myself, all the estates and the villages. Remembering made him feel strong, and he went back to thinking of an answer to whatever Psin would say.

Jouncing along on the driver's seat, Ana wept. "Why did you burn it? Why? You lived there. Doesn't it mean something to you, when you've lived there?"

Psin glanced back. They were half a day's ride from Susdal already; only the black smoke climbing into the sky marked it. The damned girl still cried. The Kipchak woman driving the cart muttered in her own tongue. Her fat brown face was grooved with disgust.

"I hate cities," Psin said. He reined the dun horse down to match the cart's pace. The baggage train was so long that he had had to form it up in a triple column. He swung around to look back at it. The thin line of horsemen stretched over the last hill. On the far side of the train the herds spread out almost to the far stand of trees. If anybody attacked . . . He bellowed to Kuchuk to bunch up the herds more tightly.

"You lived there," Ana said. She snuffled.

"Girl, I've been easy with you. You are not my slave, but you are a slave, and it's improper for slaves to bawl and carry on." He took a drover's whip from under the seat, and Ana cringed. "Djela, come with me."

Djela veered over to the wagon and said, "Don't worry, Ana. Spring will be here soon."

Psin started off around the head of the train. Djela galloped after him, yipping. The oxen were plodding along at a fast walk; their dewlaps swaying, they thrust through the wet snow. The dun wanted to stretch out, and Psin held him down tight. He could smell rain coming.

"It will be colder before it's warmer," he called to Djela. "Don't be too hungry for spring."

Kuchuk and his men were turning the cattle herd back toward the train. Their whips snapped over the bony rumps. Psin untied the thong that held his whip curled, shook it out, and pointed to Djela to ride in front of him. Djela galloped up past him. Snow flew into the dun's face, and he squealed.

"Hee-yah. Get around there, you."

The cattle broke into a trot, lowing. Beneath their hoofs the snow was churned to filthy marsh. A bull roared, flinging up his head. Psin took a piece out of his ear with the whip, and the bull lumbered hastily back into the herd.

"The horses, Kuchuk."

Kuchuk and his men dropped back to keep the horse herd from running up into the cattle. Behind the horses was the little herd of reindeer Psin had collected. The sheep and goats, butchered and trimmed, hung neatly in the carts above the heaps of gold, the stacks of fur, the chests full of folded cloth. Psin remembered the campaigns in China, when after a city fell every Mongol wore silk underwear and necklaces like breastplates of jewels.

Djela shouted and threw a snowball at a cow trying to sneak out of the herd. Psin fell back, watching her. She was heavy with calf, but she moved quickly enough getting back to the herd. Horns rattled.

Across the ridged backs of the cattle Psin could see Ana slumped on the cart seat, her hands in her lap. He sighed. When they reached Tver she would be overcome, if the burning of Susdal bothered her so much. Tver would be a greater fire.

"Grandfather, look."

Djela pointed up at the sky. Psin shaded his eyes against the sun. Vultures were circling, high overhead, their wings cupped to the wind.

"They always follow baggage trains," he said. The vultures probably thought that the train would take them to a battleground. He turned the dun and galloped down to the reindeer and back, more to give the horse some work than to check their progress. The reindeer was the totem of Sabotai's clan, and Psin meant to supply him with roasts for the rest of the campaign.

The wind was soft. Maybe spring was coming. It was too early, but . . . He remembered Mongke's saying that he had found signs of deep, hard freezes in past years—rocks and trees split. A late thaw and a freeze would do that.

Quyuk was riding at the head of the train, his reins slack, probably asleep. Psin had talked to him only once since the fall of Yaroslav, and they had said very little beyond where Quyuk would ride on the march. Psin remembered how Quyuk had spoken, that other time, when they'd talked of Novgorod. One by one, he had

lost the Altun. When he'd been unable to rule Psin, even Kaidu had
fallen away. Now only Buri was Quyuk's friend.

Tshant, perhaps. They had always gotten along surprisingly
well. Quyuk had to be the Kha-Khan; he'd lost everything between
the Khanate and misery. The deep and the peak.

He rode back to the carts for something to eat. Djela importantly
took over his place, shouting. The cattle threw up their heads. Ana
wasn't crying, but the Kipchak woman looked as sour as before.

"I'm sorry," Ana said. "I . . . lived there most of my life."

"I know." He filled up a leather jug with kumiss and slung it
from the pommel of his saddle.

"Will Tshant be there?"

"At Tver? Yes."

She smiled faintly. Psin put his rein against the dun's neck, and
the horse spun around and galloped up toward the head of the
train. Quyuk's horse jumped, and Quyuk woke up and lifted his
head.

"Shall I go scout a campground?"

"Yes."

Quyuk lashed his horse and cantered away. The dun gathered
itself to charge after him, and Psin hauled hard on the bit; the dun
squealed and bucked, lurching in the snow. Quyuk rode up a slope
and over the height of it and was gone, and the dun quieted. Psin
swung into place at the head of the train and picked up a slow jog.

Tver hadn't trusted in the Grand Duke. Three huge mounds of
snow ringed the city, and the ice of its river was chopped to shreds,
so that a horse could cross it only at a slow and careful walk.
Tshant and his army had camped before the main gate. Psin
brought the baggage train in to camp a long bowshot from the first
snowring, opposite the south gate. He could see Tshant's patrols
riding innocently along the outermost of the snowworks. Apparently Tver wasted no arrows.

"You got here fast enough," Tshant said. "Sabotai is still a day
away."

He reined his horse around and nodded to the city. "Have you
had a close look at it? You should. This one may be more trouble

than Yaroslav. They're getting wiser, these Russians."

"Too late," Psin said. His yurt rose into shape, just behind Tshant's taut face. The framework wavered, and loose felt flapped in the wind. From inside came a muffled curse.

"You seem to think we'll be here awhile," Tshant said. "If you set up your yurt."

"I like my comfort."

Djela galloped up. "Ada. I went looking for you." He slid off his horse onto Tshant's and hugged him. Tshant settled him more comfortably, his arms around him.

"What do you think?"

Psin shrugged. Ana and the Kipchak woman came out of the yurt and began to lace down the sides. Dmitri was still inside. Kuchuk was riding up, probably with questions about the herds. "I'll have to go look."

"They were careful," Tshant said. "The outermost ring is not inside bowshot range of the city."

"Yes, but once we get inside we can use the snow for shields."

"I told you to look," Tshant said. "See for yourself. They must have begun building them when Riazan fell. Otherwise they would never have had the time."

Ana was looking at him, waiting for him to say something to her, but Tshant hadn't even glanced at her yet. Psin said, "Do you want your slaves?"

"My—"

He turned and looked at Ana. She blushed.

"Yes. Send her over. She can watch Djela. And go look at those rings."

"I will."

He rode off. Ana stared after him. Psin dismounted and went once around the yurt. Kuchuk jogged after him and called, "We've turned the cattle out north of the city, on the river, and the horses and reindeer south of it. Is that all right?"

"Yes. Very good."

Ana brushed past him into the yurt. The Kipchak woman said, "Will you want your dinner now, Khan?"

He nodded and slitted his eyes against the glare of the sun to look toward Tver. Three rings.

While he ate, Ana kept close to him, serving him, taking his empty dishes. At last she said, "When am I to go to him?"

He drank some kumiss, thinking how to warn her, but he decided she would learn better if she found out unprepared. "I'll send you over when I'm done."

She nodded. Her face with its strong bones seemed almost stolid but her eyes shone with desperation. He emptied his cup. Before he had gotten to his feet, she was at the door. He followed her out. From the dimness of the yurt into the glare was like coming out of a dead sleep. He called to Kuchuk and told him to send Ana and two male slaves over to Tshant's yurt in the other camp.

"And bring me my horse."

Kuchuk bellowed orders. Psin went back into the yurt after his bow, and the Kipchak woman said, "Am I to have no help?"

"Dmitri."

"Dmitri has gone to help the herders."

"Oh. Yes. Well, tomorrow you'll have help again."

She grunted. Her hands were full of dirty dishes. "Is the little noyon to live here?"

"Only me."

She giggled, looking at him with bright black eyes. Psin stared at her, startled, and she put the dishes down. She swung her thick hips in a grotesque parody of a young girl flirting. He laughed, and she began to giggle again, until they were both sobbing with laughter so hard they could barely stand up. Psin turned toward the door.

"Don't seduce anybody while I'm gone, beauty."

"How could I look at another man when I know the Khan will be at my side?"

They both started laughing again, and Psin ducked out the door. His horse was waiting for him.

Tshant galloped up to him before he reached the snowworks. "I want to see your face," Tshant said. "Be careful. You shouldn't ride in there alone."

"Ah?"

"Wait and see."

The outermost ring was twice as high as a man, four times as thick as its height, and frozen solid. Tshant pointed to the sheer ice wall. "They must have poured water over it to melt it so that it would freeze like that."

"They were thorough."

"Very."

"What were the tunnels like, in Yaroslav?"

"As the Russian said. They built them from the riverbank into the city. For sewage, I suppose. In places they were caved in. The one I followed came up in the middle of the city. We went in at moonset."

Psin could see the tunnels in his mind, icy probably, stinking of garbage, full of rats—the torchlight flickering over the sagging walls, the bad air.

"You did well," he said.

"I know."

They rode in through a gap in the snowworks, hewn with axes. One axe still lay half-buried in the ice. Chunks of old snow cluttered the gap; it was just wide enough for one horse. Tshant uncased his bow.

"Be careful."

Psin nocked an arrow and reined the dun into the gap. Ahead was only a flat space and the next wall—lower, this one, and pierced with great wood poles slanted down toward the ground. One of the spikes was blood-stained.

Something moved in the corner of his eye, and he twisted in the saddle. A man darted back under cover and an arrow thunked into the ice beside Psin's head. He whirled the horse, but Tshant said, "Don't. He's gone by now. Come look. Keep an eye on the alley behind us for me."

Tshant jogged his horse down the space between the walls. Psin glanced over his shoulder, saw nothing, and started after him. He heard something behind him and jerked the dun around, and another arrow hissed by him. He saw the man running away and shot him. The man sprawled into the packed snow and slid along it, his face against the ground.

"Good," Tshant said quietly. "Usually we don't kill them."

The dun cantered up to Tshant's horse, and Psin leaned down. A cave bored into the wall at ground level. He dismounted and looked in and saw that it went clear through to the other side.

"I see," he said.

"Yes. We managed to cut the one gap. They run back and forth in these rings. They know all the tunnels, and they pick us off, one by one."

Psin frowned.

"I haven't got the men to pour them in here and hunt all these rats down."

"I understand." Psin straightened. "I want to see it all."

"We'd die before we got past the second wall."

"Come, now. Are we Merkits or Chinese?"

"You're a Merkit. I'm a Mongol. I'm too clever to go into a warren when I don't know all the tunnels."

"Take our horses back to the gap. I'll watch you."

Tshant stared at him. "If I hadn't seen the hole in your leg I'd swear you were shot in the head. All right. But if we die here, think of our widows."

He took the dun's rein and cantered back to the gap. Psin crouched in the mouth of the tunnel and watched, glancing up and down the empty alleyway between the walls. Once he saw a flash of bright color, but before he could swing his bow it was gone. Tshant left the horses at the gap and ran back, his head low.

"Come along," he said, and started down the wall, keeping close to it. Psin walked backward after him.

The silence was irritating. Tshant's boots made no sound on the stone-hard ice. Once or twice he looked behind him, making sure Tshant hadn't gotten too far ahead, and found Tshant so close their backs nearly touched. That made him angry. His nerves were bad if he couldn't keep track of a man walking so close to him.

"Here's a tunnel," Tshant said.

"Ssssh. Next time, just tap me on the shoulder."

They went on. He saw nothing, no moving thing, and he began to wonder if the rings were so full of Russians as Tshant believed. He counted his steps, and when they had gone thirty-seven strides Tshant tapped him on the back. He turned, saw the tunnel, and ducked into it, holding the bow lengthwise. The tunnel was so low he scraped his head on it, crawling through. When he reached the far end, he put three arrows on the ground, nocked a fourth, and looked out.

Four men were crouched against the wall across from him, at the mouth of another tunnel. He shot one, and the others whirled. An arrow bounced off the ice near his hand. He shot again, missed, and the three men were gone, and the ring was empty. He swore.

"I should do better than that." He backed out again.

Tshant said only, "Watch. We're coming to the steps."

Steps. They were all city-builders, Russians; give them a snow-fort to make and they turned it into Karakorum. He inched along the wall, wishing he had gone after his arrows.

"Duck," Tshant cried. "Look—up on the wall."

Arrows pelted around them. Tshant gasped. Psin dropped close to the wall and looked up; Russians were kneeling on the top, shooting. He put an arrow through one, and the others slid down and were gone.

"Are you all right?" Tshant said.

"Yes."

Tshant had taken an arrow through the fleshy part of his hand. He kept watch while Psin broke the shaft in two at the head and drew it out. The blood dribbled down Tshant's wrist. Psin kicked at the packed ground until he had broken off a little bit of ice. "Hold that. Let's go back."

"I knew you'd never get past this ring. I want to show you the steps. It's just a little way."

"Don't be a—"

"Come on."

Tshant ran down the wall, taking short steps to keep from slipping, and Psin followed him. He kept his head turned on his shoulder to watch behind them. Tshant halted and Psin slammed into him. For a moment they slid wildly around on the ice, clutching each other.

"Look—and then let's get out of here."

The steps were cut into the ice—broad and deep, carefully salted with gravel. They were covered with old blood sign.

"I lost fifty men here," Tshant said. "We fell back. We were beaten."

"I see. Come on."

They started back slowly, Tshant walking backward this time. A red scarf lay on the snow ahead of them, near the mouth of a tunnel. While Psin watched, a hand darted out and snatched it away.

He started to call to Tshant, realized it was a trap, and whirled, dropping to one knee. Four Russians popped out of the tunnel just beyond the steps. Psin drew his bow, saw their startled faces, and shot. Tshant was swearing at his bad hand. Two arrows skipped over the ice and careened away, and three Russians dropped. The fourth dove back into the tunnel. Psin whirled and ran; the tunnel of the red scarf was empty.

"Nasty people," he said.

"Come on."

The Russians were apparently out of tricks. They let Tshant and Psin get out of the rings without any more trouble. Their horses were waiting. Tshant said, "Now, Father, what shall we do about that?"

Psin cased his bow and gathered up his reins. "Remember it. It might come in useful sometime." He mounted. "When Sabotai comes, maybe we'll think of something." He grinned at Tshant and rode away.

The next morning, he rode to Tshant's camp. The glare from the ice walls still hurt his eyes, but now grey clouds were streaming up over the sky. He sniffed hopefully. He did not want rain. He wanted a good solid snowstorm. Rain would pour down those ice walls and turn the rings into rivers. The rats might drown in their tunnels but the Mongols would drown as well trying to fight them.

At Tshant's yurt he paused and looked around. This camp was neat, strictly ordered, and looking very permanent. Three suits of silk underwear hung to dry on a line strung between a yurt and a pole, and two young children were digging industriously and uselessly in the snow behind another yurt. He dismounted, hitched his horse, and went inside.

Ana was stirring a pot. Each stroke of her arm was like driving in a knife. He stood behind her and sniffed, and she still didn't hear him. Her hair hung across her cheek.

"Something good?" he said, in Russian.

She jumped. "Oh. Oh. You scared me."

"Did I? I'm sorry." Her face was white and taut, and her eyes were dull. "I came to ask my son if he would loan you back to me.

My Kipchak says she can't do all the work."

Tshant came out of the back of the yurt. "What are you doing here?"

"Borrowing a slave, I hope."

"She's watching Djela."

"She seems to be. Miraculous eyesight. Djela's off with the reindeer herd."

Tshant made a face. "Take her, then. Have you thought of any way to break the rings?"

"The weather will break the rings for us, sooner or later."

"Later would be disastrous."

"Maybe. We'll see. Ana, get your things, if you have any."

She got up and stumbled into the back of the yurt. Her back was stiff, as if she expected a blow.

"Quyuk is getting troublesome," Tshant said.

"Inaction. Where is he?"

"You brought him here. You should know."

"I don't. Where is he?"

"He's kicked my aides out of their yurt. He's dead drunk. Dead. Since last night. They tell me when he snores the fumes drench the fire."

"Then he can't be very troublesome."

"No. Sabotai will be here by nightfall, and there was a courier from Karakorum."

Ana came out from the back of the yurt, a bundle in her arms. Tshant glanced at her and said, "Go back behind the hanging."

She turned and crept away.

"There was a dispatch for Sabotai. A dispatch for Quyuk from his wife." Tshant's mouth worked. "And one from Kerulu to me."

Psin waited. Tshant was nervous, and that made Psin uneasy. Tshant glanced toward the hanging again.

"She says Ogodai is sick."

Psin pursed his lips and whistled softly.

"She says he will live, but he sickens. Not so much day to day: month to month, she says."

"Has Quyuk gotten his dispatch yet?"

"He's been too drunk."

"Keep him drunk. Send one of your men over there and see that he stays drunk."

Tshant's eyes glittered. "Now, listen—"

"You listen to me. Keep him too drunk to read until Sabotai hears of this."

He stared at Tshant, and when Tshant's expression altered, said, "Do as I say."

"I will. If he finds out—"

"Let him. Out here, what can he do?"

"Nothing, I suppose. There were messages for you. From the Volga camp. They must have gone there for the winter."

"Wonderful." Psin swore. "I suppose you sent them to my yurt?"

"Yes. Shall I—"

"You might, when you feel free." He lifted his head. "Ana? Come with me."

He went out into the fading sunlight. Ana followed, clutching her belongings. She would not look at him; she rode back to his camp behind him on the dun horse. She said nothing, and he was boiling because Tshant had forgotten that he could not read and sent him messages that would have to wait until the afternoon to be read. At his yurt, the Kipchak woman and Dmitri were waiting for him. Dmitri stepped forward to hold his horse.

"Your help," Psin said to the Kipchak, and shoved Ana through the door. He turned to Dmitri. "Where are they?"

"Here." Dmitri took two rolls from his belt and handed them over. Psin thrust them up his sleeve.

"Aren't you supposed to be with the herds?"

"They don't need me," Dmitri said. "And I don't ride well, you know."

"All right. I can use you. Come inside."

He went in and opened up one of the scrolls. Chan would have written it to Artai's dictation. As usual she had mixed Uighur script and Chinese characters indiscriminately. That meant over half the letter would remain a secret forever. He threw the scroll down and opened the other.

This was not from his wives. This was in plain Uighur, and the seals were Jagatai's. Psin bellowed wordlessly.

"What's wrong?" Dmitri said.

"My imbecile son. Kuchuk!" He shouted Kuchuk's name so loudly Dmitri flinched.

Tshant, excited at the dispatch, hadn't bothered to check the seals on either of Psin's messages. He had assumed, since the first was from the Volga camp, the second was also. Kuchuk came in.

"Go to Tshant's yurt and bring him back here. Tell him I have a letter from Karakorum."

Kuchuk bounded away. Psin sat down and growled. Ana said, "Dmitri, what's wrong with him?"

Dmitri shrugged. Psin said, "Nothing for either of you to know. Someday I'll have to learn to read."

"Shall I teach you?" Ana said.

"You can't read Uighur. Or Chinese, which my ignorant second wife insists on interpolating into the letters she writes."

"She can't be ignorant if she can write."

He lay down on his couch. "She is. She's the most ignorant woman I've ever known." In some ways. "What happened?"

Ana turned away. "What do you mean?"

Her face was wooden. Fresh tears clung to her lashes. Dmitri studied her and looked over at Psin and shrugged.

"You know what I mean."

She collapsed, sinking down onto her hams. "He has another woman." On the last word she nearly choked, and the tears spilled down her cheeks.

"I asked you once if you were in love with him and you said, 'Of course not.' "

"I am. I am, I am."

"I know."

She wailed. Dmitri retreated hastily into the back of the yurt. Psin lay on his side, watching Ana carry on, and wondered how much of it was anger.

"This has been happening to people since the world began," he said. "Tshant has a wife in Karakorum. If you had told me—"

"I told you." She was screaming. Her face was dark. "I just didn't tell you in words."

He got up and went to the door to watch for Tshant. "You are a lovely girl, but you should—"

"Don't tell me anything." She beat her fists on the floor. "You're a man—you take a woman and use her and throw her away—"

"Have I had a woman since you've known me?"

"You must have. You're animals. You never think about what you do, you just do it."

Tshant was coming. He turned back to her. She was staring into the fire. Her eyes, puffed and red, burnt with rage, and she snuffled.

"Go into the back. He's almost here. Stop thinking about him."

"How can I? I'm going to have his baby."

"You can very easily. If you're going to have a baby, and you can't be sure so quickly, we'll deal with that in due course. In the meantime you can work and take care of me like any other good slave. Get into the back."

She got up and shambled off. The hanging swung shut behind her just before Tshant walked in.

"I didn't see any—"

"You were too excited to think straight. Use your eyes next time." He picked up the scroll from Jagatai and handed it to him. "Read it."

Kuchuk was in the doorway; Psin glared at him and he backed quickly away. Tshant read through the scroll once in silence.

"Whom is it to, you or me? Read it."

"He says—"

"Speak dialect."

Tshant licked his lips. He probably hadn't spoken the Merkit dialect for years. Psin scowled at him.

"He says—that you are to keep Quyuk here if you can. On his strictest order."

"Read it to me."

" 'From Jagatai Khan of the Altun Uruk to the Khan of the Black Merkits, Psin. Dispatches ac-accompanying this will tell you why I . . . command you to keep my nephew Quyuk the Kha-Khan's eldest son with the army in Russia. This is my strictest order.' "

Psin nodded and switched back to Yek Mongol. "He's quick, Jagatai." Another Mongol would have understood the dialect, but Kuchuk, a Kipchak, and the two Russians wouldn't.

"Why you?"

"Who else? Quyuk would never listen to the Altun. They hate him. Besides, one of them—Kadan, for instance—would interpret this to mean that Quyuk could be killed if he tried to go back to Karakorum. Sabotai is in charge of the war and has no leisure. Jagatai thinks I have."

Tshant snorted. "That isn't why. You've shown you can handle him, and they know you won't use him."

"Possibly."

"Possibly." Tshant said a graphic obscenity. "Use him. You have the power. The Kha-Khan's own brother gives you the power. Bargain with Quyuk. If you do not keep him here, he will be the Kha-Khan, if Ogodai dies. Make that clear to him."

"No, thank you."

"Why not?"

"Because I serve the Kha-Khan, and not Quyuk."

Tshant elaborated on the graphic obscenity.

"Temujin could have killed me plenty of times. He did not. I was of use to him. If I stop being of use to him—"

"Temujin is dead." Tshant hunched his shoulders; his head sank down between them.

"Yes, but I was loyal to him when he was alive, and I am a man of strong habit. Lamentable, perhaps."

"It is."

Ana came out and said, "Do you want something to eat?" She spoke to Psin.

"No. Leave."

She went back. Tshant said, "What's wrong with her?"

"Nothing. She was upset when I burned Susdal."

"I need somebody to take care of Djela."

"Get your new woman to do it."

Tshant glanced back after Ana and looked at Psin again. One of his eyebrows cocked up. "Is that it?"

"No."

"Women are odd."

"You don't need her. Let me keep her here."

"I don't understand you anymore. I used to think I did. The older I get, the more complicated you get."

"When you've got great-grandsons I shall be worse than a Chinese puzzle. Here. Read me your mother's letter."

He tossed the scroll to Tshant, who caught it, and sat down again. Tshant settled himself on his heels. "God. She's got Chinese mixed up in it again. Unh—'Artai Khatun to her something something.' Probably most sweet husband or some other nonsense. 'We have settled ourselves in the Volga camp because of the something wretched something Chan something all since something left.'" He looked up. "Learning anything? 'Something something news makes me very proud, although something wishes—' Chan, that must be— 'you would come back.' Can't be Chan. 'The Volga camp is very something but something is very dear so that we are eating nothing but something and gruel.'"

Psin groaned. "Pork. Pork is very dear. Chan won't eat anything but roast pork."

Tshant was grinning. "'Something something something something.'" He glanced up. "Remember that. It's important. 'The Khatun and I something something all day long, while Chan plays with the cat.' The Khatun? Oh. Batu's wife. 'She wants you to give her a cat to take back to something.' Have you noticed when Chan wants something—" He laughed. "When Chan wants to tell you . . . something . . . it always comes through in very clear Mongol? 'We shall something until you return.' That's all."

"That's enough."

"It certainly is. I have to go. I'm soaking Quyuk in wine. When Sabotai comes up we'll have a conference."

"How's your hand?"

"Mending."

Tshant left the yurt. Psin looked up at the ceiling and thought of Chan playing with Batu's cats. He thought of Artai saying the words and Chan with her brush writing them down. She said she used the Chinese when it made the page look prettier. He looked at the half-rolled scroll. He wished Artai were with him. Artai would know how to handle Ana, and Artai would tell him he was right not to be ambitious, and Artai would tell him how he was going to keep Quyuk in Russia. Artai would sleep beside him at night and listen when he talked. He shut his eyes. Later. Later.

THE VANGUARD OF SABOTAI'S ARMY REACHED TVER IN THE MID-afternoon and pitched a camp opposite the east gate of the city; the clatter of their arrival lasted until nightfall. Batu and half the tumans had stayed in the north to comb out the last resistance. At sunset, Sabotai himself and Baidar and Kadan rode into Psin's camp.

"You don't know how glad I am to find you standing on your own feet," Sabotai said. He embraced Psin. "When I left you were screaming and thrashing around."

"Weakness comes to us all. Have you seen Tver's defenses?"

"Yes. Imaginative." Sabotai sat down on Psin's couch. "Ah. You heard about the battle?"

"Quyuk told us."

"All we need do now is accept the submission of some minor towns."

"The army is tired," Baidar said. "Let them rest—Psin, we are all down to two horses apiece."

"I brought a herd. And cattle and reindeer."

Kadan looked up from his wine. "Good."

"There are dispatches from Karakorum." Psin reached for the wine jug.

Baidar rose. "Shall we leave?"

"No. This concerns you." Psin looked at Kadan, and Kadan's face grew wary. "Your father is dying."

Silence. Kadan's mouth trembled; he glanced around. Sabotai got up. "Where is Quyuk?"

"In Tshant's camp, stone drunk."

"How old are the dispatches?" Kadan said.

"A month and a half."

"Then he may be—"

"Where are they?" Sabotai said.

"With Tshant."

Kadan said, "He may be dead already."

"No. We would have heard." Psin took him by the arm and made him sit down. "He's not an old man. He's not yet so sick he can't recover."

"My father . . ."

Psin handed him some wine, and Kadan took it. His hands shook. Psin went around the fire and sat down. "He's been very sick before, Kadan. And lived."

"I know. Quyuk is drunk, you said."

"Yes."

"Does he know?"

"No. Jagatai sent to me to keep him here."

"When he falls sick they take the drink away from him and he gets well very soon. Doesn't he." Kadan licked his lips. "Doesn't he?"

"He has before."

"But the women are there. My brother's wife and—"

"And your mother. Oghul Ghaimish may be a witch but she can't suborn your mother."

Kadan drank the wine. "I have to go see to my men."

Psin nodded. Kadan paused at the door and looked out.

"I would sooner be a slave than the Kha-Khan," Kadan said. "I would sooner be dead."

He went out. Psin followed him to the door and watched Kadan ride off. The dusk was thickening, blotting out Tver's walls. He felt sorry for Kadan, and he tried to think that it was stupid because Kadan was what he was by choice, but that only made him feel worse.

Mongke was riding up toward him. Psin stepped outside. The cold wind touched him. Mongke trotted up and dismounted.

"Psin. How pleasant to see you alive."

Faced with Mongke, he could not think about Kadan. "Come inside. It's going to rain."

"Yes. Splendid fortifications, those. Have you been inside them?"

Psin followed him into the yurt and called to Ana for more wine. Mongke sprawled out, sighing.

"Tshant and I went in. We got about one bowshot down the wall and turned around and came back."

"Why?"

"The walls are full of tunnels, and the Russians duck in and out and shoot at you when you aren't looking. Tshant got an arrow in the hand."

"Pity it missed his head. What will we do?"

"Don't be so eager, child. We may have to wait until the walls melt."

"That would be too bad, because we should miss Novgorod for sure, then. Where is Quyuk?"

Mongke's face was bland, his eyes wide with innocence. Psin watched Ana pour the wine. She looked even redder around the eyes than before.

"Quyuk is in Tshant's camp."

"I thought perhaps he might have gone back to the Gobi. After he and Batu had the argument. It was a display, Psin. You should have been there."

Psin studied him. Mongke's wife and his mother Sorghoktani lived in Karakorum, and because Mongke was a khan they would have certain power. The women always had ways of getting news out. "How much do you know?" he said.

Mongke arched his brows. "Why, less than you."

"That's an answer. Get out. I'm going to Tshant's camp."

"Someday, Psin, you're going to have to learn how to speak to princes, you know." Mongke got to his feet in one supple motion. "I overlook it, in view of your rough but useful qualities. Other people are not so forbearing."

Psin put on his coat. "A man has to keep his self-respect somehow."

"Why, how humble of you. I might be tempted to believe that, if I didn't know you better."

"Would you."

He went out and pulled the reins of his horse loose from the tether pin. Mongke strolled along behind him. The wind filled the darkness, and Mongke sniffed; his face in the torchlight looked suddenly tense and watchful. His nostrils flared.

"Psin," Mongke said. "When you need help, Psin, come to me."

Psin rolled back in his saddle and looked down at him. "When I need the kind of help you can give me." He kicked the dun into a trot. Behind him Mongke cursed softly.

The smell of meat cooking and the happy babble of voices followed him to the edge of his camp. Riding out between the watchfires, he felt the first icy raindrop on his face. Rain wouldn't help. He gave the dun its head and galloped through the dark toward the clot of fires at the edge of Tshant's camp. The rain was streaming down, hissing into the snow, and when the wind blew a gust of it into his face he felt the sting of ice.

Before he went to Tshant's yurt he stopped to see Quyuk. Tshant's aides had packed themselves into another yurt, leaving Quyuk stretched in solitary abandon on the couch in the middle of the yurt. Under the grate, fire flickered, and a little pot of gruel was steaming over it, but there was nobody else there. Quyuk was snoring. He stank.

Psin sat on his heels beside him and slapped his face. Quyuk groaned, licked his lips, and was still again.

A woman came in from the back and stirred the pot. Psin said, "Does he eat?"

"Sometimes." She knocked the spoon against the rim of the pot. "When he wakes up."

"How often?"

"Two, three times a day."

The yurt was clean, except for an empty jar lying next to Quyuk; a puddle of wine lay on the floor around it. The entire yurt was carpeted in cheap cloth.

"He gets sick," the woman said. "When he does I take up the cloth and burn it."

Psin nodded. "He gets no more wine. No kumiss. Water. Feed him meat when he wakes up."

"He'll beat me."

"Tell him it's my order."

"The Khan wishes."

He went outside and rode back to Tshant's yurt. The rain was steady and ferocious. His shoulders felt each drop like a small mallet. The dun kept its head low, and all around the snow and fires hissed.

Sabotai was eating. He said, "I read them. One was from Ogodai —we have complete charge of the war, you and I and Batu. It was countersealed by everybody he could find. Ye Lui, Jagatai, Siremon, Turakina, Sorghoktani—"

"Oghul Ghaimish?"

"No. She hasn't got her hands on it yet. From Jagatai: they are caring for him as usual and Jagatai thinks he will recover. This time. He repeated to me his orders to you."

"Yes. Have you summoned the Altun?"

"They're coming here. Most of them know already." Sabotai reached for a knife and cut a slice from the roast on the spit. "I'm glad you brought the reindeer. You recall the story about Jebe and the white-nosed horses."

Psin pulled his mustaches, grinning. "I was unaware I'd ever shot a reindeer you were riding."

Djela crawled out of the back of the yurt and sat down by the fire. "A story? What is it?"

Sabotai chewed and swallowed. "You've heard it, boy. About how Jebe Noyon won his name, and how he repaid your Ancestor for the horse he had shot with a herd of one thousand white-nosed horses."

"Oh. I thought it was a new one."

Tshant said, "About Tver."

"We can't do anything until the rain stops," Sabotai said. "Psin, what do you think?"

"I want to see what the rings look like after the rain."

"It's sleet," Tshant said.

"Maybe the weather will get warmer."

"Oh, God." Tshant slammed his fists on the floor. "Maybe. Maybe. The city is there. We have to take it."

"Wait until the rain ends," Sabotai said.

"I smell reindeer," Baidar said. He came into the yurt. Buri followed him, looking pale; he'd been wounded in the battle on the Sit' River. Sabotai gestured to them to eat and drew Psin to one side.

"Before Mongke gets here, I want to tell you something."

"Ah?"

"I sent him and Baidar in to push the Russians against the river— before we all attacked. The charge was late. Baidar will say nothing of it. I think Mongke hesitated."

Psin put his hand on Sabotai's shoulder and turned him so that Psin could see the door of the yurt over Sabotai's shoulder. "I think you jump to conclusions."

"Are you looking for me?" Mongke said, pleasantly. He walked over from the side of the yurt near Baidar. Psin stepped away from Sabotai.

"No. Quyuk."

"Oh." Mongke smiled. He looked at Sabotai and went off.

"He overheard," Sabotai said.

"He has ears like a cat's. And whenever you speak of him he appears—watch. He does." He walked away.

Kadan came in the yurt door, saw Psin, and walked over to him. "I meant to thank you," he said, in a low voice. "For telling me."

"Jagatai says he will get well."

"I know. I heard. Someone else might have . . . Never mind." He reached for a cup of kumiss on the low table.

Psin looked around. All the Altun at Tver but Quyuk were here. Tshant leaned up against the cabinet on the far side of the yurt, watching them. He caught Psin's eye, and Psin went over to him. Halfway there Sabotai joined him.

"What's wrong?" Psin said to Tshant.

"Nothing."

Sabotai said, "You should be pleased with the way he handled his command, Psin."

Psin frowned. "I am."

"He led the attack on Susdal. I could tell by the way he fought that he meant to have it by sundown, so that you could be cared for."

Tshant shifted his weight. "He was dying, I thought, and he was making a mess of the cart."

Psin looked from Sabotai to Tshant and chewed his mustaches. If Sabotai thought this kind of talk would get him Tshant's favor he didn't know Tshant very well. He looked back toward the center of the yurt and saw that Mongke was watching them, half-smiling.

Sabotai said, "You've never held an independent command before, have you, Tshant?"

That was a subject not to be opened up. Psin started off. Mongke came over to him and said, "Did you know I overheard, when you said that?"

"When I said what?"

"That Sabotai might be wrong when he said I'd faltered. In the battle."

"I thought you probably were. I hadn't seen you come in."

Mongke's stare wavered. "Oh. He's right. I did."

Psin said nothing. Mongke looked much younger than usual. He looked down, over at Tshant and Sabotai again, and suddenly straight into Psin's eyes. "Watch Sabotai. Be careful." He turned and started away.

Quyuk walked in. Psin stiffened. Mongke stopped dead, halfway between Psin and Baidar. Quyuk, so drunk he could barely stand, moved his unsteady gaze around the yurt. The other Altun were motionless and silent. Quyuk saw Psin and came toward him. Psin made his fists unclench. The Altun all watched Quyuk. He walked like a man under a special grace; as if he sensed their fear of him he stopped and turned his head slowly to look all around the yurt. When he brought his eyes back to him, Psin trembled. Everyone else was far away and could not help him. He set his teeth together.

Quyuk said, "Have you spoken to him yet? About Novgorod." His voice was clear, in spite of his drunkenness.

"No," Psin said. "I will."

Quyuk looked around him again. There was no sound. It was so quiet in the yurt Psin could hear people talking far away.

"You see what they think of me," Quyuk said.

"Go back and sleep it off," Psin said. His heart hammered. He will kill me, he thought.

"My father is dying," Quyuk said.

"Go back to your yurt and sleep."

Quyuk's face darkened, and he tried to focus his eyes. He swallowed. "Maybe I'm not so great as Temujin," he said.

"I gave you an order."

Quyuk nodded. "You did. You did." He turned and walked toward the door, and his voice rose with each step. "You did. You did. You did."

Psin looked at Tshant and pointed his chin after Quyuk. Tshant detached himself from the cabinet and walked swiftly toward the door. Outside, they could hear Quyuk's voice, blurred suddenly, the words unrecognizable. Psin let his breath out with a deep sigh and sat down heavily on the chair behind him.

"What did he mean?" Sabotai said. "That he's not so great as Temujin."

"Nothing," Psin said.

"He said something about Novgorod."

"He said I should ask you to reconsider your plans. If we don't start for Novgorod now we'll have trouble when the spring thaw comes. I agree with him."

"No. We'll have plenty of time to take it later."

"I'm not sure we will."

"I said no. Tell him that."

"Why not send an expedition up there—half the army. Let—"

"No," Sabotai said, and scowled. "Why fight so hard? You know I will not."

"All right." The low murmur of conversation inside the yurt had started up again. Tshant came inside.

"We should sober him up," Sabotai said.

"I left orders at his yurt. I'm tired. I'll sleep here the night."

Tshant said, "I thought he was going to hit you."

"If he did I could have handled it. Go away. I'm tired."

Tshant stared at him a moment, turned and went off. Psin put his head back and looked at the ceiling. Quyuk had frightened him. If the others saw— He shut his eyes. They had not seen. He was sure of that. If they had, by now one of them would have said something.

Quyuk leaned his head back against the couch behind him. "God. I feel rotten."

Tshant spooned chunks of meat into a bowl and handed it to him. Quyuk tried to push it away; Tshant set it on the floor beside him. "Eat it. You'll need the strength."

"To ride to Karakorum?"

"You're not going back. You are to stay here. I saw your dispatches."

"Which—"

"Both. Even your wife said that you were not to return yet."

"Reading the messages of a Kha-Khan to his eldest son is a crime punishable by . . ." Quyuk shut his eyes. "I don't remember."

"A heavy fine." Tshant watched him steadily. "I'll pay it. Your father will pay it for me."

"My father is sick. Maybe dead."

"Until you hear otherwise, you are staying here."

"Who—" He swallowed. His eyes opened but he seemed to see

nothing. "I'm . . . I feel terrible."

"You shouldn't drink so much."

"Give me a drink."

"No."

"Please."

"No."

"Am I the child of a waystation slave to be treated like this?"

Tshant said nothing. He remembered how his father had stood, while all the rest of them shook like leaves, and told Quyuk so calmly to go away.

"Are you my jailer?"

"No. I'm in charge of getting you healthy to fight."

"So it's your ox of a father. No, don't. Your great glorious most excellent—to fight. Where?"

"Here. Tver. We attack the rings tomorrow."

"Whose . . ." He gulped again. "I'm going to throw up."

"Don't."

"Whose order?"

"Mine."

"To attack the city?"

"No. Sabotai's."

"He's mad."

"Possibly."

"We can't take it."

"Psin and Mongke say we can."

"Mongke is a coward. He—"

He lurched to his feet, stumbled across the yurt to the door, and sprawled over the threshold. Tshant followed him. He stood in the door, watching Quyuk on his elbows crawl across the ground to the deep snow and be sick. The bright sunlight shone fiercely over the camp. In the street before the yurt people turned and watched, and Buri cantered up, his face flushed.

"Get him inside," he called to Tshant. "Will you let everyone see?"

"Yes," Tshant said.

Buri's eyes blazed. Tshant shifted his weight, so that he stood on widespread feet, and lifted his fists. Buri looked at Quyuk again.

"He's done. Take him inside. He's weeping."

Tshant went to Quyuk and dragged him back into the yurt. Buri galloped away. His whip rose and fell across his horse's lathered shoulders.

Quyuk said, "Give me something to drink."

"No."

"Tshant. I shall die."

"Don't."

"Were they laughing at me?"

"No."

"Buri was there. Where is he?"

"He went off."

Quyuk crept to the couch and knelt beside it, his head buried in the rucked covers, his breathing ragged. Tshant sat down by the fire. Quyuk seemed to sleep; his shoulders trembled a little, not constantly, but often. In a while he would start to talk again. The meat in the bowl by his knee was cold, and Tshant got it and poured it back into the pot and sat back down again, aware of his own patience, to wait for Quyuk's waking.

Psin paced back and forth in front of the tower, watching the gap into the rings. The clang and shrill yelling of the battle had died long before, but no messenger had come, and the rings kept him from seeing what went on inside.

"Sabotai," he shouted.

"I can see nothing. Control yourself." Sabotai was pacing back and forth on the platform on top of the tower. "They should hold the outermost ring by now."

Psin cursed him. The snow, trampled black, slurped under his feet, and the shadow of the banner on the staff above the tower rippled over the ground before him. A cluster of women muttered and watched from the space between the yurts nearby. He glanced over and saw Ana, her lips moving.

"Damned woman." He paced three strides.

The women shrieked, and he wheeled around. A horseman was galloping up from the crowd around the gap into the rings. It was Buri, his face filthy with blood and sweat, his coat half ripped off. Sabotai shouted something, but Psin refused to hear. He ran to meet the galloping horse.

Buri reined in hard. "We hold the outer ring. They are shooting at us from the walls. It's slow, building the roof."

Psin caught the horse's rein before Buri could wheel and said, "Losses?"

"Few. It's just—" Buri grimaced. "So slow."

"Go back." Psin stepped aside and turned to relay the news to Sabotai.

"Good. Good." Sabotai grinned. He was sitting cross-legged on the platform, very near the edge. "Listen."

A great roar had gone up from the rings. The women howled and called the names of their men into the bitter air. Sabotai's voice lifted over the shouting, over the rising clang of swords and shields: "The Russians are on the steps. They are trying to beat us back—"

Psin swore, ran two steps to the tower, and leapt. His hands caught the second crossbar on the tower's side and he climbed awkwardly up. The tower swayed and tipped under his weight. Sabotai roared at him, and he scrambled up onto the platform just before the tower would have fallen. Sabotai and the aide with the banners stood on the far side, balancing.

"Grandfather," Djela called, from the ground. "Can I—"

"No." Psin shaded his eyes and looked in the direction of the city.

The great rings throbbed with running men. Mongols filled the outermost, a river of men, their shields raised over their heads against arrows. He could see arrows pelting down onto the shields, but he saw no Russians on the wall and he guessed that they were shooting from the floor of the inner ring into the air, pitching their arrows to drop across the intervening wall.

On the steps the Russians were massed. They held great long wooden shields against their shoulders, and they were all armed with swords. The Mongols inside the ring were shooting at them. Psin could see almost to the bottom step, and there the Mongols were fighting the Russians hand to hand.

"Slow," Sabotai murmured.

"We're gaining ground."

The Mongol shields like a ceiling filled the outermost ring, and more Mongols poured in through the gap under the shield cover.

The shouting dimmed for an instant, as if everyone paused at once to take a breath, and Psin could hear the sound of mallets. A cart lumbered away empty from the gap, and another, full of timber, took its place. A whip curled across the backs of the oxen, and they lowed.

"Grandfather—"

"Ssssh."

A great yowl went up from the area around the steps. Psin tensed; he took a deep breath. The Russians dashed backward up the steps. Mongols charged after them. The swords flashed like the ice rings, and a cloud of lances streaked into the pack of Russians. Bodies slipped down off the wall.

"White banner," Sabotai said. "Psin, look."

"I see."

Russians were running nimbly along the wall toward the steps, coming from the west, and while Psin watched several leapt down onto the ceiling of shields. They bounced up and down on it, testing its strength. Arrows thumped the shields all around them. Some of the Russians had torches.

The Mongols on the steps knelt to shoot, but the Russians paid no attention. A single file stood on the shield ceiling. Buckets passed swiftly along it. The arrows slit into the line and here and there Russians fell, but the buckets emptied over the ceiling, and the torches fell onto the soaked shields, and flames sprang up. Djela murmured something; he had crawled up onto the platform and stood watching, one hand clutching Psin's coat.

Sabotai spoke to the aide with the banners, and Psin patted Djela on the head. "This we foresaw, noyon."

Three banners stood out from the staff. Carts lurched hastily away from the gap, and Mongols streamed out, four abreast. The ceiling remained standing behind them, shored up from underneath and braced with timbers. The fires burning on it drove the Russians back as well as the Mongols, and the men on the steps were swiftly rigging their own shelter of shields.

Outside the wall, the Mongols leaned pine trunks up against the snowbank and scampered up with buckets to douse the flames. Arrows met them, and they ducked, but the flames rose like a wall between them and the Russians. Psin could see both sides—the Russians feeding the fires, the Mongols drenching them. The flight of the Mongols from beneath the burning ceiling continued unslackened. On either side of the steps stood a shield wall, and Psin could see the men sitting safe in it, far from the fires, relaxed and talking. Their bows lay on their knees.

Buri, Quyuk and Kadan were circling around near the gap; their banners dipped suddenly. Psin said, "They're asking for orders."

"Yes. Bring them in."

To the aide with the banners, Psin said, "Raise the gold." He turned back, frowning, to look at the rings. The fires were dying slowly. Most of the Russians were gone.

The yellow flag ran up the staff, and the Mongols around the gap turned and jogged on foot back into the camp for dinner. Djela tugged at Psin's sleeve. "Is Ada coming back?"

"No. He's in command of the steps."

"But he's hungry."

"He's got food with him."

Buri was riding up, no cleaner than before. Sabotai said, "We'll have to go down and hear his report. When do you want to go in?"

"Are you going in there?" Djela's mouth described an O.

Psin nodded. "Let's get onto firm ground."

Several men were stationed at each corner of the tower to hold it steady. Sabotai lowered himself cautiously from crossbar to crossbar, his feet groping beneath him. Djela said softly, "Gandfather, maybe—"

"Ssssh."

He started down; Djela maneuvered around the tower's side just above him, nonchalantly clinging to the crossbars with one hand. "Can I—"

"No."

The sun was setting. Psin jumped the rest of the distance to the ground and faced Buri. Quyuk was behind him. Soot smeared one of Quyuk's cheeks, and a long scratch parted one eyebrow. Buri was talking about the fighting for the steps.

Quyuk said, low, "Are you still going in, Khan?"

"Yes. At moonrise."

"You're a fool."

Quyuk's slaves were gathering around him. One handed him a
cloth, and another held out a jug of kumiss; Quyuk held the cloth
in one hand while he drank from the jug, swiped disinterestedly at
the dirt on his face, and threw the cloth aside. His fingerprints in
soot stood out vividly on the white fabric. He walked away, trailing slaves. The other Altun were riding off to their yurts. Buri had
finished his report. Psin looked up at the sky. The red light from
the sun climbed from the western horizon toward the summit of
the sky, sheer as flame. Under it the fire-blackened snowbanks
turned rose-color.

"Progress enough for one day," Sabotai said.

"Do the Altun think so?"

"Of course not. They say we should have taken the city by now.
They are impatient. I don't think it's necessary that you go inside
the wall tonight."

"I'm not sure they'll do what we wish."

Sabotai's eyes narrowed. "Besides, they'll fight better if you are
there."

Psin looked at him, startled. "What makes you think that?"

"Nothing. Come along, you'll need sleep."

Tshant shook himself awake, yawned, stretched, and stood up.
He was alone on the steps; when the fires on the shield ceiling had
gone out he had sent most of his men to posts all along the roofed-
over section. The night air still smelled of charred, wet wood and
old smoke.

Behind the city wall, fires gleamed, and he saw fires in the Mongol camp, but between them lay nothing but dark. The snowbanks
even looked dark. The cold touched him, and he shivered.

The dead silence made him uneasy. He liked the quiet nights on
the steppe, the rare calm of the Gobi, nightbirds and the wind and
the whisper of grass or sand, but in this stillness his ears strained and
his back prickled as if someone were creeping up behind him. No
wind at all, tonight, and the stars looked dimmer than usual.

He picked up his fur cloak and went down the steps into the
roofed-over ring. The six men clustered at the foot of the steps
came lazily to attention. Under the ceiling the dark was thick and

foul-smelling. He walked back toward the gap, kicking at the shields blocking the tunnels through the inner wall. Tonight those shields came off.

His father was damned clever. Unless it had really been Mongke's idea, the whole thing. He doubted that. Mongke was a raider, strike and fly, not capable of something like this. Mongke was too impatient for sieges. He stopped still and listened and heard only the creaking of the timbers.

He could see little in the darkness. Ahead, far ahead, a small fire burnt in a pot, marking the gap. Boots crunched on the packed snow, and he spun around.

"Yuba," a voice called. "Sentry, noyon."

"Pass."

Yuba strode by him. A timber groaned, and the ceiling seemed to sag. Tshant dodged away. But the shields held, braced up and lashed together. He trotted toward the gap, passing Yuba again. Coming nearer the burnt section he could smell the smoke in the stagnant air, the faint odor of burnt meat: Russian bodies, maybe even Mongol.

"Who comes?" the sentry hailed from the gap.

"Tshant Bahadur."

The sentry stepped aside. Tshant ducked a jutting beam and slipped into the fresh cold air outside the gap.

Silent, motionless, a vast army of Mongols waited there. They sat on their heels in even rows, watching the gap; when Tshant came out they gave no sign that they saw him. Tshant took a deep breath. To keep so many men quiet . . . He looked for his father but didn't see him.

The silence tore at him. He wanted to shout, to bang something, just to break the stillness. With the nervousness working in him he stepped farther from the gap and looked around. There was no sign of Psin. But in the east the moon was gliding up over the horizon, huge, bright orange, flooding light over the snow.

Heavy footsteps. He looked over his shoulder and saw Psin coming, his bow in his hand. His edginess drained away. Psin lifted one hand casually to him and went in through the gap without hesitating. Tshant started after him. Behind him, the rows of the army stood and softly, softly crept into the roofed ring.

No sense asking if they all knew what they were to do. Tshant caught up with his father and walked beside him, one hand on his sword. Psin said nothing. The roof of shields caught the sound of feet behind them and made them boom. In the dark Tshant could see only Psin's shape. He shortened stride so that he did not out-walk Psin and wondered if he always did that, or if this was not some new sign of weakness.

He is old. He must slacken. He was recently sick.

The familiar anger swept over him, and from long habit he fought it down. He shouldn't hate a man because he was strong. I don't hate Psin, he thought. But he wasn't sure.

The closed ring pressed down around them. They passed a sentry, answered his low challenge, and walked on. Tshant could hear no one following them. They had passed the steps, they were nearly to the end of the shield ceiling, and the air was like cobwebs around them. Tshant's nose tickled and he suppressed a sneeze.

Psin's hand touched his shoulder. They were at the end, where the roof ended against a wall of snowblocks hacked out of the ring. Here it was utterly dark. Tshant closed his useless eyes and listened.

Now. Yes. He could hear men behind them, not talking, just moving around. He heard Psin groping along the wall to find the tunnel that was here, and he heard the timbers creak and the shuffle of Psin's clothes against his body. Something scraped—the shield that blocked the tunnel.

He opened his eyes. Psin was making a fire in the pot that had hung from his belt, to signal the men down the way that they were ready. The red glow leapt up and settled instantly, and Psin kneeling beside it cast the edge of his cloak over the pot to signal.

Down the way they had come, another pot winked, and a third. Psin sat easily waiting, his wrists on his bent knees. The glow from the fire lay over the planes of his face. He looked up at Tshant, but his eyes were expressionless and he said nothing.

The pots were winking again. Psin kicked the pot aside, wheeled, and jerked the shield away from the mouth of the tunnel. He plunged in, still wordless, leaving Tshant to find the shield and follow on hands and knees.

Psin's body blocked the far end of the tunnel. Tshant, shivering in the cold from the ice all around, shoved the shield ahead of him.

Psin took it and thrust it out into the ring before them. There was no sound. Psin waited only long enough to find out that no one was shooting at them before he scurried out of the tunnel. Tshant dove after him.

All down the wall, Mongols were plunging out of the tunnels into the second ring, into the bright moonlight. There was no sign of the Russians. The ring filled swiftly with Mongols, still quiet, but moving efficiently up and down the ring. The shields they rammed into the mouths of the tunnels in the inner wall facing them. With axes they cut handholds into the ice walls on either side of the ring, and men with bows climbed up to watch the city. Tshant scrambled up onto the inner wall and looked, and saw the city closer, all quiet, unaware that they had only one snowwall left to them.

Psin said, "No casualties."

Tshant slid down. "They didn't know we were coming," he said, and immediately cursed himself for not thinking that over. Psin smiled at him.

"Obviously."

This ring swarmed with Mongols. The wall behind them was lined with bowmen, and through each tunnel even more crawled, to jump up and run to their new stations. Tshant followed Psin down the wall.

"Only one ring left."

Psin nodded. "They'll fight to the death for it. Tomorrow."

"Why not now?"

"Because I would rather hold the outer and the middle rings, not just the outer and the inner."

"We can hold all three."

"Not yet."

The men creeping through the tunnels all carried shields on their backs, many three or four. They heaped them against the inner wall. Psin turned and held up one arm. Down the ring, someone threw up a hand in answer—Kadan. Psin pointed to the stacks of shields and made a spreading motion, and Kadan gestured again. He ran around tapping men on the shoulders and pointing to the shields.

"They've had plenty of time," Psin murmured. He jabbed his

chin toward the city.

"For what?"

"Wait."

Already the shield roof was springing up; the Mongols in rows held their lashed shields over their heads, while others dragged timber through the tunnels and braced them. Tshant paced, watching the work. The pine trunks skittered around on the ice, rolling, so that the men had to dodge and leap over them. His father was an old fool and they should be taking the inner ring now.

"The city," a man on the snowbank shouted. "They're doing something in the city—"

"Find cover," Psin roared.

The silence shattered. Tshant, filling his lungs, bellowed orders. Men dove into the tunnels and packed the space beneath the half-erected roof. Psin started toward Tshant, his eyes turned upward. The moonlight flooded the rings. Psin's shadow licked at the snow wall.

"Everybody down," a sentry howled.

Tshant flinched back against the wall. A massive hailstorm— rocks. They were catapulting rocks from the city into this ring. Psin, running, caught one on the shoulder and reeled and collapsed against the wall. The air thundered with falling rocks. They bounced and rolled on the flat ice, pelted the roof, swept the sentries from the wall over Tshant's head. Somebody screamed. Tshant dove into a tunnel. Abruptly, the storm of rocks ended and the great silence closed in.

"See what I meant?" Psin said, just outside the tunnel mouth.

Tshant crawled out. The ground around him was a field of stones from wall to wall. No sign of the ice below showed through, and in places the stones were piled up into heaps as high as his knees.

"Shake the roof," Kadan roared.

The Mongols crouched beneath the sagging roof charged to the timbers and rocked them. The roof swayed violently. Rocks bounded down, rolling, splitting on the stones beneath. The roof undulated, and most of the stones cascaded harmlessly off. Kadan stood to one side, rubbing his hands on his coat.

Tshant said, "They must have tested the catapults for distance, back when they built the rings. They knew if they could block us here we'd have trouble getting supplies through."

Psin nodded. "Better here than outside or in the closest ring. I've changed my mind. We have to take that ring tonight. Kadan?"

Kadan stumbled across the field of stones. Tshant could see the rocks turning under his feet, and he saw the stray hands, the heads and boots of men crushed under the hail. If they had not been warned . . .

"What now?" Kadan said.

"Send a man back and tell Sabotai that we have to take the inner ring before the Russians can find boulders to shoot at us. We need every man here."

"The Khan wishes." Kadan leered and plunged into a tunnel, shouting.

Some of the sentries on the outer wall of this ring were running back into position; they had run across the roof on the ring beyond to dodge the fall of stones. One shouted, "Russians coming out the city gate."

Psin chewed at his mustaches. His eyes turned toward Tshant, as if he meant to ask something, and Tshant stared back. Psin said nothing.

"More stones," a sentry yelled.

"Inner wall," Psin called. They plunged across the ring, sliding on the stones, to flatten themselves against the inside wall. Stones pelted down around them—not so strong a shower as the first. A rock bounced from the ground and struck Tshant on the hip. A man gasped, somewhere near. Stones hit something with a sound of splintering bone. They drummed on the roof, and a timber gave way, crashing down.

Psin said, "The tunnels." He lifted his great voice over the pounding of the falling rocks. "The tunnels—every man."

Tshant, kneeling, rolled away the rocks blocking the tunnel entrance at his feet. He took hold of the shield to pull it free, and the rock shower stopped. Like a voice in his ear he heard someone in the tunnel before him. He snatched out his dagger. Psin was standing just behind him. Tshant rapped him on the knee with the flat of his dagger and tore the shield away.

No one came out, so he ducked and plunged in. The point of a sword gashed his reaching arm. Like meeting a bear in its cave—he grappled with the Russian. The two of them packed the tunnel. Their shoulders cramped, they muscled each other, grunting, muffled up in their cloaks. Tshant pulled his dagger arm free and stabbed the Russian in the throat. The blood streamed over him, hot and salty, and the Russian sagged, but his hands still plucked at Tshant's eyes. Tshant stabbed him again.

"Grishka . . ."

The Russian was dead. Tshant kept him upright in the tunnel, to block the others behind him. There were several; he could hear their voices. They shoved at the dead Russian and Tshant shoved back. Psin was pressing against him.

Outside there was shouting, there were stones falling again, and a lot of men screamed. Something crashed and the ground shook. Between Psin and the dead Russian Tshant could barely move. His throat constricted. He got his feet up in front of him, planted them in the corpse's side, and shoved.

The dead man popped out of the tunnel. Tshant on hands and knees raced after, slipping on the bloody ice. Swords clashed in the ring beyond. A Russian face, yellow-bearded, thrust into the tunnel, and Tshant slashed at it with his dagger. Blood leapt from the Russian's nose and he scuttled out and vanished. Through the tunnel mouth, Tshant saw the moonlight on the ice and the city wall across the way, nothing else. The shouting had died.

"Do we stay here or leave?" he said, throwing his words behind him.

"Stay here," Psin said. "Everybody else is."

Other Mongols, wedged into the tunnels, all along the wall. Just like him. "Do we hold all the tunnels?"

"I doubt it."

A torch thrust into the tunnel. Tshant yelped, fending the blaze off with his hands. His cloak stank abruptly of burning fur. He could not back up and he howled to Psin to move, but Psin did not; Psin flung his own cloak past Tshant, wrapped it around the torch, and pulled it out of the hands of the Russian. He beat at his cloak until the flames died.

Tshant sat still, panting. He gulped for air. His face stung; the Russian had scratched him, the torch had burnt him. He took great lungfuls of air. The silence closed in again, and he shuddered. He wanted to burst out, to stand, to be in the open. His throat clogged up.

"Easy," Psin said. "Easy." He took Tshant's left arm in one hand and tore the sleeve of his shirt away. The wound there dribbled blood. Tshant clutched at his father's hand. He thought he had to hold onto something. He could not get enough air to breathe.

An arrow bounced into the mouth of the tunnel, but Psin's cloak, wadded up in front of them, shielded them. More stones pelted the ring behind them.

Psin's hand lay passively in Tshant's grasp. His fingers were cramped from hanging on so tightly, and he let go and pushed away from Psin. He heard Psin move a little.

"What now?" Tshant said.

"We wait."

"But they'll—"

"Ssssh."

I sound like a child. He soothes me like a child. He drew himself up. The silence was suddenly bearable.

Stones rolled and crunched behind them, and a soft voice from the middle ring said, "Quyuk and the rest of the army are in the tunnels." The stones crunched again, and the voice sounded at the entrance to the next tunnel.

Psin shifted his weight. "And now—"

"We die for the glory of the Kha-Khan," Tshant said, and gathering his cloak plunged out into the open.

For two strides he saw nothing and nothing attacked him; he had a chance to fling the cloak around him before the first arrows came. He heard Psin's voice roaring behind him. Out of the other tunnels Mongols charged, yipping.

A horde of Russians streamed down on them—mounted, their horses wild-eyed and their swords like scythes. Tshant swung to face them. An arrow thunked into his cloak and the heavy fur stopped it. Only a few Mongols stood between him and the Russian wave. He had his dagger ready; he took a deep breath and ran toward the oncoming horses.

"Eeeeeyyyyaaaaah!"

The horses trampled down two Mongols before Tshant and swept toward him. A sword flashed toward his eyes. He saw thrashing mane, a beard, a heaving shoulder, and jumped. His arms slid along a horse's neck and he hung on. The horse staggered, and the Russian lurched in his saddle. Something smacked Tshant across the back. He swung his legs up and booted the Russian in the chest. The horse stumbled to its knees. The Russian hurtled off, and Tshant hooked one heel over the saddle's high cantle. The horse charged on, neighing.

He waited for the sword to strike off his head, for the axe to cut him in two, but nothing happened and he managed to reach the saddle. He could not find the stirrups, and the reins flew loose around the horse's knees. All around him riderless horses galloped. He didn't stop to figure it out. He swept down toward a mass of Mongols, scattering before the charging horses; Russians poured out the gate, and more Mongols bolted from the tunnels. He caught one rein and jerked the horse down a little.

An arrow took his horse in the neck and he threw himself free just before the horse slammed to the ground. Another horse jumped across his prone body. He rolled to the wall and sat up. Overhead the air was laced with arrows, two streams merging: one from the city wall, one from the top of the snowbank. That explained the empty saddles. The horses galloped madly up and down through the heaving pack of Mongols and Russians.

Heavy Russian voices called out, and Mongols answered, high and yelping. Metal screeched on metal. A horse reared straight up, a stump where one foreleg had been, and crashed down on its side. Tshant dodged around it and into the main fighting. With only a dagger he had to get close. He rammed into a Russian on foot and put the dagger in between his ribs, and the Russian looked down at him, eyes round with surprise, and fell.

He whirled to face another. This one carried a lance, and the lance jabbed at him, nuzzling at his cloak. He knocked it aside and jumped in. The Russian struck him in the face with his fist. Tshant sat down abruptly, lunged to one side, and slashed at the Russian's hamstring. The hide boot parted under the dagger blade, and the Russian grunted and collapsed. A charging horse rushed them. Tshant dove aside, but the Russian only flung up his hands, and a great forehoof smashed the hand and the face beneath it.

Tshant jumped up and looked for the Russian's lance. The surging lines of men around him caught him like a river current and carried him in a rush toward the gate. The timbre of the Mongol shouting had changed, it was fiercer now, triumphant, and he knew that they were winning. He gasped for breath and yelled along with the rest. The moonlight made it almost as bright as day.

They rushed up against the wall, as if by their weight alone they would smash it down, and the rough wood seemed to tremble before them. On the wall over their heads, women shrieked and sobbed. Tshant paused, his hands flat on the wall, and looked up. The wall could not be manned only by women—

"Climb," someone behind him screamed. "Quickly—climb the wall."

That was Quyuk. Tshant flashed a look over his shoulder and saw him on a Russian horse galloping down toward them. The stirrups banged against the horse's sides, far below Quyuk's feet. Tshant swung toward the men around him.

"Bend your backs, now. Come on, climb."

The first row of men bent over, their hands on their knees. Tshant pushed away from them, not meaning to be a pack animal. The next line backed up a step, ran lightly forward, and leapt up onto the backs before them and bent in the same way. The third line climbed up onto their backs, and the fourth onto theirs. Tshant pulled himself up over the crouching men, using belts and shoulders for handholds, his dagger in his sleeve. The top of the wall swayed above him, painted in moonlight. He stopped just long enough to take his dagger in his hand and vaulted over.

The rampart was deserted. All along the wall, Mongols were running. Torches bloomed. Tshant ran for the main gate. His breath burnt in his throat. He stumbled over a catapult's lashings, almost fell from the rampart, and saw briefly a clot of women and children huddled underneath, their faces white as the ice. He raced to the gate.

Three or four men were already there, struggling futilely with the enormous bar across it. He paused, wiped his dagger on his sleeve, and sheathed it. The engine on the ground beside the wall was a winch. But the bar could not be worked by winch.

He yipped, calling up the Mongols within earshot, and jumped down to the gate. The Mongols followed him, leaping down from the wall. They caught the bar in their hands and with a single shout heaved it out of the cleats and flung it down. With their bare hands they tore the gate off its hinges.

Only a few Mongols came in by the gate. Tshant, watching them go off contentedly to plunder, frowned and climbed back up onto the wall.

What had happened he saw at once. Here on this stretch of wall the Mongols had beaten the Russians, but everywhere else the fighting still blazed on. Probably every male Russian able to fight was outside the wall. The Mongols streaming in through the tunnels were slowly overpowering the Russian defense, but they still fought, and in some places they were forcing the Mongols back toward the main gate. In the moonlight the Russian armor glinted, and there was no color, only black and white, even where there was blood.

He saw Quyuk on his Russian horse lead a charge straight into a mass of mounted Russians. The fighting surged up all around him. A horse screamed and reared up, and the swords hacked and jabbed at the massed bodies between the two walls. Quyuk's horse burst riderless out the back of the Russian line and galloped away. Tshant swore under his breath.

Abruptly he realized that someone was attacking him. He swung around. A dozen women with pitchforks and axes lumbered along the rampart toward him. Their faces, slobbered and stained with tears, were like the bloated faces of drowned men. He took a step backward. They screeched and rushed toward him. They could come only two abreast, because of the narrow rampart, but the ones behind shoved at the ones in front in their eagerness to get at him.

He bent his shoulders and launched himself at them, grabbed the pitchfork in the hands of the nearest, and whipped her off the rampart. She thudded on the ground. The others shrieked at him. Their eyes gleamed. Their hair flew around their heads. He jabbed the fork at them, and one woman spread her arms and smiling ran herself onto the triple tines, gasping only a little. He leapt back, jerking the fork loose, and his stomach churned.

The women came on. He could not frighten them back. He swung the fork in great sweeps, knocking them in pairs and threes off the rampart. They hardly seemed to use their weapons, only fell and smashed on the cobblestones below. From under the rampart rose the wailing of children. The last pair of women faltered, whirled, and ran away screaming.

He followed them. They began to cry out for help, ahead of him. One plunged down onto the rampart and lay still. He caught up with her and kicked her over onto her back. She stared at him, white-faced, and her mouth jerked open. She raised her hands to hold him away.

He grinned. His blood hammered in his ears, and he caught his breath. All the while the woman lay still, her great eyes pleading with him, her hair tangled on the wood of the rampart. The thought of monsters dimmed, and he knelt, one knee on each side of her waist, and dragged her skirts up.

Quyuk's breath sobbed through his teeth. Psin glanced quickly down, saw that his eyes were still closed, and whirled to drive off the Russians beating down on them. His arm ached from holding the sword so high, and whenever another sword smashed into his he felt the jar clean to his shoulderblades. The Russians spilled back, away from him, uncertain. The angle of the wall at Psin's back and the fighting all around them kept the Russians from attacking effectively. Across the little space between them and Psin they stared, their eyes shadowed under their helmets, their mouths working nervously.

"Come on," Psin said, in Russian. "Come take me, Christians." He switched the sword to his left hand and flexed the other arm; one of the Russians cocked his lance and charged in.

Psin chopped awkwardly at the lance, knocked it aside, and struck for the horse. A hoof grazed his side. The horse's head swung across his shoulder. The Russians behind the horse bored in grimly. He hoisted the sword and fended off their strikes, his legs widespread so that he could dodge from side to side without moving his feet. Somewhere far away something crashed down hard enough to shake the earth. The Russians shied back.

"Leave this one," one said. "Get a bow. Nicholas—"

Arrows came, but they were Mongol. One of the mounted Russians screamed and pitched off his horse. The others whirled and raced away. Psin looked up and saw Mongols running down the wall above his head. More Russians thundered down the space between the city wall and the snowbank, but they were fleeing and they didn't pause to attack Psin. He knelt beside Quyuk.

"I'm all right," Quyuk said. "It's my shoulder."

"Hunh." Psin helped him straighten himself out. He'd thought, when he saw Quyuk weave in his saddle, that Quyuk had another headache. "Let's get out of here."

"Are we winning?" Quyuk's face was strained, dead white around the mouth.

"I don't know. Stand up."

"Help me."

Psin took hold of Quyuk's good hand. Quyuk braced himself against it and gathered his feet under him. His right arm hung limp and his right shoulder bent at the wrong place. He rose unsteadily and leaned hard on Psin. He swayed, his eyes squeezed shut. Psin jerked off his belt and lashed Quyuk's bad arm to his side. When he picked him up, Quyuk gasped.

"Are you all right?"

"Hurts. Yes. Do it."

Psin carried him as gently as he could, but he felt each stride jarring the broken shoulder. Quyuk's hand was fisted in Psin's collar. At the nearest tunnel, Psin paused and called, "Is anybody in there?"

"Three of us," a Mongol voice said. "Nobody but wounded out here."

"I have the Kha-Khan's son; get a litter."

Horses were coming. Psin looked up and saw a band of whooping Russians hurtle around the corner and down this wide stretch. Their swords cut arcs through the empty air.

"Sleds," the Mongol in the tunnel said. "They won't fit—"

"Get out here and defend me."

"Who—"

"Psin Khan. Get out here."

The Russians, seeing them, were veering to attack. Three Mongols squirted out of the tunnel mouth. They had bows; they knelt and shot. Two Russian horses pitched forward and slid across the ice toward them, kicking. The others whirled and fled back the way they had come. Arrows hummed after them. Rounding the corner, one Russian flung up his arms and fell backward over his horse's rump. Psin sat down with his back to the tunnel, Quyuk still in his arms, and dug his heels into the ice.

"How goes it?" one of the other Mongols asked.

Psin shrugged. "Ask tomorrow." He shoved himself backward into the tunnel. Quyuk's head lay against his neck. He pushed his feet against the sides of the tunnel to keep himself moving. Someone took him by the belt and dragged him out the other side.

"Sleds here, Khan."

"How—"

"We've widened two tunnels." This was a Kipchak. He spread a cloak on a sled and thrust it over. Psin laid Quyuk on it and folded the cloak around him.

"Be careful. He's broken his shoulder."

"Are we winning?"

"I don't know."

Across the wall, in or near the city, Mongols were cheering. The moon was setting and the light failed steadily. The Kipchak said, grinning, "I think so. You look tired."

Psin pried Quyuk's fingers loose from his collar. "Take care of him."

Quyuk's hand tightened abruptly, to pull Psin around to face him. "Why is it I'm only helpless around you, Merkit?"

"Because you can afford to be." Psin jerked loose and dove into the tunnel and crawled to the other side.

The city was burning. Smoke eddied in the air above him, and embers rained down. The sounds of fighting had died for a moment. He could hear the solitary howl of a baby, inside the wall. He had dropped his sword when he picked up Quyuk, and he couldn't find it again. He had only the dagger in his belt. He jogged along the wall, looking for something else.

This section was almost empty. The blood shone in lakes and dead men and horses covered the ice. Many of the dead were Mongols. Most of them. He stopped and counted, surprised. Of the thirty-four corpses he could see twenty-two were Mongol. That was wrong. Something was wrong here.

From the wall across from him, a Mongol yelled, and Psin ran around the corner to the sounds of fresh fighting. The battle filled the space from wall to wall. Most of the Mongols were on foot, most of the Russians mounted; Psin saw two Mongols darting in and out of the packed horses to slit girths and bellies. The Mongols stood shoulder to shoulder in a breech in the city wall. The gate. Psin took a deep breath and jumped in among the surging horses.

Russian axes and swords smashed down at him. He drew his dagger and plunged it to the hilt in a horse's chest. When the horse reared he ducked beneath it and slashed at a mailed leg that swung at eye level before him. The rider attached to the leg clubbed at him with an axe. Psin grabbed the horse's bridle and forced it back, dodging the wild swings of the axe. The Russian screamed a curse, lifted the axe in both hands over his head, and swung hard at Psin. Psin dragged the horse around so that the axe clove into its neck just behind the ears. The horse screamed and plunged to its knees.

"Mongols, down—watch your heads—"

That was Tshant's voice. Psin went to his hands and knees beside a dead horse. Above him, the arched necks, the swinging arms and swords shut out the night sky. He saw a face, solemn, almost detached, above a long sword with jewels in its hilt. He flattened himself against the dead horse.

Stones pelted all around him. He squirmed, trying to get as much of himself as possible under the horse. Something—a stone, a hoof —smacked the ground beside his head. The dead body beside him quivered. A horse bugled. Something landed hard across his back. He smelled blood, horse, sweat, dead things. Metal clanked hollowly.

The noise rolled away, and he lay still, waiting. Finally he lifted his head. Stones lay all around, and dead horses and men. A Russian in armor sprawled across him, a stone buried in his skull just behind the ear. Psin kicked, and the corpse rolled sluggishly away.

"Hurry up," Tshant said. "There's fighting just down the way."

Psin got to his feet. The smoke was heavier now, and flames crackled just inside the gate. "Who set fire to the city?"

"We did. We thought if they saw it burning they might lose heart."

"They lose heart, we lose plunder. How is it going?"

"I'm not sure."

A sword lay among the stones near a dead horse, and Psin went over and picked it up. The weight dragged at his arm. Tshant was watching him, and he forced himself strong and started down the wall. His shoulders ached, and he couldn't keep his knees from sagging. The light was strange, and looking up at the sky he saw the first streaks of the false dawn reaching through the stars.

WE LOST A HUGE NUMBER OF MEN, AND WE TOOK ALMOST NO plunder." Sabotai pulled up his belt and rammed his hands inside it, over his belly. "It was a hard fight, granted, but I think we should have done better."

Psin nodded. He brushed his hair back off his forehead. The dead weariness hauled at him. He had fought until noon and it was only dusk now.

"What happened?" Sabotai said.

Psin shut his eyes. He heard Sabotai move quickly around behind him, and Sabotai's hand shook him roughly by the nape of the neck. "Come along. We have to hold a council tonight. If we two can't decide what happened, how can the pack of them?"

"I'm tired."

"I told you not to go into the city. You said you weren't certain the Altun would do what we wished if you did not. You went in, and they still did not do what we wished. They were burning the city long before we had cleaned up the Russians. Why?"

"Nobody knew what was happening. Nobody could see anything. Quyuk ordered them to climb the wall, and they did, and threw the gate open. But there were no Russians inside but women and children, and they started to plunder and rape the women and burn—"

"So. First, Quyuk should not have told them to take the city wall."

"We made out better because we held the wall. Once they got organized on top of it."

"They got inside without a commander, then."

Psin opened his eyes. Sabotai was in front of him, his stare urgent.

"They had a commander. Tshant was inside."

"Tshant couldn't keep them organized?"

"Apparently . . . he didn't see the reason to."

Sabotai murmured. "All right. There's the crux. Quyuk was wounded too early to do much damage—"

"Quyuk did well. He kept every man he could outside the wall and moving."

"Kadan? Mongke?"

"Mongke I did not see."

Sabotai settled back, frowning. "Do you think he fled?"

"No. I'd stake a lot on that."

"Baidar?"

"I didn't see, Sabotai. I know them all. I suppose they did what was there to do."

"But you know that Tshant . . . didn't."

"Yes." Psin shut his eyes again.

"In fact, on the basis of partial evidence, the whole disaster seems to have been Tshant's fault."

Psin whispered, "Yes."

"You shouldn't have gone in."

"Sabotai, he's never held an independent command before this war, and he's—"

"Neither has Quyuk. Quyuk so far has proven himself something of an excellent commander. You have more faith in Tshant than he deserves, apparently."

Psin bit his lip. "Sabotai, I won't—"

"Be quiet. He's made an error, and he has to be punished. I mean to take him to pieces in the council."

"I could punish him."

"You could, but I will. Go to sleep."

"O God. I'm so tired."

Sabotai pushed him gently down. "Sleep."

Psin sank down on the couch. In the last of his consciousness he heard Sabotai say, "You're tired. I would be dead. Go to sleep. Go to sleep."

Sabotai summoned the council in his yurt; the Altun, the tuman commanders, and half a dozen of the thousand-commanders gathered there when the moon rose. They woke Psin up, and he shouldered his way through the growing mob, found Mongke, and sank down next to him.

"Where were you in the fighting?"

Mongke looked over at him. He was sitting on a couch next to Quyuk with his bound shoulder. "I was with Kadan, down by the river."

Psin nodded. "I thought so. I didn't see you."

Quyuk glanced over, cold-eyed. Mongke was watching Psin thoughtfully.

"What's wrong?" Psin said.

"I'm waiting for you to go ask Kadan if I was there."

Psin laughed. "Why should I?"

Baidar came over and sat on his heels beside Psin's knee. "It was terrible, wasn't it."

Mongke said lightly, "Oh, well, we only lost a tuman and a half, that's all."

"And no plunder," Baidar said. "I'm just glad I got out whole. We all did. Quyuk, how are you?"

"I," Quyuk said, "am in excruciating pain, useless on a horse, powerless to carry a bow or a sword, and dying of thirst."

"You're lucky," Mongke said. "You could have died."

"Oh, no." Quyuk drew up one knee and rested his good arm on it. "Let me fall, and my nurse-jailer is there to cushion my back from the stones of the earth."

Mongke said rapidly, "Nursemaid to the Altun Uruk is a title that might become hereditary to the Khans of the Black Merkits."

"Not likely," Psin said. He looked at Tshant, who was leaning against the far wall of the yurt.

"Whose fault was it?" Baidar said.

"Mine," Quyuk said. "I ordered them up the wall."

Kadan was behind them, and Buri came toward them through the packed yurt. Sabotai on his short legs walked to the middle of the room. The noise settled and drifted away. Sabotai put his back to Tshant and said, "Tver has fallen. We have lost many men and we won little to pay us back for the blood. It was a difficult fight, complicated, and the defense was clever, but still we ought not to have lost fifteen thousand men."

Psin caught his breath. To say a tuman and a half was one thing, but fifteen thousand bodies meant something else. He chewed one of his mustaches.

"Whose fault was it, that we lost so many? And that more than three-quarters of the casualties came last night and this morning?" Sabotai looked all around. Mongke, beside Psin, lifted his eyes toward Tshant.

"Psin, what happened?" Sabotai said.

Psin stood up. "We entered the rings and went through the tunnels into the second ring. They did not expect us. We started to build the roof. Sentries on the wall warned us that the city was active, and we took cover—"

"Why?" Sabotai said. "If there were no Russians near you."

"I expected that they had trained their catapults into range on that ring. I thought they might shoot fireballs."

"They did not."

"No. Stones. Just as effective. Kadan kept the roof from collapsing. We were to take only that ring, if you remember. But I thought perhaps they would have boulders that would smash our roof. So we went on—I thought we had to take the city before they could reorganize their defenses."

"You sent to me for confirmation, very properly. Does anyone question the efficacy of the Khan's decision?"

No one spoke. Sabotai nodded to Psin, who had sat down again.

"When we went into the last ring, the Russians were waiting for us. But the sentries on the roofed-over rings used their bows and held the Russians off until enough of us could get into the ring."

"Wait. Who commanded there?"

For a moment there was silence. Finally a thousand-commander said, "Sabotai, we were told to stay there until the reinforcements came up. Mongke's order."

"Mongke was not in the force that first entered the rings," Sabotai said.

"I waited at the gap," Mongke said. "When I heard the stones fall I went in."

Sabotai looked surprised. "Very good."

Buri, hunched on the floor at Quyuk's feet, said loudly, "Mongke told me to command the bowmen on the roof. He went on in to the fighting."

Psin slapped Mongke lightly on the boot. "Good work."

"Ah, Psin Khan. For love of you." Mongke laughed.

"Psin, what happened inside the last ring?" Sabotai said.

"You know how the ring was shaped, like a crescent, stopped at either end by the river. I went in at the middle, near the main gate. At no time did we know what was happening at either end. We spent almost half the night chasing Russians up and down that sec-

tion. Quyuk organized all the men he could and cleared the area
around the main gate. He ordered the advance line to climb the
wall. Tshant was with them. They tore open the gate, but Quyuk
didn't enter the city. He and his men had enough trouble keeping
the Russians broken up and on the run. Long before dawn he was
wounded and carried back to the camp."

Sabotai nodded curtly to Quyuk. "My compliments." Quyuk
swore at him in a pleasant voice.

"After Quyuk was gone, I took over and with Tshant's help
from the city well cleaned up the Russians in that area. At noon I
left, when I found out the battle was almost over. That's all I
know."

"Who fought on the western end of the ring?" Sabotai said.

Kadan lifted his head. "Mongke and I. There's a snow barricade
there, and we were pinned up against it. We never got off it until
daylight. We couldn't catch enough horses, and the Russians had
the advantage of the terrain."

"I saw the battlefield," Sabotai said. "You couldn't have done
anything else."

"We had control of enough tunnels to keep reinforcements coming in," Mongke said. "We lost a lot of men, though. Mostly to
defenders on the city wall. Women and large children, with rocks."

"But we held the wall," Sabotai said.

"Not that section."

"Baidar?"

Baidar shifted his feet. "I was on the eastern side, and I did about
what Kadan and Mongke did. Buri kept a good covering fire up
and that helped me. I never had enough men to launch an offensive,
but we kept a lot of Russians very busy."

"Very good. Quyuk, do you have anything to add?" Behind
Sabotai Tshant's face was dark with anger. Psin waited patiently to
catch his eye, but Tshant would not look at him. Quyuk said, "I do.
Psin Khan is the world's greatest flatterer. Almost all the credit he
gave me belongs to him."

Psin snorted. "He's trying to curry my favor. Ignore him."

Quyuk socked him in the back with his good fist, and most of the
Altun laughed. Sabotai said, "Tshant, what happened that you
saw?"

"I went over the wall," Tshant said.

Sabotai waited. When Tshant said nothing, he swung to face him. "What did you do?"

Tshant crossed his arms. "After a while, I got men up on the wall to help some of Quyuk's men, the ones Psin Khan led."

"After a while. What did you do before?"

Tshant cocked his head. "I sat on the ground and made tea, like a Chinese."

Sabotai's eyes jerked up. "Don't use that tone of voice to me."

A hand fell on Psin's shoulder; looking up, he saw Baidar. Mongke said sweetly, "I doubt that will be necessary, cousin."

A thousand-commander stepped through the pack. "Sabotai, I was inside the city with Tshant. We had trouble with the women—"

Everybody roared. "Women?" Quyuk shouted. "Women gave you trouble? That's where the tea came from, Sabotai."

The thousand-commander flushed. "They attacked us."

"Who opened the gate?" Sabotai said.

"I did," Tshant said.

"But you made no attempt to gather up the men there and use them on the wall to help the others."

"I didn't think of it." Tshant's voice was steady and almost amused.

"It's your duty to think of such things."

"Psin Khan does the thinking in our family. I'm out of practice."

Sabotai whirled away from him. Over his shoulder, he shouted, "We lost fifteen thousand men, because you didn't think. Quyuk was nearly killed, because you didn't think. Baidar spent most of the battle tucked off in a corner, because you didn't think. Kadan and Mongke couldn't organize an offensive, because you did not think. Did you have good friends in Tver?"

"I am the whole world's friend."

Sabotai was fuming. His eyes raked Psin. "What shall we do with him, Khan?"

"Sabotai—"

"Answer me."

"Send him back to Karakorum. He's worthless to us, now."

Tshant pushed himself away from the wall; his smile vanished. "For the love of God, you cannot—" The blood drained from his face, and the tendons in his neck stood out. His gaze flew to Psin.

"Well," Sabotai said smoothly. "Yes. We might do that. Send him home like a badly trained horse. But I don't think we will. I think the threat will be enough."

Psin's eyes and Tshant's locked. Tshant's face was white with shame. He shoved himself into the midst of the mob and charged the door. The crowd before it parted to let him through. When he was close to Psin, he jerked his face toward him and said, "I should have let you die in Vladimir."

Psin's jaw clenched. "I wish you had."

Tshant bolted out the door. Sabotai said, "I think he's punished enough, don't you?"

"Ah, you—" Psin sank down.

"He wasn't responding to a straightforward tongue-lashing, was he?"

Psin leaned back against the couch. He could sense the confusion and tension in the Altun around him, and he made himself relax. "Sabotai, of course not. He never has. He's never responded to anything less than a beating. If you think you can talk him humble, you don't know him."

Mongke whispered, "He knows him. Watch."

Sabotai said, "He's a little old and strong for a beating."

"Didn't someone say that once of Temujin?"

The Altun stiffened even more. Quyuk said, "Do you dare compare your wretched offspring to the Ancestor?"

"I did, didn't I? And if you want to press the matter, Quyuk, come look for me when your shoulder heals."

Buri said, "It was a mistake any of us could have made. Tshant did organize the men on the wall eventually. Perhaps Quyuk himself was overeager—storming the wall before he had adequate reinforcements."

Before he'd stopped talking everybody else was muttering. The crowd stirred restlessly. In the general mumble, Baidar said, "Buri. Who put the ice in your heart, nephew?"

Buri laughed. Quyuk said, "Perhaps some of the fault is mine. My timing may have been off. But I say so because it may be true, and not because of Psin."

Kadan whooped. "Trot that past again, brother. I didn't catch it the first time."

Mongke got up and went off, tapping Psin on the shoulder. Psin followed him. Mongke took a wineskin from the masterpole and poured red wine into two cups. He held one out to Psin.

"You were sent to shepherd Altun," Mongke said softly. "You seem to be having more trouble with Tshant than any of us, though."

Psin shut out the rest of the room with his shoulders. "Mongke. How clever you are, to notice it."

"If you think I'm going to blush you're wrong. He can beat you in a fight, you know."

The back of Psin's neck prickled up. "It won't come to that."

"Oh? The way things are going, it will. Soon, too." Mongke glanced away. Psin followed his gaze and saw Sabotai. Mongke's voice sounded in his ear.

"Tshant and I. Tshant and Buri. Tshant and you. You and Quyuk. Quyuk and Batu. Every man finds his master. If he won't go hunting him on his own, Sabotai introduces them."

Psin brought his eyes back to Mongke. "Sabotai is my friend. What are you trying to say?"

"That Sabotai is out to win wars, not keep friends. Do you know how Tshant and I came to meet in Quyuk's room, that pretty day in Bulgar? Sabotai ordered him there and sent me after him."

The muscle under Psin's eye twitched painfully. He glanced over at Sabotai, now talking to Quyuk. The torchlight behind Sabotai limned his head.

"However," Psin said, "a man who liked to manipulate people might have a pleasant time splitting up the high command, mightn't he?"

Mongke nodded. "He might. I thought you'd say that. I take no offense. You'll know, soon enough. Ask Quyuk. Ask Buri. Ask yourself, Psin. What worries you most? That someone might be better than you?" Mongke smiled. "Or that Tshant might be better than you?"

Psin brought his fist up. Mongke's small hand dropped across his knuckles; Mongke stopped smiling. The skin of Psin's face felt too tight for the bones. He felt queasy, and he fought against it, but the warning tingle in his mind would not go away.

"Sabotai is making a mistake," Mongke said. He forced Psin's fist down and open. "Don't make one yourself." He went off; his satin sleeve grazed Psin's. Psin's mouth was dry. He took a gulp of the wine, tasted it, and lifted the cup and drained it in one draught.

"What do you want?" Tshant said.

"May I talk to you?"

Tshant was lying on his back on the couch; he stretched his arms over his head and snorted. "Father. The humility rasps."

Djela called out from the corner, and Psin said, "Go to sleep, noyon."

"Talk," Tshant said. "Tell me what a bad bad man I am."

Psin put his hands on his belt. In the darkness he could see only the outline of Tshant's body. "I don't mean to tell you how bad you are. You're not bad."

"Only worthless."

"I meant that you were worthless because Sabotai had torn you down in front of the whole staff. You made a mistake. So did I. I should have . . . done something other than—"

"Shut up. You sound like a woman. Kowtowing to Quyuk has given you a mouth like a fat eunuch. Get out of here and leave me alone."

Psin grabbed him by the knee and shoulder and dumped him on the floor. "The next time you talk to me like that, I'll kick your brains out."

Tshant darted swiftly out of his way. In the corner Djela whimpered.

"That's better," Tshant said. "That's more like you. Get out. It's hard enough to endure you in the normal run of things. I'm not going to put up with you unless I have to."

Psin started toward him, and Tshant coiled up. A long knife glittered in his hand.

"Stay away from me."

Straightening, Psin shook his muscles loose. He took a sliding step to one side, and Djela flung himself on him.

"No, don't. Please don't. Grandfather, please."

Tshant relaxed and the knife's tip dropped. Psin put his hand on Djela's head. The child clung to him.

"All right," Psin said. "I suppose it's better, anyway."

He turned and started toward the door. Djela still hung on to him. Psin paused and said, "Stay here."

"Grandfather. Let me go with you. I want to—"

"Stay here."

"No."

Psin picked him up, held him at eye level, and shook him. "You brat. I said you were to stay. Don't bother me. I'm not your father." Tshant was on his feet, and Psin tossed Djela to him. Tshant had to drop the knife to catch him. Psin stared at him a moment, hawked, and tramped outside to spit into the snow.

Two days later, leaving Quyuk in command of the garrison near Tver, they started out for Novgorod. The horses were gaunt from winter feeding, and the snow was deep and wet, hard to plow through. After four days of it, Psin told Sabotai that he doubted they would reach Novgorod before the thaw.

"We've covered less than half as much ground in four days as we did when I rode reconnaissance here. Look at the sky, look at the sun—spring's coming. I saw some hay from Novgorod; it was half weeds. Their springs are wet. The army is tired."

Sabotai looked out through the trees toward the west. That wing of the army stretched out across the slopes, sagging in their saddles. Already the trees were growing more thickly, and the hills were treacherously steep under the snow. He said, "We'll keep going."

They pushed on. Batu's outflung western flank made contact with them two days later. When Sabotai asked for supplies the scouts only smiled.

"We were hoping you'd bring us some."

"No matter. Tell Batu to hold this line."

The only advantage to this, Psin thought, was that the riding was so hard and the food so scanty that neither he nor Tshant had the strength to fight. They seldom met. Tshant rode in the eastern wing and Psin stayed near Sabotai in the center.

He had thought at first it would be difficult riding with Sabotai; he was sure that Mongke was right about the fighting between the Altun. But it didn't seem to make any difference between them. He and Sabotai were old friends, and he discovered that the long patterns of association between them held up easily enough even now.

Once Sabotai said, "You've fought with Tshant, haven't you."

"Yes."

"Is there no way to reconcile you?"

"Oh, there probably is." Their horses jogged side by side over a little meadow. "But there's no sense in it. We don't like each other. It's better if we don't force it."

Sabotai looked sharply at him, but the horses were on the upward slope and they both had to concentrate on riding.

The forest closed in on them, and the going was twice as hard as before. The horses stripped the bark from the trees and still neighed from hunger. At night the men crouched over their fires and made thin gruel from their grain, protecting the pots and the fires from the dripping trees all around them. The wet cold crept inside their coats and cloaks. Psin's teeth chattered all night long, and his lips chapped and bled.

On the eighth day of the ride north they woke up in the rain. It came without wind and fell like the stones of Tver. The snow, already soggy, turned to slop. Psin bundled himself into his cloak and swore.

"Don't open your mouth, you'll drown," Kadan said cheerfully. "Here. Eat."

Psin looked at the diluted gruel. "That might drown me sooner."

"How close are we?"

"A day's ride in dry weather on the flat steppe."

"Three days' ride, like this."

Psin threw down the empty bowl. "Thank you. Where is Sabotai?"

"Here," Sabotai said. "I'm catching cold."

"I hope you sneeze yourself back to the Volga camp." Psin threw his saddle onto his dun horse and yanked up the girths. "The trail from here to Novgorod is due north. It goes up a steep hill and down a steep hill and through what is by now undoubtedly a marsh deep enough to lose a horse in. Shall I lead off?"

Sabotai laughed, coughed, and wiped his nose.

Psin, riding, caught a glimpse of Tshant, a good distance away. He had left Djela behind, in Quyuk's camp, with Ana and Dmitri to look after him.

Ana had said, "What's wrong? Are you two fighting?"

"Woman, we are always fighting."

He did not know what he would do if they ever fought hand to hand. Mongke was right. Tshant would beat him. He wondered if he could bear that. When he thought of it he was filled with dread.

The rain continued all day long. Snow slid heavily down on them from the branches of trees. The dun's neck streamed darkly with water. On the slopes, bare rock nudged up out of the rotting snow. One of Sabotai's horses broke a leg in the afternoon, and they butchered it and ate it for dinner. In the marshes, the horses staggered and leapt forward and sank down to their hocks, neighing madly, while the stink of the putrefying earth stuffed up their riders' noses. Sabotai sniffled and sneezed constantly.

Toward sundown they drew up on a ridge Psin knew was only a short ride from Novgorod's lake. The sky was dark grey and no sunlight came through; the forest was full of a vast dripping. He could smell marsh at the foot of the ridge. Boulders lay tumbled all down the slope.

Two scouts came toward them, splashing through black mud. They paused halfway up the slope, and one called, "Marsh all ahead. We have a deer."

"The ravine down the way?" Psin shouted.

"Full of water."

Sabotai cursed. He had wanted to ride the ravine north.

Psin looked behind him. He could see only the first few ranks of the army. Kadan sat slouched in his saddle, his horse's hoofs on a flat rock. Tshant, behind him, looked grim and tired.

"Yes," Sabotai said. "I see what you mean." He cupped his hands around his mouth and yelled, "The road?"

They had crossed the road twice, so far, and each time their horses had sunk to their stifles in the mud. The sentry raised both hands and shrugged. "It's under water."

"Hunh." He swung toward Psin. "We'll camp the night here. Tomorrow . . ."

Psin looked up at him from under his eyebrows.

"Tomorrow we go back," Sabotai said, and sighed.

Hungry, cold, drenched to their underwear and so tired that they swayed in their saddles, they turned south. The thawing spring swept over them like a flock of birds. When they reached the place where the pine forest gave way to oaks and beeches, they found the open meadows running with melted snow. A few days later, Batu and Kaidu with their personal guards joined them. Batu had left the bulk of the army under the command of his brothers; he said they were spread across the hills to the Kama River, and that they had come decently through the winter.

"I'm glad they did," Sabotai said, and sneezed.

They swung west, to bypass Tver and the land they had already taken, crossed the Dnepr on ice that heaved and shuddered beneath the horses' hoofs, and looted all the estates on the river's east shore. These were many and rich, but even so the army's supplies shrank dangerously. Some of their horses died, so that they had meat.

"We can't stop to take cities," Sabotai said. "Look—look."

He threw his right arm out toward the forest. Through the thin sheet of dissolving snow, grass thrust, startling green. The trees were hazy with new buds. Psin nodded. The air was heavy and sweet, almost singing with warmth. Flowers showed where the sun reached in through the canopy of branches. The horses dug wildly through the shell of snow to get to the new shoots.

He had never liked Russia before, he had thought of it only as land to be taken, as grass for horses and cattle, a source of supplies, but that spring made him love it. When they had left Tver to ride north, the cold had clutched at them; now no one wore a coat. The air was so rich he could not breathe enough of it. The dun horse bucked and played like a foal, although his ribs showed and hollows lay deep under his hipbones.

They reached the margin between the forest and the steppe, turned along it, and plundered two villages in one day. Sabotai left three hundred men to keep watch on the country around them. The villages, full of tanned leather, furs, even gold and silver from the churches, gave up nothing to eat but some dried vegetables and a few baskets of grain, and Sabotai chafed.

"We're almost out of food."

"We can reach the Volga camp on what we're carrying now."

Sabotai twitched. "We're not going there. I want to summer west of it, on the steppe."

"Well, we can get there."

"No."

They forded the Dnepr again and headed due south, crossed a smaller river where the water ran cold and clear over rocks and chunks of ice butted into the green shallows to be torn apart by the current, and plunged on. Two days later, scouts reported a small city up ahead on a hill.

"Ah," Sabotai said. "How big?"

"Ask Tshant," Psin said. "He scouted this region."

Sabotai turned and passed the word back for Tshant. Psin reined the dun off some little way and let his reins slide. Tshant galloped up. The dun lowered his head and grazed; Tshant glanced at Psin and pulled over beside Sabotai.

Psin was too far away to hear what they said. He looked back at the army. The horses were tough, and on the new grass their necks were filling out, their coats regaining the shine of good health. But the men looked tired.

Tshant rode around to Sabotai's other side, and Psin trotted back. Sabotai said, "He says it's Kozelsk, on a bluff over a spring, hard to get at, but small."

"Large enough to have something to eat in it?"

"Apparently."

"I wouldn't like asking them to fight uphill."

"For food they'll do anything. It's right in our path. Let's take it."

They did not take the city in the first attack, nor in the second. Before they had regrouped—dusty, swearing—twilight rolled in, and Sabotai ordered the army to camp. Psin looked up at the city and grunted.

"You don't seem to have thought this out properly," he said to Sabotai. "You know we can't withdraw now."

"We'll take it tomorrow."

Psin glanced at him and turned back to the city, perched at the edge of the bluff. Against the luminous twilight sky the walls made a black lump. Torches shone abnormally bright on the stubby towers. The only approach lay between two great shoulders of basalt, a steep and narrow trough from the lower ground where the spring was to the thick stone walls. The Mongols could not bring their full weight to bear on the gate.

He walked the dun back through the camp and listened to the voices of the man hunched around their fires. Most of them were already asleep, their dinner bowls licked clean. The few who spoke sounded angry.

Stone walls. Tshant should have mentioned that. Perhaps he had, but Sabotai hadn't thought it worth repeating. They could not burn Kozelsk, they could not storm it; the city they were attacking for its food supply they would probably have to starve into submission. He tried to raise the energy to laugh at that.

The deep night was full of a soft wind. The sky shone, dark rich blue. Everything seemed more distinct than usual, more alive. A nightbird shrilled. He dismounted and pulled his saddle off the dun, and great swatches of loose hair came with the blanket. He rubbed the horse down. On the dun's shoulders his soft new summer coat showed in patches through the shed, three shades lighter.

If he were not on campaign he would be beside the Lake now, moving the herds slowly into spring pasturage, tending the foaling mares, counting new calves. The yurts would have patches after the long winter. Malekai's new son would have a coat made of a lamb's skin, and the meat would suddenly be tasting better, the kumiss more pungent, the game fatter.

We are hunters, he thought. We are herders. In God's name, how did we come to be here?

"Do you think we'll take it?" Tshant said, behind him.

"Eventually."

"You didn't discourage him much."

Psin kept his back to Tshant. "I didn't know it would be so hard to take."

"Neither did I."

Psin hunched up his shoulders. After a little silence he heard footsteps going away. He looked up at Kozelsk, at the black walls. It seemed to him that the land under his feet was tensing to throw him down.

Three times the next day they charged up the trough to the gate, and the Russians on the walls screamed and hurled stones and arrows and lances down on them, and they drew back, shouting with rage. Few died—Sabotai ordered them back each time just when it was obvious that to go on would cost too much.

They had to take Kozelsk now, no matter how long it took, and the army knew it and ground its teeth over it. To Tshant it seemed that the fresh wide pastures of the bursting spring lay just over the southern horizon, that the rest and food he had done so long without waited for him only two days' ride south. But they had to stay, because Sabotai hadn't judged this properly.

He rode out with four hundred men to raid the Dnepr. Psin was dispatching as many as half the army at a time to forage. Already the grass around Kozelsk was eaten down to the root. The grain was old and tasteless. Tshant didn't like the way the water tasted, metallic from the rock just below the soil. He rode slowly, letting his horse graze.

Kaidu, cheery as ever, had demanded the whole story of the campaigns against Yaroslav and Tver. In return he had told Tshant about the winter in the north. "It was cold, and we spent all day long hunting. All day long. Our grain was gone long before you came by on the way to Novgorod. The hunting is fine, up there. Not like the Gobi, but interesting. How is Quyuk?"

"Mending. He broke his shoulder at Tver. What did he and your grandfather fight about?"

Kaidu shrugged. "I didn't hear. Quyuk's an odd sort. No, I guess I'm the odd sort, aren't I? Everyone else is like Quyuk."

"Even me?"

"Oh, of course." And Kaidu laughed.

One of Tshant's scouts rode up. "There is a herd of cattle in a meadow just ahead."

"How many herders?"

"Six men and a boy."

Fresh beef. "Did they see you?"

"Yes. They sent a messenger west, on foot."

"Good." Tshant wheeled. "Kaidu, take command of the right flank. I want a crescent formation." He looked at the scout. "Is the meadow in a wood?"

"No—there are trees all around, but not thick. It's just beyond that ridge."

"Good." Tshant pointed to the dozen men nearest him. "You, you, you—when we attack, you tend the herd. Keep them bunched. Don't let them run. Nogai, take the banners and ride at the tip of the left flank."

Nogai and Kaidu began to yell, and the men riding along behind them whipped up their horses and shoved forward into the crescent shape. The ends of the formation spread out swiftly and moved slightly ahead of the center. Nogai on the far west spread out the black banner and waved it in a circle on the high pole. The band broke from its trot into a canter.

The ground below the ridge was marshy. Tshant's horse splashed through it, throwing mud up over its shoulders. If the messenger had gone on foot their help couldn't be far away. Tshant strung his bow and laid an arrow to the string. The ridge was sprinkled with beech trees. A man dodged behind one, and Tshant lifted the bow and shot. The arrow missed but the man raced away, yelling, and another Mongol shot him down. They careened up to the summit of the ridge, weaving in among the scrawny trees, and flung themselves down the other side.

The cattle were moving through the trees on the far side of the meadow. Tshant heard the high calls of the herders. They looked over their shoulders at the sound of the Mongols. Their mouths, wet, red, gleamed in their white faces. They threw down their staffs and ran, screaming. Tshant shot; his arrow flew up with four hundred others and the herders slapped into the young grass, quilled like porcupines. The cattle began to bellow.

Nogai was waving the yellow banner; he hadn't stopped to string it on the pole and it flapped in his hands. Tshant reined in. Two horses collided with his from behind, and they skidded entangled down the slope. The dozen men chosen to herd galloped by after the cattle. Nogai was riding back up to the summit of the ridge, to watch the east. Tshant leaned back to look at his horse's hindlegs, saw them still whole, and glared at the men behind him. They grinned, ashamed.

"Watch the banners, you fools."

The cattle stamped out into the meadow again, their horns swinging. The Mongols yelped and beat at them with their bows to keep them close together and moving. Two bodies lay in the herd's path, and the cattle split to pass around them.

Nogai whistled from the height of the ridge. Tshant jerked around; the blue banner was up. He filled his lungs and yelled, "Kaidu—what do you see?"

Kaidu was farther down the ridge from Nogai; he stood in his stirrups and looked east and shook his head.

Tshant gnawed his lip. Nogai was still signaling. Abruptly Tshant kicked his horse forward toward the cattle herd. He paused long enough to shout, "Drive them straight to the camp," whirled his horse, and charged toward Nogai, urging on the others with his arm.

Now Kaidu was shouting, but Tshant couldn't hear the words. He took an arrow from the quiver. His horse raced madly up toward Kaidu, who was swinging his men around to face whatever was coming. Arrows lifted from their bows. The men behind Tshant yelled. They surged up over the summit of the ridge and swept right down into the oncoming knights.

Tshant's horse smashed into another horse, reared, and plunged on its hindlegs through the pack. Armor clashed. The bow was useless. Tshant drew his dagger, ducked a swordthrust, and leaned out to swipe at a knight's jaw. An arm swept him all but out of the saddle. He clung, feeling the horse stagger beneath him. Harsh enemy voices thundered in his ears. He stabbed at the men snatching for him, hauled himself back onto his horse, and ducking swords and outflung arms bored free of the tangle.

There were far fewer knights than Mongols, he saw at once, but the Mongols could not use their bows and the knights like boulders were grinding them to pieces. The horses reared and plunged down across one another, and the swords of the knights glanced occasionally off Russian helmets. Tshant dragged his horse back, thrust three fingers into his mouth, and whistled.

The Mongols looked around toward the banner and wheeled away. Many of them could not get free of the knights and were cut down. The knights charged heavily after. Tshant's bow was broken, and he flung it down and wrenched his spare out of its case. "Shoot," he yelled. The knights wheeled toward him. Their huge eyes shone above the cheekpieces of their helmets. They lumbered along, while the Mongols got back their senses and bent their bows and the arrows hissed into the iron-clad swarm. Some of the knights tried to turn, but before they could work their horses out of the pack the arrows felled them.

Nogai on the summit was waving the blue banner again. Tshant whistled, and the Mongols looked at him, looked at Nogai, and trotted up the slope. The Russian knights did not follow. Tshant galloped after his men. On the ground behind him lay as many Mongol dead as Russian.

Never mind, Father. I'll make up for it. The cattle herd was already south of the ridge and plodding energetically toward Kozelsk. Tshant caught up with it, ranged his men on all sides, and let his horse graze while he walked.

His father would be angry. Let him be. This time Tshant had learned something worth the dead. The old man had to learn to treat him more gently, anyhow.

Long before they reached Kozelsk, the following morning, he saw the smoke in columns all down the bluff. Psin was taking no risks. Any Mongol detachment, hunting or raiding, could follow the smoke back to the camp. When Tshant and his men brought up their herd, they found the pasturage at the foot of the bluff already jammed with cattle, sheep, horses, even swine, and nearby a slaughter pen big enough to keep the whole camp in fresh meat.

"We've scoured everything for two days' ride," Kadan said, across his campfire. "Everything that walks on more than one leg is or will be slaughtered for us before the day after tomorrow."

"Have they tried to storm the wall again?"

Kadan nodded. He lay back on the ground and shut his eyes. "Twenty men could hold us off from that height. You didn't find anything to drink, did you?"

"No."

"Ayuh. I think Sabotai is deliberately keeping me sober."

"They're sending out parties to find grass for the horses, now," Baidar said. "Look at the dust."

Tshant nodded. "And we've only been here ten or twelve days."

"You lost some of your men," Baidar said. "What happened?"

"I ran into some knights."

"How many?"

"Eighty, if that."

Baidar stared at him; Tshant lifted his head, slowly, and the muscles at the hinges of his jaw tightened.

"Eighty? You had almost four hundred."

"Yes. I mean to talk to my father about it."

Kadan muttered under his breath. Tshant spun toward him. "Say something, Kadan. Anything."

"Not me." Kadan lifted both hands. "I'm too sober to fight."

"Psin is over at the spring," Baidar said.

Tshant rose. Baidar stood up with him and swung to face him.

"He's tired, Tshant. He's done too much this winter. And he was wounded. His temper's short."

"It'll be shorter."

Tshant brushed past him. He heard Baidar's blunt cursing and Kadan's low voice beneath it. Catching his horse, he rode over to the spring.

It lay in a sink just below one of the great cliffs that framed the trough up to Kozelsk, and while the water was pure there wasn't enough of it for all the horses and men in the camp. Psin was standing sentry duty on the sentries, to make sure no one broke the rationing. He sat on a bulge of the rock, just a little lower than Tshant on his horse. Sabotai was there, and Batu, sitting on the ground to Psin's left.

"Good hunting?" Sabotai said.

Tshant's head bobbed. "I met some knights—we lost twenty men."

"Ah?" Sabotai frowned and glanced up at Psin.

"In God's name," Batu said. "Is there so large a band of knights running around here? I wouldn't have thought so."

"Eighty." Tshant shrugged. "Much less, now."

"Eighty knights? You had five times that many. How did you manage to lose even one?"

Sabotai glanced up at Psin again. Tshant let his reins run through his fingers. Psin's face was impassive. He was braiding together some wisps of straw, but his eyes were on Tshant, not on his moving hands.

"We met them just below the summit of a hill—when we rode over the hill we didn't know they were there," Tshant said to Sabotai. Through the tail of his eye he saw Kadan and Baidar strolling toward them, all innocence. "We got mixed up with them, very close quarters, and we aren't lancers or swordsmen."

"And before you could pull free they had killed twenty of you."

Tshant nodded. Sabotai looked at Psin for the third time, but Psin was having none of it; he never looked at Sabotai, and he said nothing.

"How did they fight?" Batu said. "Did they try to run you down or throw you off your horses?"

"They just swung whatever they had in their hands."

Batu looked around. "Psin. What do you think?"

Psin's eyes were still on Tshant. "If he lost only twenty, he's lucky."

Sabotai murmured something. Psin threw aside the bits of straw. "Knights are heavy cavalry. If they can reach light cavalry, like Mongols, they'll ruin us."

"We've fought knights before," Batu said. "Without any problem."

"Because we could get out of their way."

Batu spat. "Their horses are slow. We can run before them all day long."

"Providing the terrain lets us. On a steppe, yes. On country we know, yes. But over unfamiliar ground, hills, forests, rivers—"

"Where do you see hills and forests that we don't know? Not even in the north."

"Europe," Psin said. "Sabotai wants to fight in Europe. You've spoken of it. The steppe breaks up, there. And the Europeans are knights. So."

He turned and stared off across the plain. Kadan and Baidar began to tease Sabotai for another drink of water. Tshant was braced, ready for a fight, but somehow Psin had gotten out of it. He scowled.

The siege dragged on through the lengthening days. On the walls at night, the Russians paced uneasily from torch to torch. Psin kept two or three men with bows watching, to shoot down any they could, but the Russians learned quickly enough not to stand against the sky. Sometimes, late at night, Psin could hear them talking on the walls.

Every day since they had first come up to Kozelsk, the city's cocks had crowed in the morning, but gradually their number thinned. On the twenty-eighth morning of the siege, only one cock crowed, and on the twenty-ninth, none. By the thirty-first day, the dogs didn't bark any more. Psin, arranging his foraging parties, shaded his eyes to count the heads behind the rampart.

"Soon," Kadan said.

"Ah." Psin turned away. "It was a mistake to begin with. We shouldn't have come up so grandly, now we have to stay until it's all over."

Mongke had been gone three days, now, and Kaidu five. The horses grazed nearly half a day's ride away. Coming back from a six-day raid, Tshant had reported a caravan moving across the edge of the steppe, far south. Sabotai did not want to attack it.

"If it's going to Karakorum it's under the Kha-Khan's protection."

"Tax them," Psin had said. "Cut their herds. Anything."

"No," Sabotai had said.

"Damn you," Batu had roared. "We are slowly starving."

"Kozelsk will fall soon enough."

Now Psin told Kadan, "Don't raid south too much. When we move on we'll need that forage."

Kadan nodded glumly and reined his horse around. His three hundred men waited, impatient; away from the camp they could find water, graze for their horses, small game not worth carrying back here but far better than what the camp lived on. Psin watched them go. The dust of the ruined pasture rolled up under the hoofs of their horses.

If it were winter they would have been forced to drop the siege long before this. No man could live in the winter on the scraps of meat and fish the rationers doled out. It was worth marveling at that no one tried to steal or hold back supplies. Most of the men spent their daylight hours sleeping in the sun and the cool nights gambling. Twice in the last ten days they had attacked the city, probing, only to retreat as soon as the shower of stones and arrows and debris started to pelt them.

Tshant was sitting beside the spring, sipping his day's cupful of water. He looked up when Psin came near and his eyes took on the stony stare he'd been favoring Psin with since the business at Tver. Psin put his hands on his belt; his temper edged him.

"Stop sulking, will you?"

"Oh." Tshant put the cup down empty. "Am I sulking?"

He stood, close enough that Psin had to look up to see his face. "I didn't know I was sulking. Can you find it in your heart to forgive me?"

Psin backhanded him as hard as he could. Tshant staggered and fell to his knees beside the spring. Psin glanced quickly around; there was nobody nearby, except for a handful of men dozing down where the pebbles turned to sand. He bent and picked up a rock just small enough to close his fist over.

Tshant lunged to his feet, his hands clenched, took a deep breath, and leapt for Psin. His right hand gathered up the front of Psin's shirt, and the other arm cocked back to strike. Psin smashed one arm up against Tshant's right wrist, and when Tshant threw his punch he ducked under it. Tshant wobbled, off balance. Psin hit him behind the ear with the hand that held the rock. Tshant fell hard and lay still. Psin looked around again. No one had seen it. He knelt, made sure he hadn't fractured Tshant's skull, and walked quickly away.

He hoped Tshant wouldn't realize that he'd hit him with a rock. Out of sight of the spring, he opened his hand. The sharp edge of the rock had torn the insides of his fingers. He tossed it away and wiped off the blood on the tail of his shirt.

"No," Sabotai said. "We leave the caravan alone."

Batu grumbled. "You're mad. Let me take half the army south, at least. Get away from this place."

Psin lifted his head, thinking about that, but Sabotai at once said, "No."

"Why, in God's name? If you mean to starve them out you cannot need so many—"

"Because we have been here so long the whole country knows where we are. How can we know there won't be an army after us?"

Batu threw his head back. "Sabotai. We have beaten their army."

"Only one. There are more. There are always more." Sabotai shook his head. "No. We stay, and we suffer through it. When the city falls we can move south again, and by the time we reach the steppe the grass will be full grown and the game ready for hunting."

"If we can find the men to hunt them with."

Psin said, "Sabotai is right."

He looked at his hand, at the scraps of dead flesh clinging to the insides of his fingers. He hadn't seen Tshant since the fight.

Baidar, across the table, leaned forward and said, "We can wait a while longer before it becomes entirely impossible to hold this position. Maybe we can storm the city before then."

"What have they been burning?" Sabotai asked Psin.

"You've smelled it."

"Yes, but my nose is older than yours."

"Wood. Nothing else. No garbage. No meat."

"Meat, burning?" Baidar said.

"Their dead," Batu said. "We may not live to see it."

"We haven't lost a man, a horse or a cow to starvation," Psin said. "Or to thirst, which is the worse of the two. If it would rain—"

"It rained itself out when we rode to Novgorod," Baidar said.

Footsteps crunched the sand behind Psin. He recognized them; he didn't look up.

"Where have you been?" Batu said. "I wanted you to play chess."

"I was by the spring," Tshant said. His voice rasped across Psin's ears. "You didn't look hard enough."

"Who goes near water he can't drink?" Batu laughed. "Come along. We can play now."

"Not right now," Tshant said. "I have something else to attend to."

His hand fell to Psin's shoulder, and Psin leapt away from the table, whirling; he snatched the dagger out of Tshant's belt. Before Tshant could draw his fist back Psin had the dagger up, the tip against Tshant's breastbone. Tshant froze.

"Go attend to it," Psin said. "Now."

Tshant looked down his nose at the dagger. The jewels in the hilt caught the sunlight and threw bright color over Psin's hand. Psin's arm shifted a little, and the point indented Tshant's coat. With all that weight behind his arm Psin could gut him in a single lunge. Tshant opened his eyes wide and smiled.

"Yes, of course. I would love to play chess with you, Batu."

He backed up two steps, and Psin lowered the dagger. Batu was rising. Tshant turned halfway toward him. Through the corner of his eye he saw Psin reverse the dagger to fling it onto the table. He spun around, threw his whole strength behind his fist, and knocked Psin head over heels.

The others bounded up, but Sabotai's voice held them back. Tshant dove after Psin. He caught him just rising and smashed him flat again, face to the harsh sand. He wrapped both arms around Psin from behind, pinning down his arms, and pulling his face back away from Psin's shoulder took a deep breath.

Beneath him his father's tremendous strength flexed smoothly, and he felt himself rolling helplessly over. A heel struck him in the shin, and one of Psin's arms ripped out of his grasp. He braced himself just before the elbow crashed into his ribs. Psin was breaking free. His weight held Tshant under him.

Tshant whipped his legs around and wound them around Psin's. That elbow smashed him in the mouth; blood spurted over his tongue. Psin, his back still to Tshant, heaved himself off the ground and fell back on Tshant's chest. The breath exploded out of Tshant's lungs. He lurched up, grabbing for Psin's forearms, and Psin fell on him again. He could hear his father's breath hissing through his teeth. Psin was squirming around to face him, and Tshant straightened his legs to keep his hold tight. Psin clubbed him on the knee with one fist and flipped himself over, belly to belly with Tshant.

Somebody yelled, far away. Psin was dragging one arm up. Tshant could not hold him; every time he managed to wrap his arms or legs around his father Psin in a violent convulsion tore loose. Psin reared up, planted one knee in Tshant's stomach, and drew his fist back. Tshant saw the fist coming, and he saw that Psin had another rock in his fingers.

He flung himself to one side. The fist grazed his ear and crashed into the rough sand behind his head. He heard a howl of pain. He swiped one arm awkwardly around and got a hold on Psin's belt. The knee in his stomach was grinding his guts through his backbone. He wrenched, and Psin slipped sideways, and Tshant flung him off and lunged to his feet.

He gulped for air. His mouth was full of blood, and he spat it out. Psin came up on one knee, panting. He was stronger than Tshant, and faster than he looked. Tshant made himself relax. If he let Psin get in close he'd never beat him.

The look on Psin's face puzzled him; it was as if Psin didn't recognize him. Wary, he backtracked a little. Psin got to his feet, arms dangling. He'd never seen his father look so harsh.

He glanced up at Sabotai, wondering when he would stop this, and saw him, up there, his face cold and remote. He remembered the fight with Mongke—the fights with Buri—

Psin hit him, and he reeled back. Psin was coming in, crouched and reaching. Tshant backed up fast to get out of his way, ducked, feinted, and hit Psin cleanly in the face. Psin wobbled, but when Tshant bored in got both arms up to protect his face and kicked Tshant's legs out from under him. Tshant landed on his side and rolled.

He felt the hands on his coat and the strength behind them, ready to drag him up, and getting one foot under him he sprang forward. He butted Psin in the jaw. Psin started to fall, and Tshant hit him twice in the belly. Psin kicked him in the knee and raked one elbow across Tshant's face, but Tshant, collapsing, brought his father down with him and rolled and finally had Psin underneath him, face down. He clenched his fingers in Psin's hair and drove his face against the ground.

He could feel Psin coiling up beneath him. He jerked Psin's head back and pounded his face against the sand again. This time Psin wouldn't get away. He could feel his strength ebbing. He let go of Psin's hair, swung his shoulders back, and drove his fist into the back of Psin's head. His knuckles split. He gasped at the pain shooting through his arm, but Psin no longer moved. He almost cried out in triumph; he drew his fist back to hit him again.

They threw him off, wrestled him back, away from Psin, shouting at him. He couldn't hear the words. He swung his weight against them, but they were fresh, and they flung him up against the basalt and roared in his ears.

"He's your father," Baidar shouted. "Do you want to kill him?"

Tshant's head swam. He panted; his lungs burnt. Baidar and Batu stepped back, their faces taut. All the exultation was gone. He looked down at Psin and saw the blood pooled under his head, soaking into the sand. His stomach contracted.

"Why did you let me do it?"

Batu said, "If you can't—"

"Shut up," Baidar said. "Is he all right, Sabotai?"

Sabotai was beside Psin, his fingers pressing against Psin's skull. "Why did you let me do it?" Tshant said.

"I think he would have done it to you," Baidar said softly. "He was frightened of losing."

Tshant couldn't catch his breath. Sabotai came up toward them.

"He's only sleeping." His eyes rested on Tshant. "You hit him hard enough, that time, to murder him."

Tshant spat in his face. Batu murmured. The bloody spittle dribbled down Sabotai's beard. Tshant turned and went off down the slope, stumbling. His legs felt weak, and he could barely see. It was only when he was nearly to his own fires that he realized he was weeping.

"You have a skull like a piece of rock," Tshant said.

"Is that fresh water?"

"Yes." He squeezed out the cloth and pressed it against the mess of Psin's face. "I didn't mean it."

"Remorse. And the nursing on top of it. If I could find my right arm I'd break your neck."

"I didn't know you were so strong. If you weren't so strong I wouldn't have lost my temper."

Psin's eyes glittered feverishly. Whenever Tshant put the rag to his face, he flinched, shivering. The sand was embedded in the raw meat of his cheek, and he'd bitten the inside of his mouth to shreds. Tshant rinsed the cloth and started to soak out the sand, but Psin's left hand caught him around the wrist.

"Why? I've got friends enough. I don't need you working over me."

"Because of your friends," Tshant said. "The way they look at me, I may get an arrow in the back the next time I turn it."

The grip of the fingers loosened. "It was Sabotai." Psin shut his eyes.

"I know. I finally figured that out."

The blood ran freely down into Psin's hair. His limp mustaches clung wetly to his jaw. Tshant picked up Psin's right hand and bandaged it, hoarding the water.

"Baidar, Batu, Kaidu and Sabotai all gave up their water ration for you."

"Tshant. I'm tired of fighting with you."

"You're sick. You wouldn't say—"

"I am. I don't want to fight anymore."

Tshant paused. He stared down at the wreck of his father's face in the wavering torchlight. That Psin might weaken he had never considered. His hands trembled; he could not bear that, that Psin should weaken.

"I must be . . . older than I thought," Psin said. He shut his eyes.

"No."

Psin's eyes slowly opened. His lacerated cheek stretched into a smile; his fingers moved and caught Tshant by the wrist. "Unnatural," he said. "Unnatural. You came by it naturally enough, monster. I'd rather fight you than the Russians. Go away. I'm tired."

Tshant stood up, uncertain. Psin pulled his sable cloak over him and shifted his weight a little; his eyes shut again. The torchlight lay now on the better side of his face. Tshant gathered up the cloth and filthy water and went away.

Mongke walked up out of the darkness. "I hear you beat him."

Tshant stopped, surprised. Mongke had come back from patrol after sundown. If he knew already the whole camp knew. "Who told you that?"

"Many, many. Did you beat him?"

Mongke of all people should have been gleeful, but Mongke was not. Tshant grimaced. "No. I knocked him cold. That was all."

Mongke's teeth flashed in a grin. "I didn't think you had." He went on by. Tshant looked after him, thinking of following, but after a while walked on up the slope.

*   *   *

Psin leaned back against the warm stone. After forty days of siege there was no reason to be hasty. The lines of the city wall stood out unnaturally clear against the blazing sky, unblurred by smoke. Behind the thick parapets no heads moved. That wasn't unusual. The Russians had learned early not to make targets for the Mongol bowmen.

He glanced down the slope, to where Sabotai, Batu and Mongke were crouched talking over a dead fire. Kaidu and Baidar were off raiding; Kadan was with the horse herd, moving it still farther off, and Sabotai had sent Tshant to forage immediately after the fight. He said that it was because the Altun in the camp were likely to do Tshant damage for nearly killing Psin.

"He didn't nearly kill me."

"It looked as if he did."

Sabotai was angry because the fight hadn't settled much of anything. Psin had heard about Tshant's spitting in his face. Sabotai would have to find another weapon. He stood and went down there, by habit circling the area that the Russians could reach with their arrows.

Mongke said, "Enjoying the sun?"

"Very pleasant."

Batu had been describing a battleplan with small sticks and pebbles. He stood up. The boredom of the siege was eating at him: his face was sour with it. "Do you smell burning meat?"

"No." Psin turned to Sabotai. "I don't smell anything at all."

"The wind's wrong."

"There was no smoke yesterday, Sabotai. No smoke today. No heads on the walls. No sound."

Mongke's eyes narrowed; he turned and looked over his shoulder at the city. Sabotai stood up. "Anything else?"

"Isn't that enough?"

Sabotai nodded. "Mongke, go down and get the men in the lower camp up here. Batu, you command on the right flank. Psin, go back and watch."

Psin nodded and walked back up to the place he'd just left. The wind was still wrong. He moved in closer, moving as quietly as he could. Usually at this time of day the wind changed.

The men from the lower camp were trotting up, bows in their

hands, swords clanging at their heels. Russian swords, most of them, from Moskva, from Vladimir and Susdal and the Sit' River and Tver. Running, the Mongols went into formation, under orders barely spoken.

A head moved behind Kozelsk's rampart, and a thin shout rose. Nobody answered in the city. Across the forming ranks of the Mongols Sabotai yelled to Psin and Psin pointed to the city and nodded. Mongke, running neatly over the rougher ground beneath the basalt height, shouted and led the others up the trough.

Psin stood up. On the wall men appeared, bows and rocks in their hands—but fewer, much, much fewer even than three days ago. The rocks and arrows pelted down, and the Mongols flung up their shields. Batu's men were already bending to let the men behind them scale the wall. The Mongols around Sabotai shot back at the Russians. Psin pressed himself against the rock. The Mongols swarmed up the wall and ran along the ramparts, and the Russians retreated before them, not even shouting any more.

The wind had changed. Psin took a breath of it and nausea swam in his throat. He whirled and waved to Sabotai. "Get them back out here!"

Sabotai frowned, not understanding, and Psin plunged down toward him. Before he reached him the gate to the city burst open and the Mongols charged out, yelling, fright in their voices. The men still outside the wall faltered, whirled, and ran away.

"Plague," Psin yelled. He dodged in next to Sabotai. "You can smell the stink—"

The army was streaming back from the walls. Russian dead hung over the rampart, all of them probably dying before the Mongols cut them down. He realized he was standing stiffly and shuffled his feet. Sabotai said, "Pleasant thing to find."

The last of Mongke's ranks were out of the city. Mongke himself jogged along behind, red in the face, looking as if he didn't care at all that the city was full of plague. He swerved over and stopped beside Sabotai.

"It stinks in there. Psin, your nose has gone bad on you."

"It's been living too near the rest of me too long." He laughed, shaken. "Silly end to it, isn't it?"

"If it gets to the army," Sabotai said, "it will be a not very silly end to everything."

It was over. In one brief charge and flight, the whole siege was over, and he was still twitching because it shouldn't be. No smoke —because there was nothing to cook, no corpses burnt because the living dared not go near the dead to drag them to the fires. He turned back to the city. The gate yawned, and through it he saw a wide street, small buildings. Empty. Dead, and full of ghosts.

"We have to get out of here," Batu said. "Let's march. Now. Leave sign for the others to follow us."

Sabotai nodded.

We have to get out of here. Dead, unappeased, untended. The wind swept down from the city and the full stink made Psin turn his face away. The men were already down on the flat plain, and Mongke and Sabotai were running after them to send for the horses.

The wind hissed softly over the rocks. Nothing moved between Psin and the city; on the walls a loose shirt flapped sluggishly, as if it were sick as well. Not even the carrion birds would come to Kozelsk. The open gate with the glimpse of cobbled streets and buildings fascinated him. He was sick with it. So long sitting here, waiting for that gate to open. All he had to do was walk up there and in. It was his city. He had waited for it.

"Come along," Sabotai shouted. "We are done here."

Psin turned his back on the gate and went after him down the slope. The horses were coming. Most of the men were running to meet them. Psin kicked three fires to pieces, waved Sabotai on, and rummaged for a flat stone. In the space between the two basalt cliffs he laid the stone on the warm sand and scratched on it with the tip of his dagger.

South, the scratches said. He arranged sticks alongside the stone: Don't go into the city. Follow us. He scratched the Yek Mongol totem onto the flat stone above the signs, and beneath them cut in his own clan sign, the mark of the ox.

"I've got your horse," Sabotai said.

Psin rose, sheathed his dagger, and mounted. Ahead of them, the army moved off to the south; many of them were singing. The fresh wide plain lay ahead of them, and the whole long summer. He couldn't help but smile.

Part Three

PSIN

Temujin said, "When it is necessary to write to the rebels and to send envoys to them, do not threaten them with the strength and great size of your army, but say only: If you will submit yourselves obediently you shall find good treatment and rest, but if you resist—as for us, what do we know? The Everlasting God knows what will happen to you."

ANA STABBED THE AWL INTO THE LEATHER AND DRAGGED IT through. The Kipchak woman said something in her own tongue, and Ana said, "If you're talking to me, speak Mongol, will you?" She looked over at Djela, currying Psin's dun horse in the shade of the yurt.

"I wasn't talking to you," the Kipchak said. "But if you want, I will. Have you told the Khan yet that you're pregnant?"

"Now, how did you know that?" She flapped the leather out in front of her to straighten it.

The old woman grimaced, delighted. "Do you think I'm stupid?" She nudged Ana with her toe, and Ana slapped at her foot, making a face.

"If you keep me from working, I'll see the Khan knows of it."

The Kipchak mumbled again. Ana sighed in mock exasperation. She lifted her head to check on Djela again and to look across the camp. The size of it overwhelmed her. Psin had said that Sabotai's couriers took a full day to ride across the camp and return. Each yurt had a great yard around it, a floor, and a shed for hay and grain to feed the horses not kept with the herds.

"Have you told him?"

"I told him once and he didn't believe me." She hadn't really known it was true but that didn't matter. "Why should I tell him? He'll find out soon enough."

The sun was warm on her back, warm on her strong brown arms, and she smiled for no good reason. The Khan's wives were coming, and when they got here she and the Kipchak woman and the other slaves would have to put up another yurt, but until then they had little enough to do.

"He might think of selling you," the Kipchak said. "He can't, if you bear a child to his son."

"Am I his or Tshant's?"

Djela trotted over and sat down beside her. "Can I—"

"No," the Kipchak said. "If you've finished with the horse, find something else to do."

Djela pouted, and Ana reached out to touch him. "What do you want?"

"Just something to eat. I—"

"Your father says you're not to eat between meals."

Djela leaned his head against her shoulder. "Tell me a story."

The Kipchak cackled. "Tell him the story about how his grandfather got his face bashed in."

"I know that," Djela said. "It was in the war. Tell me another story."

Ana glared at the Kipchak. "Djela, don't bother me. I'm working."

He snuggled up against her. She was proud that he'd chosen her to tag after instead of the Kipchak or his father or one of his Altun relations. He and she were very close. She bonked him lightly in the head with her elbow, and he giggled.

She remembered when she had first seen Psin, after the army came at last onto the steppe and made its camp; she'd seen him first in torchlight, the good side of his face toward her, and when he'd turned and she saw the chewed, scabbed wreck of his right cheek she had gasped.

"You should have seen me when it was raw," he said, and in a high good humor had gone off with Tshant and the others to drink until they dropped.

Three little boys on foot raced around the corner of the yurt opposite theirs, screamed to Djela to join them, and tore down the crooked street. Djela leapt up and bounded away. His voice rose in the screech the Mongols made when they were winning a battle.

"Like puppies," she said. Djela and the others vanished in a cloud of dust down the street.

"Ayuh," the Kipchak said. "The herd of them. From the Kha-Khan on down."

"Ssssh." Quyuk's yurt was to their left, and Quyuk was sleeping on a rug outside in the sun.

The baby inside her would be no bigger than a worm now. She settled her weight more carefully. Perhaps she should tell Psin.

"Horses coming," the Kipchak said. "Look."

Ana looked up. Three horsemen were charging down toward them; one of them was Tshant. He whipped his horse up toward them and jerked it to a halt. "Is my father here?"

"He's inside, asleep."

"He's got a hangover, you mean. Hunh." Tshant dismounted and went to the door. "Father. Wake up, you old pig."

The Kipchak cackled.

"I'm awake," Psin yelled, from inside the yurt. "What's got you out in the heat of the day?"

"Mother and Chan are almost here."

"Unnnh?"

Something heavy hit the floor inside, and Ana with her back to the door heard Psin's footsteps coming. She smiled at her hands holding the awl.

"How did they get so close without anyone's telling me?"

"They're just at the edge of the camp. With the carts they'll be two days getting here."

"Have you seen them?"

"Buri told me. He'd heard from Kadan."

"Loan me some slaves. God above. Where am I going to put another yurt?"

"Have you got another yurt?"

"Yes. Somewhere. No planks for a floor. Which woman do I put in the yurt without the floor?"

Ana turned to look at him. He wore only a cloth draped inartistically around his waist. His immense chest and shoulders were sunburnt pink as a baby's skin. He backed up to look behind this yurt. "Ana, how much space is there behind us?"

"Enough," Ana said. She wondered what his wives would say about his half-healed face.

Quyuk had woken up next door. He hooted something across the space between the two yurts, and Psin whirled and shouted, "Just remember, while you're consoling yourself with a slave, I've got my women here, and not in Karakorum doing my bribing for me."

Tshant laughed. Quyuk was making obscene gestures. Psin turned his back. To Tshant, he said, "My male slaves are both with the herds. The yurt is in the cart under the platform. Ana and the Kipchak can supervise putting it up, if you'll give me the slaves to do it."

"Where are you going?"

Psin ducked back into the yurt. "To get them, naturally. The carts can come later."

Tshant grunted. He looked down at Ana. "You'd better go find a pig. My mother will eat anything, but Chan is fussy." He lifted his head and called, "Father. Send a slave when they get here."

"I will."

Chan had brought cats; two of them yowled in baskets lashed to the cantle of Psin's saddle. Ana, at the door of the yurt, saw dim shapes moving behind the bars of the baskets. The dogs across the way began to bark, and Psin swore.

"You see?" he said, to the cloaked and hooded woman on the horse beside him. "You always cause me trouble."

The woman said nothing. In the deep summer darkness Ana couldn't see her face. The other woman was already dismounted, and Ana rushed to help her. The Kipchak was inside keeping the food warm.

"This is Ana," Psin said, while she helped the older woman sort out her bundles. "She'll take care of you until your own women get here. Ana. Watch out for her. She's old and feeble."

"Humph." The woman turned her face toward Ana and smiled, openly, warmly. "I am Artai, and when I am old and feeble the Khan will be bones under the earth. Do I smell pork?"

"Yes," Ana said. "You must be tired."

"Hungry, too, but we've been eating pork all winter." Artai went to the door. Ana glanced back; Psin had lifted the cloaked woman down from her horse and was standing with one arm still around her. In the darkness she couldn't see if he was smiling.

"Where is my son?" Artai said. She ducked in the door ahead of Ana and shed her cloak. "Hunh. My husband might have been sick, but he got his share of plunder. You Russians make lovely things. The wood is beautiful."

"Tshant is four yurts north of us," Ana said. "Do you want kumiss?"

"Please." Artai sat down with a plunk. Ana poured kumiss into a cup and held it out, and when Artai took it she saw with a start how gnarled her hands were. Artai sipped. "Is the weather always this good? Sit down, girl. You make me crane my neck." She smiled again, patted the couch beside her, and nodded when Ana sat. "We had a very pleasant ride, until my husband came and swept us off like a hawk with two rabbits in his claws."

The other woman came through the door, advanced two steps, and let her cloak fall. Expressionless, she looked around the yurt. Ana stared; when she realized she was staring she drew her eyes away, but she kept looking back. Chan glanced over and their eyes met and held. Psin had come in behind Chan, and his hand rested on her hip. The lamplight caught in the jewel at Chan's throat and lay softly on the white silk of her gown.

"Don't stare," Artai whispered. "It only puffs her up."

"She's beautiful."

"Yes." Artai patted her shoulder, her fingers light and strong.

Chan looked up at Psin and said, "Is she yours?" She pointed at Ana with her chin. Psin looked over.

"Yes. Don't fight. Sit down, and when you've eaten I'll take you over to your own yurt. It's not as fine as this one."

"I am only the humble second wife," Chan said. She sank to her knees and folded herself neatly down on her legs. The tone of her voice and the look of her eyes were not humble. She turned her face toward Artai. "He says the dogs will eat my cats."

"They ate them in Serai. Why should they lose their appetites here?"

Ana went after the plates with the pork. Tshant burst in the door, Djela in tow, and Artai leapt up. They embraced. Babbling, Djela danced around them. Chan turned her face away and drew the corners of her mouth down. Half-sitting on a chest, Psin watched her and smiled.

"I don't know if I can bear to look at you," Chan said sweetly to him. "You are so ugly."

Her voice was extraordinary; it reminded Ana of gold filigree, each word distinct and precise.

"You are indeed," Artai said. "What did you do—get dragged?"

"Yes," Psin said.

Artai frowned and looked up at Tshant, and he blushed. Artai said, "That dun horse is a demon." She glared at Tshant; her back stiffened.

Djela said, "Grandmother, we had the best fun. Ada, can I tell her about the snowfort?"

"When I've eaten," Artai said. She cut her meat. "Here, chew on this awhile."

Djela took the meat from her fingers and swallowed it. "Grandfather and Ada had a fight."

Tshant jerked. Chan looked at him and tilted her face up toward Psin's, and Ana saw her understand. Djela went on serenely, "Ada made a mistake and everybody was really angry and Grandfather said he should go back to Karakorum, but it's all right now. Isn't it?"

"Yes," Tshant said.

Artai was eating slowly, her eyes flitting from Psin to Tshant and back again. Her face, creased with wrinkles, looked suddenly lean and fierce, like a man's. Ana sat down, ready to take the plate for more food if she wished it, and saw Psin look at Artai and smile; the lamplight raked his gouged face.

"I'm not hungry," Chan said. She put her plate down, and the Kipchak woman came for it. "You haven't enough slaves."

"I'm a man, I don't need more than two or three. You'll have to bear up until your own get here."

"Am I to sleep all alone in a strange yurt?"

Tshant pretended to choke. Psin said softly, "Sweetness, I've got you so hedged around with guards and slave women a charge of Russian knights couldn't reach you."

"Quyuk is right next to us," Tshant said to Artai. "And Quyuk is moderately fond of looking at her."

Psin slid off the chest he'd been sitting on. Chan rose, turned, and shot a look at Ana. She started out, and Psin went after her and took her by the hand.

Artai said, "Ana, will you take Djela home and put him to bed? Thank you."

Ana stood and with Djela's hand in hers went off. Just before she stepped out of the light she heard Artai say, inside, "Now what have you done, Tshant?"

Artai said, "Tshant says you fought."

"Meddling old woman." Psin sat on the couch to take off his

boots. Artai squirmed over to the inside of the couch and smiled at him.

"Is it so impossible for you to get along with him?"

"Yes."

Ana came in and lowered the flap over the door. She looked shyly in their direction, murmured something, and slipped behind the curtain into the slaves' quarter of the yurt.

"She's a pleasant girl," Artai said. "Where did you get her?"

"Tshant took her in Susdal." Psin stripped off his tunic and slid under the light cover. "She fell in love with him, and naturally he got himself another woman in the next city, and she was miserable, so I told him to give her to me."

"This must have been during a calm spell. At least you don't always fight."

Psin put his head down on her shoulder. "Not always. I'm glad you're here."

Her arms pressed him against her. "You make me very happy."

"Good."

"Sometimes."

Batu had gone back to the Volga camp; his two younger brothers were in command of the garrisons in the north. Most of the Altun followed him immediately. Sabotai suggested that Psin go as well, to keep watch on Quyuk.

"When we were fighting it was different. If he left his assigned post he was liable to punishment, and he knows it. But now . . . ."

"That I should live in cities in the winter is almost unbearable," Psin said. "But in the summer—"

"He's restless."

Psin cast around. The cattle herds stamped over the plain past the horizon, with more being driven here every day. Sabotai had sent out orders for horses to be rounded up, broken, and conditioned, but the first herds hadn't arrived yet. "Who is to command the camp, if I go?"

"I will. Am I so old I can't handle a handful of yurts and a few—"

"Twelve full-strength tumans. Their women, their slaves, their—"

"Well." Sabotai shrugged. "The Kha-Khan's orders were to you, not to me."

"Hunh. The orders came from Jagatai, not Ogodai. My women won't like it. They came out here just a few days ago."

Sabotai's horse stamped, and he reached down to crush the fly clinging to its neck. "If anyone had told me that you, of all men, should be worried about—"

"I'll go," Psin said. He gritted his teeth.

Tshant had already packed up his yurt and his slaves and rumbled off to the Volga. Djela had stayed behind with his grandparents, and Psin gave him three horses and a pack of food enough to banquet on and sent him on the two-day ride to Batu's city to tell Tshant they were coming. Djela, flushed and strutting, galloped off the morning before they were to leave.

Ana stood looking after him from the top of the platform; the laundry was drying on the wood behind her. Psin narrowed his eyes thoughtfully, studying her figure.

"Isn't he young to be riding off alone?" she said.

"He's a Mongol. Are you practicing for motherhood, girl?"

She blushed and hurried back to her work. Psin grunted. The Kipchak was right.

Chan came out of her yurt and sat down in the warm sunlight. A cat curled limply in the crook of her arm. Psin watched her through the tail of his eye. She wore a gown of the light cloth he'd taken from Moskva, and against the pale yellow her skin glowed. One of her women sat down behind her and began to brush her hair. With each brush stroke Chan's head lifted. The cat began to lick its paw, rolled deftly onto its tail, and slung its right hindleg up past one ear.

Psin went over to her. The cat lifted its head and watched him, its pupils narrow as lances. Chan said, "If I had known we were only to go back to the Volga I would never have come."

He sat down cross-legged in front of her and rested his elbows on his knees and his chin on his hands. "I know."

"It's very hot. This is a terrible country."

The cat flopped over on its side and yawned. Psin poked it with one forefinger and the cat slapped at his hand. "If it's so hot, go inside."

"I like the sun too much."

Psin laughed. "Would you like to ride?"

"Ride? Where?"

"Khan," Artai shouted, "will you come help me?"

"Later," he called. He straightened up, smiling down at Chan. "Down by the river. Come on."

"Perhaps," she said, "you should help your first wife instead."

"Perhaps I should not. Come on."

She stood up, and the cat bounded away. Within the loose robe her body moved like the cat's inside its skin. She gave Psin a long, reckless stare and went into the yurt to change her clothes.

Beneath the trees by the river, it was cool, and the wind stirred the branches so that the dappled sunlight on the ground glittered and blended into patterns like a carpet's. The river ran almost silently. Half a day's ride down, it met the Don River, which Psin said was as wide as the Volga. They had passed a few people fishing.

She let the horse graze and watched the river slide between its banks, dark brown water over furry brown stones. A bird was singing on the far side, low and warbling, as if it had taken the river's voice.

Within days they would be back in the Volga camp. She frowned at the river. It would be happier to live here, to have a little yurt on the plain she could see boiling in the sun just beyond the trees, to have some cattle and a few sheep and horses, and to spend all day lying beside the river and thinking. Artai could take care of the yurt and she would think. She thought about getting off the horse and trailing her fingers in the smooth water.

She turned her head and looked up the ridge; Psin was there, the dun horse massive in the half-shade of the trees. His bow jutted up from the sheath on his saddle. He had said there might be enemy Kipchaks or Alans around, spying on the camp. His face was in shadow, but she knew he was looking at her.

Toy, she thought. I am a toy.

She brought the whip down hard on her horse's barrel, and it bolted. Ahead the trees grew down thicker around the bank, and she collected her reins, steadied the horse, and sent it plowing through the underbrush. She crouched down over its neck to keep from being raked off by the branches, heard the dun cantering after her, and kicked her heels into her horse's sides to keep it running. The trees were so close together her knees rasped against them. She glanced back, saw no sign of him, and jerked her horse to a stop. He was coming, but more slowly—bigger horse. She dismounted and lashed her horse across the flank. The horse pounded off through the trees. She crouched down in the midst of some high sweet-smelling bushes.

They had thorns, and the branches crackled if she moved. She held her breath. Hard, unripe berries hung before her nose. The dun jogged up toward her, and she heard Psin's soft curse.

The dun stopped dead, and Psin yelled her name, furious. She wrapped her arms around her booted legs. He passed so close she could have touched his stirrup, and she had to bite her lips to keep from laughing. She drew a soft breath, inhaling the smell of the horse, the smell of Psin himself, and covered her mouth with her hand.

He went on by. A little farther down the bank, he shouted again, and this time his voice sounded worried. He had seen her horse with the empty saddle.

He was coming back. The brush crackled and swayed. She pushed deeper into the berry bush, hoping the sound of his horse would cover the noise she made. He was shouting with every breath, so that the trees rang with his voice. She crouched on knees and elbows.

"Hunh."

He was right opposite her. She held her breath. Through the screen of thin stems and leaves she saw him bend out of the saddle to look at the ground, and his eyes moved, following her track, until they stared directly at her. His hand on the reins lifted, and the dun whirled. She crawled backward, careless of the thorns tearing her arms. The dun was pounding into the thicket.

Under her weight the ground crumbled, and she fell rolling into the river. She yelped, and the water flooded into her mouth. Her feet struck the bottom. The water was as soft as milk, warm, gentle. She stood up to her waist in it and scowled at the bank. Psin on the dun horse began to laugh; his eyes squeezed shut and his chest bounced with laughter.

"You dog," she said.

He gasped out some words, but she couldn't understand. The dun horse, to his belly in the tangled underbrush, shifted and started to back away from the bank. Chan waded to the edge and dug mud out of the river bottom. She took two steps backward, moulding the fine silt in her hands, and flung it at him.

He stopped laughing. The mud splattered his shoulder and the bad side of his face, and he scraped it off, sputtering. She put her hands on her hips.

"Help me up the bank."

He brushed off most of the mud; his mustaches were caked with it. She saw him start to dismount and went nearer to the bank. He dropped his reins, walked to the edge, and bent, holding out his hand. She grabbed it and jerked him in.

He yelled in midair and made a splash that got the dun horse wet. She scrambled away from him, upriver, flailing at the water with her hands. Losing her footing, she went under and tasted the softness of the water again and pushed herself up.

He stood dripping in the middle of the river, glowering at her. He hated water. She laughed.

"Come here," he said.

She drove the heel of her hand into the water, so that it splashed him. "No."

"This is ridiculous."

She laughed again. "You are, certainly." The water streamed down his face, and his hair was plastered to his head, his clothes stuck to him. "You look like an angry panda bear."

"I am angry. I'll beat you."

She splashed him again. "You can't catch me."

He plunged after her, clawing at the water with his hands, and she backed away. She made for the other bank and he plowed after her. She scraped up another handful of mud, feinted to throw it at him, and when he ducked hurled it at the dun horse.

Psin howled. The horse reared up, whirled, and galloped off, crashing through the brush. They heard him neigh once, and after that only the diminishing thunder of his hoofs.

"Now I am angry," Psin said.

She mimed terror. He started after her, and she vaulted easily up onto the bank. He lunged. She danced back out of the way, grabbed a long branch, and poked it at him.

"Stay there until I am ready to let you out," she said.

He stood still, watching her. He chewed on his mustache. She saw him dart a glance upstream, toward the camp, from under his sodden brows. "You're making a fool of me," he said.

She nodded happily. He started up the bank, and she stabbed at his face with the branch until he backed off again.

"Chan. Let me up."

"What will you give me?"

"I'll break my hand over your backside."

"I want two cream-colored ponies and a cart with gold trim."

"No," he roared. "I'm your husband. Let me up."

"And I want a big dog. Black as jet, with a white face."

He charged up the bank. She clubbed him with the branch; his arms fended it off. When she hit him over the head the branch broke. She whirled and ran. The brush blocked her way, and he was right behind. She swerved, ducked behind a fat tree, and looked for a trail. Just two strides away was a little clearing. She leapt for it, but he caught her ankle and she fell, hard.

When her eyes had cleared he was lying on top of her, pinning her down. "Hah," he said in her ear.

She twitched, experimenting, but she was flat on her face and couldn't move. Her nose pressed into the soft earth. She said, "I am tired. Take me home."

"Beg." He got off her, one knee across her back.

He would spank her. He had before. She screwed up her face, squeezing out two tears, and looked up over her shoulder at him. "You're hurting me."

He looked dubious, but he eased his weight off the knee in her back. She squirmed around, sat up, and put her arms around his neck. "Please take me home, husband." She burrowed her face into his neck.

His arms tightened around her, and he laid his cheek against her hair. "You're silly."

She leapt up and dove for the brush, but he had her by the wrist. "Oh, no." He dropped her flat on her back. His weight descended on her. "Not yet."

Through the branches over their heads the sun's rays shot like staircases. He pulled at the laces of her shirt.

"I worked hard enough," he said. "Don't I deserve a reward?"

THEY REACHED THE VOLGA CAMP FIVE DAYS AFTER DJELA. TSHANT had gotten a house for them, next to his and Mongke's, and across from the wall around Batu's palace. Tshant deposited himself in a chair in the garden and watched while the slaves carted goods and furniture through to the rooms. Djela was with him, full of stories about his ride from the camp to the city.

"The Russian princes have been coming in since the thaw," Tshant said. "They're making their submission. Batu is enjoying himself tremendously. What's that?"

Psin looked; four slaves were lugging a closed chest through the gate. Artai walked briskly beside them, directing them.

"Gold, probably. It's heavy enough."

Tshant stretched out his legs. "Your pet is not fit for human company."

"Who?"

"Quyuk."

"God. He's not my—"

"He's roaring drunk all the time, and he does nothing but shout about what he will do when he's Kha-Khan. Mostly kill us all off. Incidentally, messages have come. Kerulu says Ogodai is much better. He wrote to Quyuk and I guess they're nearly reconciled."

Chan with two of her women came out into the garden; three cats trailed them. Chan sat down, her back to Psin. Tshant was watching her. "Buri is supporting Quyuk against all comers. There are plenty of comers, too."

"Who?"

"Kadan. When he's sober, which is rare. Baidar. Is he older than I am? He acts it. Kaidu—he's gotten ambitious, Kaidu. He talks about his grandfather's chances of being elected Kha-Khan." He lifted his voice. "Good day, stepmother."

Chan ignored him. Tshant snorted. "Anyway, everyone's been saying that Quyuk will have to shout a little softer when you get here."

"I'll see what I can do." Psin tried to catch Chan's eye, but she was resolutely staring off. She called to Ana and sent her after something, which was what Psin had wanted her to do in the first place. When Ana was gone, he said, "You know that Ana's pregnant."

Tshant frowned. "I didn't. Is it yours or mine?"

"It's yours. I've never touched her."

"I suppose not. You'll have to give her back to me, then."

"I will."

"She gets along very well with Djela. Doesn't she?" He reached out and ruffled Djela's hair.

"Yes." Djela's head bobbed. "I like her."

"It could make trouble." Tshant looked back at Psin. "Your face has healed."

"I'll have a nice set of scars, though."

Tshant looked at Psin's right hand. Across the knuckles scar tissue grew like a shield, slick and paler than the other skin. He had almost told Psin that he was relieved that he was in the Volga camp. That surprised him. He'd been drinking all day, but he hadn't realized he was drunk.

Ana said, "They were sitting very amicably in the garden, the last time I saw them."

"It goes like that," Artai said. She passed the knife swiftly around the edges of the pattern and laid it aside. "They don't fight all the time, they have to work themselves up to it."

"Have they always fought?"

"Ever since Tshant was old enough to talk." Artai sank back on her heels. "He was such a little boy—I was afraid he'd die before he grew up. And full of mischief. The other two boys were much older than he—Tulugai and Kinsit."

"I didn't know you had other children."

"Tulugai and Kinsit are dead. My daughters are all married."

Ana picked up the felt to cover her surprise. Psin had once mentioned his other sons—somehow she hadn't connected them with Artai.

Artai said, "Tshant would break something, or get in someone's way, and Psin would roar at him. You know how loud his voice is when he's angry."

"Yes." She remembered him shouting, when he was sick in Susdal.

"Tshant always roared back. The other two . . . never did. I thought when they died that Psin would die. He and Tulugai were . . . He and Tshant have always fought."

She was staring off, and her mouth twisted unhappily. Ana said, "I'm sorry. I shouldn't have made you remember."

"I remember every day." Artai smiled and patted her hand swiftly. "Don't be sorry."

She got up stiffly, and Ana gathered the cut-out felt. Artai said cheerfully, "So you finally thought to come see me."

Ana turned; it was Tshant. He hugged Artai, but his eyes were on Ana. He said, "Mother, will you keep watch on Djela while I talk to Ana?"

"Of course," Artai said, surprised. She turned and beckoned to Ana.

I don't want to go, Ana thought. The big room, full of other women, seemed a haven against Tshant. But she went over toward him, and he said, "Come along. I want to talk to you."

"What—"

He took her by the arm and steered her out the door and across the corridor into the room opposite. There was no one else there. He let her go, and she went immediately to the couch at the far end of the room, wheeled, and said, "What do you want? I haven't done anything wrong."

"I know. Don't fidget." He shut the door. "My father says that you're pregnant."

For a blind moment she thought he meant to kill her, to hide it. "Please, don't—"

"What's wrong? Are you afraid of me? I'm not going to hurt you. Sit down. Are you going to have my child?"

"Yes." She sat down, short of breath.

He came farther into the room. "I can't take another wife. Kerulu is a granddaughter of the Ancestor and reasonably proud. I'll give you your own yurt and slaves, and you'll have the same rank as my brother's second wife."

"You don't have a brother," she said.

He stopped in the middle of a stride and turned to face her. "What?"

"Your mother says—"

"Oh. I mean my half-brother. Chan's son."

She gulped. Suddenly it occurred to her that he was offering to take care of her and the baby. That surprised her as much as his summoning her. She looked at the carpet in front of her, confused.

"The baby will have the same rank and privileges as Djela. If I am the Khan when my father dies, which is likely, your son will come first after my sons by Kerulu. You are entitled to a fifth of my plunder in a war and a third of my herds and the spoils of my hunting. There's a lot else, too, but that's the most important."

All through his speech she had been concentrating on the idea of Chan's having a son old enough to be twice married. She looked up.

"It's very generous."

He shrugged. "It's in the Yasa. Do you want to come to my house tonight or tomorrow?"

"I want to stay here."

He said nothing. He was in front of her, and she lifted her face toward him.

"I'm not ungrateful," she said. "You're being kind. But I like it here."

He sat down on his heels. "There's no place for you here."

"I can help. I—"

"What is my father going to do with a woman who can't be a slave and who isn't his wife, and who will have a child not his—You are under my protection. You can't stay here."

"Isn't there any—" She stood up. "I'll stay a slave. I don't—"

"You can't. It's against the Yasa." He rubbed his face. "Every person has a place. Your place is in my camp."

"But—"

She stopped. He was shaking his head, slowly, and he looked angry. He said, "Women. I will leave you here until the child is ready to be born. You have to have it under my roof. It's the law. Do you love my father?"

"No." She laughed, uneasily. "No."

"Tell him to tell Chan that the child is mine, or Chan will make you miserable."

"She's very nice. She—"

"She's jealous. And whose could it be but his?"

He got up and prowled around the room. "Chan is . . . different than most women. Don't think she's just what she acts like."

"Oh," Ana said. "I've discovered that. She and the Khan were by
the river one day, and they came back soaking wet and muddy and
laughing like children."

"Hunh." He wheeled back. "Do you understand? About why
you must come with me."

"Yes." She would ask Artai.

He sat down next to her, and she shrank away. He picked up one
of her hands and closed his fingers over hers. "You're acting like a
little girl. I won't hurt you. I won't sleep with you unless you want
me to." He put her hand in her lap and stood up. "Don't be afraid
of me. I don't like that." He left the room.

She sighed. Once she'd gotten over being surprised, she decided,
she hadn't been afraid of him. But she didn't want to go live with
him. There had to be a way to avoid it. She would ask Artai. Rising,
she crossed the room to the door and went out into the corridor.

Psin put his feet up on the table. "Kadan, you stink."

Kadan howled, tiptoed like a girl, and plunked into a chair. "Psin
Khan, it's the very b-best perfume—my Russian woman wears it
and I go mad."

The Altun rocked with laughter. Buri picked up a pear and
hurled it at Kadan, who ducked. The pear splashed on the far wall.

"Stop wrecking my room," Batu called. "And quiet down. How
can we play—"

Buri gathered up two more pears and hurled them at Tshant and
Batu, crouched over the chess board. Tshant threw up one hand
and knocked one pear off course. "Check."

Mongke walked past Psin, paused long enough to say, "Look at
Quyuk," and moved on. Psin looked over at Quyuk, who was
sprawled on a couch. Across Quyuk's slack face the expressions
marched: surprise, momentary fright, and intense pleasure. His
eyes were unfocused. Psin put his feet down and stood up.

"Don't go near him," Baidar said. "It's the hashish."

"He's fun to watch," Mongke said. "And it keeps him quiet."

Kadan shouted, "That is our next Kha-Khan."

Quyuk looked over, smiled beatifically, and spoke a long sentence of gibberish. He lay back.

"If Sabotai were here," Mongke said, "things would be much less merry."

"You are so right," Kadan shouted. He blinked. Mongke winced away from his voice; Kadan was right beside him.

"You needn't yell. I can hear—"

"I'm not yelling," Kadan yelled. He reached for his cup.

Psin put his feet up again. He thought of Temujin, of Temujin's harsh law against drink. But even Temujin hadn't considered hashish. Slaves trotted in with huge platters of meat, and the Altun attacked them before they could set the food on the table. Psin dove into the tangle and emerged with a roast pigeon. He retreated to one end of the table, near Tshant and Batu, and with his dagger cut up the bird. Tshant said, "And check."

"Hmmmm," Batu said.

Psin glanced over at them. Tshant hadn't told him what had come of the talk with Ana, but Artai said that Ana didn't want to move into Tshant's house.

Kadan was shouting at Mongke. Mongke sat back and listened, half-smiling, as if Kadan were making sense. His eyes danced with amusement. Psin looked over at Quyuk again, and saw that he was still in the hashish fog. His lips moved soundlessly. Psin got up and went around the table to Mongke.

"If you'd moved the horse here," Batu was saying comfortably, "I'd have had a great deal more trouble—"

"Oh, shut up," Tshant said.

Psin knelt by Mongke's chair. "What's he like when he recovers?"

"Who? Oh." Mongke glanced at Quyuk. Kadan went on shouting, his eyes shut. Mongke said, "He'll be groggy and bad-tempered and nervous. He's no trouble."

"Then I'll leave."

"If anything happens I'll send for you."

Psin nodded and got up. A platter of meat had spilled and the floor was covered with juice and bits of roast animal. He stepped on a chicken wing, slipped, caught himself, and went out the door. In the corridor the noise from the room was only a muted rumble.

Sentries jerked up their lances in salute when he passed, and two of them pulled the front door open for him. He stepped into the cool night air, breathed deep, and started off toward his own house.

In the middle of the night Chan woke up from a bad dream and lay, soaked in sweat, and cried. When she couldn't cry any more, she curled up with her face buried in the covers, afraid to go back to sleep. Two of her cats slept in the hollow behind her knees. The other usually slept on the windowsill, but now it leapt down, walked across the floor, and jumped up beside her to lick her face. She stroked it, and the cat arched its back, purring.

She couldn't remember the dream. She thought it had been of monsters. She pulled the cat under the covers and the cat immediately struggled out again.

Across the house, Psin slept with his arms around Artai, his face against her skin. Chan felt the tears harsh in her eyes. Artai was old and ugly, but Psin still went to her, once out of every two nights.

When I am old, she thought, he will not come to me.

She wondered if that were really so. He was fond of her, she was sure of that. But he did not love her the way he loved Artai.

The cat walked up and down her back, purring, and eventually curled up against her and went to sleep. Through the window the moonlight tumbled onto the rug, onto the couch; the bright colors of the daylight vanished into blue-silver and black. She threw the covers off and got up.

It was cold. She pulled her cloak over her shoulders, shivering, her hands frozen. The cats were lumps on the rumpled covers. She went into the antechamber, moved softly past the three women sleeping there, and slid between the lattice screen and the wall, through the door.

The corridor was empty. She ran down it, her bare feet soundless on the timber floor. Through one window she saw the garden under the moonlight, like a blasted city—the stone benches, the stark black shrubs. Ash heaps. Somebody was coming. She pulled the cloak tight around her and waited.

It was a sentry; he stopped and said, "Who is it?"

"Chan Khatun. Let me pass."

He pressed himself against the wall so that she could get past him without touching him. She caught a glimpse of his face, young, the eyes round with awe. She walked away with all the dignity she owned, turned the corner, and ran. The door to the garden was bolted. She swore at it, using a curse Psin sometimes used, and climbed out the window.

Artai's window was straight across from this one. She went along the edge of the garden, avoiding the places where the brick in the walk was loose. Her feet were cold. At Artai's window she stepped in among the tended plants and rapped lightly on the shutter.

Silence. She shivered. Something moved in there, and she tensed to run away. She shouldn't be here and he would beat her, probably. Most likely. The shutter opened swiftly inward, and Psin with a dagger in his hand looked out.

He stared at her, and she stared at him, until she wondered if he thought he was dreaming. Finally he put one finger to his lips, nodded at the couch, and climbed out the window, naked.

"What's the matter?" he whispered.

"I had a bad dream."

"Oh." He looked around. "Well, wait here."

He climbed back into Artai's room. She heard Artai say something in a sleepy, comfortable voice, and he said, "I'm just going outside. I'll be right back." Artai mumbled and rolled over. Psin crawled out the window, his coat loosely wrapped around him. He took Chan by the hand and led her toward the far door.

"Are you angry?" she said.

"Livid."

He stopped in front of the door, tried the latch, and swore. He used exactly the same words she had, and she laughed.

"What's funny?"

"You."

He snorted, climbed through the window, and unbolted the door from the inside. The noise apparently woke a sentry, who called out, and Psin said something to him. He opened the door and Chan went in, walking very straight.

"What was the dream about?"

"You."

He said nothing. She tried to think of something to say if he

asked why she had come running to him when she'd had a night-
mare about him, but he never asked. They passed the same sentry,
who flattened himself against the wall once more, and all three of
her women woke up when they entered her antechamber.

Psin ignored them. He pushed Chan into her room, scooped her
up, dumped her on the bed, and said, "Stay here." He turned on his
heel and walked out. Chan pulled the covers over her, glared at the
door, and shut her eyes, furious.

The noyon of Novgorod said, "I have come to ask the terms of
our submission."

Psin glanced up at him and went back to eating the orange. Batu
on the table behind him said in his formal voice, "The terms are
those we offered your uncle, the Grand Duke Yuri. One quarter of
your goods now, one tenth of your young men to train for our
army. A yearly tithe thereafter in the name of the Kha-Khan."

The prince looked tired. His eyes never left Batu's face, and his
voice was almost bored. "These terms are unacceptable to us."

Psin looked down the table. Kadan was not there, being too
drunk to look pretty before Russians; Mongke and Baidar and Buri
sat ignoring the noyon. On the dais, at Batu's table, Quyuk
slouched with his head on the back of his chair. Batu said calmly, "I
think you'll find them acceptable enough."

"We are of Novgorod the Unconquered," the noyon said.

"Would you care to test it? Did we destroy all that lay between
the inland seas and your little lake to bend before your pride? We
offer you much, boy."

Psin looked quickly at the noyon, but he didn't react at all to the
insult. The men behind him in their ceremonial robes frowned a
little. The noyon said, "You offer us only slavery."

"If such is slavery," Batu said, "then we all are slaves. The Kha-
Khan's will is the will of God. Defy us, and you defy God. Submit,
and we throw the shield of our protection over you. In our peace
you will prosper without such distractions as foreign or domestic
war."

Tshant came in behind the Russian delegation, circled them and bent to talk to Psin, one hand on the back of Psin's chair. "Messages from Sabotai."

Psin nodded. He turned to catch Batu's eye; Batu was saying, "The alternative is, of course, the same your uncle chose, noyon. We looked among the dead beside the Sit' River, but we couldn't find his body to send it to you for proper burial."

He glanced at Psin and nodded, and Psin rose. Following Tshant to the door, he heard Batu's deep voice rolling on, describing in detail how Novgorod would benefit from the protection of the Mongols.

Tshant said, "Was that Yuri's nephew?"

"Yes. Alexander Something-or-other-evitch."

"He's not like these Southern Russians."

Psin smiled faintly. They went down the corridor to a small room where the messenger waited, and while Tshant took the rolls of messages and dismissed the courier Psin brought in a chair from the next room and sat down. Tshant was reading quickly through the first roll.

"He'll be here before sundown. He wants to talk to you about the new campaign. Before he sees Batu. Reconnaissance, envoys, the usual. He asks is Rijart here." He looked over, his brows arched.

"One of the Kha-Khan's Europeans. We sent for him in the spring."

"He says he has trained Kipchaks until he's sick for the sight of a Mongol face. The horses have come in from the south. He wants to attack Kiev this coming fall."

"That I know." Psin rose. "Go back and take my place at the audience. Quyuk looks in a bad temper."

"What am I to do with him?"

"Nothing."

"When are you going to talk to Ana?"

"I'll go now. She'll understand. You didn't explain it right, that's all."

"I hope so. She's big as a mare already."

"She'll be in your house tomorrow. What are you going to do about Kerulu?"

"I'll handle my own household. You were leaving?"

Psin laughed and went out.

*   *   *

In her antechamber, in the midst of her women, Artai was making felt. She beamed at Psin when he looked through the door. The women rose and moved discreetly off into the next room, and Psin shut the door after them.

"Ana told Tshant she won't go with him," he said. He sat down on the floor, just behind Artai's shoulder, so that he could see her quick hands kneading.

"She told me. She wants to stay here."

"Do you think . . ."

"You take too much trouble over slaves."

"She's not a slave."

"Let them alone. Let her come to it herself." She measured out size and mixed it into the hair. "Are you fighting again next winter?"

"Yes."

"Take me with you."

"No."

"You have women in the baggage trains. Take me."

"We have slaves with the baggage. It's too dangerous."

"Dangerous?" She turned her head toward him. "When we were first married, the Yek Mongols were hunting Merkits like birds from tree to tree. Whenever we made a camp your father had us tethering the horses to our wrists while we slept."

Psin frowned. "My father was overexcited."

"Ah? There used to be fifty clans of the Merkits. How many are there now?"

"We are Mongols now."

"Two." She thrust the felt away from her. "Your beloved Temujin. I want to go with you. How can it be so dangerous?"

"Do you think I would take my women in a baggage train?"

"Better than languishing here, like—"

"No. If I took you I would have to take Chan."

"She would go."

"She's too fragile."

"She's as fragile as a yak. Didn't she keep you pinned down in a river for—"

He felt the heat rising across his face, and Artai grinned. "Oh, yes. We heard about that. The Khan's favorite bit of thigh—"

"Did she tell you?"

"No."

"I'll beat her."

"No, don't. She didn't mean to. I just asked how you'd gotten so wet."

"She could have lied."

"Don't hurt her. You'll be sorry if you do."

"You sound like Djela." He got up and went out of the room.

He sent a slave to bring Ana into the small room opposite Chan's; if he left the door open he would see her when she came in from the market. His blood ached in his ears. He could picture Chan telling Artai the story, laughing, adding small touches out of her imagination, and the serving women giggling in the background. In his rage he hardly noticed Ana come in.

She said, "Khan."

He swung around. "Oh. My son told me that you refuse to go to his house."

"I want to stay here."

"You can't." He sat down on a chest. "There is no place for you here."

She was twisting her hands together. "Please let me stay."

"Every day you stay here is a mark against me and Tshant. Pack up your clothes. You'll move there before sundown."

She flinched as if he had struck her. He stood up again and went over to her. He tried to make his voice gentle. "You're a Mongol now. You have to do things the way Mongols do them."

Her face was turned up toward his. He hadn't noticed how she had filled out—her cheeks were rounder, her eyes brighter. She said, "I'm not a Mongol. I'm a Russian."

"Not any more. Don't make me lose my temper. I'm angry with Chan and I'm in a bad mood. Go pack. You'll be happier with Tshant." He put his hand against her cheek. "That's my grandchild you carry. Be careful."

She put her hand over his. "I will."

"Good." He turned and walked toward the window, his hands behind his back.

"Do you . . . do you remember when I said Mongols were ugly?"

"Very well."

"You aren't," she said, softly. When he turned to look she was gone. He sat down again, watching the door, willing Chan to come back.

A horse clattered into the garden. He leapt up and threw the window open. It was Quyuk. He dismounted, let his reins trail, and stamped toward the main door into the house. Psin leaned out the window.

"Quyuk."

Quyuk spun. He stared at Psin, jerked his eyes around toward the gate into the garden, and strode over to the door next to Psin's window. The front of his blue tunic was wet. He let himself in and slammed the door behind him.

A slave caught Quyuk's horse; Psin turned away from the window, leaving the shutter open. Quyuk came into the room, took two steps forward, and said, "Batu is an old woman and I'll see him bastinadoed."

"Really? What is it now?"

Quyuk pitched himself into a chair, crossed his legs, uncrossed them, and leapt up again. "He drank before me. He's been careful before this. We've always drunk together. But he drank the first cup. Before me. I am the son of the Kha-Khan—what is he but the son of a bastard?"

"The eldest of the Altun," Psin said.

"Depending on whether you believe Juji was Temujin's son."

"Don't be a fool."

"My honor is in this." Quyuk walked swiftly around the room, his hands tugging aimlessly at his belt. "You see?"

Psin nodded.

Quyuk reached out for the shutter and drew it closed. "Before the rest of the Altun and the Russians from Novgorod. I won't let him get away with it. Before—"

He sat down again. "Before you came I could have overthrown him there. In his own palace. They would have supported me. Baidar and Mongke. They were afraid of me before you came. It's your fault I had to run."

"Buri didn't—"

"Buri. What is he but a loudmouth?"

Psin sat down on the chest, his hands between his knees. Quyuk's face was working.

"They all stand in my way. My father puts up Siremon like a wooden doll and won't give me my due. They block me, everywhere I go they are blocking me. Psin, I am the Successor. Not Siremon. No one but me has the right to be my father's heir."

Psin said nothing.

"Whether I am good or bad does not matter. Only the blood matters."

"And the will of Heaven."

"Psin, I am the Successor."

Quyuk's eyes blazed, and under the steady strong glare Psin grew uncomfortable. The eyes were Temujin's eyes. He turned his face away.

"Let me stay here," Quyuk said. "Batu will throw me into prison if he can get hold of me. You owe me this, Psin."

"I do not."

Quyuk's eyes half-closed. Before he could speak, other horses galloped into the garden. Psin went quickly out of the room and through the door just beyond it. Mongke and Tshant were there, sliding down from their saddles, and behind them, just outside the gate, rode Batu's personal guards.

Tshant said, "Has Quyuk come here?"

"He has."

"Did he tell you—"

"He told me. He stays here, under my protection."

Tshant came three steps forward. "He cursed Batu to his face. In his own ulus Batu is supreme, and Batu has ordered him taken."

"I will not permit it."

Mongke called, "Buri is in Baidar's custody. Let Batu say that Quyuk is in yours."

"Quyuk comes and goes as he pleases," Psin said. "He is a guest under my roof and he has my word for his safety, but he is not my prisoner and never will be."

Tshant came up beside him. His eyes darted toward the house. Swiftly, he said, "Batu has sent a messenger to Karakorum. Let me tell him that you hold Quyuk for him. Quyuk doesn't have to know. Batu forgets easily—it will all be mended before the autumn."

"Tell him Quyuk is my guest." Psin backed up a little. "Tell him what I told you."

Tshant frowned. "What do you think you're doing?"

"Who are you to question me? Go on."

Mongke shouted something, and Tshant turned and jogged back to his horse. The guards in a mob backed away from the gate. Tshant and Mongke rode through. Psin heard a high, questioning call, and the horses galloped off.

Quyuk was in the room where Psin had left him; the window was open. He said, "I will cause you no trouble."

"That's very kind of you. Stay away from my women and don't mistreat my slaves, and you'll keep my good will."

Quyuk nodded. "You'll enjoy this, I'm sure."

"I'll try," Psin said.

Chan came back, and he tried to work up his anger at her, but he could not. She stood in the midst of her purchases and listened to him yell and smiled and without a word went into her room. The night before he had spent with Artai, so he consoled himself he would take some revenge on Chan when they went to bed.

But Sabotai arrived shortly before the sun went down, right after he had taken Ana to Tshant's house, and they spent the evening arguing about Quyuk and the night talking over Kiev. When Psin finally went to bed the light spilled blue over the windowsill and he was too tired to do anything but lie next to Chan and wish that sleep were not so long in coming.

"My father is ruining us all," Tshant said.

"What has he done now?" Ana poured wine for him, and he took it, absently.

"You know that he has Quyuk under his roof. Batu is furious. He says that Psin of all men should know Quyuk is treacherous."

"Is he?"

"Quyuk? No, of course not. Batu doesn't care what he calls his enemies, so long as it's bad. But we're fighting again soon, and Batu could decide to interfere with everything my father says or does."

"Fighting? Am I going with you?"

"No. You'll stay here. God. I hope—"

He broke off and stared, and she waited for him to go on. He was sprawled across the couch; lying down he looked as long as a whip.

"What?"

"Nothing. Go on, go do something."

She got up and left the room. In this strange house she found herself by habit turning left to go to her room—she had turned left in Psin's house—but the room was to the right. She passed Qo'a on the stairs, Tshant's Alan girl, and Qo'a sent her for some oil. She knew she shouldn't go after it; Qo'a was only a slave. But it was easier to obey, more familiar, and she was almost glad to do it.

Chan settled down in the shade and took out her box of paints. Psin's garden made a little leg off to the south in one corner, full of trees, and in the heat of the noon it was a good place to sketch. She rolled out paper and poked through her box after a brush. The heat shimmered in the full sunlight in the middle of the garden, but here it was almost cool. She sketched a clump of trees in the middle distance of her paper.

She shouldn't have told Artai about the incident beside the river. He was still angry over that. But Artai had been upset because Chan's orange cat had eaten up the stew meat, and Chan had had to appease her in some way. She didn't like Psin to be angry with her.

The gold lace on her collar itched, and she undid the hooks down the front so that she could pull the robe off her shoulders. She looked down at herself. The upper halves of her breasts showed over the taut line of the displaced robe. She looked out toward the center of the garden, but there was no one there, and the low shrubs shielded her from a casual glance. She dipped her brush in ink and carefully drew Psin's face on the smooth curve of her left breast. The brush's soft touch made her hot. She drew long mustaches, like Psin's, down toward her nipple.

Somebody moved behind her. She looked back and saw Quyuk, leaning against a tree, watching her. His eyes were slitted; the curve of his mouth trembled.

She clenched her teeth. He was in her part of the garden. He was in her favorite place. She stared back at him. "Go away."

He moved his feet, but he stayed leaning up against the tree. She shrugged her robe back up. "Go away. This is my place."

He said nothing, and she threw the paintbox at him. Ink splashed across his face, but he did not move. He was staring as if he could see straight through the heavy cloth of her robe.

Abruptly, he looked past her, and his face changed. She knew by the mixed guilt and fright on his face what he saw. She hooked up the front of her robe as fast as she could. Her mouth was dry. She was afraid to look up.

Psin said gently, "Get out of here, Quyuk."

She glanced toward him through the corner of her eye. He was standing right beside her. His fist opened and closed.

"I went in under the trees—when I came out she was here," Quyuk said. "I didn't mean—"

"Go wash your face."

He didn't sound angry. His fist was still opening and closing. She looked down at the ground. Her hands felt cold. Quyuk almost ran past them.

"He did nothing," she said. She licked her stiff lips.

"The way he looked at you, you might have twins."

His soft voice chilled her to the soles of her feet. He crouched and jerked her around to face him. She shut her eyes so that she wouldn't have to look at him.

"Don't come in here again. Do you hear me? Don't come here again."

"I like it here," she said. Her voice quivered, and she fought against it.

His hands on her shoulders softened. He stroked her hair, so roughly she almost cried out. "I know," he said. "I know. But he's dangerous. Obey me. Don't come here again."

He hugged her, crushing her against his chest. She put her arms around his neck. She was still frightened, and she began to cry. He gathered her up and carried her into the house.

*   *   *

"I didn't mean it," Quyuk said. "I came out of the trees and she was there."

Psin rammed the maps into his bowcase and put on the top. "How much did she have on when you saw her?"

Quyuk flushed. Psin could feel the hot bile in his throat. He said, "If you were any but the Kha-Khan's son, I would kill you for looking at her like that."

"I couldn't help it."

There were still ink stains on his face. Psin slung the bowcase over his shoulder. Quyuk looked up. "I'm sorry. I . . . Let Batu take me."

"Don't whimper. We're late for the council."

He went out, and Quyuk trailed behind him. In the twilight, their horses stood waiting. Psin said, "If you couldn't help it, perhaps Batu should."

"I know. That's what I mean. Being the Kha-Khan's son is bad training, in ways."

"Ask Kadan. He'll tell you how bad." Psin mounted. "I know it was a shattering experience, being put off by a woman, but you're not taking it well at all. If I were a gambler I'd bet you four good horses that the next time you see her you'll look at her just the way you did today. Get on that horse. We're late."

When they came to the door into Batu's council hall, Kaidu was there; he took a long look at Quyuk and said, "This is an insult."

Psin threw out one arm to keep Quyuk back. "Let us by."

"No. This man abused my grandfather to his face."

"This is a war kuriltai, not a camp." Psin took Kaidu by the arm and threw him against the wall. Kaidu rebounded, sputtering, and ran shoulder first into Psin; Psin did not move, but Kaidu bounced off and tripped and fell. Psin shoved Quyuk through the door into the hall and followed him before Kaidu was back on his feet.

The hall was dead quiet. All along the table, the Altun sat in their gold and silver splendor, staring at Quyuk. Batu's brothers, down for the kuriltai from their posts in the north, got to their feet in unison. Quyuk walked steadily to a chair at the foot of the table and sat down.

"You dare—" Batu said.

Psin dragged over a chair, stood it behind Quyuk's, and sat down. The veins in Batu's neck swelled into ropes. Mongke, Tshant, Baidar and Kadan were looking anywhere but at Psin and Quyuk.

"Stop fighting," Sabotai said. "We have much to do. Buri, sit down."

Buri, halfway to Quyuk, turned and went back to his chair. Sabotai stood beside Batu, and Batu seemed to relax. Mongke leaned forward to get his winecup and grinned down at Psin. Kaidu had come in. The silence droned on, until Batu cleared his throat and said, "We are here to talk of the plans for the next season's war."

Psin exhaled and put his hand to his face to shield his relief. Before him, Quyuk's shoulders twitched.

"We are to take Kiev and gain control of the grasslands west of the Dnepr," Batu said. "This should require no more than a few months. Already all the princes of the Slavs east of the Dnepr have sworn allegiance to the Kha-Khan, and they are sending us men. The Kipchaks have been trained. Two clans of the Kipchaks fled across the Dnepr and have taken refuge in Hungary."

"Enough of that," Sabotai said. "The problem is Kiev, not the lands west of it." He sat down again. "The land we will fight on is mostly steppe. North of Kiev is a great series of marshes. At Kiev another river joins the Dnepr, and up river from the juncture, on the tributary, in marsh, is a city called Chernigov, which we shall take. Downriver from Kiev is Pereislav, which we shall also take."

He looked at Psin and nodded. Psin rose.

"In those cities the people don't want to fight us. I talked three days ago with a man from Pereislav who told me if we attack them before the autumn the people will probably open the gates as soon as we appear. Chernigov he said is the same. The cities are like the ones we burnt last winter. They will have to be destroyed."

He pulled his chair a little forward and sat again. "They have few knights. In the fall last year, when Tshant raided there, a large number of knights ambushed him, but these seem to have come from Kiev. Kiev will not surrender to us; we sent an envoy and he hasn't returned yet. They've probably killed him and his escort. We can siege Kiev until the Gobi turns to ocean."

"We won't have to," Sabotai said. "I believe we can storm it."

"The steppe west of the Dnepr is rich, and Kiev will be full of plunder. The city is part of the trade route from the south. When we have cut her off from the south we should have no trouble with her, as Sabotai says. But we must cut her off. The army that takes Pereislav will continue on west into the farm country beyond the river, as far as the next major river, the Dniester, and hold the line against that river until the main army catches up."

Mongke said, "How likely is it that they will have help from the west?"

"Extremely unlikely." Psin put his forearms on the table. "We are sending a small embassy to the court of the Hungarians, beyond the mountains west of the Dniester."

"They killed the last envoy we sent," Tshant said. "I hope your ambassadors are expendable."

Psin said, "We have reason to believe that they will be more friendly this year. Not enough to surrender to us, but willing to talk. The ambassador will be Rijart the White, whom some of you probably met in Karakorum. I'll ride in his escort."

Tshant slouched back and looked at Sabotai. Sabotai said, "Psin will travel under another name, as a common soldier. Due to the nature of the Hungarian steppe, we can't make the usual reconnaissance raids. It's important that we find out what we're likely to meet."

"Nonetheless," Mongke said. "Rijart they might kill, for all I care, and welcome to him. If they kill Psin, the army suffers."

Psin said, "The Hungarian King knows that we mean to attack him. He's been crying for help from all the other khans in Europe. Would he provoke us further by killing envoys? No."

"Kiev did," Tshant said.

"Certain men governing Kiev believe that they can withstand us. They killed our people in a deliberate attempt to bring us down on them, and it was against the wishes of their overlord, the khan of the Galicians. The sentiment in Hungary is much different from the sentiment in Kiev. This we are sure of."

"The point is settled," Sabotai said. "Now. The attack on

Pereislav will be under Baidar's and Mongke's command. The attack on Chernigov is Batu's. I will ride with Batu. Quyuk goes with Baidar and Mongke, and Kadan with Batu and me. Buri with Quyuk. Tshant goes with Batu, Kaidu with Baidar and Mongke. After the two cities have fallen, one half of the southern army, under Quyuk's command—"

Batu squawked. Sabotai kicked him in the shin.

"—Under Quyuk's command, will turn north and meet with Batu and me across the river from Kiev. When the ice freezes we will cross and take the city."

Baidar and Mongke leaned back; Mongke's eyes flew from face to face. Buri leaned forward and whispered something to Quyuk, and Quyuk shook his head. Baidar rose.

"In the southern army. Do Mongke and I take our own tumans, and Quyuk his?"

"Yes."

"Then how can Quyuk not share in the command?"

Sabotai grunted. He poured kumiss into a bowl, took a little jar from his coat, unstopped it, and let honey drip into the kumiss. Half the table yowled. Sabotai mixed the honey in with his little finger and said, "You and Mongke are the commanders, named in this kuriltai. Quyuk is subordinate to you. Is that clear?"

Baidar swung toward Quyuk. "Is that clear?"

"Cousin," Quyuk said. "It's murky only to you."

Psin could tell by the tone of his voice that he had recovered from the experience in the garden. Baidar sat down. "Mongke and I stay with the southern wing, then, after Quyuk leaves."

"Unless something develops. Batu's brothers will of course be with him."

Batu's brothers scowled, all together.

Kaidu said, "Quyuk is under disfavor."

Somebody laughed at the wording, and Kaidu bristled; Sabotai said, "This is an army, not a khanate."

Psin said, "The army camped along the Dniester will scout the land between the river and the western mountains. When I come back from Hungary I'll meet the army there."

"If you come back," Tshant said.

Psin glared at him. Mongke said, "Ah, we'll welcome you, Psin, like the cream on the fresh milk."

Psin made a face. Mongke put his hands behind his head and grinned. Tshant called in a slave with wine and began talking about the defenses of Pereislav, and from the high end of the table Sabotai looked down at Psin, nodded, and sat quietly to listen.

R IJART WAS TALLER EVEN THAN TSHANT, YELLOW-HAIRED, WITH quick pale eyes and a smooth smile. Psin, who did not like him, had known him in Karakorum; Rijart had taught him Latin once.

Now Rijart said, "Do you remember the Latin? It might be of some use, on the embassy."

"You'll have to refresh my memory."

"The Khan wishes." Rijart smiled. They were hardly out of the Volga camp. The tracks of the latest caravan headed west printed the road before them. Two Nestorians had come with the caravan from Karakorum and were taking messages on to the princes and priests of Rome from the Kha-Khan and Batu. Psin had talked with the Nestorians all the night before, but they knew little more of Rome than he did. They thought it was a city, but also that all the people in Europe called themselves Romans as well as Christians, and therefore it could as well be a nation.

Rijart recited words, and Psin repeated them. Kaidu listened, grinning. He would ride with them as far as the Dniester, commanding their escort, which they would pick up at Sabotai's camp north of the Caspian Sea. After the embassy had crossed the Dniester Kaidu would scout the country back toward Pereislav and meet Mongke and Baidar there to start sieging the city. Psin glared at him to keep him quiet and repeated what Rijart had said.

The steppe was thriving with the summer. In the tough, grey-green grass small blue flowers bloomed, and shrubs sprouted, reddish-leaved, in the hollows around the springs. By noon they had shot enough grouse to make a good dinner. Once, in the afternoon, a courier raced by, the bells jingling on his bridle, and they pulled off to let him pass without hindrance. The wind swept away the dust of the horse's churning gallop. Only a little way on, they reached the new waystation, where the courier had changed horses; it looked like every waystation between here and the China Sea, except that Russians manned it.

"We've already made our mark on the land," Rijart said.

Psin grunted. He resented Rijart's acting as if he were a Mongol. They watered their horses, changed their saddles to their led remounts, and rode on. Rijart was a patient teacher and by nightfall

Psin remembered enough Latin to ask questions.

They spent the night in a hollow of ground beside a spring. When the sun went down, the grass bending in the wind turned red and gold; it reminded Psin of the Gobi in the late summer when the tamarisk bloomed. Except that the low mountains of the Gobi would have looked wrong on this undulating plain.

"Rijart, what is Rome?"

"Rome is a city," Rijart said, and ran through the forms of the Latin for city. "The Pope reigns in Rome—"

"The Pope."

"The chief priest." Rijart turned the spit; fat exploded in the fire.

"Who are the other princes?" He knew all the Latin but the word for other, and Rijart told him.

"There is the Emperor, who rules Germany, which lies west of Hungary. He is also the King of Sicily. That's the southern half of Italy. Rome is in Italy, about in the middle."

He said it all in Latin, gesturing, and Psin nodded that he understood.

"Each nation has its own king," Rijart said. "There are many nations."

"They fight all the time."

"I don't know. I've been away too long to know."

"Where were you born?"

He used the Mongol word for "born," with a Latin ending; Rijart told him the Latin and said, "In England. I was born in England. That's an island that lies off the far western coast of Europe."

"Enough. I can't remember all the words yet." Psin took the meat off the spit. "How did you come to Karakorum?"

"With a caravan."

"Why didn't you go back?"

Rijart smiled. "I am an outlaw in the Empire."

"But you are an Englander."

"Englishman. Yes. But I'd have to pass through the Empire, and they watch for me."

"Who is the Emperor now, do you know?"

"Frederick Hohenstaufen. He's an odd man. You'd probably like him. He speaks Arabic, so you could talk to him. They say he's irreligious."

"Is he a Muslim?"

"No, he's a Christian, or supposed to be. But he's too learned to be a God-fearing man. They say he's called Christ a fraud."

Psin pulled the meat off the breastbone of his grouse. His mind went seeking after this Emperor. A rival Kha-Khan, maybe, like Jamuga, back when Temujin had not been called Genghis. "Have you ever seen him?"

"Never. They say he has red hair and green eyes."

"Hunh." Psin stopped chewing. "But he's round-eyed? Like you?"

"Yes."

Kaidu said, "Red-headed like the Altun?"

Rijart said softly, "Like most of the Altun."

Kaidu flushed; his hand drifted toward his dagger. Psin watched him steadily until Kaidu looked away and lay down, his face buried in his arms. The night wind sang in the grass on the top of the hill behind them.

A round-eyed Temujin. Psin took another bird from the fire and ate it thoughtfully. Too learned to be God-fearing. That was strange; most of the learned men he knew were devout. Rijart was going off from the fire, and one of the Mongol soldiers going with them to Hungary got up unobtrusively and followed. A horse wandered over to the spring and drank, swishing its tail across its hocks. Psin lay down and drew his cloak over him and slept.

The next evening they spent in the waystation at Sabotai's big camp, and just before dawn rode west with their escort of one hundred men. Kaidu was taking this command seriously and spent the morning wearing himself and his horses out herding the escort into formation. Rijart made up Latin sentences and Psin repeated them, asked questions, and wished Kaidu would send out men to hunt. But Kaidu apparently forgot about it, and they ate gruel for dinner.

"Tomorrow," Psin said, "hunt."

Kaidu nodded. He slurped up the contents of his bowl and smacked his lips. "I suppose we'll have to save the gruel for a delicacy."

"And post sentries. We're not on our own ground now."

Kaidu arranged for sentries, and the next day he sent off a party of men to hunt birds and antelope. They moved steadily over the plain, their bows loose in the cases. By noon each day the heat drove them all to strip off their coats, but the nights were clear and cold. Psin, learning Latin at the trot, thought he'd know enough to eavesdrop effectively when they reached the Hungarian capital.

The scouts reported walled houses—the estates of Russian nobles —and they circled to avoid them. Occasionally they saw horsemen far across the plain, and once a band of knights rode parallel to their track almost half a day, but could not hold the pace.

They reached the Dnepr in the morning of their seventh day riding; broad and full of silt, the river ran sluggishly between sandy banks. Kaidu wanted to send scouts to find a ford, but Psin thought they could swim the river. The horses balked at the bank, and they had to whip them down. The bank crumbled under the hoofs of Psin's horse, and with a wild neigh it slid into the water. The water sloshed up across Psin's saddle. He lashed the horse on the neck, and the horse struggled out a little into the river and stood to its belly in the slow current.

"It's not deep at all," Psin called. "Throw me my leadrope."

Several of Kaidu's men plunged their horses down the bank where Psin's horse had caved it in and made it easier. Rijart tossed Psin his remount leadrope. The dun braced its legs, flattened its ears back, and refused to jump. Rijart raised his whip.

"Jump back when you hit him."

Rijart brought the whip down across the dun's rump, and the dun kicked back. With a yell Rijart pitched out of his saddle. The dun bolted down the bank, dragging the other horses on the line with him. They splashed into the river and started across. Psin laughed at Rijart, who was scrambling into his saddle, and reined his horse after the remounts.

In the middle of the river they had to swim. Psin slid out of the saddle and held onto his horse's mane, letting it drag him through the water. All up and down the river, horses' heads split the brown water. The river smelled of dirt and fish, and Psin kept his chin high so that he wouldn't get any water in his mouth. He felt his horse's hoofs strike ground, hauled himself into the saddle, and braced against the drag of the rope when the dun charged up the far bank.

The horse beneath him shook itself so hard Psin almost fell off.

He stood in his stirrups and looked around. There was no sign of any enemy. Two of the Mongols going with him to Hungary were laughing at the third, who had gotten separated from his horse in midstream. One of the men coming after him had scooped him up across his saddle.

"Eh," Psin called, "Mago. Do you find that more comfortable than sitting up?"

Mago sputtered. His hair hung in his eyes. Psin remembered Chan and the episode beside the river and turned hastily away to organize the scattered escort.

In the following days they rode over plowed fields; they saw peasants by the drove, who fled at the sound of any horsemen. One night they chased a family out of their hut and spent the night there, eating the chickens and drinking the sour red wine, while the mother and her daughters wept and howled in the bushes just beyond the field and the father and his sons rode their plow stock for help. In case they found any, the Mongols set fire to the hut and burned the fields on their way out. Psin looked back and saw the wife and her narrow-shouldered children crouched in the yard, weeping, bright in the glow of the fire.

"We'll be back," he yelled, in Russian.

Kaidu was excited. "This is a fat land," he said. "Ripe for us. Have you seen their cattle? And the fields—a man could sit on a good-sized horse in the middle of that grain and never be seen."

"Don't underestimate them," Psin said. "People with something to defend tend to be zealous about it."

They passed a large town, and people shouted at them from the walls; they could hear the bells in the church tower ringing. The gates opened and a band of men rushed out, waved their lances, and ran back in again. Kaidu laughed.

"Someday we'll have it all," he said. "Someday when a Mongol rides through here they will rush out to bow and scrape and give him presents."

Rijart smiled.

They reached the Dniester, and Kaidu with his hundred men turned back. "We'll see you before Kiev," he called. "Don't linger in Hungary."

"Be careful. It's not so easy here as you might think."

"Pfft." Kaidu galloped off. His men strung out behind him, and he headed back east, shouting at the top of his lungs. His standard-bearer rode beside him, and the blue banner flapped wildly against the darker blue of the sky.

"He'll get in trouble," Rijart said.

"No. He's lucky, and he's more sensible than he acts. I think. Come along."

They rode upstream at full day, until they were opposite the town where they were to meet guides, and there they crossed the river. The governor of the town would not let them inside the walls. He sent the guides to them in the early morning, so that they left before the sun was up. Psin rode behind Rijart with the Mongol standard: there were no more Latin lessons. The guides spoke to Rijart in Latin, most courteously, and to each other in Russian; the dialect was hard for Psin to understand, but he followed most of it and their discussion of the Mongols amused him.

"Rough, savage, ugly," they said, on the first day.

On the second day they complained of the pace Rijart set and decided that only a dull brute of a Mongol would ride so fast by choice.

On the third day they didn't talk at all, but bit their lips, nursing their saddlesores and clinging to their reins.

Before them, the mountains rose on the horizon like clouds, but denser than cloud. One of the guides complained of sickness and they left him behind in a village where they spent the night. Under the horses' hoofs the ground began to climb. Trees grew on the rolling plain, strange to see after the treeless steppe, and the small streams they passed bounced white over the rocks, cold from the mountain snow.

They camped one night in the foothills. Psin and the three other Mongols huddled together under their light summer cloaks, their teeth clacking. The stars burnt like points of ice and the rock shoulders of the mountains heaved up against the sky around them. Psin thought of his sable cloak, stored away in a chest in his house in the Volga camp, and shivered. The man pressed against his back stirred in his sleep and whined. If he had the sable cloak, he couldn't have used it anyway; it was a sign of his rank.

When he finally slept he dreamt of Chan, like an ice carving, watching him expressionlessly, and behind her Artai looking withered and much, much older.

They climbed steadily toward a great pass. Eagles soared over the bare rock of the mountain heights. There was little grass, and the horses grazed all night long to keep fed. Goats browsed on slopes so steep Psin couldn't see how the goats kept all four legs under them. The guides began to get used to the pace and chattered on, making fun of the Mongol horses.

"Look at them. They're tiny. And you could shear them for their wool."

Psin's dun horse scrambled up a little rockslide and paced along a ledge no wider than Psin's shoulders; the guides' horses refused the tumbled slope and they had to ride around to an easier, longer trail. Rijart went with them, but the other Mongols with the led horses followed Psin. They waited, their legs thrown casually across the pommels of their saddles, for the guides and Rijart to catch up.

"What are they saying?" Mago asked Psin.

"They're disparaging our horses."

The others laughed. Psin shaded his eyes with his hand and looked up and down this slope. Just north of them the trees grew like a living fence, their branches interlaced. He could hear the wind sobbing in them; the smell of pine reminded him of Novgorod. They were still well beneath the pass. The guides reached them and they went on.

The air grew steadily colder. Psin took his kumiss jug from his saddle, drank some, and with a gesture offered it to the nearest of the guides. The guide looked at Rijart. Rijart smiled and said something, and the guide took the jug. He sipped at it cautiously, smacked his lips, and handed it around to the others.

"What is it?" he said in Latin.

"Fermented mare's milk," Rijart said.

The guides all screwed up their faces in disgust. Psin took the jug back and hung it on his saddle. One of the guides said to the others, "Do you suppose they eat horseflesh as well?"

That night, just before they camped, a knight came down the trail from the pass; they were to have an armed escort from the pass to the city of Pesth. Psin took Rijart aside while the guides were cooking their meat.

"Discourage him. Tell him we don't need an escort. Tell him they'll only slow us up."

"They are adamant," Rijart said. "They won't let us ride without a guard."

"Try, at least."

Rijart shrugged. Shivering, Psin went back to the fire and ate.

The next morning they rode into the pass, and while Rijart argued with the leader of the knights waiting to meet them, Psin looked back over their trail. The trail they had taken was steep enough to discourage anyone, but from here he could see that the guides had deliberately led them up by the roughest way. They had come from the southeast, but a trail broad and gentle as a caravan's ran due east down across the foothills. And this was not the only pass.

Rijart had lost the argument. He turned and said, "This is the Knight Denes. He asks me to introduce you to him."

"Change my name," Psin said.

Rijart nodded. He pointed to Psin and said, in Latin, "Targoutai, my standardbearer." A ghost of a smile touched his face. Psin stared blankly at the Hungarian knight; he doubted anybody so far west of the Gobi would know that Rijart had just named him after Temujin's first and greatest enemy. "Mago, Vortai, Kobul."

The knight bowed and made a short speech. The wind screamed across the barren pass beyond it, and the armored men on their great horses shifted uneasily. Their eyes poked curiously at the Mongols. When the knight was through, Rijart replied, bowing and making a lot of fancy gestures, and the knight waved them on. The guides had drawn aside and were chatting to some Hungarians on foot.

The knights on their big horses reined up on all sides of the Mongols. Psin studied them, his ears full of the groaning of their armor; if they weren't stupid, they would be formidable warriors. The Russian knights had been only imitations of these, who were better armed and better mounted. He hoped they were as stupid as the average Mongol. The chain armor looked thick enough to stop an arrow at any but close range.

Beside him rode a young man, watching Psin as curiously as Psin was watching him. His helmet clanged on his saddle's great square cantle. Abruptly, catching Psin's eye, he said, "Targoutai?"

Psin nodded, confused. Rijart turned. The young man put one hand on his own chest and said, "Gabriel." He pulled off his glove and held out his hand. Psin recoiled.

"Take him by the hand," Rijart said. "That's how they greet friends here."

"I'm not his friend." Psin rubbed his hand over his chest.

"Pretend. He'll be angry if you don't."

Psin clasped his hand around the knight's, and the knight shook his hand hard, up and down. He had strong fingers. Laughing, he said something to Rijart, and Rijart said, "He says he would like to see you fight, sometime. You have strong hands."

"He may. Don't tell him that."

Rijart said something to the young knight, who shrugged. He called out in his own language to one of his friends. They rode on through the pass, beneath the wall of a stone fort that stood at the summit, and down toward the foothills on the far side. Psin edged his horse to one side and looked between two knights. Before them the hills lay tier on tier, falling away from the pass, the gullies clogged with trees. Just at the horizon he could see the flat plain. Steppe land. He settled back into his saddle.

They reached the plain by the hardest route again, but Psin caught enough glimpses of the way the hills folded around the main trail to know where it was. Two days after they had reached the summit of the pass they rode out onto the grassland. Immediately the Mongol horses began to graze, thrusting their heads down into the high grass, and Vortai with a great show of relief leapt down from his saddle and pressed his forehead to the flat ground. Blushing, Rijart yelled at him, but Psin laughed.

The knights were careful not to let them see anything but flat pasturage. The mountains grew dim on their backtrail, and the steppe unrolled before them. The knights set the pace. Psin thought they were deliberately going slow to fool the Mongols about distances, but Rijart said that many of them were complaining about how fast they were traveling.

The second night after they left the hills, they stayed in a stone tower. Psin judged the walls to be as thick as a horse was long, and they rose smoothly to a peaked roof at least five storeys off the ground. The walls were slit with narrow windows. Around the foot of the tower was a ditch half-full of scummy water and lily pads and spanned by a little wooden bridge. The gate was doubled, the inner gate blocked by an iron grille so heavy it needed a winch to lift and lower it.

Rijart said, "All Europe is filled with these towers. Do you think Mongols could take them?"

Psin stretched out and shut his eyes. They were alone in the room, except for the other three Mongols. "Yes." He thought Rijart wasn't sure whom to be loyal to, his own people or the Kha-Khan. When they got back to the Volga camp he would have to tell Sabotai of that.

"I feel terrible," Ana said. "And I don't know why." She put her head down on her arms. Artai stroked her hair, undid the ribbons on her braids, and let them out.

"It's because of the baby. You'll be happy when the baby is born."

Ana sighed and shifted her ungainly weight. "I feel as if the whole world is falling away from under my feet. All I want to do is cry."

"Do you want to go back to your own house?"

"No." Ana looked up at her; her long face was drawn and new lines rippled her forehead. "No. I want to stay here. There's nothing in that house that's mine—only Qo'a." She burrowed her head into Artai's lap. "I want to stay here."

"We're all unhappy when the men are gone." Artai took the comb from the table and untangled Ana's hair. "They'll come back."

"It's different for you. I was happier when I was a slave. I had things to do, and friends—the Kipchak woman and I, we spent the afternoons . . . And Djela. I had someone to look after."

Her body trembled, and she began to cry. Artai pulled the robe up over Ana's shoulders and rocked her.

"He took me back because of the baby. Because of the Yasa. I'm a jug that carries something precious for him, that's all."

The door opened; Artai saw someone move in behind the lattice screen, and Chan with a cat walking beside her came into the room. Chan gave Artai an inscrutable glance and sat down on the floor beside the couch. She had her paintbox in her sleeve. Ana was trying to smother her sobs. The cat leapt up and mewling walked along the edge of the couch, its tail perfectly erect.

"Don't cry," Artai said. "When the baby comes you will have all you want."

Chan stared at her, sat so that her back was against the couch, and put the paintbox on the floor. The cat sat down on her shoulder.

Artai said, "Why are you here?"

"Because I am lonely." Chan didn't look up. She unrolled a scroll of paper and anchored it with pots and a slipper.

"Cats walk differently than horses," Artai said. "They move both legs on the same side at once."

"Sometimes," Chan said. She began to draw.

Ana snuffled. "How do horses walk?"

"Each leg separately," Artai said. "One hind foot, then the same forefoot, then the other hind foot and the other forefoot."

"Sometimes cats do that," Chan said.

Ana shoved the cat to make it walk. The cat only gave way and settled back, purring. Artai leaned forward to see what Chan was doing, and saw behind the quick brush a river with trees on the far bank.

"What is she doing?" Ana said.

"Drawing."

Ana lay still awhile, no longer crying, and finally pushed herself clumsily up on one elbow. Chan had put mountains behind the river, and between them, small horses.

"Where is that?"

"China," Artai said. She pressed Ana gently back into the covers. "You may stay here, with us, until they come home. Shall I send for your women?"

Ana shook her head. She got a cloth out of her robes to clean her face. Chan sat still, her brush poised.

"When she and the Khan were first married," Artai said, "Chan would draw pictures of Kinsai burning, just to anger him."

"He commanded me to stop," Chan said. She put the brush lightly to the paper and started a horse in the foreground. The brush slipped. Artai frowned. She had never seen Chan botch anything before. Leaning forward, she saw that Chan's eyes were shut, the lashes stuck together with tears.

The Mongols with their escort of knights reached Pesth in the midafternoon. The city streets were packed with people, who stared at them and yelled back and forth. The knights rode with their lances at salute, as if the mob would at any moment charge the Mongols. Under their helmets their cheeks glistened with sweat. The air was heavy with the odor of the crowd, of smoke and houses and the river.

All the noise made Psin's dun horse nervous, and it started to canter, as slowly as the other horses walked. Psin kept a tight hold on the reins. While the dun horse rocked along, he judged the size of the crowd. Their clothes were far richer even than the Russians'. Their houses stood well apart from one another, high strong buildings, their windows stuffed with people. All the ox-like faces and the round, glaring eyes made him uneasy.

The King met them at the gate to his palace and when he appeared the people began to yell and throw their caps into the air. Their arms waved like the stems of flowers. Beside the King stood a younger man, full-bearded. They spoke elegantly to Rijart. Psin looked around at the palace wall and the buildings beyond it. He was glad to see that it wasn't as strong as the tower on the plain.

They dismounted and went into the palace. A flock of women in brilliant colors stood on the balconies over the courtyard. The windows were wide, and the corridors flooded with sunlight. Everything glistened, clean and tended. They walked into a large room, out into another courtyard—where women clustered and giggled —and on into a hall hung with tapestries. A white stone table stood along one wall, covered with trays and bowls of food; at the north end of the hall was a dais draped in a cloth-of-gold.

The King sat on the dais, and the younger man stood behind him. The knights lined the Mongols up formally in a semi-circle facing the King, and a lot of people said things to Rijart. He bowed. A priest in black read from a book and made a sign over them. Psin didn't listen to the Latin; he was too busy judging the plunder they could have from this one place alone.

"They are rich here," Vortai said softly, beside him.

"Ssssh." Psin looked at the table again. The dishes were surely of gold. Two women were standing in an alcove at one end of the table, and seeing him looking they laughed and stared boldly back.

Rijart was introducing them. "Targoutai, my standardbearer. Vortai, of the Borgijin clan of the Mongols, and Mago and Kobol of the Darbin clan."

The young man behind the King said something in a high, cold voice. The King smiled.

"My brother Colomon says that your men should bow."

Psin shuffled his feet so that he could pretend he didn't understand. The King spoke slowly, as if he wasn't good in the language either. Rijart said, "My lord, the Mongols bow to no one but their Kha-Khan, the Lord of the Earth, the Master of Crowns and Thrones."

"Hmm." The King folded his hands over his chest. His dark eyes snapped. "Ask them what they think of my court. Ask him, the old one."

Rijart said, in Mongol, "Did you understand?"

"Yes. If I am old he is half in his grave. Tell him to a man who has seen Karakorum all this is nothing more than a glorified waystation." Psin kept his voice soft; he'd seen a man off to one side of the dais. "And watch what you say to me. I think that's a Kipchak and he might speak Mongol."

Rijart nodded. "Are you sure—"

"Damn you. Yes. Tell him what I said. I want to hear what he answers."

Rijart translated what Psin had said, and the knights around them muttered. The King's brother took a step forward. Rijart said, "Targoutai is sometimes rough in his speech."

The King smiled up at his brother and said something soft to him. To Rijart, he said, "I'm sure he's a fine soldier. You have the freedom of my court. Later we shall talk over the issues between us. Now, eat, drink, and talk among yourselves."

He rose and went down the steps of the dais. The group before him parted to let him through. His long coat swished metallically. Music burst out, somewhere, and Psin winced. Rijart beckoned to them, and they followed the King to the table.

Mago said, "They are staring at us, those women. Eh. Rijart. Ask the King if he will give them to us."

Psin glared at him. "The Christians aren't generous that way. Don't make trouble."

The women were mingling with the men. The King directed boys in fancy clothes to cut meat and sent one with a plate to Rijart. Rijart bowed, smiling.

"You bow," the King's brother said.

"I am no Mongol," Rijart said.

Now a boy in red and gold was holding a plate toward Psin, and Psin looked at Rijart, surprised. Rijart said, "Take it."

Psin took the plate. The heavy gold was cool to his hands. The King said, "Tell your standardbearer his answer pleased me. I'm surrounded by courtiers and the rough words of a simple soldier are sweet to my ears."

Rijart smiled. "Did you hear that, simple soldier?"

"Rijart. When we are back in Russia maybe I'll have molten lead poured into your ears and mouth."

A young woman had come up behind the young knight Gabriel; she spoke to him softly. Gabriel patted her hand. She looked at Vortai through the corner of her eye and smiled. Vortai stopped chewing and stared at her, his cheeks bulging with food. The King laughed; he said to Rijart, "Your men seem quite taken with our women."

"They are unused to seeing women moving so freely among men, my lord."

"Oh. Well, tomorrow we'll have manly sport. We'll hunt. I've seen Mongol bows, but never in action."

Leaning toward Psin, Vortai said, "What would they do if we took their women?"

"The women would stop you. They entice you and slam the door shut in your face. Rijart warned me against them. We aren't pretty enough to them, he said."

The Kipchak was pushing his way through the crowd toward them. He said, in loud Russian, "King Béla is misled, to let Mongols lay hands on his gold."

He was talking to Rijart; his eyes swept around the four Mongols. Rijart, who spoke no Russian, frowned and looked at Psin. Psin translated it into Mongol.

The King called out sharply, but the sudden intrusion of yet another language had thrown Psin off and he didn't understand the Latin. Rijart spoke to the King in a level voice.

In Russian, the Kipchak said, "Here is one of the butchers of Vladimir. Do the Hungarians shelter such animals?"

Psin alone understood him. The excited voices of the others rose like bird calls. The Kipchak looked all around. He was darkening with frustration. Psin took a bite of his meat. If the Kipchak could speak Mongol, he would. He was too angry to dissemble. Psin said, "I'm the only one here who speaks Russian. If you don't go away I'll tell them you are telling us you will join us to plunder Hungary when we cross the Carpathians."

The Kipchak's mouth fell open. "You Tartar pig."

"You Kipchak coward. Rijart—"

"No. I'm going."

The Kipchak turned and plowed through the mob. The courtiers were almost screaming; their eyes followed him, they shouted to one another. The King stepped forward and calmed them with a word. He spoke to Rijart, and Rijart turned to Psin.

"What did he say?"

"We . . . exchanged insults. Tell the King that it was the Kipchak who started it."

Rijart nodded. "Watch out. If he spoke only Kipchak and Russian there is probably someone here who speaks Russian and Latin." He swung back to the King and with a bow and many gestures explained.

Psin ate. Rijart was right. They wouldn't have let the Kipchak in if he couldn't be understood. A small man with a bald head was standing just behind the King; the King's brother turned to him, and the bald man spoke in a quiet voice. The brother nodded. Psin chewed thoughtfully. Rijart was clever. The King's brother and the bald man saw him watching and he looked away.

They stood around and ate and drank until the dark drove the King to order torches lit. Finally they were led off to rooms. Rijart was given his own chambers but the four Mongols were thrown together into two small rooms. Their saddles lay tangled on the floor waiting for them. Psin sank down onto a bench, sighing when the weight left his legs, and said, "Straighten up the gear. Vortai, tomorrow we hunt. You and I will shoot. Mago and Kobol, leave your bows here."

"Why?" they asked, together.

"Because we can't risk a miss, and neither of you is good at long shots. Vortai. We shoot as deep as we can. Can you draw my spare bow?"

"Yes," Vortai said. "But I'd rather use my own. The pull's not so heavy, but I'm good with it at maximum range."

"I know." Psin drew his bowcase out of the tangle, pulled the bow out, strung it, and drew it a couple of times. "We'll keep a sentry posted until we're sure of them. Mago, you first. Kobol second, Vortai third, and I'll go last. Stay inside the door, though."

Rijart talked with the King in the morning, but he said that they spoke of nothing but the weather and the possibility of sending envoys directly from Hungary to Karakorum. They did not mention the Kipchak. In the afternoon, they went to the King's park, where beaters drove the game right to them. Psin and Vortai took turns killing the few deer they saw long before they came within range of the Hungarians' stubby little bows. The Hungarians swore, murmured, and shrugged as if it were a trick to shoot so far.

A deer waded out into the tall grass at the edge of the wood, saw the line of archers, and turned to dive back. Psin raised his bow and shot. The arrow struck the deer just behind the shoulder, and it leapt and fell dead.

"Good shot," a man said behind Psin. He spoke Latin. Psin looked over at Rijart, and Rijart translated.

Psin looked back at the man who had spoken; he was a knight, brawny in his mail. He wore a white cloak with a black cross sewn onto the left front.

"Perhaps you would like to try one of our bows," the knight said. He smiled pleasantly, and Rijart translated.

Psin nodded. The knight reached over and with a soft word took one of the odd little bows from the man beside him. The bow had a horn box built into it, from the grip across to the nocking point of the drawn string. The knight said, "Turn the handle, here," and Psin, taking the bow, just remembered to wait for Rijart's translation. He stopped listening to the knight's Latin. The harsh, deep voice so close to his ear bothered him. He cranked, and the string wound back to the nocking point.

"The bolt goes here." The knight slipped in the short arrow. "Aim. No, that's too far. Try that tree." He guided the bow. The tree loomed up before him. Psin moved his shoulder until the butt of the bow fit better. "Sight through those prongs. Mary Mother, this one's quick. Now. Pull the trigger. This."

Psin pulled, and the bow shot itself. He swore. The bolt traveled faster and flatter than the Mongol arrows. "Ask him if that's the full range."

Rijart did so, and the knight smiled and nodded and went away. Psin gave the bow back to its owner and whirled to watch the knight walk back toward the tethered horses.

"What did that mean?" Rijart said. "Who is he?"

"I don't know." The knight had come here, to the park, to the hunting, for this one purpose. He was already riding away. Psin chewed his mustaches. He picked up his own bow, nocked an arrow, and drew the bow as full as he could. The game wasn't running any more, and the others on the line turned to watch. He lifted the arrow until the point lay against the sun and let the string fly. The arrow whistled straight up toward the sun. At the top of its trajectory, it stood like a hawk in the air; against the sun's brightness he could see it turn and fall. The Hungarians sighed. The arrow had fallen out of sight, in the wood. Psin looked at Rijart, but Rijart only shrugged and turned away.

The court at Pesth quickly grew boring. They were not permitted to ride by themselves in the town; the King said that the people would do them some harm. The days drifted by, full of meaningless chatter and overcooked food and the thick red wine, while Rijart and the King discussed minor points of courtesy and the people of the court stared, muttered, probed and laughed at the Mongols. Mago chased a woman into the garden one night, and only Rijart's frantic explanations kept the knights from killing him. He hadn't touched the woman. She retired from the court, sick, they said, of the awful shock. Psin listened to the Latin and remembered words he hadn't heard before and asked Rijart what they meant, when Rijart came in the evenings to tell him what had gone on between him and the King in their private sessions.

"Nothing," Rijart said. "Nothing. Today, at least, we reached the question of the Kipchaks who fled here. He says that they were given refuge as an act of common mercy. I say they are fugitives from the Kha-Khan and must be returned. He says he can't. I say he can. He says he will not. I say the Kha-Khan will be angry. He says that's too bad."

He raked his fingers through his hair. Psin said, "Did you tell him what comes of people who anger the Kha-Khan?"

"He said that the Hungarians were steppe people until nine generations ago, and that they still fight like steppe people. He says when we come they'll serve us better than they do now."

Vortai said, "When will we fight here? This place is rich enough to keep us all in booty for the rest of our lives."

Mago nodded. "And I'd like to pay that girl back for the trick in the garden."

"Be quiet," Psin said.

Rijart sat down on the one cushioned chair and put his feet up on the little table before him. "This is useless. I hope you're learning what you came here to find out."

"I am. Did you ask him why they put us up in this sty?" Psin kicked at the wooden bench. "They treat us like servants."

"They think you are. They have no slaves here, and they think you must be my servants. To them these are good quarters for servants. Their own live like beggars. I couldn't have questioned it without telling them you hold rank."

"Hunh."

"How is your Latin?"

"Good. I understand almost everything. I can't speak it because I've had no practice."

"You learn fast. Soon now we'll go home. He's almost done talking, this King."

But they stayed. The summer was slipping past, and Mago and Kobol began to fight like two dogs in the cramped little room. Psin understood; he felt the walls packing him in and the air growing stale, and he dreamt at night of horses galloping wild over a plain that did not end. The rhythm of galloping horses filled his mind even when he was awake. When Mago and Kobol fought he whipped them with his belt and kicked them until they stopped.

"Are we going to die here?" Kobol said. "In this pen, like somebody's menagerie?"

"Just a while longer."

That day, in the hall where they were eating, Psin saw the tall knight in the white cloak again. The man lifted his head and smiled, across the rows of the seated court. Psin frowned. The knight was unlike the Hungarians—too tall, too fair, too deliberate in his walk. Psin distrusted him.

"I want you to speak to your father for me," Quyuk said.

"About what?"

Quyuk looked back toward the camp, strung out a day's ride over the plain. Tshant followed his eyes. The late sunlight blurred everything; it was hazy, golden, the way everything was in the Russian autumn. A train of carts was straggling up to the eastern edge, and the dogs there began to bark. Djela was riding toward him and Quyuk.

"I want him to support me for the Khanate," Quyuk said finally. "I think he will, if I can only . . . get to him. Before Batu has me carted back to Karakorum."

"Don't get me to talk to him for you. If I say anything he'll take the other side. By habit."

"I thought you were friendly again, after Kozelsk." Quyuk kicked apart a mushroom. "Breast to breast, I thought."

"It never lasts."

"You shouldn't fight with him. He'll only beat you."

Tshant glanced around at Djela, who was still far down the rise from them. "My son doesn't know about the fight. And I beat him, at Kozelsk. God, he bled—"

"So I heard. He still runs your life, doesn't he?"

Tshant caught himself before he could get angry. There was something wrong in the way Quyuk was approaching this.

"I have nothing but awe and respect for our gallant Psin," Quyuk said. "So much that I think I'll have an easier time at the electing kuriltai if he supports me. Tell him, Tshant, that you will not support me."

"That's the truth."

Quyuk moved deeper into the shade of the tree, toward their tethered horses. "I know. I've been working hard, Tshant. I have Baidar back again, you know. And Sabotai is coming to me. Mongke goes with Psin, like a matched team." He laughed harshly. "Badly matched. Good afternoon, noyon."

Djela reined up. "Hello, noyon." He looked curiously at Tshant.

Quyuk drew his reins over his horse's head, gathered them at the withers, and mounted. His horse turned in a quick circle before he got his other foot into the stirrup. "Your father and I have been talking, noyon. Who will be the next Kha-Khan, do you think?"

Djela's mouth had been slightly open, as usual, but now he pressed his lips together. Tshant went over and took hold of his horse's rein, near the bit. Djela said, "Ogodai is the Kha-Khan."

Quyuk's brows twitched. "But who will be the—"

"Ogodai is the Kha-Khan," Djela said. His voice was so neutral Tshant almost did not recognize it.

Quyuk snorted. He whipped his horse into a gallop and plunged down toward the camp.

"What's the matter?" Djela said. "Why were you here?"

"I came up to get out of the camp," Tshant said. "He followed me. That was a good answer."

"I couldn't—I mean, there was nothing else to say."

Tshant nodded. He remembered telling Ana that Quyuk was not treacherous. "Of course not," he had said. But Psin had given Quyuk shelter and protection and it sounded as if Quyuk meant to start them fighting again, him and Psin. He couldn't think of any other reason for what Quyuk had said—the way he had said it.

"Have you seen Baidar with him lately?"

Djela shrugged. "They're always together, aren't they? All of them. Ada, come on, let's go hunting. I brought my new bow."

Tshant nodded. He patted Djela's horse and went to his own. They rode away from the camp, down toward the river where the marshes began in the broad curve of the bank. When they were almost there, Tshant heard the hoarse call of geese over his head and looked up. A great flock was sailing overhead, in a V pointing south. Djela was staring at them with bright eyes.

"Do you remember when we hunted the geese, that time by the Lake?" Tshant said. "With your grandfather."

"Yes."

The geese were already only flecks in the vast sky. Their cries were dim in his ears. Djela said, "When is Grandfather coming back?"

"Before the snow falls." Tshant kicked his horse up. Beyond, in the marshes, a heron stood on the margin of the water; at the sound of the horses coming, it flapped its wings, took two awkward steps on its stick-legs, and rose softly into the air. It had been nearly this time last year when he had left the Lake. Only a year . . . he thought of Kerulu with a fierce, fresh longing.

Rijart said, "It's over. I have six packets of messages to take back, none of which says more than I've already told you. The news came today that we took Pereislav and Chernigov, and they say that we come smiling to talk about peace and friendship while we burn and loot and destroy in the background."

"Hunh." Psin stretched out his legs. "We've told him often enough peace and friendship come only when he submits to the Kha-Khan. He was just—"

Somebody knocked on the door. Psin leapt up. Rijart raised his brows, and Psin nodded. He went to sit on the wooden bench against the blind wall.

Rijart called out, and the door swung inward. The knight in the white cloak came in. He smiled quickly at Rijart, glanced around, and went to stand behind the cushioned chair. Rijart stood in the center of the room, frowning.

"My name is Arnulf," the knight said. "I am a knight of the Teu-

tonic Order of Saint Mary of Jerusalem, and I am here as the agent
of the Emperor Frederick. King Béla knows nothing of this visit. I
have messages to give you, to be relayed by word of mouth to
whomever commands the Mongol armies in Russia, and through
him to the Kha-Khan. The King is to remain ignorant."

Psin leaned back against the wall. The knight was speaking
slowly, so that a novice at Latin could understand, but he would
know that Rijart was no novice. The other three Mongols watched
curiously from across the room. The knight sat down, and Rijart
perched on the bench across from him.

"You trespass on the King's courtesy," Rijart said.

"So do you. We have information that a certain Mongol general
has crossed the Carpathians. We suspect that he is among your retinue, traveling discreetly as a servant. Spying, in short."

"I know nothing of it," Rijart said.

"Our information is good. We know, for example, that the Mongol is named Psin. And that he is one of the men who planned the
attack on Russia. And that he speaks Arabic and fought in your
campaigns against the Turks and Syrians."

"You insult me." Rijart's neck was red.

"Oh? Why should we talk to an underling when we could treat
directly with a Mongol khan?"

Rijart's shoulders quivered. Psin drew one knee up and rested his
arm on it. He wondered who the Emperor's spies were. They even
knew about the ambiguous command in Russia. Rijart's voice
croaked, "I have never heard—"

"Outside this room," the knight said, "are four crossbowmen.
Presently I shall call them in. We will shoot your retinue, one man
at a time. I don't think you will allow your general to die when one
word could save him. We shall start with the young man over by
the window."

Psin did not look at Vortai. He saw Rijart tense; Rijart turned his
head, looking desperately to Psin for help. The knight leaned back,
smiling.

"You fool," Psin said.

Rijart clamped his jaws shut. The knight reached out and pushed
him gently to one side, so that he could see Psin better.

"We knew it was you, of course," the knight said. "But we
weren't sure you spoke Latin."

"What do you want?"

Vortai said quickly, "Who is this man?"

Psin got up. "Some hireling of the Emperor's. Rijart let him know who I am. Don't hurt him. We'll give him to the Kha-Khan to hurt, when we get back." He drew a chair over and sat down on it, forcing his mind back to Latin. "If you speak Arabic, that's better."

"Yes." The knight went on in Syriac Arabic. "My master the Emperor received messages recently from your Kha-Khan. Through the Muslims. I have replies."

"So you said."

"First, you may tell your superiors that the signs of disunity within the Christian world that you've undoubtedly seen are not signs of weakness. We are strong and we will fight to the last man to resist you, if you attack us. You shouldn't take that lightly. You have fought the Muslims; they are good warriors, and they set you back once or twice. We've fought them too, and beaten them as well as you have."

"I've heard. Tell your master that if we had flinched at the thought of hard fighting we would not hold more of the world than he dreams exists. Tell him that his knowledge of my name doesn't surprise me. His name might be known within his own country, but mine is known from here to China, and I'm not a very important man."

"You malign yourself." The knight smiled. He took the silk cap off his head; his pale hair gleamed in the late sunlight. His blue eyes were direct and intelligent. "But you recall the crossbow you shot. With your own bow you were killing deer at a range fully four bowshots longer than ours, certainly, but I doubt I could bend your bow, and I'm accounted a strong man. The bow I showed you how to shoot a woman could handle. And women shall, and children, if you ride against us."

"They'll die before they come close enough."

"Oh? Europe is thick with forest, Khan. West of Hungary is nothing but forest. You've hunted in the trees, I'm sure. How often do you get a long clear shot in a forest? The branches deflect the arrow, the trees hide your game. And we need not be strong to kill."

Psin cocked his brows. "A good point. I'll think about that. But it is God's will that the Kha-Khan rule the world. One sun in the sky, and one lord on the earth, no more."

"God's will. To rule the world, perhaps. Or, perhaps, to be a terror to it, scourge the peoples for their sins, and afterward to return to whatever the hell you sprang from, to be heard of never again."

"Who can know the mind of God? You are a good advocate for your Emperor."

"I? No. I only say what he told me to say."

Psin started to rise, surprised, but sank back again. He smoothed his mustaches along his jaw. "He told you what I would say, and how to answer?"

The knight nodded. "The exact words of my answers."

Psin studied him. The knight was not lying. "Rijart said he was a great man."

The knight's broad smile flashed again. "Also, he wants to send envoys to your Kha-Khan to discuss an alliance against the Turks."

"Oh." Psin shrugged. "We know that the Turks have asked you for an alliance against us. I'll send that on, but the answer is no."

The knight nodded. "Your Kha-Khan sent to the Emperor that the Emperor should come in person to Karakorum and make his obeisance. To that the Emperor said, 'Tell them this: that I think I know enough about birds of prey to serve as falconer to the Kha-Khan.'"

Psin laughed. "Good. Tell him this. From me, not from the Kha-Khan. When we ride into Europe, I will come for him, because I think I would like to talk to him. And that he should wait and not run, when all the cities burn around him."

The knight rose. "I will tell him." He bowed. The sunlight lay on his shoulder, across the black emblem of his Order. "I doubt you'll find our cities burn as well as the Russians'." To Rijart, in Latin much more fluent than before, he said, "I'm sorry I had to trick you. In any case, I would not have harmed your men. We knew it was he. The description was explicit." He turned back to Psin and bowed again and left, shutting the door quietly behind him.

W ELL?" TSHANT SAID.

Psin nodded. "I saw enough. Where is Sabotai? I didn't see his banner, when I came through the camp."

"He's gone back to the Volga camp until the ice freezes. It's been quiet. We had dispatches from Karakorum, the usual thing. Everyone is well. Apparently they hadn't gotten Batu's letter about Quyuk when they sent them." Tshant spat. "He's driving us all wild."

Psin dismounted, groaning. He did not want to go on to the Volga camp, but if Sabotai was there . . . "Who, Batu or Quyuk?"

"Quyuk."

Djela galloped up, whooping, and flung himself out of the saddle. "Grandfather. I knew you'd be back soon. How was Hungary? How do you like my new horse?"

"He looks fast." Psin glanced at the tall black horse and back to Djela. "God's name. Have you grown, or have I shrunk?"

Djela grinned. "I've grown. Ada says I'm eating him poor."

Tshant said, "He eats twice as much as I do. Stay here awhile."

"No. I have to find Sabotai."

"Well, you'll stay the night, at least. Go see Quyuk. That's his yurt. He'll be there."

"Take my horses."

Psin went to Quyuk's yurt and called through the door. Quyuk's voice came back, rough-edged: "Come in."

The yurt was dim and smelled of sweet hemp. The fire cast a red glow over the gold and brocade cushions. Against the wall to the left, Kadan sat, hunched over, his eyes on his brother. Quyuk was pacing up and down the other side of the room.

"And if you will not," Quyuk said gently to Kadan. "If you will not—Psin. How pleasant. You look disgustingly well. Sit."

Psin sank down on his heels just inside the door. "If he will not what?"

Kadan said, "The self-proclaimed Successor wants allies against Batu."

"Oh. Are you still at that?"

"Yes. I'll still be at it the day before Batu dies."

"God above. Remind me not to run foul of you. You're like a jackal with a skullbone worrying out the brains. It must be hard work to be always angry; why don't you try being sweet and calm, just for the change?"

Quyuk's ears grew red, and he glared. Psin laughed.

"You might find it restful. Stop looking ugly. I'm not going to be here long enough for you to work any revenge. I hear your father's well again. Perhaps you'd better court us, instead of bullying everybody you know."

He got up, nodded to Kadan, and went out into the cool autumn sunlight again. He heard Kadan laugh and Quyuk swear. For a moment he wished he had let Quyuk alone. He glanced back; Kadan was coming jauntily out of the yurt. He waved, and Psin saw the flash of his teeth when he smiled. He waved back. In a way, it made him angry to see ordinary men like Kadan laughing in Quyuk's face.

He spent the night in Tshant's yurt and rode on the next morning. The clear chill was turning into the bone-deep cold of the coming winter. When he left the camp, frost lay thick over the dry grass, heavy enough that the horses left sharp prints in it. Tshant had said that the road to the Volga camp was as safe as the streets of Karakorum; Psin rode alone.

He was beginning to feel it; all the hard riding. His bones grated against one another, and in the cold mornings his muscles twinged. The horses trotted quickly over the frozen ground. The dun horse was hard as horn from exercise and jogged up even with the horse Psin rode. On his dark winter coat the line down his back was blurred.

Tshant had said that now they had more than enough horses to mount each tuman on its own color. Blacks, bays, duns, greys. He reined up on a ridge to let the horses blow, and the dun immediately ducked its head and snatched a mouthful of the crisp brown grass. Quyuk had gotten one of the rare spotted horses from the east; his wife Oghul Ghaimish had sent it to him for a gift. The horse was dark grey, except for the white blanket across its hips covered with big grey spots.

"Skittish," Tshant had said. "Especially when the light's bad."

Psin had never seen a spotted horse that didn't have bad eyes. Their lashes were sparse and pale. He wondered why he was lonely, out there on the steppe.

He spent the night at the new waystation, exchanged one of his remounts that had gone lame, and left before dawn. When he went back to the Dnepr from the Volga camp he would take his sable cloak. The horses trotted along around him, their round dark eyes on the eastern sky.

That there should be many Kha-Khans made no sense. There was only one God; there could be only one Kha-Khan. For a moment he was frightened; he could see order in the world, and there should be no order, because all the world did not accept the Kha-Khan. He thought, I am guilty. He thought, if I can believe that, I am safe.

Broken light spilled up over the horizon, grey, uneasy. The air turned pale. Low clouds rolled back from the east, and he heard the growl of thunder. The sun grew steadily stronger. He dismounted and paid his homage to it, and remounted. Now he could see the slopes and heights of the heaped clouds. Lightning shimmered there, green-white.

But it was noon before the storm reached him. He slid down from his saddle and stood in the midst of his horses, the reins and leadrope in his fists, while the heavy rain smashed down on him and the wind roared past. He looked up at the sky, letting the rain hammer his face, into the curling clouds. Lord God, Tengri the Eternal Sky. He remembered what the knight Arnulf had said of God's purpose.

Why us, then? There were other tribes, thousands of them. Everywhere we go we fight a tribe that has been fighting another tribe for generations, east, west, north, south, that we shall have to fight. Each tribe had its own circle of wars, enemies, friends, land to graze, hills to hunt in, forests for hiding: each of them thought its small circle the center of God's purpose and was surprised to find things happened, far away, beyond their knowledge, that mattered more to them than the quiet events within their own horizons. So far west, who had marked the election of Temujin Kha-Khan?

The storm passed, and he mounted and rode on. The rainwater ran off across the hard plain, pooling in the hollows. He passed a puddle and looked down, and saw reflected in it the grey-black clouds and a streamer of blue sky. Through it, the sun poured, and through it, he could see the white tops of the clouds that looked so black underneath.

The Mongols had cut across the circles, opening them up into one another like a river running from sea to sea. Temujin had said that God meant them to rule. To end the circles, to make all people Mongol. He, who had been born a Merkit, was one no longer, even though he called himself one and the Altun used it to insult him. He thought of the Emperor in the west, who had known without knowing Psin what he would say to the knight's words.

Under the clearing skies, he rode on, unsure.

When he reached the Volga camp, he went first to the house where Artai and Chan stayed. The slave that took his horse looked grim. He went on into the garden and saw the fires there, tended by slaves, in front of the side door. Before each fire a lance stood tip down in the dirt. His heart contracted, and he almost ran to the main door and threw it open. The Kipchak woman was there, her hands in her lap, and she had been crying.

"Who is it?" he said.

The Kipchak shook her head. She rose and went off. Psin filled his lungs to yell at her, but before he could she reappeared with Artai.

"What's wrong?" he said. "Is it Chan? The fires—"

"Ana," Artai said. She put her arms around him, less ardently than usual. "She's had the baby, and she's dying."

The Kipchak sank down in her chair again. One hand groped for her mending. Artai said, "She's calling for Tshant. He didn't come with you, did he."

He shook his head. "He doesn't know."

"I sent a message when the baby was born. Six days ago, with dispatches from Karakorum. They went by an arrow messenger. He knows." She pulled at him, and he went after her down the hall. Her shoulders looked rigid.

"He didn't know when I left there." But he must have.

She glanced at him; her face was locked up against him. She

jabbed her chin at the door. He hesitated. If Ana died while he was in the house he would be impure for months. Artai glanced at him again, her eyes bright and cold. He went into the room.

Ana lay wrapped in furs, her face whiter than the white bearskin beneath her. Psin strained his ears, but he could hear no baby crying, anywhere. He sank down beside the couch and touched Ana's face. The skin was rough and parched.

Her eyelids fluttered. "Is it you?" Her voice was so weak that he had to put his ear almost against her lips to hear. "Is it you?"

"Yes," he said.

Her mouth trembled. She dragged one hand free and put it on his. "I knew you would come."

He took hold of her hand. Her breathing was shallow, and every few breaths she would try to take in more air, but her throat would catch and sigh. He turned and saw Artai and Chan there in the doorway.

"I'll be right back," he said. "Don't worry." He put her hand back under the furs and went to the door.

Chan was watching him distantly. He thrust them both into the hall and whispered, "Get out of this house. And take all the slaves with you. Now. Do you hear me?"

Artai said, "Someone has to—"

"I will. Go. Now."

They went off down the hall. He turned back into the room, frowning. He heard the pale girl on the couch murmur, but he couldn't hear the words. He went over and sat down next to her.

"I knew you would come," she said.

He smoothed the hair back from her forehead, said something reassuring, and wondered how he was going to communicate with Sabotai when he was under ban. He felt her fingers, dry as spider webs, touch his, and he held her hand. Her breathing grew fainter with each breath. He was relieved she thought he was Tshant.

"The baby," she said. She tried to open her eyes. He bent to hear, but she said nothing more. Her lips parted slightly. He thought, I should have gotten here tomorrow. She lay still, but she wasn't dead. He could feel the tiny wobbling beat in her wrist.

He was small and mean. She wasn't dying to inconvenience him. He remembered how she had tended him at Susdal, a great inert sick heap she couldn't have moved by herself, with an oozing wound and a flighty stomach, and how she had wept when Susdal burned. He started to speak to her, but before he could call up the words she was dead.

He sat still, hoping for the pulse to come back. Beside her dead cheek the fur shone glossy and rich. Finally he tucked the robes up over her and went out.

The house was empty. In the garden, the household stood, and the shaman was sitting on the bench beside the fires. Psin went out the side door, walking between the two fires, and the shaman called out, "Khan, you are unclean, from now until the ninth new moon."

He nodded. Artai came over to him, and he stepped to one side of the fires.

"What will you do?" she said.

He shrugged. "The law says I can't go into a chief's camp, that's all. I'll have to meet Sabotai in the open air."

"The baby is a boy. He's healthy, for now. Tshant should have come."

"He will, probably."

"He will not. We'll have a message that he is busy. He isn't busy. What was she to him? He'll be glad she's out of his way."

Psin frowned at her, but she took him by the arm; her fingers dug into his forearm muscles. "Won't he? It will be easier to explain a baby to Kerulu than a new woman."

Her face was tight, graven into angles like a stone head. He said, "You blame him too much."

"Blame him? He took her. He gave her the baby. You— Did you think she thought you were he?"

"Of course she did."

"She knew who you were. She wanted you to come, more than Tshant. She never said so, but we understood. Now you're preening yourself because you were generous enough to risk a ban that Sabotai will surely set aside, and you sent us away because you knew that we could be with you if you were under ban, but you couldn't have us if we were."

"What's wrong?" he said. "You're shaking."

"You're wrong. You and Tshant. She's better off dead. You ruined her, you and Tshant."

"We didn't—"

"She was happier when she was a slave. At least she could still be a Russian. Go away. I'm angry with you."

He stared at her. Her face was full of implacable energy. He looked over her head at Chan, standing a little apart from the slaves, shivering with cold. Expressionless, she stared back. After a moment he put his hand on the back of Artai's head and drew her gently against him, and with her face against his coat she cried.

After a lot of confusion and the running of slaves back and forth, Psin met Sabotai in the courtyard of Batu's palace. Sabotai had a fur robe around him against the light cold, and a slave came after him with a chair. He looked furious.

"How did you manage to get yourself mixed up in this? Dead women—"

"Talk to Batu's shaman. Maybe he'll lift it."

"I already have. He says he could not purify the Kha-Khan himself from the dead ban. If you'd spat out gift meat or defiled running water— Never mind. It's all right. You'll have to pitch your yurt apart from everyone else's, in camps, but the shaman says that clean persons can come to you, if they pass between fires going away. We'll have to hold our councils in your yurt. What did you see in Hungary?"

Psin took the King's messages from his coat and handed them to Sabotai. "The usual. He will not return the Kipchak refugees. Kotian Khan lives in high regard just outside their capital. Rijart jabbered with him about the envoys they killed, that time, but the King said they were spies."

"Oh. Was Rijart useful?"

"Moderately." Psin told him about the Teutonic knight. "But that might have been for the good. What did he mean, 'I think I know enough about birds of prey to serve as falconer to the Kha-Khan?'"

Sabotai shrugged one shoulder. "What do you think?"

"I think it was a most courteous way of telling us we could boil the Kha-Khan and eat him, for all the Emperor cares."

"So do I. This one sounds more interesting than most of them. What else?"

"You know I talked to merchants and such before I left. All I saw confirms what they said. There are many tribes, and they're all at each other's throats. The way the Hungarians talk of the Germans, Rijart says, would make you wonder why there are any Germans left. And the Germans hate the Franks—"

"I thought the Franks were all the people of Europe."

"So did I, but it seems they're just one tribe. And the Franks hate the Englanders—Rijart's people. The Hungarian King is kin to the noyons north of him, the Poles, and south of him—the Bohemians. And to the Moravians and a lot of others. They took us in through a pass I'm sure we can force, if we come at it properly. They've got the pass garrisoned. We could send men south, between the mountains and the sea, through a river basin that runs east to west. North is only marsh and plain."

"The knights. How do they fight?"

"Like little fortresses. I would not like to face one at close quarters. But kill their horses and they'd be helpless." He told Sabotai about the crossbows. Sabotai snorted. "I think he's probably right," Psin said. "Hungary is the last of the flat ground; beyond that we have forest to fight in."

"Yes. Are their cities like the Russians'?"

"Stone walls, huge gates. The cities themselves aren't so defensible. Their stone towers would be impossible to storm."

Sabotai made a face. "Oh, my."

"I doubt they would wait to be sieged. I think we can bring them out onto ground of our own choosing easily enough. They're wild to show how well they fight. And as long as we have room to run from them we can beat them."

"This Emperor. He'll defend his people, won't he?"

"No. He's fighting their head priest. Don't ask me how a head priest can withstand a kha-khan long enough to make it a war, but apparently this one can. The Emperor's son is the King of the Germans, but the Hungarian King owes him homage and Rijart says the usual run of things there is to let a defiant man get beaten so he'll have to crawl to the others for help."

"Supplies?"

"We can winter and summer very well in Hungary. In the north they say the springs are very wet, but the foraging shouldn't be too bad. West of Hungary . . ." He shrugged.

"Forests."

"Forests, hills, rivers, more forest. And a lot of cities. I don't know. We could have trouble. We would have to lay siege to the cities."

"What did the river look like, when you passed Kiev?"

"It's not frozen yet. Soon."

Sabotai grunted and gnawed his lip. "Interesting. Interesting. We have fifteen full strength tumans, of which six are at least half heavy cavalry. The Kipchaks made splendid heavy cavalry. We gave them Russian swords. They think they're finer than khans. How are your relations with your son?"

"Good. Since the fight."

"He's penitent, he thinks he almost killed you. He'll forget, soon enough."

"Quyuk is badgering everybody."

"I know. Batu asked the Kha-Khan to recall him. Jagatai sent you a message. Did you hear of it?"

"No."

"You're no longer Quyuk's nursemaid. He wants your opinion of Kadan."

"What for?"

"I don't know. Maybe Siremon is less than they'd hoped. The Kha-Khan is strong but he's not long this side of the grave. Would Kadan make a good Kha-Khan?"

Psin laughed. "People might have trouble saying it."

"I'm beginning to think Quyuk is the only one of them who can be elected."

Psin studied his face. Sabotai cocked one eyebrow. Finally Psin nodded. "I know what you mean. He has the . . . way about him."

"Well. We'll see what happens. Are you fit? Are you tired? We'll go west tomorrow."

"Slowly."

"Yes." Sabotai laughed. "Stay in Tshant's house tonight. They won't have your goods purified until tomorrow anyway." He rose and slapped Psin on the shoulder. "I'm glad you're back. Just don't get mixed up with any more dying women."

* * *

"Call him Tulugai," Psin said.

Artai nodded. The slaves had brought in what they would need while they stayed here, and the little room was packed high with chests and boxes. Dmitri was carrying the child around in a sling.

"I didn't mean what I said," Artai said.

"You did. You were probably right, too." He hooked his elbows over the windowsill. The odor of meat stewing drifted in from the other room, where Chan's slaves were cooking dinner. He had written Jagatai about Kadan; he had given the shaman the gift for purifying the house.

"No," Artai said. "She was just a silly girl who didn't understand too many things."

"Everything that happened to her happened to Chan," he said. He remembered Ana's soft voice, telling him she wanted to stay in his house.

Chan looked in the door. "What is he saying about me?"

"That you are like Ana."

Chan's brows drew down perfectly straight. She stared at Psin until he had to grin at her, moved inside the room, and sat down with her hands in her sleeves. "Bring me something to drink," she said to him.

Psin called to Dmitri, in the next room. Artai said, "Tell me again that she is like Ana."

"I never said—"

Dmitri came in with three bowls and a sack of kumiss. He had the child tucked up neatly in the crook of one arm. Psin took the baby and held it while Dmitri poured kumiss for them all. Chan picked up her bowl.

"I am not like her," she said.

"Where are we going to sleep?" Artai said. "This house is so crowded, there are no empty couches."

"Here," Psin said. "What, do you need more room to stretch out?"

"Hunh," Artai said. She picked up her bag of things to be mended, pulled out a sock, and inspected it closely. Psin took the baby into the kitchen; Dmitri followed him.

"Khan," Dmitri said.

Psin turned. The baby squirmed in his arms, and he handed it to a woman.

Dmitri fidgeted a moment. "Ana was Christian, Khan. She should have a Christian burial."

Psin nodded. "I've seen to that."

"Oh. I . . ." Dmitri glanced around and switched abruptly into Russian. "May I go, when they bury her? And pray for her."

"You were never such friends with her."

"No. But she was Russian, like me. And . . ."

Psin waited for him to go on, but Dmitri only reddened, and Psin said, "What?"

"I think maybe we shared the same sin." Dmitri thrust his hands into his belt. "We shouldn't have submitted to you, but we did. Maybe if I pray for her, she will pray for me."

"She's dead."

"If she is in Heaven, she will pray for me."

Psin sighed. "Of course you can go."

"Thank you. I knew you would let me."

"You shouldn't think it's wrong to submit to us. It's wrong not to."

"Maybe. I don't know. Thank you."

Dmitri bowed and went off. Psin chewed his mustaches. Of all the people they had conquered he would have thought Dmitri the happiest. Dmitri had become so much a part of his household that Psin had almost forgot he was Russian. But now Dmitri said he was unhappy over it. He shook his head and went back to the room where Artai and Chan sat.

Tshant said, "How in God's name do you think you're going to do anything out here?" He flung his arms wide, and his eyes blazed. Beside him, Djela looked up in awe.

"Sit down," Psin said. "Stop yelling. By the Yasa I am not permitted to live in the camp, but there's no law against people coming out here."

"A day's ride from the center of the camp," Tshant said. "We all live in the center of the camp—Quyuk, Mongke, everybody. You could have leapt out the window, couldn't you? Taken the damned girl out into the garden to die?"

"The Yasa says—"

"The Yasa says that anyone under the same roof when someone dies is unclean. In the garden you wouldn't have been under any roof at all. Except the sky. And that would make us all unclean."

"Ada—"

"Sit down. Stay out of my way."

Djela went over to sit next to Psin, and Tshant paced up and down. "I thought perhaps I could depend on my own father to—"

"What's going on?"

"If you were capable, I'd say that you should wait and see." Tshant sank down on his heels. "I'm fighting Quyuk."

"You're fighting Quyuk."

"Yes. I don't know why. I don't know when it started. Since you came through here, from Hungary."

"How?"

Tshant shrugged. "Whenever we're all together, he manages to set me up against him. Anything I say he denies, everything he says I have to deny. Then he chops at me, so that all the others have to admit that I'm wrong."

Psin wondered quickly if Tshant were imagining all this. He went to the masterpole and took down the skin hanging there a˗˗ poured kumiss. Djela said, "Maybe we can live out here with Grandfather."

"Be quiet," Tshant said.

Psin handed him one of the bowls, gave another to Djela, and sat down again with the third in his hands. "When the fighting starts again there won't be time for—"

Tshant's head jerked toward the door. "Horses coming."

"Djela, go see who they are."

Djela got up. Through the open yurt door they could hear the frantic beating of several horses' hoofs, and somebody called out sharply—Mongke. Psin rose.

"It's my cousins," Djela called. He leaned out the door. "Have you been hunting? What are you doing out here?"

Quyuk, bending to get through the door, swept Djela up and set him down again to one side. "We came to see your illustrious ancestor." He was drunk. Behind him, crowding into the yurt, Buri, Kadan, Mongke and Kaidu were all drunk as well. They bellowed and clapped Psin on the back and made remarks about people who stayed around when other people were known to be dying; Buri with a skin of wine under one arm went around filling cups for them all. Tshant sat like a rock in the middle of a rushing stream.

"In-law," Buri cried, and embraced Tshant noisily. "Dear husband of my father's sister, glory of our clan." Tshant shoved him hard, and Buri tripped backward and fell.

Quyuk was smiling with one side of his mouth. He presented his cap to Psin and drank. "How can we express the joy of having you back with us, Khan? Especially since you know and will surely tell us what Sabotai means to do, after we hold Kiev. Where do we go next, hmmmm?"

"You'll hear at the kuriltai," Tshant said.

Kadan slumped down to sit with his back against Psin's couch. "We are the kuriltai, we here." He held out his cup to Buri to refill.

"With the exception of Sabotai, Batu, Batu's brothers, and the tuman commanders," Psin said, "you are the kuriltai."

"We." Quyuk draped one arm across Psin's shoulders and squeezed. His hand flopped beside Psin's cheek. "We. You are part of us, Psin. Altun Uruk."

Kadan cheered, and the rest joined in. Djela said, "So am I. So am I."

"Right," Kadan said, and dragged the boy into his lap. Tshant stiffened.

"So," Quyuk said. He breathed in Psin's face. "Tell us what will be said at the kuriltai."

Psin looked past Buri, toward the door. Mongke was rolling his cup gently between his palms. For once he was not smiling. He looked steadily at Psin; Psin cocked his eyebrows. Mongke said nothing, did nothing, only stared back.

"No," Psin said.

"No?" Quyuk squeezed the arm that lay around Psin's neck. "No what?"

"I will not tell you what Sabotai will say at the kuriltai."

"Ooooh."

Buri and Kadan growled and made faces. Psin thought them so

drunk they didn't understand anything said. Quyuk's arm was tight around his neck.

"Tshant," Quyuk said. "Tell him to tell us."

"No," Tshant said.

"What a family this is. They all say no. Kadan."

Kadan was rocking back and forth, sightless, murmuring to himself. His arms lay loose over Djela's shoulders. Djela looked as if he were getting ready to bolt.

"Kadan. Hey. Brother. Listen to me."

"Uh?"

"They say no, Kadan."

Buri roared. Behind him Mongke's face was blank, but whenever Psin looked over, Mongke was staring straight back at him. Kaidu had said nothing. His eyes shifted from Quyuk to Psin to Tshant and back to Psin again.

Kadan had wrapped his arms around Djela and was rocking him. "They can't say no. Not to us."

Tshant put one hand on the ground, ready to spring up, but Psin shook his head at him. He thought Kadan didn't know what he was doing. Djela's face was white, and he was looking beseechingly at Tshant.

Quyuk said, "Tell us. What harm will it do?"

"No harm," Psin said.

Kaidu's voice rose, higher than usual. "Then tell us."

"No."

Djela said, "Father, make him let me go."

Psin spun around. "Kadan."

Kadan's face turned toward him, and his arms loosened. Djela slid free and ran to Tshant.

Quyuk said, "Tshant, ask if he will tell you, when we have gone."

"He won't," Tshant said. He had Djela by the arm, and he made him sit down.

"Ask him."

"No."

"Is that all you two can say? It must be the Merkit blood. They do say that the first Merkit was a snake hatched in the dung heap of a—"

Tshant leapt for him, hauled him up onto his feet, and hit Quyuk in the face. Quyuk's head snapped back, but Tshant still held him by the front of his tunic. Tshant looked over at Psin, surprised, and with great precision hit Quyuk again. He dropped him and went back to his place and sat down.

The others were all staring, open-mouthed. Buri swung toward Psin. "Why did you let him do that?"

Quyuk sat up, rubbing his jaw. He blinked rapidly several times. Psin put one hand to his mouth to hide his grin. He watched the surprise wash over Quyuk's face, and Quyuk wheeled toward him.

"You didn't stop him."

Psin laughed. "No. Why, should I have?"

"I was . . . expecting you to." Quyuk glared around. "Or I would have hit him first."

Mongke laughed. "Tell us, Quyuk. Tell us how you would have trampled him into fishbait."

Psin said, "You were discoursing on the origins of Merkits, Quyuk Noyon. Would you care to continue?"

Quyuk's mouth tightened. Psin expected him to walk out. Buri was already on his feet; Quyuk rose, and Buri started toward the door.

"There are no Merkits," Quyuk said. "There are only Mongols. Buri, where are you going?"

"No place," Buri mumbled, and sat down again.

"Yes, you are," Psin said. "You're leaving. Now."

Quyuk sank down on his heels. "I think we'll stay."

"Get out or I'll throw you out."

"No. Now I say it. It's not just a Merkit word."

Tshant lunged; Buri shot to his feet, a dagger in his hand. Psin grabbed him by the wrist and whipped him around and jammed Buri's wrist up between his shoulderblades. He could see the sweat start out all along Buri's neck. Tshant was circling Quyuk, who had his own knife out. Psin started to yell to Tshant to stop, but Djela dodged in behind Quyuk and tripped him.

Quyuk sprawled backward. Tshant took a step to one side, astonished, and Kadan hooted. "The whole family's poisonous."

Mongke said, "I'm leaving, and so is Buri. Aren't you?"

Psin shoved Buri out the door. Mongke and Kaidu followed him.

Quyuk, rising, looked over at Djela, and Djela brought both fists up. Quyuk laughed.

"First blood. He should be blooded. Am I bleeding anywhere?" He bounced up and started across the yurt, still laughing. Kadan staggered after him. At the door, Quyuk whirled.

"I made a mistake." His eyes moved from Psin to Tshant. "I should never contest the strength of oxen." He wasn't laughing anymore. He turned and left.

Kadan, weaving, got himself stuck in the small doorway and blocked it, so that Tshant couldn't go after Quyuk. Psin decided Kadan wasn't as drunk as he seemed. When they finally got him straightened out, Quyuk was riding off on his spotted horse.

Tshant said, "Why didn't you stop me?"

"You're full grown. You've got to learn when to stop yourself. Besides, he wouldn't have provoked you unless he thought I'd protect him. He knows you can beat him."

Djela said, "Did I do well?"

Tshant said, "I'm not sure. You gave him a way to get out of it. Didn't he?" He looked at Psin.

Psin nodded. "He'd worked himself into a trap, this time. I think he'll be more careful with us."

"I thought awhile ago that he was after you, but he's not."

"After me? You mean, to finish me?"

"Yes. But he's not."

"No." Psin went back into the middle of the yurt. "He's got reason to be after me but he's not that kind of man."

"What?"

"Chan."

Tshant sank down. "Has he . . . gone sniffing after her?"

"Yes."

"What is he trying to do, then?"

"I don't know. He won't have the leisure before we start fighting again to work out a new means of attack, anyway. Sometimes I think he's just playing some kind of game. Shall I tell you what's happpening at the kuriltai?"

Tshant's eyes widened. "Why?"

"Because I wouldn't tell them."

For a moment Tshant thought about that. Finally he nodded.

"Yes." He grinned. "And I'll see that they know I know, of course."

Psin smiled. "Of course."

Sabotai said, "The ice is hard. We'll cross tomorrow night—the moon will rise early."

Psin nodded. He went around behind Sabotai to look over his shoulder at the map on the table. Sabotai's forefinger moved swiftly over the paper. "Here, and here. And here. By dawn we should have the city surrounded. I have burning lights to signal with."

"It might not be clear," Psin said. "Just because it snowed yesterday—"

"If it's snowing we'll have to change plans. The point is that we can expect Kiev to be ready for us. Their army will probably be waiting outside the city. How many men?"

"Up to one half our strength."

"Hmmm. And we have to consider an attack from within the city as well. Mongke led the vanguard at Chernigov, and he did surprisingly well. He can do so again."

"Let Quyuk lead the vanguard."

"Quyuk? Why?"

Psin sat down on the couch. "There was a courier today from Karakorum. I heard the bells. What did he say?"

"That's . . . secret."

"That Quyuk is to return to Karakorum? As soon as any war operations he's involved in are over?"

"Yes." Sabotai leaned on the table.

"And you're using three flying columns with a detached vanguard. So the vanguard will see the heaviest action."

"God's holy name," Sabotai murmured. "Are you trying to get him killed?"

Psin laughed. "No. But he does well in heavy fighting. I want him to go home leaving the Altun with a good impression of him."

"Why?"

Psin shrugged. "I like him."

"The rumor is that he and Tshant fought, and Tshant messed him up a little."

"Rumor."

"Well." Sabotai looked down; he made a mark on the edge of the paper with his grease pencil. "Yes. You're probably right. No one should be permitted to laugh at the Kha-Khan's son the way Mongke and Kaidu are currently laughing at the Kha-Khan's son."

"Especially when he's liable to be the next Kha-Khan."

Sabotai shook his head. "It would be much simpler just to tell him you support him."

There were horses coming. Psin rose. "Dmitri, go see who that is." To Sabotai, he said, "If I support him now he'll take it as a sign of weakness. I plan to bargain with him for my vote, when it comes to that. Dmitri?"

"It's Mongke and Buri," Dmitri called. He went back to the slaves' quarter of the yurt.

Sabotai said, "What do they want?"

"Not the same thing."

Buri came in. "Sabotai, it's all over the camp that Quyuk has been called back to Karakorum."

Sabotai said, "The dispatches are secret."

"He told me himself. I want to go with him."

Psin shut his eyes and sighed. "Back straight as a lance, he rides off into exile."

Sabotai made a small shushing noise. "Yes. If you want to, Buri."

Psin opened his eyes and stood up. Buri looked at him over his shoulder. "He has no friend but me."

"And it's all my fault. I know."

"No," Buri said. "He's . . . changed, a lot. But he still doesn't have any friends." He turned back to Sabotai. "Thank you." He went out the door. Mongke came in immediately after.

Sabotai said, "I suppose you want to go too."

"I? Hardly." Mongke looked around for a chair and sat. "Psin, are you going to let him fight at Kiev?"

With a snort, Sabotai rolled up the map. "I'm going. Clearly I'm not wanted for this discussion. Psin, we'll hold the kuriltai out here tonight."

"Bring some kumiss with you."

"I will." Sabotai went out the door.

Mongke said, "You can't let him fight. He might win too much.

You have to keep him where he is now."

Psin cased the map.

"Why, where is he now, Mongke?"

Mongke got up. "Psin, listen."

"No. You listen. The batch of you should have been drowned the day you were born. I'm sick of you. Stop entangling me and my son in your little family feuds. The next time I see a member of the Altun who isn't related to me by blood, I may knock him down and stamp on him."

Mongke went sheepishly to the door. "I only wanted—"

"I know. You only wanted to keep Quyuk looking silly. Get out."

Mongke left.

Tshant said, "He what?"

Mongke nodded. "He told the rationers to give Quyuk's tuman and two others grain for their horses."

"But that means—"

"That Quyuk's tuman is to ride vanguard."

Tshant gnawed on the inside of his lower lip. "How did you find this out?"

"Oh, I happened to be down by the commissary when Quyuk's men went in for their war rations."

"Just happened. You aren't supposed to do that."

"No, I'm not. But I thought it wise. He wouldn't tell me if Quyuk was to fight, and I thought if I went down there I'd find out."

"His tuman is staying here through the fighting for Kiev. He may not be leading them."

"His slaves took his ration for him. I know his slaves well enough to recognize them."

"He can't do that."

"He is. They are, I mean. Psin and Sabotai."

"And Batu."

"Two hawks to your bay horse Batu had nothing to do with it."

Tshant turned his head and called to a passing slave to get his horse ready. "Two hawks to your grandmother Sabotai had nothing to do with it."

Mongke nodded. "Psin, of course. Where are you going?"

"To tell him not to."

"Don't. It won't accomplish anything."

"Why did you come here to tell me if you didn't want me to go face him over it?"

"Because I thought you might know what he's doing."

Tshant settled back. "He's proving that when he snaps his fingers Quyuk jumps. What else?"

"More than that."

Tshant spat out the door. "Name it."

"He likes Quyuk."

"He hates Quyuk."

"Does he? Why did he keep him from Batu, that time in the Volga camp?"

"Quyuk went asking his protection. Psin's just. He does what he thinks fit, no matter who it is."

"I don't think he thought it fit. Batu was right. The justice lay with Batu, and Psin should have let him take him. I say that Psin likes Quyuk. If Psin does, I shall make it a point to like Quyuk."

Tshant studied him. Mongke was the shrewdest of the Altun; he was probably right. "Psin would be a fool to try to brace up Quyuk now."

"Now is the best time. Quyuk is leaving right after we take Kiev."

"In disgrace."

"Or with the glory of having led the vanguard that crushed the Russians. Take your choice. Psin chose."

Tshant stood up. Mongke snatched at him. "Don't try to talk him out of it. You'll just get into a fight."

"Let go of me." Tshant backed away from him. Mongke sat down again. His mouth twisted.

"Who's the fool? At least wait until after the kuriltai, when it's common knowledge, or you'll get me into trouble."

"You should have thought of that yourself." Tshant left the yurt.

* * *

Psin's yurt stood to the east of the camp; horsetracks cut through the new snow toward it, like strings tying it into the other yurts. Tshant rode out at a canter. Dmitri was shaking out wet laundry, in the lee side of the yurt, and looked up when he heard Tshant coming. Tshant kicked his horse, but before he could get to the yurt door Dmitri had gone in.

Psin came out before Tshant had dismounted. He squinted against the sun and said, "What's happened now?"

"What do you mean?" Tshant pulled the reins over his horse's head.

"You look like a storm thinking about thundering."

"I've heard Quyuk's tuman got grain rations for their horses."

"Do we have talkative quartermasters?"

"Mongke told me."

"Just talkative Altun. Yes. What of it?"

"Is Quyuk commanding them?"

"Yes."

"You told me yesterday that Mongke would probably command the vanguard."

"Sabotai changed his mind."

"Sabotai, or you?"

"Sabotai is the commander."

"Why?"

"Mongke commanded the vanguard at Chernigov. There's no—"

"Because Quyuk has been recalled to Karakorum? Because you don't want him to leave here like a beaten dog?"

Psin's eyes rested on him a moment. "I don't know what you're talking about."

"You lie."

"Well. I lie. What concern is it of yours, anyway?"

"If my father acts like a complete fool—"

"Who's the fool? Mongke told you what's happened and told you exactly how to interpret it, and you do just what Mongke wants, you run up here—"

"I didn't—I mean, what Mongke said has nothing to do with it. He even tried to keep me from coming here."

Psin smiled. "How hard?"

Tshant took a deep breath. He remembered what Mongke had

said. "He told me he wanted to know what I thought of it, that he didn't want to cause trouble between us."

"Did he ask you what you thought of it?"

Tshant's temper rose; he could feel it pressing against his ribs, his heart. He opened his mouth to speak, but Psin said, "You are so predictable, my heir, that whenever the Altun want something of me they're too cowardly to ask or force me to do, they go to you. Mongke plays you like a pipe. Try thinking before you do things. It has a wonderful effect on the mind."

He turned and went inside the yurt. Tshant shouted, "Stay here and—" The door shut. He stared at it awhile; Psin had painted the ox totem on it in red and yellow. Finally Tshant got up and rode back into the camp. He went hunting Mongke, but he couldn't find him, and at last, giving up, he went by Quyuk's yurt to play chess until the kuriltai.

THE DUN HORSE SNORTED, AND PSIN STOOD IN HIS STIRRUPS TO look ahead of them. Blue in the moonlight, the river lay like a wide road between the fringes of trees on either bank. The bluffs cast a shadow over the far side. Two horsemen were threading through the shadow; they were Mongols, and he settled back into his saddle.

He had forgotten how many men three tumans were. All down the bank around him, horsemen waited. They weren't supposed to move, but the trees were full of motion, and it was warmer here than out beyond the pack. He glanced at Buri, carrying the staff with the lanterns. All four were shuttered.

"Rocket," Mongke called, far down the line, and Psin reined his horse forward. Over the bluff the tail of the rocket hung like a long star; no one not looking for it would have seen it. It burst with a thud, and blue, green, red and yellow light dappled the black sky. The dun bolted, crashing through the brush at the edge of the bank, and with all his men packed behind him Psin charged over the river.

For a moment the army fought and staggered and shoved on the ice, yelling. Psin with the front rank broke through onto the far bank and scrambled through the trees there into the level pass. The rest streamed after. The dun caromed into another horse, neighed, and bucked. Overhead, the burning lights were fading, sliding down the sky. They hurtled onto the flat plain, wheeled around a spur of the bluff, and charged along the flat ground beneath Kiev's walls, where Quyuk and the vanguard were fighting Russians.

Buri's lanterns flashed wildly. Psin nocked an arrow and shot. Quyuk and his men were nearly surrounded; the Russians were throwing them back against the steep slope. Voices rose over the rattle of weapons. The arrows hissed in the air. The dun horse swerved violently, and Psin kicked him straight. He shot quickly, keeping his arrows low. All around him bowstrings sang.

"Yip-yip-yip—"

He reined the dun back hard, trying to see what was going on. The screams and shouting beat against his head. Buri and half a dozen other men were on the high ground before the city gates, where the army could see the lanterns. Psin whirled the dun and crowded him through the pack toward Buri. Abruptly the red lantern flashed three times, and the Mongols whirled all around Psin and flooded back, away from the fighting. The pack carried Psin with them a little way up the slope, until he broke loose and galloped up to Buri.

"We got separated," Buri shouted. "I thought you would come when— Green lantern."

The man now holding the standard pulled a cord, and the lantern flashed. In the light Buri's face looked like a corpse's. Psin looked over his shoulder. The Mongols were regrouping down the plain; they whirled and charged back, yelling, and their bows filled the air between them and the Russians with arrows.

"Look at Quyuk," Buri said.

Psin turned his head. Quyuk had pulled his men out of the middle of the Russian army, back when Psin's tumans retreated. They packed the steep road to the city, motionless, shooting downhill. The Russians howled and slewed away from them.

"Where's Mongke?"

Buri jabbed his chin toward the western tip of Psin's line. Psin stood in his stirrups. Mongke was charging his men around to encircle the Russians, but the knights veered suddenly to meet him. The Russians were already firming up their lines against the new attack from the south. "White lantern, four short."

Buri said, "Where is Sabotai?"

"Coming. Look."

He pointed to the sky. The moon was setting, and the high arch of the sky was blacker without its light. A rocket was streaking across between the stars. It burst, and green light showered down over Kiev.

"Drive them north," Psin said. He looked back toward Mongke's flank. They were charging around the Russians, shooting wildly, but the line was dangerously thin. The Russians in a mob attacked, and down where Mongke rode a lantern flashed.

"What's he doing?" Buri yelled.

"Wait and see—look out. Give Quyuk's sign and two long blues."

The gates of Kiev were opening. Quyuk's men, still shooting into the Russian army, had their backs to the city. The blue lights glared. Buri said, "He doesn't see them."

Psin picked up his bow and nocked an arrow. "Keep flashing." He lifted the bow. Buri yelped angrily, and Psin shot. The arrow skipped into the mass of Quyuk's line; heads turned, and somebody shouted. Quyuk's men whirled around.

Out of Kiev another army streamed, shouting and waving bright swords. Torches flared on the walls. Quyuk's men, facing a charge down hill, spun their horses and raced away. The Russians whooped.

Psin swung back toward Mongke's flank. It had split neatly in half before the Russian charge, and the knights had met nothing but the snow and the wind. On either side, the Mongols flew lightly back, their arrows tearing through the Russians.

"Mongke's sign, and a long yellow."

Buri said, "He won't do it." But he ordered the signal.

"Watch."

"We should watch. Those Russians—"

Psin looked quickly back over his shoulder. The Russians coming out of Kiev were chasing Quyuk down onto the flat, but one wing had swerved toward Psin and Buri.

"All lanterns shut. Let's go."

He turned the dun and whipped him straight down the slope. The horse bounced snorting across the snow ridges, between the trees. Buri and the others pounded after him. The Russians were gaining on them, and he heard their hoarse triumphant calls. He dropped his reins, nocked an arrow, and twisted in his saddle to shoot. The dun ran straight on.

"Yip-yip-yip—"

That was Buri. The high call ranged over the Russian shouts and the distant noise of the fighting. Psin shot again, and a Russian horse somersaulted into the snow.

Nobody was coming to help them. Psin gritted his teeth. The dun reached the flat ground and stretched out, running for the gap between the two tangled battles—Mongke on the south, Quyuk and the second Russian army to the north. The Russians chasing him and Buri were almost close enough to throw their lances.

A great roar went up from the south. Psin had an arrow drawn to his chin, and he released it before he looked. Mongke's army was surging back and forth across the trampled snowfield, and he could see no single Russian in their midst. The Mongols' highpitched screams mounted into the thin dawn light. A lantern flashed, somewhere.

The Russians after Psin faltered. Behind them, up the slope toward Kiev, stretched a trail of bodies. On the flat ground the Mongol horses were faster; they had no hope of catching them. They wheeled and galloped heavily off toward their main army, to the north.

Mongke's lanterns were flashing all over the field. Psin reined up and waited until Buri and the standardbearer were beside him. Buri said, "He did do it. I didn't think he would."

Psin nodded. He was panting, and his lungs hurt from the sharp icy air. He looked back toward Quyuk, who was leading the remaining Russians madly north.

"Mongke's sign, and two short greens. Maybe Sabotai feels like fighting."

"Maybe we should warn him."

Psin shook his head. He swung the dun horse around and headed west, to get out of the way of Mongke's army. Buri and the others pattered after him. "He'll be looking. He couldn't see a rocket now anyway."

Mongke's army was grouped up again. They started off after Quyuk. Mongke had spread out the line wide enough that the Russians could not double back without being seen. Psin and Buri and the standardbearer rode a little apart from the army, and as soon as it had settled into its trot Mongke galloped over to them.

"You saw more of it than I did," he said. "When you ordered us in, I thought they were still almost intact."

Psin laughed. "It looks that way, sometimes. No. There were less than two or three thousand of them left, and they were spread out enough."

"So I found out."

"You could have come and helped us," Buri said. "Eight of us, with a thousand Russians right behind. They chased us clear across the field."

"I didn't notice," Mongke said sweetly.

"They made us look ridiculous. Two separate battles, and the command post being chased."

The sun was nearly up. Psin looked at Mongke's face and saw the faint smile. Mongke said, "Who will laugh at us when all the Russians are dead?"

Psin said, "Take down the lanterns and get the banners out. Mongke, your line is ragged. Your black horses are riding the same formation they used crossing the river. Tell them to fill up the gaps."

Mongke held his horse back so that he could yell to his standard-bearer. Psin watched the lines pull together. It was a good mark for the tuman on the black horses if they kept formation until ordered to change it. The other two—one on bays, one on greys—had automatically closed up, filling the holes left by the men who had died.

"What color horse is Quyuk leading?" Psin said to Buri.

"Chestnuts with light manes."

"Hunh."

Buri shrugged. "It's a common color, at least. And Sabotai has a tuman mounted on chestnuts with red manes."

"The day will come when we search from here to Korea for bay horses with black points and white stockings on the hindlegs, just to keep each tuman different. The drawbacks to leading large armies."

A flock of birds sailed overhead, piping. Psin shaded his eyes to look after them. The sky was almost yellow from the sunlight in the haze.

Ahead, the rearguard of the Russians was nearly out of sight. The snow had turned to mud where their horses had churned it up. Psin squinted to see the Russians; he thought he saw a banner past them against the sky, but the Russians carried banners too.

"We should have left some men back by the city," Buri said.

"The city will be there when we're done here. No reason. And they might turn."

By now the Russians knew they were trapped. They could see the Mongols coming along behind them, and probably they could judge numbers well enough to know that this army was bigger than Quyuk's, which they were chasing. They would be wondering why Quyuk didn't wheel and hold them still until Psin and the others caught up. Maybe they had guessed.

To the east, the ground rose steeply into another bluff. The river was probably just beyond it. Psin looked west. Sabotai choosing his ground wouldn't have passed this up. He turned to the standard-bearer.

"Get the black banner ready. Buri—"

"Look. On the bluff." Buri turned to yell to Mongke.

On the bluff stood several beech trees; suddenly one of them flared up into a gigantic torch. Black smoke rolled back from it. Oil, Psin thought. Waiting until we came into sight. "Gallop," he said. "Don't charge."

They burst into a short gallop. On the bluff men on foot were forming a line beneath the trees. Psin could smell the wood burning from here. Mongke raced up and shouted, "Let me swing the western wing out more. Keep them from running out."

"No. Sabotai's over there. Look—there they go."

The Russians, up ahead, were turning, racing back toward Psin's army. Psin pulled the dun away toward the west. Buri and the standardbearer veered after him. Mongke charged up to the head of his line, shouting. The Russians pounded down toward them, and beyond them, Psin could see Quyuk's army and another, two full tumans, with their banners snapping over their heads.

"Black banner," Psin said. He jerked the dun to a stop three bowshots from the far edge of Mongke's line. The standardbearer waved the black banner on its pole, and with a yell the Mongols charged. The driving Russian line staggered under the wash of arrows.

"They'll charge up toward us," Psin said. He looked behind him. They could run before the Russians all the way back to Kiev. The dun shied, and he looked ahead again, counting. He could count only eight tumans. There were supposed to be nine.

"In God's name," Buri murmured.

Out of the middle of the plain to the west, horses leapt. They came up out of the snow itself, a flood of them, all up and down the plain from Psin, all chestnuts with red manes. The Russians, swerving west, fell back screaming through their own lines. Sabotai's tuman howled, raised their bows, and started shooting. The cloud of arrows threw a shadow over the snow; Psin looked up and saw them like a moving roof over his head. The Russians were milling frantically. The snow turned black with their bodies. From the west Sabotai's, from the north Quyuk's, from the south Mongke's —Psin's horse reared up, excited. A column of Russians broke from the churning mass and drove for the narrowing gap between Sabotai's line and Quyuk's. With each stride another horse collapsed into the snow. Armor flashed in the sun. Psin saw a man fling up his arms against the river of arrows, take three shafts through his forearm, and sag forward over his horse's neck. The remnants of the column broke through and raced away, and Quyuk's west wing wheeled to follow. In the center of the closing trap, the Russians left alive had thrown down their swords in surrender.

Buri turned toward Psin. "Do they live?"

"Kiev killed our envoys. They all die."

Buri nodded. The black banner came down, and the yellow spilled out across the staff. The Mongols encircled the Russians thickly and kept on shooting. Psin heard the Russians bellow in rage and fear. He turned and rode over toward Sabotai.

"That worked well," Sabotai called. "They were too surprised to meet us."

Psin jogged up to him. "Ravine?" He looked back at the scarred snow.

"River. Or a canal. Something. With a steep bank. The only other place was well up the river, where the forest closes in."

Mongke cantered up. "Where did you come from? You came out of nowhere."

Sabotai explained, his face glowing with pleasure and exertion. Quyuk was sitting his horse a little way off, watching them. His leather armor was fouled with blood.

"Are you all right?" Psin called.

Quyuk nodded. "It's my horse's, mostly. They killed one under me."

Sabotai said, "He's always in the middle of the fighting, that one. Let's go take Kiev."

"Ada," Djela said. "Isn't Grandfather's time up yet?"

"No. Catch." Tshant threw the end of the felt toward him. Djela picked it up and dragged it out full length. Tshant was lacing it to the yurt framework beside the door.

"Well, when?"

"When what?"

"When will Grandfather be—"

"Not for another eight months. And more." Tshant put one foot against the masterpole and pulled the lace snug. "Get out another length."

Djela trotted over to the packhorses and pulled down the top roll of felt. He looked toward Kiev, frowning. The line of yurts circled the city from river to river, and his father was probably right that the Russians wouldn't leave the shelter of their walls. But the one yurt on the approach looked so lonely. It was closer to the city than to the first row of Mongol yurts, almost within bowshot of the walls.

"Djela."

"I'm coming." He towed the felt over, and Tshant unrolled it.

Horses clattered by, on their way up to the lines forming to attack the wall. "Is Grandfather—"

"Stop talking about Psin. Help me get this up."

Djela sighed and stretched out the felt on the ground. Tshant held the laces in his teeth, pulled the end of the felt up against the poles, and lashed it. He worked his way along the yurt, lacing, while Djela straightened the felt and held it against the framework.

A great shout went up from the city, and Djela whirled. Tshant said, "Look. They've got the shield braced up. That was quick."

Djela nodded. All that morning every slave in the camp had been lacing shields together into a huge mat, and now they had carried it up to the gate and staked it firm with lances. He shaded his eyes. Beneath the shield roof, men chopped furiously at the gate.

"It's hot under there," he said. "Quyuk's not got his coat on." Quyuk had come out from under to look at the wall and ducked back beneath the shields when the defenders threw stones and filth at him.

"Hurry up," Tshant said. He had brought over another roll of felt.

Tugging at the roll, Djela craned his neck to see the city. The gate was monstrous, made of brick, but the walls were only of wood; Russians mobbed them. Suddenly they began to chant in unison. From under the shield roof, Mongols streamed, and one—Mongke—grabbed a horse and galloped down toward them.

"What are they saying?" Tshant said. "The Russians."

Djela strained his ears. "I don't know the words."

"I'm sure it's something pleasant."

Mongke charged by. A clod of earth spun up by his horse's hoofs struck the half-covered yurt. Tshant shouted, but Mongke did not pause to answer.

"Here come the damned women," Tshant said. He pulled Djela back, away from the yurt. Their slaves jogged up, baskets of grain on their shoulders, set down the baskets, and went to work on the yurt. They had been sewing shields.

"Ada, can I—"

"Yes." Tshant was staring up at the city. "Just be back before dark."

Djela whooped and ran off toward the tethered horses. He wished he had understood what the Russians on the wall had said; still, that Tshant had asked him pleased him. He jerked his horse's leadrope loose from the line and scrambled up bareback. The only trouble with knowing Russian was that it reminded him of Ana. But his father had said he had a new brother in the Volga camp, and that was worth not having Ana anymore.

He jogged through the belt of yurts around the city, looking for his grandfather. Psin wasn't supposed to come into the ordu, but they were having trouble with the great gate, and he might have sneaked in to confer with Sabotai. Three women hanging out wash yelled at him for splashing mud into their baskets, and one set a dog on him. He galloped away, leaving the dog barking in the street behind him. When he reached the place where the plateau dropped off into a steep slope, he reined in and looked toward the city.

There was a wide stretch of flat ground between the gate and the slope, and most of the Mongol army was packed onto its western rim. The gate itself was coated in copper, so pitted and dirtied now it didn't shine even when the sun shone full on it. The shield roof jutted out from it like a tongue from a mouth. While he watched the shield roof shook and swayed, and the Mongols beneath it bolted free. Other Mongols raced up on foot with bows, to keep the Russians off the wall.

The teeming action delighted him. The whole plateau seethed
with men and horses running. Overhead, ravens circled, waiting for
the dead. Quyuk, his coat draped over his shoulders, cantered his
horse down toward Psin's yurt; Mongke was riding up from the
lower camp, and Tshant and Sabotai trotted together to meet them.
They would be changing their tactics. Djela drew a deep breath
and let it out in a whoop. The cold wind and the wild action made
his blood sing. He whipped his horse into a flat run and bounded
down the rocky slope toward the open plain.

Quyuk said, "I have enemies enough. You've been just to me,
and I trust you, even if you hate me."

Psin glanced at him. In the darkness Quyuk's face was unread-
able. "I don't hate you."

Behind them, in the forest that clogged all this slope, two tumans
shifted and murmured in the dark. Quyuk said, "You set Tshant
against me. We used to be friends."

"You set Tshant against yourself. You shouldn't have tried to
bully him."

"Do you think we'll take the city tonight?"

"Yes."

"Tshant is . . . I don't think between here and Korea there's a
better fighter."

"There isn't."

"But he doesn't use it to effect at all."

"He's under a disadvantage," Psin said. He pulled the top off his
quiver. The sword dragged at his belt, and he eased it. Quyuk said
nothing, and Psin said, "Why don't you ask me what it is?"

"Because you'll tell me anyway."

"It's that he is my son."

"Tell me something I don't know. You take it so seriously.
We're all working under the same disadvantage. Consider
Mongke."

Psin laughed.

"What was your father like?"

Psin looked up at the city. Its walls were rimmed with torchlight,
and he could see the sentries marching along the ramparts. "Big,

strong and stupid, like me."

"That sounds like something I said to you when I was drunk. If I did I didn't mean it."

Under the shield roofs, it would be hot, close, and noisy. If a horse stumbled or a man fell, there would be no rising. Sabotai was suddenly enamoured of night fighting, probably because of the burning lights.

"I was very fond of my father," Psin said. "Everybody said it was unusual. It runs in my blood, the sons always hate the fathers. But my father died when I was young, just thirteen. Maybe that was it."

Quyuk's horse pawed at the ground, and Quyuk whacked it on the shoulder. He jabbed his chin toward the torchlit wall above them on the crown of the bluff. "They must know we're coming."

"Sabotai thinks they've lost their heart for fighting." Most of the Kievan men had died in the fighting outside the city. Besides, half of the Mongols were gathered up in front of the copper gate; they'd been unable to break it, but during the afternoon they'd built another shield roof here, on the south, and chopped the gate-doors to pieces. Once inside, Psin was supposed to see that the copper gate was forced from within. He doubted Kiev had enough men to defend both gates simultaneously.

"Did my grandfather kill your father?"

"Yes," Psin said.

"Would you be angry if I asked why you were spared?"

"When I went back to my people, after my father was dead, I had two choices. I could go for protection to Totoqua, the Grand Khan of the Merkits, or to Temujin. I went to Temujin."

"Even though he killed your father."

Psin nodded. "There goes the rocket."

"Why?"

"I didn't feel like dying." He jerked his head to the standard-bearer. "Two short blues."

The standardbearer pulled the strings on the lantern, and overhead the rocket exploded. Fountains of light poured down on Kiev.

Every Mongol on this slope yelled, and the sound lifted Psin and Quyuk like a wave and carried them headlong up the stony slope. Sentries rushed madly around toward the south gate. A shower of stones pelted them. Psin took a deep breath and held it. They charged in under the shield roof. The dun tried to swerve away but the weight of horses behind them thrust him on. The air under the roof was stale and stank of hide. Horses collided in the dark and neighed, and a man screamed. The things falling on the roof made it drum. Through the smashed gate faint light glimmered, and they struggled toward it. Horses kicked out. Quyuk yelled, "Slow down, behind," but the pressure only increased, until Psin and Quyuk squirted through the gate and into the narrow open.

"Watch your head," Psin shouted. "Let's go—up the wall."

He wheeled the dun, whipped him close to the wall, and jumped. The defenders were running away—they were old man, children, women. The rampart lay naked and open. Psin hung at arm's length from the rampart's edge, swung himself up, and for a moment lay flat, trying to catch his breath. With a crash the barricades fell apart under the sheer weight of the men rushing through.

Quyuk was beside him, and the standardbearer. The streets leading off from the gate were mobbed with horsemen. Psin couldn't see a Russian anywhere.

"Two reds, two blues," he said. "Quyuk. Round up as many men as you can and clear the wall."

"It's already—"

The building opposite Psin exploded into flames. Heat washed over him, and he staggered back. Quyuk was running north along the wall, shouting, and half the men packed into the street below him scrambled up onto their saddles and leapt onto the rampart. They drew their swords and charged off, yelling. Psin peeled off his coat. The light from the blazing building would make it hard for Sabotai to see his lanterns.

"Douse the lanterns. Nobody can see them. We'll have to yell." He looked back over the wall. The next tuman was mounted on bay horses. The standardbearer was trimming his lanterns, lined neatly against the inside of the rampart. Psin said, "Climb up on the gate frame and tell me what's happening."

The man rushed off. Psin knelt and called down to the men moving through the gate. "Who is your commander?"

"Buri."

"Here," Buri said. He rode up. "Where do I go?"

"Get up on the wall and clear it. Go west." Psin pointed. "No prisoners, remember." He stood up again and looked down to Sabotai's post. The lanterns ranged there were blinking steadily.

Buri charged off. On the gate frame, the standardbearer called, "I can't see any resistance anywhere. Maybe in the houses. The square is full of people. Women, children. Old men."

"Any Mongols there?"

"No."

"The copper gate. What's there?"

"Sentries. A barricade."

Psin bent down and hailed the nearest officer, a thousand-commander from Buri's tuman. "Take your men and ride to the copper gate. Force it. There will be men on the outside waiting. There is a barricade and sentries."

He straightened up and looked down the slope toward Sabotai. The lanterns there were signaling that he didn't understand Psin's signals. He swore. The building behind him was still flaming. He took three lanterns, strung them together, and lowered them over the outside of the wall.

"There's fighting on the wall near the copper gate," the man on the gate frame shouted. "Buri and his men."

Psin nodded. He pulled the strings on the lanterns, and Sabotai's winked back to confirm. Half a tuman broke out of the ordered ranks behind Sabotai's post and rode toward the south gate. Psin sent the next thousand-commander through the gate down to help Buri.

"Psin," Mongke shouted. He galloped through the gate and whirled his horse to look up. "There's no fighting—what do I do?"

"Standardbearer, how do you get to the square?"

"Take this street all the way down," the man called from the gate frame. He had hooked his legs over the crossbar and was swinging lightly; every time a new band of Mongols struggled through the gate the timbers quaked.

"Go to the square," Psin said to Mongke. "It's full of people. Remember that they are not to live—none but the smallest children. And loot the houses."

Mongke galloped away, and his men raced after him.

"The copper gate's fallen," the man on the gate said. "Tshant's tuman is coming through. Batu is with them—I can see his banner."

Only Batu would bring banners into a city in the middle of the night. "What's burning?"

"Only this building."

"Good."

"Batu is signaling—he's sent Tshant to clear the eastern side. Yeeow!"

The gate was coming down. The man clung with both hands. Men streamed through the gate—Kadan, Kaidu. Psin bawled to them to get clear. The frame shook, swayed, and collapsed grandly into the city. The standardbearer leapt clear just before the crossbar broke in half.

Kadan was yelling, and Psin bent to hear him. Kadan cupped his hands around his mouth.

"Sabotai says that we are to start looting if you think—"

"Yes. Go. Start at this end. There shouldn't be anything burning yet. I haven't seen a Russian since I came in."

"He wants to know why you don't signal."

"I will. Go on."

They scattered into the streets around them. Psin drew back to the wall. The standardbearer was climbing back up, unhurt. The roar of the fire across from them was dimming, and Psin could hear the timbers crashing inside. There was no sound of fighting.

"One yellow, three red," he said to the standardbearer. "The lanterns are all over the side.

The man leaned over to see. The last of Kadan's tuman dribbled through the gate and galloped off. The silence was unnatural, pricked through with yells and the sound of this fire. There was nobody in the street beneath Psin.

He sat down, putting his coat on again. The standardbearer said, "Two white from Sabotai."

"Two white." Psin rubbed his jaw.

"Withdraw," the man said, helpfully.

"I know. Can you see Batu's post from here?"

"No."

"See if you can rig up a mast and run the lanterns up on it."

"It would be easier to—"

"Wait. Here comes Mongke."

Mongke rode up, alone. Psin called, "Go over and find out what's happening in the southern part of the city. What have you done?"

"We are killing them." Mongke's mouth drew crooked. "You know I have no stomach for it. Ask if we may spare the mothers of the children. Otherwise it would be more merciful to kill them all, to the last infant."

"Yes." Psin turned to the lanterns and swung back. "My order. All the mothers of suckling children may live. Go find out—"

"I will." Mongke rode back toward the square to change his order.

Psin sat down on his heels. By the Yasa every creature in Kiev had to die, because of the Mongol envoy killed. But Sabotai had said that the children should live, and now the mothers were to live. The law was losing its meaning. Tuli, Mongke's father, had cut the heads off all the corpses in Nishapur, so that none could live by feigning death. "Consider Mongke," Quyuk had said.

Women, weeping and screaming, pushed down the big street toward the gate. Mongols herded them. Three men galloped up to stand guard by the gate, and the women started through. The weeping had died abruptly, as if they were all too tired to cry. Their faces were slack with despair. Most of them clutched children, but none of them held more than one, and several had none at all. Psin chewed his mustaches. Mongke was stretching the order. The women filed out beneath the eyes of the guards, who kept them from shoving or stopping. One woman paused, just beneath Psin, to wait until there was room; she held a child of two or three years in her arms. The child's head lay on the woman's shoulder, and its big eyes stared up at Psin. It looked neither frightened nor angry, just tired. The woman found a place in line and went on.

Mongke rode up. "Batu has told Tshant that he and his men could loot in the south. There is no resistance. All the men are dead."

"Send all your men out. We're supposed to withdraw. Go back and tell Batu, will you?"

"Withdraw? It's not looted yet."

"Kadan and Quyuk will do the looting. We'll split it up afterward. Go on."

Mongke called over his shoulder to a thousand-commander and sent him to Batu. Psin said, "If you're going out, make sure these people don't get into our camp."

Mongke waved and rode out after the women. Buri and his men rode up and organized themselves into double columns to leave. Mongke's gate guards had gone with him. Batu cantered up with his men and went out before Buri. Psin saw him collecting the women and moving them to a place to camp. He was playing khan, protecting his people as soon as they became his people. It made an interesting point: when did a conquered Russian become the responsibility of his khan?

Kadan and Quyuk appeared, and wagons moved in through this gate to transport the plunder. They would loot street by street and burn it all afterward. Psin stayed on the wall until he was sure everyone was out who was not with Quyuk and Kadan. When he left, the moon was rising, a thin scrap of pale yellow. Down in the Mongol camp, dogs began to bark, and a little inside the city wall, Russian dogs answered.

QUYUK IS GONE," KAIDU SAID.

Psin nodded. "Did Buri go with him?"

"Yes."

Tshant moved a pawn, and Psin frowned at the board. He did not like chess. He always did well enough at the beginning but when the game drew out his mind drifted on to other things and any child could beat him. Djela, hanging over the edge of the table, said softly, "Grandfather, look." He pointed to the threatened elephant.

"Will he be the Kha-Khan when Ogodai dies?" Kaidu said.

"Who, Buri?" Tshant slapped at his son. "Djela, don't tell him what to do."

Djela folded his arms on the edge of the table and rested his chin on his hands.

"No. Quyuk, of course."

"Turakina will have it for him, if she can," Psin said. "And Oghul Ghaimish."

"The sorceress," Kaidu said. "Who drives out men's souls from their bodies." He pulled over a stool and sat down.

Psin remembered Oghul Ghaimish, her face with its treacherous mouth and the long flat eyes. They said that Quyuk had married her under a spell.

"There are better men for the Khanate than Quyuk," Kaidu said.

"None in the bloodline," Tshant said. "Quyuk is very capable."

"Quyuk is a drunk. Batu—"

"Check," Tshant said.

"Grandfather," Djela said, in a pained whisper.

"Don't you think Batu should be the Kha-Khan?" Kaidu said.

Psin looked up, amazed. "No. Of course not."

"He is the heir of the eldest son—"

Psin got up and pulled Kaidu away from the others. He heard Djela arguing with Tshant; Djela wanted to finish Psin's game. Near the window, Psin looked out and saw no one and turned back to Kaidu.

"You know the story about Juji. Batu will never be the Kha-Khan. Nor any other of Juji's blood."

"No one ever proved—"

"Temujin was sure. Why else would he call him the Guest? Borte was almost a year in somebody else's yurt. Don't mention it. There's bad blood from here to Lake Baikal about it."

"Batu—"

"Batu would like to be the Kha-Khan. So would all the Altun."

"I am of the Ancestor's blood."

Kaidu's face was flaming, and his mouth grew tight. Psin said, "I believe it. You know that Borte was thieved away by Merkits— When I was a child I knew the man Temujin thought was Juji's father. There was nothing of him in Juji."

"Then why—"

"When the Merkits attacked, Temujin fled. He left Borte behind. He had less than a dozen men—he couldn't have defended her, he would only have died. It was his fault she was taken, and he always knew it. But he wasn't a man who liked to be reminded of his mistakes. Juji reminded him."

"It's unjust."

"Boy, Batu's ulus is richer and stronger than any to the east. You will come to it, probably. Why yearn after the Khanate?"

Kaidu said nothing. Psin shook him roughly.

"There are things not to be longed after. Learn that. And don't remind people of that story."

He went back to the chess table. Djela said, "And then I would move—"

Tshant said, "I don't like him."

Psin looked over his shoulder; Kaidu had gone out. "Why not?"

"He's like all Juji's kind. He isn't like us."

"Maybe."

"Temujin was right. Juji wasn't his son."

"I think it was a lie."

"Can you prove it?"

"No. It was Temujin's lie. And it's come to the best, like everything Temujin did." He moved a pawn, and Tshant's archer flew down and whisked an elephant off the board.

"Check."

"And mate. Let's go outside. It's stuffy in here."

Part Four

THE MONGOL
GENERALS

Temujin said, "My descendants will go clothed in gold; they will dine on the choicest meats, they will ride superb horses and enjoy the most beautiful young women. And they will have forgotten to whom they owe all that. . . ."

DJELA SQUIRMED, SWALLOWED A YAWN, AND STARTED TO FIDDLE with the laces of his coat. Tshant slapped his hand. "Sit still."

"I'm—"

"Sit still."

Djela thrust out his lower lip. The bench he was sitting on was hard; his rump itched. Across the half-circle, Sabotai looked almost asleep, and Kadan beside him was weaving from side to side. Djela had pointed that out to Tshant, just before the reception started, and Tshant had said, "He's drunk."

The two Russians in their fur cloaks droned on. For days, since Kiev fell, the Russian noyons had been riding in to pledge their submission to the Kha-Khan, and Djela didn't understand why he had to be here. "You are the great-grandson of the Ancestor," Tshant had said. So he had to wear the coat with the gold hooks and the gold lace around the collar, which jabbed him if he moved.

Tshant said, "What are they saying now?"

Djela listened. "That they will grow grain for us and send us all we need. They say their land is rich enough to feed us all and feed them and still fill the warehouses full."

Mongke, on Tshant's other side, murmured something under his breath. He smelled richly of flowers. Tshant had been wrinkling his nose all through the reception. He said softly, "Mongke. You smell like my stepmother."

"Oh?" Mongke lifted one arm and sniffed the sleeve. "I like it."

"Ssssh," Baidar said. He leaned past Mongke to nudge Tshant.

The two Russians knelt and touched their foreheads to the ground in front of Batu. Batu's two interpreters began to speak, telling the Russians how fortunate they were to be the servants of the only God-sent Khan and describing the benefits the Russians would receive under Batu's rule. Djela leaned against Tshant, put his head down, and dozed.

After a while, Tshant shook him awake again. "What are they saying?"

Djela straightened up. "They're talking about the—the Russians who ran away when we attacked. They say they couldn't stop them." He frowned, trying to follow the Russians' quick voices. "They went west, to Hungary."

Tshant nodded.

Baidar had been with the southern wing of the army at the Dniester. Tshant said that now that he was back they would talk about going on west. Djela scratched his neck where the stiff lace had roughened his skin.

Batu's interpreter said something, briefly, about the refugees. The Russians bowed. Batu lifted one hand and made a sign that showed he took them under his protection. "Stand up," Tshant said. "They are leaving."

Djela slid off the bench onto his feet. The Russians bowed to each of the Altun in turn. None of the Altun bowed back. The Russians turned to Tshant and Djela and their heads bobbed. Djela looked up at Tshant. "Now can I—"

"Ssssh!"

They stood until the Russians had backed out of the semi-circle. As soon as the reception was over, Tshant sat down and undid Djela's coat.

"He's old enough to take care of himself, don't you think?" Baidar said.

"The first thing he'll do is get the coat dirty so that he won't have to sit at any more receptions." Tshant pulled the coat off. "He didn't inherit that from my side of the family. Go play."

Djela ran off, headed for the horse lines. After the city had fallen, all but two of the tumans had gone off and pitched their camps farther south along the river, so that the horse herds were much thinner than before. He caught his horse and bridled it and climbed up.

The Russians were riding off, and he wheeled to gallop along beside them, a short bowshot away. One of them pointed to him, and he saw the man's mouth open, but he couldn't hear the words. With a yell he spun the horse and raced back up the slope toward Psin's yurt.

Psin hadn't come to the reception because of the ban. Usually he spent the afternoon talking to men from the west, but sometimes he was alone. Djela slid down and knocked on the door.

"Who is it?" Psin called.

"Grandfather, it's me. May I come in?"

"If you keep quiet."

The door opened, but through it he saw strangers, dressed in the clothes of merchants. He backed away.

"I sat down all day until now," he said. "Can I come tomorrow?"

"Any time you wish, noyon."

The door shut. Djela put one foot on his horse's knee and scrambled up onto the bare back.

There was nothing to do. Batu had told Tshant to come to his yurt after the reception ended, Psin was busy, and the few boys Djela's age in the camp were all slaves. He jogged up and down the road beneath the ruined gate, wondered if he dared go bother Mongke. Sometimes Mongke would tease him and play with him, but when he was in a bad temper he threw rocks. He was probably in a bad temper today, after sitting through the reception. Kaidu and the others were too serious to be fun.

He turned the horse and galloped across the slope, screaming the Mongol warcry. If anybody even heard him in Psin's yurt, no one came out to see what was happening. The horse carried him on around the slope and down to the hollow between the bluff and the plain. He sighed.

In the end he rode along the river, singing songs Ana had taught him in Russian. Most of them were sad and full of low notes, which he thought he sang rather well. His father roared when he sang, but everybody knew Tshant and Psin didn't understand music.

He remembered the times they had hunted along the rivers, in the summer past, and the heron that had lived just east of Chernigov. He couldn't remember if there were herons in the rivers around Lake Baikal. That reminded him of his mother and his throat filled up. She wouldn't know him when he got back, he had grown so big.

"Have fun, and obey your father, and when you come back we'll have long stories to tell each other, won't we?" He could remember exactly how she had stood when she said it, how her hair had shone in the light, how soft her cheeks had seemed. When he tried to remember what she looked like, he had to think of special times, or he couldn't summon up her face.

The horse snorted, and he looked around. A hare was bounding off into the brush beside the river. It was almost dark. He tightened up his reins. If he got back after dark Tshant would yell and threaten to beat him. He galloped back along the riverbank, hanging onto the mane.

The snow muffled the sound of the horse's hoofs. In the trees he passed he heard the high calls of birds nesting for the night. Low clouds were thrusting up from the west. He sniffed the wind, wondering if it would snow.

He hadn't realized how far down the river he'd ridden. The bluff where Kiev stood was still a long way off. The dark slid in from the east and stars began to shine. He was too late. The rule was that he had to be home before the first star shone. If the clouds had come earlier, so that the stars were blotted out, he could have argued the point.

When he reached the pass by Kiev's bluff it was full dark. There wasn't any sense in hurrying now. He let the horse pick its way through the tangle of trees and brush at the foot of the bluff. They had come out higher up than Djela had meant to, on the flat ground midway between the camp and the dead city.

He could go hide with Psin. He rode up to the isolated yurt, keeping it between him and the camp in case Tshant was looking for him. There were no horses tethered next to Psin's yurt. Djela frowned. He slid down and knocked on the door; Dmitri answered. Psin had gone off somewhere and Tshant was looking for Djela. "You had better go home."

"Let me in."

Dmitri shook his head. "Go home."

"I am a noyon of the Altun Uruk. Let me in."

Dmitri grinned. "You're a little boy who is afraid his father will beat him for staying out late. Go home. I'm the one who'll be beaten if you hide here."

"Oh."

Dmitri shut the door. Djela looked down toward the camp, glowing with banked cooking fires. Everyone would have eaten by now. His stomach pinched him. And he was cold. If he went down and crawled in through the back of the yurt, under the felt, he might be able to convince Tshant he had been in the back all the whole. Except that Tshant knew about that trick and usually searched the yurt before he went out looking.

No matter what I do I'm going to get yelled at.

There was one other chance: if he didn't come back until morning. If he stayed out all night, Tshant was usually so worried he forgot to yell, he just hugged him and fussed over him, glad he'd gotten back at all. He turned the horse and trotted up the road toward the city. He could hide all night there, go home tomorrow, and meanwhile think of a good story. The Russians had captured him and he'd had to escape and ride home. That was good. Even Psin would admire him for escaping from Russians. He dismounted and led the horse into the city, through the wreckage of the gate and the rotting shields.

It was colder in the city than outside. He stood still, thinking. His stomach growled.

Maybe I should go back.

But he looked up at the sky; it was deep black, the stars were gone, and the wind howled through it. It was too late to go back. Maybe he could have escaped from the Russians right after they'd caught him. But the Russians would still have been in the camp, and he couldn't imagine Russians stealing him in the middle of Batu's camp.

He mounted up and rode deeper into the city, looking for a place where he could make a fire and be warm. They had started burning Kiev a few days ago, but the snow had put the fire out before more than half the city had gone down. The horse fretted, and he whipped it on.

The horse's hoofbeats were awesomely loud. In the camp below they had to have heard them. Hoofbeats sounded behind him, and he whirled. The street was empty.

The horse tugged at the bit and walked on. Djela sat stiffly listening. He could hear other hoofbeats behind him, clear and strong. He whirled around, nearly falling off, and saw nobody.

His skin crawled. He reined the horse down a little crooked side-street, to see who was following him, but the horse took two steps and refused to go farther. The air here stank of charred wood, and the buildings on both sides were only shells. He turned the horse around, and it bolted.

The clatter of hoofs swelled up like drumbeats. He wrenched at the reins, dragging the horse to a halt. Even the horse was afraid.

He looked behind him, saw nothing, and bit his lip to keep his teeth from chattering.

On his right was a huge old building, hollowed out by fire. Only two walls stood. Through the windows he could see the black sky. The windows were like eyes. He eased up on the reins and the horse started forward quickly.

Inside the burnt building, something rustled, snarled, and fled scuttling. A timber crashed down. The horse shied, and Djela clung with hands and knees. His heart was just behind his tongue. The horse wheeled to face the building, and its ears pinned flat back and its forelegs braced. Djela looked until his eyes ached.

His back prickled. Something was looking at him. Wicked, mean eyes were staring at him. He had a swift vision of slavering fangs and blood dripping from a narrow ribbon of a tongue. He was afraid to look back. He turned the horse—slowly, slowly—and started down the street toward the gate.

In a sidestreet, something screeched. The horse half-reared, neighed, and galloped on. He could feel it quivering between his knees. The reins slid through his fingers, and the horse stretched out. The gate was far away, and he bent over the horse's withers.

Abruptly the horse leapt to one side, twisting, and Djela went off. He landed hard on the stones of the street, clutching the reins. The horse dragged him along the rough ground. He contorted, trying to avoid the hoofs, trying to get to his feet. At last the horse stopped and he leapt up, bounded onto its back, and charged straight for the gate.

Behind him every foul thing under the sky was watching. Dead cities. People had died here and not been . . . The walls loomed, sweeping toward him. He shut his eyes. Noise billowed out of the streets around him. The horse skidded to a stop, and he opened his eyes, cold with what he might see. But the horse was only trying to find a way through the rubble around the gate. He clung, praying, while the horse stepped over fallen timbers and circled a mass of broken stone. They would never get through, something horrible would leap on him before they got through. His clothes stuck to him, drenched with sweat.

The horse leapt the last line of trash and galloped down the road. Cool, free air swept over him. He dared not look back; he aimed the horse like an arrow at Psin's yurt. The horse slowed to go around it, and Djela jumped off. The door popped open and Psin looked out.

"Where have you been? Wait until your father—"

Djela flung his arms around Psin and wept. Psin hugged him. The great strong arms surrounded him and held him safe.

"It's not so bad," Psin said. "He won't hurt you. What's—"

Psin dragged him into the light. "You're bloody. What happened? Djela, come out of it. Dmitri, get me some water and a cloth. And grease. And—never mind about Tshant, the horse will bring him. Djela."

"Don't let me go. Please don't let me go." Djela burrowed his face into Psin's chest. He hung on as tight as he could to Psin's belt.

"It's all right. You're all right here." Psin pried his fingers loose. "Tell me what happened."

"I went into the city. It's full of monsters." Djela wailed, remembering. "Don't let them get me."

Dmitri was back again, with a bowl of water. Psin sat Djela down on the couch and wiped his face with a wet cloth. "How did you get scraped up?"

"My horse dragged me." Djela sniffled. "There were monsters. With wings and claws."

"You shouldn't go into a dead city. And you were riding without a saddle again. Weren't you."

"Yes."

Psin put his fingers under Djela's chin and tipped his head to one side. "If you don't watch out, you'll be a scarface, like me. Why did you go into the city?"

"I was going to hide. Until morning."

"Oho." Psin threw a robe around Djela's shoulders. "Dmitri, bring him something to eat. You're a fool, Djela. You should have come back and taken the scolding."

Djela curled up under the robe. "He said he'd beat me if I did it again."

"He wouldn't have. You know he wouldn't have."

"He keeps saying—"

A horse was coming at full gallop. Psin took the bowl of stewed meat from Dmitri and shoved it into Djela's hands. "Here he comes. Don't lie, either."

The aroma of cooked meat was delicious. Djela stuffed his mouth. "I won't lie. I'm almost grown up now."

Psin stared a moment, trying to understand what Djela had said through the mouthful, and suddenly laughed. "Grownups lie."

The door flew open, and Tshant said, "I knew he'd be here. His horse came down and I knew he'd be here. Djela—"

He looked furious. Djela cringed. "I didn't mean—"

"You never mean to." Tshant took the bowl away from him and stood him up on the couch. "The next time you do this, I'll make you wish— God's name. What happened to you?" He looked at Psin. "What happened to him?"

Psin said, "He went up to the city to hide, and he fell off the horse and was dragged."

Tshant shut his eyes. "He went into the city. He was riding bareback, or he'd never have fallen off. And he stayed out after dark." His voice rose to a howl. "Do you ever do anything right?"

Djela burst into tears. "I can't help it. I try, but it just comes out wrong."

Tshant cuffed him. "Go outside and wait. Beside my horse. On the ground. Both feet on the ground, both arms at your sides, head up. Understand?"

Djela nodded, sobbing.

"Stop crying. Go."

Djela stumbled down from the couch and went to the door. He stopped crying. He wiped his nose on his sleeve and glared at Tshant. "I hate you."

"Go outside before I—"

Djela dodged his slap and ducked out the door.

Sabotai looked around at each of the Altun, frowned until they stopped talking, and cleared his throat. Mongke and Kadan, who were drunk, imitated him, and Sabotai flushed. "Don't anger me."

"Sabotai," Mongke said. "We dread your anger. Would we incur it voluntarily?"

Psin put his hand up to his mouth to hide his grin. Batu leapt up.

"This is a kuriltai," he said. "You came into this yurt between two fires. Don't make a joke out of your elders."

Mongke opened his mouth, and Psin, guessing what he would say, shouted, "And keep in mind that this is my yurt and you are all my guests."

The Altun laughed, and Sabotai said, "Why shout?"

"To keep you from hearing what he said," Psin said. He pointed to Mongke with his chin.

"What did you say?" Batu said.

Mongke cocked his eyebrows. His eyes widened. "I? Speak in the presence of my elders? Come, Batu. You think ill of me."

"Be quiet," Sabotai said. "We have plans to make."

Kadan said, "Plans to agree to, you m-mean. The plans are already made."

"Y-yes," Psin said. "So be qu-quiet and l-listen."

Kadan laughed. "I'm drunk. At least I have an ex-ex-ex-" His face reddened with effort. Mongke shoved him.

"Ssssh. Listen."

He turned his bright eyes on Sabotai. Baidar and the others sniggered. Sabotai shut his eyes; his lips moved.

Psin said, "Batu Khan, Sabotai is communing with the Eternal Heaven. Why don't you explain the plans?"

Sabotai sat down with a thump, and Batu rose.

"Now that Kiev has fallen and the Southern Russians have paid homage to the Kha-Khan, we hold all of Russia. It is the Kha-Khan's will that we go farther west. Sabotai and Psin and I—"

A chorus of hoots interrupted him. He growled at the Altun until they quieted. Psin glanced at Tshant, sitting in the back of the crowded yurt. Tshant looked bored. He caught Psin's eye and made a face. Psin shrugged.

"Sabotai and Psin and I," Batu said, glowering, "have decided that the best way to strike west is to—"

"You have no talent for explaining things," Sabotai said. "Sit down." He rose and pointed to the rug at his feet. "Psin, get the map of the west."

Psin got up and pulled the map out of his bowcase. "Due west of us lies Hungary. North of Hungary are the Poles, the Lithuanians, and the Germans. South of the Hungarians there are several small tribes. Between us and the Carpathian mountains is Halicz, which hasn't yet submitted."

He unrolled the map, and Sabotai put one foot on the far edge to hold it down. "Here is Kiev. Here is the Dniester River. These are the Carpathian Mountains. To the north is a stretch of flat marsh-land, and a river called the Vistula. On it are two cities, Sandomir and Cracow, which we shall take."

He looked up quickly to make sure that they were paying atten-tion and saw them all leaning forward to see. He pointed to the Carpathians. "This is the pass we shall force, probably. We'll need hay to feed the horses; it's a rugged climb. On the other side is steppe, though."

Sabotai said, "Batu and I, with the main army, will force the pass. Psin and Mongke go with us, and Batu's brothers. Go on, Psin."

"South of Hungary there are more mountains, very rugged, al-most impassable in the winter. But a river cuts through them, the Danube, and the basin is open enough to travel through."

"The southern wing of the army invades along the Danube," Sabotai said. "Three tumans."

"West of Hungary," Psin said, "is forest. That will come next winter. The objective for now is to take the end of the steppe— Hungary—and whatever we need to make our position tenable there."

"What do we fight?" Tshant said.

"Stone cities. Problems, of course, but I believe we can bypass most of them. Sandomir and Cracow lie in positions to cut our sup-ply routes across the Vistula and must be destroyed. But most of the cities we can simply cut off from contact with each other."

"The armies?" Mongke said.

"Knights."

"Oh, well."

"Don't underestimate them. These are not like the Russian knights. They're big men, heavily armored, and they are born to one purpose, which is fighting. Some of them are even made priests, so you see how dedicated they are. They will charge, try to close quarters, and fight hand to hand. They use swords, and they're heavy enough to bash in a bull's skull. Sometimes they use lances, but they don't throw them. They try to run into you with them."

Kaidu laughed. Baidar lifted his head and said, "It may sound funny, boy, but I for one wouldn't like to have a horse and a big man in armor crash into me at all, much less with a sharp lance in his hands."

Psin sat on his heels, looking at the map. "I never saw them fight, these knights. But if they are anything like the Russians, and if what I overheard is any indication, they don't take orders on a battlefield. They charge, and the fighting breaks up into individual combats. They are not very mobile, either. They ride stallions—"

Tshant snorted. "Can they control them?"

"I said I didn't see them fight. Can you control a stallion when he's hot? I'd guess they just gallop around bashing each other's brains out. They use bits that would make you go white—solid-mouthed things with shanks this long."

Baidar said, "Can they defend against siege?"

Psin glared at him. "I've said about six times I've never seen them fight. I should think that if they were sieged they'd die before they hid behind their walls. What good is a horseman behind walls anyway? They're like stallions themselves: in a siege they'll fret and get hot and take the first chance they're given to attack whatever's sieging them."

Baidar grinned. "Easy."

"Not so. Just because they ride stallions and use monstrous bits don't think they can't ride. They do things with those big horses you'd never dream of teaching yours."

"What?" Mongke said, interested.

"I saw one knight pick his horse up into a rear and make it hop six strides on its hindlegs. I suppose if they're in the middle of a fight and want to get out they do that. And the horses rear up and kick out behind. Don't get too close behind them."

"Tell them about the bows," Sabotai murmured.

"Yes." Psin held out his hands in front of him. "Their bows are about this long, and they have boxes on them perpendicular to the grip and cranks to wind up the string to the nocking point. They shoot much flatter than ours do, and their range is about one third our bows, but I think their arrows will go through almost anything within range. It takes them a long time to load."

"Have all these areas been scouted?" Mongke said.

Psin shook his head. "I scouted the pass through the mountains. Merchants told me the rest. I don't trust them, so I checked everything carefully with as many different men as I could find. You'll have to do your own scouting in the south and the north."

Sabotai said, "Exactly. Now. Batu's brothers are coming south with the best of the troops we left north of the Volga. We'll have fifteen tumans. The Kipchaks, Alans and Bulgars have cut their herds early to provide us with remounts. They should be here within a few days."

"By tomorrow," Batu said. "I passed them, riding in from the Volga camp."

"Good. Three tumans will invade Poland across the Vistula, having taken the cities Psin mentioned, and drive west. One wing will raid into Lithuania to keep them busy. The main army will locate and destroy the Polish armies and anybody who comes to help them."

"Who commands?" Mongke said.

"Kaidu and Baidar."

Tshant growled. Psin almost laughed. Batu had demanded that Kaidu be given a command; since Quyuk had left he'd grown bolder. Mongke looked at Psin, and Psin nodded.

Kaidu said, "I want Tshant with me." His eyes were bright with pride.

"I'm not going to fight Lithuanians," Tshant said.

Baidar said, "We want Tshant to command our vanguard, if he cares to come with us."

Kaidu nodded happily. Baidar glanced over at him, curled his lip, and immediately pulled his face straight. His eyes and Tshant's met, and they both nodded.

Psin said, "Tshant will have to do your reconnaissance. I'm not sure where either of the cities are, and I've not got the faintest idea how far west you should go."

"To the sea," Mongke said. "Eventually. All right. What else?"

Sabotai lifted his head. "Where is Kadan?"

Mongke looked around. "He was—"

"He's in back of you, on the couch," Tshant said. "Under the yak skin."

Mongke and Kaidu pounced, delighted. Kadan had curled up behind them and gone to sleep. They shook him until he sat up again, groaning and striking at them.

"Kadan will command the southern wing," Sabotai said. "Kadan, are you listening?"

Kadan nodded. "Give me something to drink."

"Not unless you listen," Sabotai said. "You are to take three tumans and go south until you reach the Danube and follow it west, locating and destroying all resistance to us."

"Oh," Kadan said. "Of course. Certainly. Give me something to drink."

Batu said, "How can he—"

"Shut up." Baidar thrust a bowl of kumiss into Kadan's hands. To Sabotai he said, "He wants his brothers to command, doesn't he. I say we ought to vote on the commands and who should have them."

Sabotai drew himself up angrily. "The commands have already been decided. If you have any objections, take them to Karakorum. The Kha-Khan—"

"Just so long as Batu's brothers don't command," Baidar said.

"What's wrong with my brothers?" Batu shouted.

Mongke looked up. "This is a joint campaign. All of us are equals. If your kin command all the wings of the army, it's unbalanced. Besides, your brothers take orders from no one but you."

Psin said, "Stop fighting. Nobody has any more power in this than anyone else of the Altun. Kaidu needs the experience, so we send him north with capable advisers."

Batu said, "It's my ulus. And I'm the only one of you with the rank of khan."

"That's not so," Mongke said. "Psin is a khan. So am I."

Batu said, "Well, Psin isn't of the Altun, and—"

"Pick at straws some other time," Sabotai said. "This is a kuriltai, not a session to discuss rank. The main army will invade Hungary through the pass Psin mentioned. Immediately we reach the steppe, we will divide into four separate columns. Mongke will command one, to raid through the south of Hungary to the Danube and meet Kadan there before turning north. Batu will lead another group, with his brothers, which will swing through the north along the foothills. I will take the third and ride straight toward the Hungarian capital, destroying whatever resistance we find. Psin with the vanguard will have gone to the capital at all speed and will invest it and cut their lines of communication and supply."

"If they attack him," Mongke said, "does he fight them?"

Psin shook his head. "I will retreat until the rest of you reach me. They'll have a large army, and I'm not going to fight them with only one tuman."

"Is that clear?" Sabotai said.

Everybody nodded; Kaidu said, "Yes."

"Good. Go back to your yurts. Tomorrow, at your convenience, bring your tuman-commanders and thousand-commanders to Psin for a conference. He'll explain each situation in detail. I'll be here most of the day to listen and comment. The northern wing will take the three tumans camped northwest of here and move out within three days. Questions? Good. Go home."

Psin reined up. The plain stretched on to the western horizon, ridged and furrowed with snow. "I'll leave you here. Whatever you do, don't let Kaidu get carried away with his new opportunities."

Tshant nodded. He looked back at the army that jogged after them. "Baidar and I get along well enough to control him." He looked again at his father. Under the grease, the scars on Psin's face were almost invisible.

"You've got the best of the thousand-commanders, although I don't like any of your tuman-commanders," Psin said. "But with three of you you should be able to keep them to one side."

"I'd feel better if you'd done some reconnaissance up there."

Psin looked surprised. "Do it yourself. You're good at it." He lifted his reins. "Just keep moving, that's all. You know."

Djela said, "Be careful, Grandfather."

"I will." Psin wheeled his horse and started back south. Tshant watched him go. In his session with Psin the day before, Psin had stressed that all his information came from merchants whom he did not trust. "Just keep moving." To go into country no one knew anything about . . . "You know."

Father. I do not know. Damn you.

He swung around to follow the vanguard, already well past him. Djela pattered along beside him. The sky was overcast and the wind was getting colder.

Djela began to sing, and Tshant said, "Stop that."

"No."

"Go away, then. Let me think."

"What are you thinking about?"

"Kaidu." Tshant looked north, trying to pick out the front edge of the vanguard. His scouts were due to report.

"You said you didn't like Kaidu."

"I don't." He settled back. "When did I say that?"

"To Grandfather. After we took Kiev. You know."

"Don't tell anybody."

"I won't." Djela grinned.

Tshant looked at him doubtfully. Djela had never yet told anybody anything he shouldn't have. When he talked to his grownup cousins he usually made up elaborate lies about his adventures. Everybody but Mongke ignored him; Mongke invented even more elaborate stories, which Djela took for solid truth because Mongke told them with a perfectly straight face. Tshant wished that Mongke had come with them.

"You know most of the things Mongke tells you are lies," he said.

Djela shook his head. "Oh, no. I like Mongke. He wouldn't lie to me."

Tshant threw his head back and laughed. He kicked up his horse into a canter. Djela began to sing again, Russian songs. Tshant opened his mouth to tell him to stop, changed his mind, and listened. Djela must have learned the songs from Ana.

She shouldn't have died, he thought. She was going to be happy.

No. She had not been happy, and she wouldn't have been happy. He felt as if he had a stone in his stomach. It wasn't my fault. How could I have done anything?

"Ada, what's wrong?"

"Nothing."

He thought, She was unlucky. Anybody but me. Anybody else she might have . . . He did not know what she might have done, what might have happened. It was a blank in his mind, like the

Muslim sign that meant nothing. He rode away from Djela to keep him from seeing his face. His nerves were leaping in his face. There was something wrong with him, if he could not—

He didn't know what it was he was trying to think. It was something entirely new. It wasn't fair; nothing the elders had told him fit, and they were supposed to . . . protect him.

"Ada, are you all right?"

"Yes. I'm fine. Go away. I'm thinking."

The sky was immense, and the plain stretched on almost featureless in all directions; in the middle of it he felt helpless and small. He was not in the middle. It looked that way to him, but to someone standing on the far horizon, he was on the edge and that someone was in the middle.

"Ada. Here come the scouts."

"Good."

He slowed his horse. The action cleared his mind. He gulped in the crisp air. The fear that had slipped into his head vanished. He wouldn't think about it again. Whatever it had been that he had thought about.

THE SNOW HAD STOPPED FALLING BEFORE NOON, AND A SICK PALE sun coasted through the flying clouds. Psin with his standard-bearer and five couriers stopped to change horses; the main body of the vanguard was stretched out across the plain to the northwest. Psin had two tumans, one mounted on bays, the other on skew-balds. He threw his saddle onto his remount and said, "Any sign of the scouts?"

The two couriers already mounted stood in their stirrups and looked around. "Not yet."

"Hunh." He swung up. "We'll canter to get back into position."

They loped off. The sky was a dull, smoky color, and the wind lifted the fresh snow like dust. The dun horse, flying along at the end of Psin's lead rope, snuffled and kicked at the horse nearest him.

Since they left Kiev they had met nothing, no enemy scouts, no enemy messengers come to deliver up this territory without a strug-gle—no people at all. They had ridden into one village but it was deserted. Newly deserted, with some of the fires warm and fresh dung in the horse pens. The tracks had run off west. They were still following them.

"Scouts," a man near him said.

Psin looked up. Across the treeless steppe a horseman was gallop-ing toward them. Psin threw up one hand, and the horseman reined in and turned sideways to the oncoming army. All down the front line of the vanguard horses neighed and men called out. The scout stood in his stirrups and gestured hugely, carefully. Psin squinted to see.

"Read it," he said.

The standardbearer cleared his throat. "Villages. Just ahead. A string of them. Three—four. Running north to south. No resist-ance."

"Signal it read. We'll lope."

One of the couriers pulled out of the group around Psin, so that the scout could see, and gestured to him. The standardbearer dipped the white banner twice. Psin looked north and saw that the standards all down the front line were dipping. The vanguard shifted smoothly into a slow canter.

The scout had whirled and ridden off west. The sun was breaking through the clouds, and the wind veered around. In the snapping wind the banner crackled as if it were frozen. West, where the white steppe met the white sky, the horizon was uneven. The villages. Or village; he probably would see no more than one.

"Speed," Sabotai had said. "Strike them quickly and go on, don't stop until you reach the mountains. You know what to do. Let them think nothing travels faster than a Mongol army."

"Do I let them run?"

"Oh, naturally. Let them run and tell the people in the west what terrors we are."

The southern wing of the vanguard was out of sight and, hopefully, riding half a day behind Psin, a little ahead of Kadan's army far to the south. The whole design was elaborate enough to entertain a Muslim. Sabotai had said, smiling, "If we can't have fun fighting, we may as well enjoy the deployment."

"Why do we have to enjoy it at all?"

"Psin. How petty of you." That had been Mongke, curled like a mink on the couch.

"Fields," the standardbearer said. "Look at the snow up ahead."

The snow was rippled evenly from just before them to the horizon. Psin nodded. Now he could see the separate huts of the village, the pens for the animals. There were no stockades. No resistance, the scout had said. "Hang the sign for torches."

The standardbearer took the ribbon pennant out of his pouch and hooked it to the staff just above the white banner. Immediately the white banners floating at intervals to the north swung down and rose again, with the ribbons streaming out.

Entertainment. The horses stumbled in the fields, caught themselves, and plunged on. With the village ahead, the loose rocking energy of the army gathered itself and steadied. Psin heard their harsh voices calling out, asking if there might be plunder or at the very least women. The tempo of the hoofbeats picked up. Torches glowed here and there in the dark mass of racing horses. He could smell the biting smoke.

Banners dipping. The standardbearer said, "The fourth thousand of the skewbald tuman is moving north, Khan."

"They know their orders."

His horse bolted. Psin yelped; the sudden flash of speed pitched him back against the cantle of his saddle, and it took him three strides to get back his seat. He hauled the horse down, but everybody else was moving faster too. The village was just ahead of them. One man down near the second thousand from him yelled a warcry, and the whole army took it up. Psin's horse neighed. Psin leaned forward to look around the front edge of the army and saw that the line past the fifth thousand had sheared abruptly north and was galloping away. They must have sighted another village. His horse swerved; they were in the ring of huts.

The men behind him all carried torches. Before he could look to see if there was anything left here the village was in flames, one single flame. When he filled his lungs to shout the hot air stung his throat. He bellowed to the standardbearer to pull them out of the village—it was so crowded many of the horses were screaming from the heat. If there had been anything left alive in the village it was dead now. The Mongols poured out into the cold clean wind of the steppe. The flames roared in Psin's ears. He jogged out between two burning huts and looked north. Three columns of smoke stood in the sky on a line with this one.

The tremendous heat from the fire hurt his eyes, and he could feel the sweat pouring over his body under his clothes. He rode farther away and circled around to catch up with his standardbearer.

At sundown, couriers started riding madly back and forth along the vanguard's front ranks. The army camped in a straight line, so that it was well dark before Psin heard the reports, sixth hand, of the northernmost thousands. There had been six villages, all but one deserted, and all had burned. The smoke still hung over the eastern sky, blurring the stars. A handful of farmers had tried to stop the charging line but as far as anyone knew there had been no fighting at all: the Mongols had ridden them down.

Psin tugged at his mustaches. The wind was colder after the fire and he had smeared grease on his cheeks, so the mustaches were too gummy to chew. "Are they all back in line?"

"The seventeenth—seventh of the skewbald—camped just

within sight of the sixteenth, more north and a little west."

"Get them back into position by noon tomorrow."

Everybody else was sleeping; the men around his fire huddled together like baby chicks. But he had to hear the reports of the scouts, who rode in all night long. He dozed off between reports. It seemed to him that he no sooner sank into a dream than someone would shake him out of it.

"A river to the west. It's frozen but not to the bed. We can ride around it."

With the tip of his dagger he cut signs into a smooth piece of wood, locating the river and giving the scout's and his own opinion of the advantages and disadvantages of crossing weak ice. The scouts reported villages, and he asked them for precise distances. They said they did not know. He asked them questions that proved they did know but were unaware of it. For the third time he explained to them, as patiently and painfully as a father, that they should talk together before they came to him, to organize everything. They nodded, looking tired, and he sent them off to sleep.

In the dead black before dawn two couriers rode in almost together from the south and the east. The southern wing had run into an army of peasants and smashed it in one charge. In doing so they had gotten rearranged so that they were now a full day's ride south of where they were supposed to be. What did he want them to do? He swore at the courier and told him to wake up one of the five men sleeping around Psin's fire and send him off. The southern wing was to be back in position by the sundown after next. The courier blanched. Psin glared at him and turned to the other.

"Halicz has fallen," said the courier from Sabotai. "There was no problem. His advance scouts are picking up your reports."

The latest report lay under Psin's elbow. He nodded and sent the courier off to sleep. In the east pale light showed. He pulled his cloak over his shoulders and shut his eyes.

The lack of sleep gave him a headache, and the jouncing all the next day drove him nearly out of his mind. They camped alongside the half-frozen river that night, and again he slept only in snatches. The scouts were as disorganized as usual. His head was splitting neatly in half, and he expected at any moment to find his brains rolling down his nose. The stretch of territory across the river was

packed with villages, estates and a few minor towns that he would
bypass, and he had to make plans, give orders, send couriers, leave
wooden messages in obvious places. By dawn he was having trouble
seeing. He commanded the vanguard to break into thousands and
cross the river in twenty widely separated places up and down the
bank. Once on the far side they were to burn, pillage, cache the
plunder, take no captives, harass any large group of fugitives, and
band together again at the foot of the main pass through the Carpathians. The tuman commanders frowned at him.

"How will we find the pass, Khan?"

"You will look."

The nearer of the two opened his mouth to protest, but the expression on Psin's face stopped him. He shrugged. "The Khan
wishes."

"In two days, you will be under the mountains. Without fail."

"The Khan wishes."

In the crisp light the vanguard divided up. Psin stayed where he
was, sitting on the ground beside his fire, and rested his head in his
hands. He dozed a little. The pounding of hoofs and the shrill cries
dribbled into the half-dreams and kept him jerking awake. When
they were all gone, he started up again, ordered his standardbearer
and the couriers off due west at an even jog, and told them to hold
the scouts with them until he caught up. They made no protests at
all, but they stared at him as if he were speaking Chinese. He
growled at them; they left. All alone on the east bank of the river,
he turned out his hobbled horses, rolled himself up in his cloak, and
slept soundly for the first time in days.

The flames were higher than Djela had ever seen them before.
He remembered Moskva and Susdal burning, but Sandomir burned
even higher than those, like steeples made out of fire. It was the
wind, his father had said.

Between this little hill and the blazing city the Mongols waited,
dark against the red-gold of the fire. He could see them turn their
heads occasionally to see if the banners were up yet. Tshant was
filing his arrowheads, and the standardbearer, Jube, knelt on the
ground folding banners so that he could pack them up again.

Djela shivered. He had charged with the rest, through the storm of the defenders' arrows and stones, and he'd taken four arrows in his shield. It had been so quick that he still wasn't sure what had happened. Tshant said that the defenders had lost their courage, seeing the Mongols charge. They'd deserted the wall and the main gate. It was silly to be afraid now.

"You see why I don't want you to fight in cities?" Tshant said.

Djela nodded.

He remembered the close quarters when they broke through the gate, the streets jammed, and how his horse had lunged and fought trying to get through. But it had all happened so quickly.

"What are we waiting for?"

Tshant looked up, not at Djela but to the east. His mouth was set hard. "Kaidu. I sent him notice when I attacked. He's so damned slow. . . ."

He bent again and the file rasped across the arrowhead. The sound made Djela's back prickle up. His own arrows were all sharp, and his bows tended, and his shield patched. There was nothing left to do. He slid down from his saddle and checked the hoofs of the second horse on his remount string, preparing a detailed answer if anybody asked him why. Nobody did.

Tshant swore. The standardbearer threw his pouches across the pommel of his saddle and lashed them, his eyes on Tshant's face. Djela scrambled back into his saddle.

"Red banners," Tshant said. "And call up the thousand-commanders. We'll leave the plunder here. They can collect it when they come past."

Djela said, "Where are we going?"

"Southwest. Toward Cracow."

The red banner flapped open, booming, and the mass of horsemen between them and the city broke into a jog. For a moment there was no order to it, but suddenly the even lines appeared, and the ranks closed. It was fun to watch. They all started off purposefully toward the river.

"I thought you didn't want to go to Cracow."

What he could see of his father's face was stiff with anger. "I don't."

"Then why—"

"Because Kaidu is in command. I wish you'd stop doing that."

"Stop what?" Djela reined over closer to Tshant's trotting horse.

"Asking questions you already know the answers to."

"But I don't—"

"Shut up."

They were angling down to ride abreast of the first ranks of the army. The thousand-commanders galloped over; two of them were new, and Tshant had to be told who they were, which thousands they commanded, and how their predecessors had died. Both had been knocked in the head by furniture thrown out of windows in the city. Tshant described the formation he wanted and the commanders whirled and rode back to their men to arrange it.

· "Well," Djela said, "when will the courier be here?"

"He should have reached us already."

Djela started to ask what could have delayed him, but his father was definitely angry. Djela already knew: Kaidu and Baidar were arguing. It had happened twice before, when Tshant had wanted to do something and had sent to Kaidu for the permission. Baidar always took Tshant's side.

"I thought Grandfather said—"

"I told you. Kaidu has changed the order of march."

Djela had asked why before, but Tshant had only sworn at him. He looked at the army. It was spread evenly toward them from the river in ranks a hundred men wide. Up ahead, trees grew close to the river, and they would have to circle. Djela looked at Jube, riding just behind Tshant, but Jube hadn't gotten the banner out yet.

Tshant said, "If he doesn't reach us by tomorrow . . ." He took off his glove to take the stopper out of his kumiss jug. The side of his hand was blistering from a burn. "Maybe by— Hold up! Jube, red banner—"

Djela wheeled to look south. His breath caught in his throat. Around the clump of trees knights were riding. Their shouts rose like wolves' howling. Tshant was calling out orders, and the banners were streaming out in Jube's hands, but the knights were closing fast. He couldn't judge how many there were. The whole wood seemed full of them. Their horses looked huge. He jerked up his bow with the arrow set and shot.

"Follow me," Tshant said. "Djela. Come on."

Djela dragged his horse around. Tshant was galloping west, across the front rank of the knights. Behind them the Mongols were splitting in half, one half charging along the bank of the river, the other flying after Tshant. Before the knights lay only empty plain and the far, burning city. The knights bellowed. Djela shot again, but he couldn't see where the arrow went.

"Shoot at the horses," Tshant yelled. "White banner, Jube."

Jube shouted back and tore at the hooks on his pouches. The horses were running flat out. Djela held his breath, aiming. The knights were only half a bowshot away. They were aiming themselves straight for him. He let go the string, and this time saw the arrow all the way in. It bounced harmlessly off the armor on the horse's chest. He could see the bright pink in the nostrils of the knights' horses.

Tshant reined in suddenly, so that Djela swept past him, and came up again on Djela's other side, between him and the knights. They were still riding across the knights' charge, and the space between was getting narrower with each jump. Djela forgot to shoot, only clung to his reins. Tshant drew his bow. Behind him Djela could almost duplicate his point of aim; he saw the bright filed arrowhead center on a horse's breast. He heard the bowstring whine, and the red fletching on the arrow streaked across the gap. The arrow shattered the armor and the horse fell sprawling, throwing its rider. Djela cheered.

"Black at the dip," Tshant yelled.

Jube's shout rang in Djela's ears. He looked back. The five thousands following Tshant were bunching up, shooting into the oncoming knights. But the knights were within strides of reaching them. The swords glittered.

His horse turned on its haunches, with the knights so near their individual voices hurt Djela's ears. He drew an arrow, swiveled to shoot over his horse's rump, and saw, from here to the river, the thousands of Mongols doing the same thing. His fear slid away and he shot. His arrow skipped off armor again, but thousands of other arrows struck through armor and flesh and horses crashed into the snow. The knights were falling back.

"Yip-yip-yip—"

"Who's in trouble now?" Tshant called.

Jube bellowed something and pointed toward the river. Djela pulled out another arrow and shot into the knights. Tshant veered close to him, signed that he should stay with Jube, and sat back in his saddle. Djela gasped. Tshant's horse stopped dead so hard its forehoofs left the ground. Before they struck again the Mongol line was as far beyond Tshant as he was beyond the screaming knights. He spun the horse, his whip rose and fell, and the horse bolted toward the river down the gap between the Mongols and the Polish knights.

"Father—"

"Stay here," Jube shouted. "In God's name, do you think any Pole could outride him? Use your bow."

The knights were giving up the chase. Djela shot as quickly as he could, trying to hit the unprotected necks of the stallions. Jube cocked the bannerstaff to slow the Mongols, so that they wouldn't ride out of range.

"They won't turn their sides to us," Jube called. "They know we'll shoot their horses out from under them if they do. Can you see what's happening?"

Djela shook his head. All he could see was the wide curve of the Mongol line and the swarm of knights behind them. They were past the burning city; he could see its smoke in the sky off to the south. He dropped his stirrups, crossed the leathers over his saddle, and got his feet wedged into the shortened irons before Jube could stop him. The plain ahead looked even enough.

Jube was red in the face. "What do you think—"

Djela stood up. The wind almost knocked him down, but he leaned into it, holding his arms out to balance himself, and looked. Now he could see over the heads of the men around him: thousands of horses running, and the knights slowing down. They were starting to turn, down by the river. He dropped back into his saddle. Jube's eyes were shut.

"They're wheeling," Djela called. "Don't worry, I do that all the time."

"If your father—" Jube brought the bannerstaff down across his saddlebows. Far down the Mongol line, blue banners fluttered. "They were driving us, I thought. Into some trap. But I guess not." His hands moved efficiently, and the blue silk shook free. He raised the staff and waved it, so that the others could see it; the wind was blowing straight off the river.

Djela brought his horse around. He was dead last in the line, and the knights were riding away at an angle. Before he could shoot even one arrow they were out of range. He swore at the top of his voice. Off north a herd of riderless, saddleless horses galloped—the remounts, cut loose when the knights attacked. He crouched over his horse's withers and set all his energy to catching up with Jube.

"Banners," Jube roared. "I can't read them."

"Turn south," someone shouted, up ahead. "They've got the east wing pinned against the city. Cut south, outflank if you— Watch out!"

Djela looked around. The knights they had been chasing were swerving around again. They had pulled together into a compact mass. Jube with the staff lowered shouted something Djela couldn't understand. The Mongols whirled north, to ride away from the knights. Djela's horse, overlapping Jube's to the girth, didn't turn fast enough, and the two horses crashed together so hard Djela's horse went clean off its feet.

Falling, Djela heard Jube's voice but not the words. He kicked his feet out of the stirrups and landed on his shoulders, well away from the horse. The ground shook under him. The thunder of hoofs was all around. He remembered that the knights' stallions were iron-shod. His horse was up, but even before he scrambled onto his feet big stallions charged between them. The knights swarmed all around him.

He kept his feet—the stallions shied away from him, and he forced his rigid arms to flail up and down to keep them scared. His tongue was sticking to the roof of his mouth. Steaming flanks and armor edged like swords filled his vision. He thought of his mother and his grandmother. A great iron-mesh arm swung down and hoisted him up onto the saddle. His face pressed against cloth that lay over chain links. The high pommel thudded into his stomach. They were taking him away—he'd never get back again. The knights were shouting over his head in their thick voices, laughing.

They spun their horses again. Clutched in the knight's rough arms, he turned upright and got one leg on either side of the saddle. They didn't maneuver like Mongols, their horses caromed together and fought and everything got tangled up. His knight reined the horse in hard. Under the armor the stallion was running with sweat, and the pumping breath of the horses all around was like a bellows. They were galloping back toward the river.

Djela could see nothing beyond the clanking bodies around him. The sky in front of them was stained with smoke. They were close to the city. He stared at the wide shoulders of the knight directly in front of him, and while he watched a long arrow with blue and yellow fletching thunked into the knight's spine. He winced. They would surely kill him now. His mouth was full of dust.

The Poles cried out. Djela wrenched at the arm holding him, but he couldn't budge it. The knight squeezed him hard and his ribs cracked. He felt sick to his stomach. The knight yelled something in Polish into his ear. Other arrows sliced into the mass of knights, and saddles emptied. There were Mongols in front of them—a yellow standard. Djela screamed for help and the knight clouted him on the side of the head. The Mongols in front of them parted, and the knights charged through the gap between them, and more arrows struck them. Djela prayed that one might hit him, so that he wouldn't have to go into slavery. His knight grunted; he had a shaft through the elbow. He shifted his reins to the hand that held Djela and yelled to the other Poles.

A horse surged up alongside, and the Pole on it plucked Djela out from in front of the first knight. The horses turned again, laboring, and started off west. Djela's face was crushed against a wool cloak. He could barely breathe, but when he tried to pull his face away from the cloth the knight only pressed his head down harder. He thought about dying; he began to cry. He could tell by the way the knights rode that they were running for home.

The wool in his face made it hard to cry. One of his legs was asleep, and when he shifted the knight whacked him on the head. That hurt. He lost his temper. One of his arms was wedged between his body and the knight's, but the other was free, dangling down the horse's side. He reached around in front of his head, caught the knight by the belt, and wrenched himself out of the knight's grip. The knight yelled. Djela slid headfirst out of the saddle, still clinging to the wide belt. He twisted, got himself right end to, and took a good deep breath. The ground was streaming by. He let his feet hit, bounced, and swung up behind the knight on the horse.

The others were reining over. Their great paws scrabbled for him. He snatched the dagger out of the knight's belt and drove it to the hilt into the man's throat. The Pole screamed, and his horse reared. Djela tossed himself lightly to the ground. A horse vaulted him, and he leapt up and ran.

He could see only a little in front of him. They were below the crest of a small hill, and the close horizon was of trampled snow. He looked over his shoulder and saw the knights charging after him, but they'd taken so long to turn that he was well ahead. He laughed back at them and settled down to run. His own dagger was still in his belt. He shortened stride to keep from slipping and got to the top of the hill.

Over by the city, there was still fighting. It was a long way away. He made himself breathe properly. A few Mongols were galloping toward him, still much nearer the city than to him, and he flung up one arm to signal them. The knights pounded along after him. They were catching up, but their horses stumbled with weariness. Djela didn't lengthen his stride. The Mongols had seen him and were racing forward.

A Polish voice shouted. He glanced back and saw them wheeling, their horses sluggish and unhandy. They were fleeing. He stopped and watched them go. When they were out of sight beyond the hill, he jogged up to the crest to see. They were headed off as fast as their horses could move. On the slope behind they had left the man Djela had killed. His chest swelled with pride and triumph.

Jube trotted up. "Thank you."

Djela looked up at him, puzzled.

"For rescuing me," Jube said. "The Yasa says I can't leave my position, even to help a fallen companion." He grinned. "The Yasa doesn't take into account that the fallen companion might be my commander's young son. Here, get up behind me. They're just cleaning up down there, and we can plunder a little."

SABOTAI SAID, "YOU LOOK FIT."

"Hah." Psin rose. "I've been squatting here for three days waiting for you. We've cleared out everything for two days' ride to the north. Those foothills are full of fighters. It's like digging out weasels. My southern flank is still half a day east. They chased two or three hundred peasants up here ahead of them, and I let them go through."

"Good."

"Any word from the north?"

"Sandomir has fallen. Cracow has been burned. Tshant fought a Polish army that had outridden his scouts, if you can imagine that, and tore them to ribbons. A large army. Kaidu believes they were from both Sandomir and Cracow. You were right. They don't like to be sieged. That should make it easier. Kadan has run into no trouble at all in the south. His main problem is moving slowly enough that he doesn't lose contact with us."

"Were your couriers from Kaidu or Tshant?"

"Kaidu. Why?"

"I was wondering how the divided command was working."

"No one's complained."

Batu, flanked by his brothers, galloped up and slid out of his saddle. "I've been to the pass. Berke says we have hay enough. When do we fight?"

Psin looked past him at Berke. "Where is the hay?"

"Packed up in bundles on the mules," Berke said. He thrust his hands at the fire. "The wind's raw. Psin, you rode that path in the summer. It's covered with ice."

Batu said, "It's not so bad. But the fort at the top—"

Psin got up. His camp was on a rise higher than the ones around it, and he could see the fires and the men around them all to the northern horizon. He had gone up to the pass. The Hungarians in their fort had yelled at him and thrown rocks and offal. The pass was wide, and the footing decent, if it didn't snow. But the peaks had been hung with clouds for days now, and the wind rushing down from the heights cut like an icy rope. He looked back at Batu and saw him arguing some point of attack with Sabotai. His brothers behind him looked dissatisfied and wary.

"If we try to break through without taking the fort," Batu was saying, "they'll only cut us in two, leave the half caught inside the mountains to whatever's waiting below, and starve us off this slope."

Sabotai nodded. "But how do we take a fort made out of that rock? We can't starve them out. The far slope can supply them until we die of old age."

Psin walked along the rise until he reached the place where he had cut the trees down; through the gap he could see the upper reaches of the road to the pass. If these were Mongols they fought he would know for certain that they had word of the fighting in Poland, but the Hungarian lines of communication were supposed to be slow and unsure. He went back to the fire. Sabotai was nodding impatiently, waiting for Batu to stop talking.

"Psin. Have you sent scouts into the mountains? To find other passes?"

Psin sat on his heels and poured himself wine. His kumiss had gone bad the day before. "They found passes. I've sent scouts into Hungary itself. They aren't back yet."

"So," Sabotai said to Batu. "We will know for certain what waits for us on the other side. If nothing—"

"Nothing? They know we're coming." Batu frowned. "Are they fools?"

"They don't fight the way we do," Sabotai said.

"That's mild," Psin said. "They fight every man for himself, and they are used to choosing the ground and ending the whole war in one battle. I don't think they'd choose the ground at the foot of a slope, do you?" He sipped the warm wine.

"When will your scouts be in?" Batu said.

"By tonight. I hope."

Sabotai reached for the wine. "If they don't come in tonight, we can't wait for them. We can't risk a storm."

Batu said, "Can we use burning lights?"

"I've only got two left, and they're both soaked from being dropped in a river when I didn't take Psin's advice. We'll use lanterns."

"They'll see us coming," Batu said.

"The path is hung over with trees," Psin said. "Until just below the pass."

"Good." Sabotai put his gloves in his belt. "We can use the trees for bannerstaffs."

"Where's Mongke?" Psin said.

"Sleeping. He rode scout for me last night."

"I'm going to get some sleep," Batu said. He turned his horse and his brothers silently followed.

Sabotai said, "I don't want you in the vanguard when we ride. It's going to be nasty, up there, especially if it snows. That wind's like a waterfall—you've been sitting under it for three days?"

"Yes."

"I wish I trusted Mongke enough to send him up first."

"Trust him. Send him."

"Psin. If the vanguard falters, we'll be in a mess. But Batu doesn't think fast enough."

"Send Mongke."

Sabotai pursed his lips, his eyes steady on Psin's.

"Or send both of us—him and me."

"I'll send Mongke. His honor guard is in my center. If he takes them—"

"No. They've not fought under him for two years, and they were leery of him in Korea. Send my skewbald tuman."

"Which of the two you've been working with do you want to take to Pesth, when we get across?"

"The others—on the bays."

"Good. Now. Suppose we send him up to the fort, in an attempt to storm it."

"Impossible. He can't."

"Just an attempt. In the meanwhile, under the cover of his attack, we move Batu's men in behind him and to either side. Mongke can retreat, get into some sort of tangle, and fall back through the middle. Would the knights attack?"

"They might."

"Leave the fort?"

"Maybe."

"We can try it, at least. If Mongke's retreat looks like a complete rout, of course they'll come out. Don't you—"

A horse was cantering up the slope toward them. Psin leapt up. "It's one of my scouts. Nejai."

The horse was staggering in its weariness. The scout sat back, and the horse stopped so abruptly Nejai nearly fell. He slipped down. His face was grey, and his lips were so stiff he could barely talk.

"I've been to the—to the far side. They have a supply sta-station. Knights—no more than twenty. A lot of—of peasants." He shut his eyes. "Wood. Hay. Grain, and herds. I . . . went back toward this pass a little. Nothing."

"Good," Psin said. "Go get some sleep. Eat. Don't even bother to go. Stay here."

The scout opened his eyes and grinned. "The Khan wishes."

He curled up beside the fire, pulled his cloak over his face, and slept. Psin bellowed to a man passing to take care of the horse. Sabotai said, "How did he get across the mountains?"

"There's a gorge half a day's ride north that leads to a stream bed that goes down the other side. He took four horses with him. From the looks of this one, he rode the others to death."

"If he got through, can we suppose it's unguarded?"

"The reports say it's so narrow and the trail so rough nobody ever uses it. They might not even know it's there."

"Ah," Sabotai said gently. He rocked back on his heels. "But you do."

The gorge twisted in through the heart of the mountains, clogged with rocks, slick with ice from the stream that had carved it. They had already lost two horses. Psin kept one eye on his remounts, crowded in behind him, and the other on the trail. So far they had found one place where three horses might walk abreast. Everywhere else was like this: the horses, snugged up on the lead-lines, scraped their sides on the rock cliffs.

Ahead of them, above the spruce trees and the lower slopes, there was a mountain with a sheer rock face that he was heading for. Up there, Nejai had told him, they would find the other trail. He couldn't see the mountain anymore, because of the dark and the clouds, but Nejai had said it would be dawn before he reached it. He let his dun horse pick its way around a mass of icy rock.

"Two short flashes," he said. "There's a dead horse up here."

The man just behind him craned forward. "God. He couldn't drag them off the trail, could he."

"He was in a hurry, damn you." The dun horse was snorting at the stinking wet body, and Psin kicked him on past. The rocks were coated with ice that glowed dimly, like the waves on Lake Baikal in the dark. The dun slipped and went to his knees.

"It's snowing," someone called.

"Lovely."

He knew why the Hungarians hadn't bothered to guard this gate into their precious country; no sane man would try to ride through it. Ahead the two sides of the gorge came down to a point. There was no level ground at all. The horses tried to refuse and he whipped at them, leaning back out of his saddle to reach his re-mounts. Wet snow drifted in under his collar. They scrambled noisily along the naked stone. Lantern light wobbled over the trail in front of them, showing the edges and broad sloping surfaces of the rock. Clumps of moss hung from the cliffs and swept across his cheek. It was almost dawn.

Probably, out in the open where people were supposed to live, it was dawn. The cliffs towered up over him, but he could see the pine trees along their rims. The horses inched along, swaying from side to side, their heads low. The dun snatched for a mouthful of moss.

The snow falling in the light of the lantern obscured the trail. He could see rocks thrusting up out of the bed of ice. Ahead, a tree had fallen into the gorge and lay across it, the trunk end still high up the side. He rode toward the high end and bent over, his cheek against the dun's shoulder, so that the horse could squeeze through. Branches raked his back. The dun missed his footing and almost tripped headlong, and he called back, "Watch out."

Beyond the windfall, the gorge made a sudden turn; he reined up to be sure his men were getting through. He had left the camp in the middle of the afternoon, and he was glad he'd pushed the pace. Before the snow had gotten deep enough to stop them, all or nearly all his thousand men would be on the way down the trail. The snow wasn't falling thickly yet.

They pushed through the turn, where the cliffs pinched the trail to a thread, and turned into the force of the wind. Tears sprang to Psin's eyes. He leaned forward, bunching his cloak around his neck, and jammed his hat down hard over his forehead. The dun tucked his nose in to his chest. But the ground was opening up a little, and there was springy moss underfoot. He glanced back and saw the men moving after him gasp when the wind struck them.

A small furry animal darted out of their way. The dun didn't shy, but the horses behind him did, reeling around in blind unison. Whips lashed behind him, and the dun threw all his weight against the leadline to drag the horses forward.

"Call out," Psin shouted.

"All straight back here."

The snow was falling more thickly; it whitened the front of his coat and built up into a crest along his horse's mane. Ahead it was light enough to see the trail without the lantern, and he shuttered it. The trail curved. Up ahead, where the gorge walls widened, he could see the horned mountain above the nearer crowns of rock. The snow fell across it and almost shut it out.

Before them, the trail threaded up a face of ice. He reined the dun to one side of it, and they scrambled up. He could hear the men behind him yelling and whipping their horses. He turned to look back and saw the gorge full of men as far as he could see. The wind froze his ears, and he tucked them deeper under his hat.

The gorge petered out. The trail drove straight for the mountain over rounded hills. The few trees were sheaves of icicles from the wind and the snow. The dun broke into a jog, but the men behind yelled to Psin to wait, and he drew down again. The snow was still too light to hurt. They wound down a steep slope and up another and came out just below the horned mountain.

"Ride to the north of it," the scout had said. Psin started up a snow-covered rise, unshuttered the lantern, and pulled down the red pane. There were no trees; they were above the timberline. The wind swept down off the crag and sledged into their faces. The dun sank to his knees in the snow.

"Call out," he yelled.

Call out, the echo said. Call out, call out.

"Behind you," someone shouted up, and the echo caught it. Every man in line was shouting in turn, so that they would keep together. He glanced back and saw the long snake of riders down this slope, up the next, and over the crest into the one beyond. Swinging back, he tried to see where they were going, but the storm was getting worse.

The dun staggered along, dragging the remounts behind him. Psin could feel the rough ground beneath his hoofs. The snow was crusted in spots almost thick enough to bear the horse's weight, but every third step it would break, and the dun would stumble. The horse's black mane turned dead white.

Ahead, something like an antelope trotted across their path, stopped, sniffed, and bolted away. Psin shouted again and heard the calls ring out behind him, just a little distance behind him, until the sound was muffled in the falling snow. Now, in front of him, he could see ridges of black rock breaking through the snow. The dun was laboring against the steep slope. Psin squinted against the snow and saw the arched face of the mountain to his left, almost beside him.

The dun stopped dead in front of the upthrust of black rock. It was too high to climb over. Psin rode along it, fighting his remounts, until they came to a place where the rock had broken. The dun put one forehoof on it, crouched, and jumped across. He skidded through the snow, turned sideways, and fell. Psin landed hard on his shoulder. The bannerstaff snapped under him. He rolled over and stood up. The horse was on its feet, shaking each leg in turn. His men were pushing through the gap in the rock.

"Look," one shouted, and pointed.

Psin turned. The storm ended here, as if there were a wall to stop the clouds. To the west the mountains fell away in a series of sheer drops into the timber. Sunlight glittered on the snow. He could see the trail Nejai had taken, off to the north. He mounted up and rode toward it, trotting the dun a few steps to make sure he wasn't lame. The trail was steep and icy but if the storm didn't follow them over the going wouldn't be as bad. The dun went into the trail without hesitation. Psin worked his shoulder carefully, found nothing broken, and settled down to watch the trail.

*   *   *

By dusk of that day they had reached the Hungarian supply station. The knights were all half-drunk, and the Mongols stormed through in one charge. Immediately they turned their horses out and went to sleep.

After midnight, Psin woke up and with three other men rode the trail up to the Hungarian pass. There was no way to tell Sabotai that they were here, and Sabotai wasn't sure the burning lights would work after being dropped into an icy river. The closest the Mongols could get to the pass was the foot of the trail up the last slope; if they came closer the knights would know they were there. Psin went back to the supply station and sent half his men up to the slope to watch.

"Sabotai is attacking today, isn't he?" one of his men said.

Psin nodded. "At noon, he said."

"We're tired. That was a terrible ride."

"What do you mean, tired? You had a pleasant trip through some pretty hills, with a nice fight at the end and a good rest—"

The man laughed. "Of course. Are you aware there's no wine?"

"No wine. That's bad."

"And very little meat."

"Damn you. Don't bother me with these things."

It was nearly dawn. Psin went back inside the hut at the supply station, roused out the rest of his men, and led them all after the first five hundred. He was hungry, and his horse was tired; half a night's rest had only made them all irritable and groggy.

If they couldn't draw the knights out of their fort, taking the pass would be more difficult and take longer. The knights certainly wouldn't leave the walls if they knew a thousand Mongols were waiting just below the pass on the western side. He couldn't charge up at the first signs of fighting in the pass. He put two men into trees where they could see into the pass, but they called down that the fort was out of sight. He swore.

The sun rose. Light streamed over the mountains; they could see it in the sky although their slope was still deep in shadow. Clouds blustered off toward the west, too light for snow. Two of Psin's men shot a wooly goat and cooked it, splitting it with the others so that they all got no more than scraps and a taste of crisp fat. The smallest owl Psin had ever seen caught a mouse almost at his feet. The wind lulled.

"It's warmer here than on the other side," one man said to him.

"Yes." Psin squinted toward the pass. "Look out. Here comes a knight."

He turned and yelled to a group of Mongols beside a little fire. They bolted toward their horses. The knight was cantering toward them along the road, his reins slack. He hadn't seen them yet. Psin's men vaulted into their saddles and started to meet him.

The knight caught sight of them coming and stopped his horse dead. Psin stiffened. The knight whirled back toward the pass. His horse took two great bounds, and an arrow brought it down. The knight pitched into the snow. The Mongols trotted over to him, looked down, and turned. They were well up the road to the pass. Psin's throat was tight with fear they'd be seen. He gestured to them, and they jogged their horses down toward him, without bringing the knight or killing him. One rode straight to him.

"Did you leave him up there to crawl home and tell them where we are? What—"

"He's dead. He broke his neck." The Mongol dismounted.

"Khan," one of the men in the trees called. "They are fighting, in the pass."

Psin swore. He stopped the wild plunge toward the horses and made his men sit down again. This was another of Sabotai's stupid ideas. He did them no good, sitting down here unknowing. He paced up and down, trying to hear the sounds of fighting, could not, and sat down.

"Can you see what's happening?"

"No—all I can see is Mongols."

Psin groaned. He jumped up and went toward his horse. His men started forward, eagerly, and he gestured to them to stay still. Mounting, he rode up the road a little, standing in his stirrups.

He saw nothing, but the closer he got the more he could hear. The pass rang with shouting and the sound of horses. Rock clattered, somewhere. He rode closer. Eagles circled above the pass, and a loose horse bolted down from it, neighing, its reins flying. A Mongol boot was still caught in one stirrup.

"Yip-yip-yip—"

That had to be Mongke retreating. He turned and rode back to his men. "Now. Mount up. Let's go."

They piled into their saddles and charged even before he gave the signal. The road was broad and even, and the horses reached a full gallop within a few strides. They bolted past the dead knight. The screams and howls of the Mongols in the pass reverberated from rock to rock, and beneath them were the high calls of the knights. He heard metal grate on metal.

Horses spilled down over the western edge of the pass—the knights' horses. The knights were still on their backs. They were running, headed straight into Psin's column. He hauled out his bow and fit an arrow. The knights were coming like an avalanche. There was no place for the Mongols to go to get out of their way. He shouted, "Full charge!"

He shot, and saw the arrow slam into one knight, but before he could nock another arrow the full force of the knights hit him. A huge horse ran into his horse, a sword swiped at his head, and his horse staggered back, still on its feet. He ducked, his bow useless. The knights swarmed around him. He heard his men yipping. A hammer crashed into the small of his back, and he lost his sight. Clinging to his saddle, he weaved back and forth. His horse was rearing and kicking out. His eyes cleared, and he steadied his horse. Knights surrounded him. He jabbed at their eyes with the tip of his bow. His back hurt every time he moved. The knights' horses rammed into his, and his horse was lifted off its feet and carried back down the road and deposited on its feet again.

"Eeeeeiiiyyyyaaah!"

He drove his horse to the side of the road and dove from the saddle into the heavy brush. He heard the whistle of arrows in flight, and getting to his feet he saw the knights falling before the shower. Mongke's men, shooting steadily, streamed down the road after them. Psin's horse stood beside the road, reins trailing, and he vaulted on and charged with the others.

The road was covered with bodies—knights, Mongols, horses. The remnant of the fleeing knights raced on ahead of them. Arrows thudded into their backs. Psin caught up with a knight, reached out, and got his fingers around the man's belt; he tugged, and the knight flew off his horse and landed under the hoofs of the Mongol charge. Psin lost his balance under the weight and nearly went off. He got one arm across the pommel of his saddle, hooked his heel over the cantle, and hung on. The horse began to slow, leaning against his weight, and he pulled himself up again.

The last of the knights was so far ahead that they would never catch him; he was even out of bowshot. Psin stopped his horse and drew off to let Mongke's men by. Mongke saw him and rode over.

"What happened?" Psin yelled.

Mongke laughed. "They took the first chance they saw to leave the fort. They were dying to run, so they did, and we chased. We wouldn't have caught them if you hadn't slowed them on the road."

"I think I lost all my men. They were on top of us before we saw them."

"You slowed them, though."

Psin looked around. He could see nothing but skewbald horses. One bay trotted along with the rest, but it was riderless. He rode off to the place where he and his men had waited that morning, and found two or three hundred men there, all wounded.

Mongke had come with him. "Are you all right? There's blood all over your back."

"Oh." Psin felt his back and winced. "Something hit me."

"Get down." Mongke dismounted. "Here come some more of your men."

Psin, on the ground, looked over and saw fifty more men on bay horses jogging into the meadow. "Too many losses."

Mongke helped him pull off his armor. "Bruise. Nothing broken. It's bleeding, though."

"That's all right. If nothing's broken—ouch!"

Sabotai with his staff, Batu, and Batu's brothers galloped into the meadow. "Psin. God above. Is all that yours?"

Mongke said, "He's got more blood than a fall pig. Yes." He was wrapping bandages around Psin's middle. Psin was suddenly weak in the knees; he leaned against his horse. Mongke explained what had happened to Sabotai.

Batu said, "We're in now. Psin, will you be able to ride? Berke—"

"No," Psin said. "I can ride." He stood away from the horse. Sabotai, watching him, grinned and nodded. His eyes were bright; he always looked happy when one of his stratagems had worked out well.

"Fill up your ranks from the skewbald tuman," he said. "You can leave for Pesth when you're rested."

"Good." Psin pulled on his armor. "There's no wine in the supply station anyhow."

Batu said genially, "There is something I've meant to talk to you about for a long while, Psin Khan."

"Oh, really?"

"Your grandson is a charming boy. I've got a little granddaughter, some younger than he."

Psin stretched his legs out flat on the ground. It was a pretty day, and he wished Batu hadn't spoiled it. "They are of the same bone, unfortunately."

"Oh, well." Batu smiled. His broad face was bland. "For the Altun such things are of little moment." He took the plug out of a jug of fresh kumiss and held it out. Psin took it and drank.

"I have a son unmarried yet," he said. "Until Sidacai marries Djela stays a bachelor."

Batu's face clouded. Psin raised the jug again to cover how sharply he was watching him. Finally, Batu said, "This is the son of your second wife, isn't he."

"Yes." Psin lowered the jug; he hadn't drunk.

Batu was fussing with the hooks on his coat. Kaidu had a younger sister. Psin didn't think Batu would mention her. The sun had risen over the mountains behind them, and the bright, clear light made the snow sparkle. Psin got up.

"I have to move out soon."

"Oh. That's right." Batu rose. "You're riding vanguard again. Sabotai trusts you much more than the rest of us. You should be honored."

"Terribly much." He slung his saddle onto his horse's back and reached under its belly for the girth.

"Kaidu has a sister as yet unpromised. Perhaps——"

"Why don't we talk about it after the campaign? Sidacai's old enough now to make his own marriage. I'd rather he were around when I talked about it."

"Keep it in mind," Batu said. "You won't find anything so good for him—not for the second son of the second wife." He put one hand on Psin's arm, smiled, and went off.

"Hunh."

Psin hooked the breastplate to the saddle. His standardbearer was jogging over toward him, and seeing him pass the thousand-commanders trailed after. Sunlight glinted off their metal gear. If Sidacai married without Psin's permission, Psin could annul it at any time. Anyway, Sidacai was in the Kha-Khan's guard and not liable to meet any girls of good family. He met plenty of girls of bad family, but them he could not marry. Psin picked up his chest armor and draped it over his shoulders.

"Do we break camp, Khan?" the standardbearer said.

Psin nodded. "I'm going to find Sabotai. We have a full tuman. Form them up into three columns." He put his foot in the stirrup and swung up. The horse turned and started off at a trot before he had settled into the saddle. He reined him off across the camp, toward the north.

Sabotai was arguing a point of strategy with Mongke, sitting beside a fire. Batu's brothers hovered behind him. Psin didn't wait to hear what it was they were discussing. He dismounted, got between them, and sat on his heels.

"I'm leaving. Anything more?"

"No."

"I'm not going to scout for you, so don't hunt for reports."

"You're not supposed to be here," Sabotai said. "You're under ban, and this is my fire." He got up and walked away. Psin followed him, grinning. Sabotai had done this twice before; it was a good way of getting Psin out of earshot of the other Altun. Some fifteen steps from the fire Sabotai turned.

"There was a courier in last night from Karakorum. Late. I couldn't very well send for you, and it was too cold to go riding."

"Any news of my women?"

"They're both well. Your new grandson is thriving. There were letters from Kerulu for Tshant. And from Ogodai. He's still strong.

very active, as usual. Very pleased with the way the war is going."

"What about Quyuk?"

"Quyuk is sitting with his hands in his lap. Jagatai says that they are keeping him under guard—supposed to be an honor guard, of course. His mother is slightly out of favor and his wife is no longer permitted the Golden Yurt. Has Batu been courting you?"

"Yes."

"They are disappointed with Siremon. That's why. The older Siremon gets the more obvious it is that there's no clear successor to Ogodai, except perhaps Jagatai."

"And Quyuk."

Sabotai sighed. "Yes. Yes. Incidentally, Quyuk sent word to you. Just greetings, and hopes that you'll have good fighting."

Psin's jaw dropped. "He what?"

"Exactly. To no one else. Not even his brother."

"Well."

"There was another courier in from the north. Tshant disobeyed every order Kaidu gave him—just ignored them—and caught an army of Poles outnumbering his three to one and smashed them to rubble."

"My, my." Psin put one hand to his mouth to hide his grin.

"You seem to have bred a rebel."

"I always knew that."

"And something of a general. I thought you'd want to know. Well. Good-by."

"Good-by. I'll send couriers when I'm at Pesth."

"Yes." Sabotai started back toward his fire. Psin stood watching him. The slow trudge of Sabotai's legs suddenly looked funny. He thought, Tshant the genius. It was interesting. Tshant had commanded so rarely before this. . . . He wondered if Sabotai's instigating feuds had made him any better. More confident, maybe. Beating me. He touched the scars on his cheek. Maybe.

Baidar said, looking toward the city, "You've made Kaidu angry. You ought not to have."

"What's wrong with him now?"

"Well, he told you to stay within a day's ride of him, and you ran it out to three days and proved he was wrong in the first place. He's too young to be in command."

Tshant nodded. He wasn't interested in Kaidu's immature jealousies. "How many do you think they have, in there?"

Baidar's horse ducked its head, and he jerked it up again. "Two tumans at least. He has a legitimate complaint against you. You lose too many men when you fight."

"My father's said so."

Behind them, Tshant's army and a half a tuman of Baidar's waited, eating jerked meat and drinking the wine from the town they had taken the day before. They had been waiting before Liegnitz since dawn, and so far no one inside the walls had shown a sign of noticing them. A collection of huts and larger buildings stood outside the wall, and Tshant had suggested attacking them, but Baidar had said no.

"He's worth handling properly," Baidar said. "Kaidu, I mean."

"Where is he now?"

"With his men. There's an army coming up from—from Bohemia. Or someplace down there." Baidar's eyes flew toward the city. "Here comes someone."

Tshant looked around. The gate had opened, and sixteen or twenty knights were riding out in double file. At their head rode a man carrying a white banner. Baidar called back to the army behind them, and Rijart trotted up, smiling.

Batu and Sabotai were in Hungary, and the courier who had brought that news had said they were meeting no resistance. The entire Hungarian army was drawn up before their capital. Psin, riding vanguard, had reached Pesth in three days flat from the great pass and was keeping watch on the King's army until Sabotai caught up. Kaidu had sent a man back to tell Batu that he could not join the main army in Hungary until he had disposed of the Poles in Liegnitz.

As well. Tshant shifted in his saddle, watching the knights approach. Sabotai could deal with the Hungarians. All this work in Poland was only a diversion; there was no sense in letting Kaidu share his grandfather's triumph. Tshant looked back to find Djela and saw him chattering with one of the standardbearers, who had orders to watch him.

The knights drew up their big horses a little way down from Tshant and Baidar. All but two of them wore white surcoats and cloaks with a black cross on the breast. The other two looked richer and less like fighting men. One of these rode forward, with a big blond knight behind him—one of the men wearing the black cross. The advance rider called out in a harsh voice, and Rijart translated.

"I am Henry, the Duke of Silesia, and my liege is the King of the Romans. What brings you to Liegnitz?"

Tshant grinned. Baidar nudged his horse forward and said to Rijart, "Tell them we come because they have an army here. They think to resist us, the chosen of God. Now they must lay aside their weapons and do homage to the Kha-Khan, God's only prince on earth."

Rijart shouted, and the knights mumbled under their breath. The big blond man tilted forward from the waist and spoke to the Silesian, who gestured impatiently. He spoke again. Rijart said, "We are all the children of God, but His only chosen is Our Lord Jesus Christ and those who follow him. If you will accept Christ, we will welcome you like the strayed lambs into the fold. Otherwise we offer only death."

Tshant said, "All this proves is how many different ways a man can say the same thing. Tell them to go."

Baidar nodded to Rijart. "Tell them what he said."

The Silesian listened and said, "We outnumber you."

Baidar laughed. "It's not the number that matters, but God's hand on the bow. We are sworn to conquer the world, and to do so we will fight until the sun falls."

The knights heard it in silence. Their faces behind the arcs of the nosepieces on their helmets were drawn and set hard. The blond man, who wore no helmet, reined his horse forward, said something to the Silesian, and jogged past him a little. His hair glistened in the

sun, and he looked Tshant and Baidar in the face. He said something; in the midst of it Tshant heard the word "Psin."

"What does he know of Psin?" he said to Rijart.

Rijart rubbed his chin. "I know this knight. His name is Arnulf,
and he is of the Teutonic Order. He met with Psin Khan in Pesth."

"My father mentioned him."

"He says if Psin is with this army he will fight him in single com-
bat, for the greater glory of God."

Baidar grinned. "Tell him Mongols don't fight like that. And
Psin Khan isn't in Poland."

Rijart called to the knight, who listened gravely and answered in
a calm voice. Rijart turned back toward Baidar.

"He says that he will fight any of the Mongols. He asks which of
you two is the stronger."

Tshant said, "I'll fight him."

"Don't be a fool," Baidar said. "Look at him. You could take him
with an arrow, but hand to hand he'd mash you. He's armored like
a tortoise and he's twice your size."

Tshant scowled. "He'll think us cowards."

"Let him. When the fighting's over there will be none left to
think anything."

Rijart spoke, firmly, and the knight nodded. He swung his horse.
The Silesian turned and rode back toward the city, with the
knights trailing neatly after. Baidar said, "Now all we have to do is
bring them out of the city."

Tshant said to Rijart, "What did my father think of him? The
knight."

"I had the impression he admired him."

"Unh."

Baidar was riding off; the melting snow squished under his
horse's hoofs. Tshant shaded his eyes to see the city wall. Now they
had to meet with Kaidu. He wheeled and rode back to Jube, to set a
watch over the city while they made plans.

Kaidu said, "Tshant will burn the huts outside the wall. If they
come out to attack him, he will give ground slowly enough to keep
in constant contact with them. When they are far enough from the

city to be taken on either side, Baidar will strike from the south, I from the north."

Tshant had one foot braced up against the pommel of his saddle. He ran his thumb over his jaw, glanced at Baidar, and said, "And I am to ride in the contact line, of course."

"If you wish," Kaidu said stiffly.

Tshant grinned. "I will. Good. How long will it be before you're in position?"

"Your confidence is reassuring," Kaidu said.

"Why, thank you."

Baidar said, "There is no need for Tshant's men to be in contact except intermittently. We cannot stand up to the knights' charge. That much we've learned."

"Sometimes it's necessary to . . . sacrifice some men for the good of others."

Tshant put his foot down and fished for his stirrup. "I said I'd go. Don't depend on my being sacrificed, Kaidu."

Kaidu glared at him. "I hope you return safely, of course." He turned and rode off.

Baidar said, "I told you you should handle him carefully."

"He's not worth—"

"He's trying to get you killed."

"He won't."

"God. You are too sure."

Tshant snorted, turned, and rode back toward his men. He had a little over half a tuman left. All the others were dead or wounded, back in the long drive across Poland. All his men carried swords, hung in clumsy scabbards from their belts. He found Djela and told him to stay by him, no matter what happened.

"I will."

"Jube, white banner. Torches lit."

Djela said, "What are we going to do?"

"Burn everything outside the walls. Pull them out of the city."

"Where is Baidar?"

"Over there." Tshant pointed south with his chin. He took a torch from the heap on the ground and lit it. He thought, Maybe I am too confident. He thought of sending Djela away.

The Mongols were trotting forward. He gestured to Jube to

spread them out. The river sparkled in the sun, just beyond the city. The ice was breaking up already in it. He had to remember not to get pinned against it.

Riding down, he could see the people running back and forth on the walls. A shower of small round stones pelted him. Over the wall he could see the upper half of a mangonel frame. He swung up his shield and charged in among the huts. His men were screaming, waving their torches. The huts went up in flames all at once, and immediately the heat was enough to bring out the sweat on his face. He looked for Djela and saw him cantering along just behind him.

Among the huts were small haystacks, pens for animals, old sheds. He threw his torch into a haystack and wheeled. His men began to yell. The mangonel fired again, and two Mongols pitched out of their saddles. Tshant started back out of the city. An ember floated down onto his horse's mane and he crushed it out.

Outside the ring of huts, he turned and looked back. His men were racing along under the walls of the city, shouting, throwing their torches up and over the ramparts. He called to Djela and started back down again. Jube broke out of the ring of blazing huts and started toward him.

Abruptly the Mongols veered toward him; they had seen the banner. The gate was opening. He cantered down toward the city. His men followed, pulling out their bows. Knights charged out the half-open gate and with lances set headed toward the Mongols. Tshant nocked an arrow.

Flocks of arrows hummed into the air. Most of them glanced off shields and armor. Here and there Tshant saw a knight fall. He set another arrow to his string and drew it. Over the point he saw the knights' faces, their glittering eyes and the wet red of their open mouths. He took a deep breath and shot. The arrow drilled into a face, but the mass of armored knights were already on him. Their horses loomed over his. He jammed his bow into the case and snatched out his sword. His horse swerved, and he leaned hard and brought it spinning around away from the knights. They ranged up on either side of him. A lance passed over his shoulder. He stabbed with the sword and felt the edge turn on mail. His horse reared up.

The knights crowded him in. He could see nothing but iron

bodies. A mace crashed down on his saddle. He whipped his horse once, dropped the rein, and with both hands on his sword drove it into the flank of the knight's stallion, where they was no armor. The stallion screamed. A lance thrust up at Tshant, aimed straight for his chest. For a frozen moment he imagined it breaking through his ribs and out his back. He threw all his weight into one stirrup and wrenched himself around and the sleek tip of the lance slid by. The knight holding it was laughing. Tshant raised the sword and slashed it down like an axe on the knight's forearm. There was no blood, but he felt the bone cave in under the sword's edge.

Banners—the red banner was snapping in the sky. He took a deep breath and charged south, trying to pull out of the pack of knights, weaving and bending out of their way. A fist came at him, steel-knuckled, and he ducked, but not fast enough. The fist crashed into the side of his head. He hung onto his saddle; he could see nothing. Blood filled his mouth. The shrill noises of the fighting fell suddenly away, and he could hear his own horse's hoofs on the ground.

"Yip-yip-yip—"

They were all racing south. He rubbed at his eyes until his vision cleared and looked around. Djela was far down the field, untouched, well out of the reach of the knights. All across the flat ground the Mongols were fleeing Liegnitz. A heavy cheer rose behind them. Tshant slowed his horse, looking for Jube. The knights were thundering after them. He pulled his bow out and started shooting.

His mouth was full of blood, and he had a loose tooth. He wiggled it with his tongue, all the while shooting into the broad front of the oncoming knights. Jube galloped over.

"What now?"

"Kaidu wants constant contact."

Jube dipped the banner. All down the line, the Mongols slowed, so that the knights could catch up with them. Tshant stood in his stirrups to see. Many of his men were wounded. Several of them rode double with other men, who held them on their horses. He jabbed his horse in the mouth to make it slow, shot once more, cased the bow, and grabbed his sword.

The knights surged up beside him again. This time he kept them at arm's length, so that he could parry with his sword. His arm was tired already. A knight drove a lance at him, and he dodged, and the momentum carried the knight on past him. An arrow took the man in the throat and he fell off his horse.

The arrows were coming close to Tshant. He let his horse drop back even more, so that a row of knights shielded him. The knights were spread out so that it was possible to fight only one at a time. He smashed his sword into one man's chest, and the knight swayed but kept in his saddle. Tshant drew his arm back to stab him, but the knight pulled out of reach.

Just to his left rode a pack of the knights in white with the black crosses; they were fighting on the run with a much larger group of Mongols. Tshant veered his horse toward them. He caught sight of Djela, galloping along just ahead of the south wing of the Polish army. Abruptly trumpets blared in his ears. They startled him, and he whipped his horse into a flat run, afraid that more knights were coming up behind him.

The knights in the white cloaks yanked their horses around, turning south, away from him. He stood in his stirrups to look and saw Baidar's tuman, sweeping down toward the knights. Arrows darkened the sky.

"Eeeeiiiyyyyaaah!"

The scream almost lifted him out of the saddle. The whole north flank of the Poles was collapsing in toward him under the pressure of Kaidu's attack. He reined down to a trot, looking for Jube. Most of his men were caught in the middle of the Poles, where the knights were still spread out, but the ranks were tightening up.

Jube was riding toward him. Tshant yelled, "Let's get out of here," and swung his arm. He saw the bannerstaff slant down, saw Jube reach for his packs; Mongol arrows rained down on both of them, and Jube pitched out of his saddle. His foot caught in his stirrup and his horse dragged him straight into the heavy fighting.

Tshant swore. He whipped his horse east again. The two Polish flanks caved into the middle just after he raced clear. He drew his bow out of the case, turned his horse, and started shooting into the thickening mass of knights. Kaidu's and Baidar's columns had them completely surrounded. The knights stopped moving forward. Tshant could hear the ring of arrows striking armor. Many of his men had been caught between the two wings and crushed. He shot high, hoping one of his arrows would lift over the Poles and hit Kaidu.

"Ada, Ada, I've been hit."

His breath caught. Djela galloped up, holding one arm. Tshant raced toward him. If it were a Mongol arrow, he would fry Kaidu. But it was not; Djela had a crossbow bolt through the flesh of his upper arm.

"Where did you pick that up?"

"I went back toward the city."

A column of Mongols raced past them, all carrying swords: Baidar's heavy cavalry. Tshant took Djela by the wrist, shoved the head of the bolt out through the skin, and snapped it off. Djela whined.

"You've been blooded," Tshant said. He dipped his fingers in the blood and made an X on each of Djela's palms. "Go wait for me."

"I'll find Jube."

"Jube's dead."

He cantered down toward Baidar's end of the battle. The knights, at a standstill, were drowning in the flood of Mongol arrows. They were steadily retreating into the middle of their circle, leaving a broad ring of bodies all around. Many of them dismounted. Tshant saw them develop a charge toward the head of Baidar's column, but before the Polish horses were beyond the limit of the sprawled bodies all the charging knights were dead. The arrows did not slacken. He pulled up beside Baidar.

"Kaidu says no mercy," Baidar said.

"Has he built a shambles for them all?"

Baidar shrugged. "How many of your men survived?"

"Not many. He was overshooting when he attacked, and he killed a lot of us."

"He's dead green."

"Oh? He smells ripe enough to me."

"Maybe. Don't fuss with him about it. Look."

Tshant looked. The knights in the white cloaks, all on foot, had broken out of the circle. They carried their shields high and close together, so that the storm of arrows could not penetrate it. The Mongols charged them. Like a tortoise the group of knights walked

steadily onward, and the Mongols wheeled away, shooting harmlessly.

Baidar said, "Green pennant here."

His standardbearer hung a long green ribbon on his staff and
swung it up. Baidar said, "They could walk back to Liegnitz like
that."

Tshant nodded. He glanced toward the rest of the knights and
trotted up toward the tortoise knights, ranged in a double rank, and
saw them steadily dying. Two thousand of Baidar's heavy cavalry
charged.

The tortoise stopped, braced. Whooping, the Mongols slammed
into them. Their swords chopped down across the shields. The
knights staggered back; gaps opened in their formation, and the
Mongols howled. Tshant leaned forward, ready to signal the bowmen in, but before he could open his mouth the tortoise pulled itself
together again, heaved, and threw the Mongols back almost bodily.

"Yip-yip-yip—"

"Those damned Kipchaks," Baidar said. "Yipping when there's
no chance of losing." He bellowed at them, and the heavy cavalry
reorganized itself and charged the tortoise again. When they struck
there was an audible clang. Tshant saw three Kipchaks break into
the shield ring; on horseback they were visible well above the
knights. Before they had penetrated more than a few strides they
were killed.

Tshant gathered his reins, called to the Mongol archers near him,
and started down toward the knights. He rode at a low trot, his
bow in his hands, circling the knights. The heavy cavalry pulled
back again. Tshant moved in so close he could see the color of the
knights' eyes when they peeked over their shields, drew his bow as
full as he could, and shot. His arrow hit a shield, and it thundered,
but it did not break. He stopped his horse dead and nocked another
arrow. The Mongols who had followed him circled the tortoise,
came in as close as he was, and drew their bows.

The knights, understanding, lunged toward them. Tshant aimed
for the bits of shoulder and face he could see over the shields. One
knight fell, but Tshant had to back his horse up quickly to get out
of the tortoise's way. He shot for an eye, and the arrow skipped off
the helmet and plunged into the throat of the knight behind. The

tortoise was charging him, the knights running, and he turned to
trot along ahead of them and shoot back over the horse's rump.
This time he shot at a mailed arm, and the arrow tore through the
mail and passed all the way through the muscle underneath.

The tortoise was growing smaller; when a knight fell the others
closed ranks. They stopped again, catching their breath, and
Tshant and the other Mongols could find nothing to shoot at. They
backed off to let the heavy cavalry charge in again. The Kipchaks
looked grim. They smashed their horses into the shields and
through them. Their swords hacked down. Blood fountained across
them. One knight leapt up behind a Kipchak and threw him aside.
Tshant lifted his bow, but before he could shoot five other arrows
whammed into the knight from all sides. The knight slid down into
the broken tortoise, now only a puddle of bodies in bloody armor.

"Fall back," Tshant yelled. "Baidar—"

The heavy cavalry drew back. Tshant rode into the mess, looking closely at faces. He thought he recognized a pair of heavy
shoulders and dismounted and turned the knight over. It was the
knight Arnulf, who had spoken of Psin. Tshant pulled his helmet
off. Two arrows jutted from the knight's chest, but he was still
alive.

"You and you. Come drag this one out into the open." Tshant
stepped over a body and mounted again. The two Mongols he had
pointed to came in and hauled the knight out onto the clean snow.

Baidar said, "No mercy, remember?"

"Kaidu's arrows killed my standardbearer. He owes me a blood
debt. Let the knight pay it." He dismounted again and watched the
two men strip off the knight's cloak. They broke the arrow shafts
and worked the chain mail up over them so that they could get that
off too. The arrows were low. Tshant picked at a scratch on his
cheek, wondering where he'd gotten it.

"They missed the lungs," one of the Mongols working on the
knight said. "He's lucky."

"Very." Tshant knelt on the knight's chest. The man's eyes
flickered open. Tshant took hold of one of the shafts and
wrenched it loose. The blood drained out of the knight's face but
he made no sound. When the other came out, with flesh clinging to
the triple barbs, the knight fainted.

Tshant looked at the arrowhead. "Mangghut. Do they think they're killing fish?" He threw the shaft away. The two wounds looked bad, but they were clean and he thought the knight would live. "Baidar. What's happening?"

Baidar looked off down the field. "Kaidu is still killing the others."

"How many left?"

"A few hundred."

Tshant looked down at the knight. The pain had woken him up again. His wide blue eyes were calm, staring up at Tshant's, and only the white line around his mouth showed that he hurt. Tshant knelt suddenly beside him, put his mouth against the deeper of the two wounds, and sucked at it. The knight did not move. The other Mongols whispered, amazed. Tshant straightened up, spat the blood from his mouth, and went over to his horse. "Bandage him up. You saw what I did. He is mine."

Baidar said, "Kaidu needs help."

"Then let's go help him."

The slow killing went on until well after sundown. Djela wept and hung his belt around his neck, in mourning for Jube; his own wound was festering and Tshant made him soak it in a bowl of wine. In the morning, the knight was brought to him, wearing a Mongol coat. His shoulders were too wide for it, and the cloth strained over his chest. Tshant sent Djela to get Rijart and motioned that the knight should eat. The man sat down and said something quietly in his own tongue and took meat from the pot. Tshant studied him, but it didn't seem to make the knight uncomfortable.

Rijart trotted up on foot and said, "How may I serve Tshant Bahadur?"

"Is this the man who spoke with my father?"

Rijart sank down and crossed his legs under him. "Yes. His name is Arnulf." He spoke to the knight in some other language, and the knight answered. "He says he should thank you, but he would rather have died back there with his brothers."

Djela sat on his heels beside Tshant, staring at the knight. Tshant said to him, "Ask this man if he speaks Russian."

"Don't you trust me?" Rijart said.

"I don't like you."

Djela smiled at the knight and said something, and the knight looked puzzled. He didn't understand, obviously, and his eyes moved to Rijart.

"He speaks Arabic," Rijart said. "Don't you?"

"No."

"Your father doesn't like me either."

"He probably has the grace not to say so."

The knight spoke, and Rijart nodded. He swung back to Tshant.

"He says you must be a man of—" His mouth twisted. "Of kindness. There's no word in Mongol for what he means. Honorable, generous, upright."

"Tell him I am not."

"He asks you to kill him. He says if you mean to question him he will kill himself, but that's a sin, and he would prefer that you kill him, so that he need not blemish his soul more than it is."

Tshant laughed. "Doesn't he think he can stay silent under torture?"

While Rijart translated the knight watched Tshant. His smile deepened, and he answered one word. Rijart said, "He says—"

"I can guess. He's clever. Tell him he won't be tortured or questioned, but he won't be killed either. He's my slave now. Tell him I mean to give him as a present to the man whose name he called before Liegnitz."

The knight listened expressionlessly. Djela said softly, "To Grandfather?"

Tshant nodded. When Rijart finished, the knight shrugged.

"Did you tell him who I am?"

"No," Rijart said.

"Tell him."

Rijart turned toward the knight and said something, including Tshant's name and Psin's. The knight jerked his head up and stared at Tshant. Tshant laughed and went off with Djela.

Psin let his reins slide through his fingers. His coat was lashed to the cantle of his saddle, and the warm wind rustled his shirt. New leaves in a green fuzz covered the trees around him.

"They've got the wagons chained together," he said.

Mongke nodded. "Interesting. What do you think they'll try to do?"

"They followed me all the way up here from Pesth, they must mean to fight." Psin shrugged. The Hungarian army, camped inside its ring of wagons, lay just opposite the only bridge on the big river. There were two rivers here, flowing together just south of the Hungarian camp, and the spring thaw had filled both of them to the tops of their banks. Batu was camped in between them.

"You made it from the mountains to Pesth in three days, I heard," Mongke said. "That's fast riding."

"I follow orders."

"Excellently. Where is Kadan?"

"Still far to the south."

"Oh. We'll have to wait until he gets here, won't we."

"Sabotai's timing is better than that."

Psin rode down toward the Hungarian camp. Horses filled the marshy pasturage around it, and at the sight of the Mongols a great roar went up inside the wagon-ring. Mongke, jogging stirrup to Psin's stirrup, said easily, "Do you think they made that wall to keep us out or themselves in?"

"Ask them." Psin cut around to cross the bridge. They had come over it from Batu's camp that morning, and the knights hadn't interfered, but now a number of men in armor burst out of the ring of wagons and started toward the bridge. Psin and Mongke whipped up their horses.

The knights' great stallions galloped over the sloppy ground, splashing through puddles. Standing in his stirrups Psin tried to figure out which would reach the bridge first—he and Mongke or the knights. He put one hand on his horse's mane and the horse stretched out, flying over the marsh. The knights yelled and waved their swords.

They were going to get there together. He pulled out his bow and dropped his reins on his horse's neck. Two knights rode ahead of the others; he could see the spurs flash at their heels. He brought the head of the arrow down to a point just over the leader's helmet and six strides beyond him and shot. The arrow screamed in the sky. Mongke yelped happily. The knight rode into the oncoming arrow and pitched to the ground; the man behind him faltered.

They were so close Psin could see the designs on the Hungarians' cloaks. He chose another arrow. Mongke shot, and the horse of the leading knight stumbled and fell. The Mongol horses strained forward. Psin steered his horse straight for the bridge and nocked an arrow. They charged onto the bridge right under the noses of the Hungarian knights. He and Mongke shot at the same time, and two knights threw their hands to their faces and flew backward off their horses into the marsh. The bridge clattered underhoof.

Mongke cheered. The Hungarians were turning back, slowing their stallions only with difficulty. Psin reined in on the other bank and watched. His horse was barely panting. The Hungarian bits fascinated him; all the stallions ran with their mouths wide open.

Sabotai was waiting for them near the horse herd. He and Batu had caught up with Psin's tuman three days before, and Psin could see that Sabotai was beginning to fret. He came over and held Psin's reins while he dismounted. His eyes were full of purpose.

"A courier from Kaidu. They've come up to a town called Liegnitz and they expect to fight the last of the Poles—I mean, they have fought them by now. And a dispatch from Baidar, commenting unfavorably on Kaidu's command. What's the ground like, west of the Hungarian King's camp?"

"Flat and no forest. They can run all day without finding a refuge." Psin sent a slave off to bring him his dun horse.

"Good. Batu's brother Siban got here while you were gone with two tumans. We have enough men to take any army on earth. Can we seize that bridge and hold it?"

Psin looked toward the bridge. "Maybe. I don't like the idea of standing up to their charge."

"Nor do I, but I want that bridge. I've got a few mangonels and catapults built, and they've cut wood for a bridge, if we can't hold this one. Come along. I want to show you what I have in mind."

In the thick, milky darkness it was hard to see. The fog sprang up out of the marsh on the far side of the river. Psin walked back and forth, slapping his hands against his arms; he refused to put his coat

on, because it was too warm. Sabotai was watching from the platform behind him.

"They're across," Sabotai called. "Here come the Magyars.
They've got a lot of footsoldiers. I can't see much."

The groaning of the bridge came muffled through the fog.
Abruptly the harsher, wilder sounds of fighting struck back to
them. Psin leapt up onto the platform and strained his eyes. The
Mongols who had crossed the river were milling around before it,
and a huge detachment of Hungarians on foot pressed against them.
A long curved blade flashed in the uncertain moonlight. The manes
of horses tossed. The Mongols started yelping.

"They're losing," Sabotai said. "Watch."

A column of knights galloped up toward the bridge, veered, and
rammed into the packed Mongols. Psin saw them give way, scurrying back onto the bridge and the bank of the river. A horse neighed
on this side of the river, and immediately the whole herd began to
whinny. The knights were passing like a wedge through the Mongols. A Hungarian warcry rang out. Psin's arms ached, and he realized he was tensed as if to fight. The knights were forcing the Mongols back so fast the horses had no chance to brace themselves.
Three horses slid down the bank into the river, and the fog covered
them.

"Mongke," Sabotai called. "Bring up the catapults and order out
the two tumans under my banner."

Mongke rode off, shouting. Psin pointed toward the bridge.
"They've cut off a good half of the column there."

"Yes." Sabotai turned to the standardbearer. "Blue lantern, four
short. Psin, is the river drowning them?"

"No." Already Mongols were scrambling up this bank. Their
horses shook themselves all up and down the river.

The Hungarians roared triumphantly. A band of footsoldiers ran
onto the bridge and chopped at the Mongols there. A burning arrow killed a man in the midst of the infantry, and he made a sort of
torch; Psin could see that the Mongols were beaten. They were
crammed onto the bridge so tightly they couldn't move. A horse
pitched over the rail and splashed into the river.

The detachment that had been cut off was galloping away from
the knights pursuing them. They swerved and rode into the river.

The rear of the column on the bridge, without room to turn their horses, backed off, spun, and rode away to give the others room. The bridge emptied rapidly. With a shout the Hungarian footsoldiers tried to follow, but a shower of arrows drove them back.

Batu cantered up to the platform, soaked through. He bellowed for kumiss and climbed up beside Sabotai. His felt socks squelched when he walked. "We can't use the speed of our horses this way. Let's drop back and make them come to us."

"No," Sabotai said. "Let's beat them on their own ground. Psin, can you use powder shells?"

"Yes. I learned about them in China."

"They've left a garrison at their end of the bridge," Batu said. "I say we wait until daylight, go upriver, and cross there."

"No," Sabotai said. "I have half a dozen shells. Here come the catapults."

"I'll need half a dozen to find the range," Psin said.

"All we need is one good hit. Batu, when you're rested, can you lead another charge?"

"I can lead one now."

"Not now. Psin. You know what I want done."

Psin nodded. "Where are the shells?"

"In my artillery cart." Sabotai jumped from the platform. A slave held his horse ready. "Let's hope they think we're licking our wounds. I'll see you tomorrow, if all goes well."

He rode away; Mongke was waiting for him, at the head of his two tumans. Lanterns flashed. All the Hungarians but the garrison on the bridge had gone back to their own camp. Psin estimated the garrison at two hundred knights and twice as many infantry. From the splashing along this bank the infantry carried bows.

"What's going on?" Batu said.

Psin sat down on the edge of the platform, looked at the sky, and shrugged into his coat. "It's past midnight now. When the moon sets, I'm going to start bombarding the Hungarian end of the bridge. If we can drive them off, you'll lead all the troops left here across. They'll come out to meet you. When they do, you must hold them. I'll give you all the support I can from this side of the river."

"The powder shells ought to make them flinch."

"I hope so. If I had fifty of them we need never commit a man against the knights."

The catapults were coming up; forty men dragged each one to the bank. Psin went over there on foot and sent a passing man for his horse. The catapults were of raw wood, still green, and he could smell the pitch running from the beams. He put his hand on one and got splinters all through his palm.

"Move it toward me a little. A little more. Good." He dug out the splinters with his teeth. "Hugar, that rope doesn't look strong."

"We're out of rope, Khan."

"God above. Well, no shells in this one."

A wagon rumbled up, loaded with stones and wood soaked in naphtha. Psin held his nose. "Make sure you don't keep torches near the wagons. Put it there. Back farther. Yes."

His horse came up and he mounted. The dun bucked, but he made it buck in the proper direction. With the spring coming the dun couldn't be expected to behave. The next catapult was too near the bank, and he made them drag it off a little. The beams groaned; the men around the machine leapt back.

"Put out that torch. No light here, I don't want them to see. And there's naphtha in those wagons." He managed to get the dun behind the catapult and sighted along it. It was aimed roughly into the trees north of the Hungarian camp. "Swing it to my left. And knock the block out from under that front strut."

Two loose horses ambled over, ears pricked up, and started gnawing on the green wood. Psin shooed them off and they kicked at him. The dun squealed.

"Catch those horses. And nobody is allowed here who isn't assigned to a catapult. That means you, Berke. Go away."

Berke snorted and rode off. Two wagons collided neatly and the drovers lashed one another with their whips. The axle on one wagon was broken. Psin ordered men over to help carry it into position. One of the catapults broke while they were hauling it along the bank, and he had the wood chopped up and thrown into the ammunition wagons.

"Now." He climbed up onto the wagon with the powder shells. "Let's see what we have here."

There were eight of the shells, each so heavy he couldn't lift it alone. The two halves were bolted together through a heavy collar. From a hole in the collar ran a length of twisted silk. He put his nose close to the hole and sniffed, to make sure there was still powder inside.

Batu shouted, "The moon is setting, damn you."

Psin stood up straight. "Don't yell at me. You're wooing me, remember?"

Batu's face split into a huge grin. "Please, beloved, may I go fight now?"

"Wait a little."

The fog was gone, at least, but it was getting colder. He wondered how Tshant was doing. If Tshant were here, he'd feel better about this maneuver. It was more Tshant's kind of fighting than Batu's: Batu hated to lose men, but Tshant got his killed faster and dirtier than any other commander, and they loved him for it. The couriers had said that he had force-marched his tuman four days straight in Poland and fought hard at the end of it.

"What are you thinking about?" Batu said.

"My son." He got down from the wagon and mounted. "I'll send a slave to you when we're ready."

He rode along the line of machines. Only two had dependable ropes, and he had put them closest to the bridge. The Hungarian garrison would realize that something was going on. With luck they wouldn't look elsewhere. The moon was all gone below the horizon. He got up onto the platform. "Red lanterns up."

"Do they all know the signals?" the standardbearer said.

"They must. Let's see."

The red lanterns ran up the pole, and around the catapults men jumped to load up. "You see? Of course they know the signals." He sent a slave after Batu. There was a lantern for each of the catapults and a Mongol for each lantern; he walked along in front of them.

"You're one, you're two, you're three, and you're four. Don't get confused. If you do, you'll be beaten. All numbers, white flash."

The lanterns gleamed. With a yell the engineers pulled their levers. The catapults went off with a rattle and a crash of wood on wood, and splashes erupted out of the river. Psin saw one stone smash into the midst of the garrison.

"Number one. Yellow lantern. Two and four, blue. I didn't see three. Who saw three?"

"Short and to the south, Khan."

"Three, red."

On the Hungarian side of the bridge shouting broke out. Shadows darted back and forth. A volley of arrows thudded into the bank of this side of the river.

"White flash."

The first catapult went off at once, and stones pelted the Magyars. One rail of the bridge caved in. The second catapult, with a block under its front strut, shot to the right range but well south, and Psin flashed the red lantern for them. The third hit dead center. Hungarians screamed.

"Three, four yellow flashes."

Hungarians were coming onto the bridge. Their bows were out of range, and they were trying to get closer. Batu and his men were lined up behind Psin's platform.

"Four is still short. Blue."

"White flash, Khan?"

"Yes."

The two engines that were sighted in fired almost together; one shot a powder shell. Psin could see the fuse sparking. He missed four's shot, watching. The shell exploded behind the Hungarians with a clap of noise and a flash that lit up the whole end of the bridge.

The Hungarians screeched. A herd of them poured off the bridge toward their camp. Psin could hear their officers' voices, rising, fierce, but the wild retreat plunged on. He whirled and pointed to Batu.

"All engines sighted in, Khan."

"White flash."

Another shell burst over the garrison on the bridge, and in the pallid light he saw the shattered bodies and the men struggling to retreat. When the light faded the dark was thick as felt, but another shell exploded immediately. The bridge was deserted.

"All colors, three flashes."

Batu's men galloped onto the bridge. It swayed under their weight. Psin could hear the Hungarian trumpets, the pound of drums. Batu, leading the charge, drew his men off to the north a little; the Mongols swept in a shallow curve from the bridge to Batu's position. Their voices rose.

"Get the naphtha," Psin said. He jumped down from the platform and ran back and forth along the catapults, realigning them so that they couldn't hit the Mongols. "Put another block under your struts. Be careful. You'll blow us all up if you take a torch near those wagons."

"The Khan wishes." They grinned at him. He went back to the platform and got up onto it again; it was getting light in the east, and a raw wind blew.

The Hungarians charged straight for Batu's line. Confidence showed in every move they made. Their warcries were heavy with triumph. All the arrows of the Mongols didn't turn them back, although they lost men and horses.

"White flash," Psin said.

Batu's line broke into a canter and started around behind the Hungarians. The knights lumbered heavily after them, and the infantry bunched up. Psin's engines groaned and shot, and the naphtha flashed in the air like fragments of ghosts. In the Hungarian army men howled. Horses shied wildly away from the dripping fire. When the naphtha struck it set horses and riders on fire, and they fled across the field, screaming. A burning horse flung itself into the river. Steam rose from the water. Psin could smell burnt meat. "White flash."

It didn't matter where the catapults were hitting; the naphtha was enough. A catapult started burning, and slaves with buckets dashed up to douse it, their faces damp with fear.

Batu's line had gotten too close. Trumpets blared and the Hungarian lines hurled themselves against the Mongols. Before their drive the Mongols scattered like dust. The knights roared. Their swords chopped through Batu's men, and their big stallions lifted the lighter Mongol horses off their feet.

"White flash." Psin swore. Batu was letting the Hungarians move away from the naphtha. This volley struck only the edge of the infantry. He thought of putting another block under the catapults' struts, but aimed so high they would surely shoot wild.

A column of knights charged the Mongols to the north, and for a moment they fought hand to hand. From the east and west other

Mongols raced down to shoot their bows. The knights plunged on. Early light glinted from their armor. The Mongols clung to them like dogs hanging from the throats of aurochs. They were running into a morass, where reeds grew, and tangled brush. The Mongols gave way in a rush, and the knights followed. Their horses sank to their hocks in the thick mud. When they lurched and clawed to get free they only worked themselves deeper. Dancing along the edge of the marsh the Mongols shot at them and brought them down, one by one.

"White flash." It hardly mattered, because the Hungarian army was out of range. And the naphtha no longer bloomed in the air, because it was almost dawn. Psin backed up to see better.

The footsoldiers in an ordered block trotted toward the bridge, and Batu himself rode to cut them off. Arrows streamed back and forth. Even in the air the difference between the two kinds of arrows was startling—the one long, deep-fletched, and the other short and feathered with wood. A Mongol horse took a bolt through the chest and reared up, shrilling. The infantry drew in on itself and kept on shooting.

"All colors flash. We're wasting ammunition."

Batu was still harrying the infantry. His men had the Hungarians almost entirely surrounded, but whenever the knights charged the line broke and ran before them. Loose and wounded horses trotted across the bridge to the Mongol camp. Psin sent a dozen men down to catch them and turn them out with the herd. His dun was pawing up the ground where he stood.

"Khan. Over there."

Forty Mongols were racing toward the river, with as many knights right at their heels. At the riverbank, the Mongols wheeled, drawing their bows. The knights smashed into them and hurled them into the water. Heads bobbed in the current. Psin called, "Number one catapult, swing around and shoot."

The knights paced up and down the riverbank, shouting. On this side wet Mongols and horses pulled themselves onto dry land, looking stunned. Some of the men remounted and jogged up toward the bridge to cross over again. The catapult shot. Naphtha slithered down on the knights, who fled.

"They're breaking."

The Hungarian infantry ran in disorder back toward their camp. Arrows pursued them. Wheeling, the knights followed; they battered their way through Batu's men and set out down the plain. Banners spread out all through the Mongol army, and with a cheer they started after the Hungarians. They seemed to lose all order, but Psin could see each hundred drawing together, and each thousand. Some of them slowed to give their horses a rest. A single rider was racing up from the direction of the Hungarian camp. Dust hung in the sky there.

"Get the catapults on wagons. Can you take them apart? Let's go. Move, down there. Do you think it's over?"

The courier pulled down to a jog to cross the bridge, which was full of holes and clogged with dead. Psin sat on his heels at the platform's edge, and the courier came straight to him.

"Sabotai and his men crossed the river well to the south and have moved up to lock the Hungarians in their camp. They came out to meet us but we threw them back. We had no trouble crossing the river, you were right about the current there, Sabotai says."

Psin nodded. "I'm going down with the engines. You can help."

When he and the catapults reached the Hungarian camp, Sabotai and Batu had it surrounded. All the Hungarians were inside the ring of wagons. Sabotai, looking thoughtful, sat his saddle a little way out from the Mongol army. Psin jogged up to tell him where the catapults were set.

"I didn't use all the shells. Shall we use them now?"

"Yes. Good. You cleared them off the bridge quickly enough."

"They were afraid of the noise, I think."

"Here they come." Sabotai turned and yelled to his standard-bearer. The wagons almost opposite them were drawing in, and a band of knights charged through the gap. Sabotai called for a yellow banner. He reached out and touched Psin on the sleeve and pointed.

The Mongols flew to the place where the knights were emerging, bunched up on either side of the gap, and started shooting. A mass of Kipchak heavy cavalry galloped up from the southern side of the ring. Before the storm of arrows the knights faltered, and the close quarters hampered their horses. Sabotai said crisply, "Red banner," and the Mongol archers dropped back to let the heavy cavalry through. The Kipchaks struck the knights with a crash that made Psin laugh. He could hear the voices of the Hungarians inside the ring. The knights scuttled back through the gap in the wagons, and the heavy cavalry trotted off, waving their swords.

Fire arrows thunked into the wagons, and many of them began to burn. Inside the ring horses neighed. A catapult went off and sprayed the whole Hungarian camp with naphtha. Stones bashed in the few tents.

"Well," Sabotai said.

Psin shrugged. "They aren't quite beaten."

"It worked rather well. I'm very pleased with that."

"You're tired, too. I can tell by the way you're talking."

"Oh, I'm worn out. I've not slept for—anyhow. Shall I get some sleep? You give the orders. Use the same signals I did to get men to a gap in the ring. I'll be in a cart somewhere."

Psin watched him ride off. Sabotai's instincts were flawless; if he thought he could sleep they had beaten the Hungarians. He trotted the dun up and down to work off its high spirits.

Batu rode up, beaming. "I told your catapults to use shells. They're shouting at us on the other side. Maybe it's a diversion."

"They tried to break out here."

"Let them keep trying. Where is Sabotai?"

"Sleeping."

"It was a good strategy. I would never have thought of it. I'm not good at that. I—"

There was a courier coming; Psin could hear the bells. He dragged his horse away from Batu's. A man on a piebald horse was cantering around the western end of the wagon ring. The even triple beat of the horse's hoofs grew louder, even through the uproar around the camp. He reined up before Psin, saluted, and said, "I come from Kaidu Noyon. We have beaten the Poles and the Silesians near Liegnitz. We filled nine sacks with the right ears of the slain."

Batu cheered, and the man within earshot looked around. He galloped off to tell them. The courier said, "Kaidu Noyon says that he will burn Liegnitz and wait until the northern flank of his army meets up with him. The one that went north to the Lithuanian Sea. They'll split up and ride south in small bands."

"Good. How is my son?"

"Well. Very well. And your grandson. Tshant Bahadur says he has a gift for you, when he comes." The courier grinned.

"Oh? What?"

"I'm not to tell you."

"Well. Good, go rest."

The sun climbed through sparse crowds. Wagons burnt in the ring near Psin, so hot that he had to move back. Some knights tried again to break out of the ring, but they were thrown back even more quickly than before. The catapults ran out of ammunition.

Just before noon the circle of Mongols began to move around the Hungarian camp. They started off at a walk, broke into a trot, and were galloping within a dozen strides. Psin tensed. There was no reason for it—riding they shot and screamed, and their horses grew dark with sweat—but he'd seen it happen before. If nothing stopped them they would charge the camp, uncaring of the fires and the desperate men inside; it was a kind of blood fever. He galloped around the ring and found Batu.

"Open the west end of the ring. We may as well let them make a run for it. The remount herd is across the river, send your men over to change horses."

Batu nodded, yawned, and roared for his standardbearer.

The aimless, shifting circle stopped turning. When the banners spread out, half the Mongols rode obediently away to get fresh horses, and the rest stayed still, confused. Many of them got dried meat from under their saddles and ate it. Psin thieved Batu's kumiss jug while he wasn't looking and drank almost half of it. A gap opened up in the west side of the Mongol army. Everybody looked the other way, ignoring it.

For a while nothing happened. A burning wagon collapsed, showering sparks over everything, and two riderless horses burst out of the camp and raced away. Suddenly a dozen Hungarians charged for the gap. Their faces were wild with fear. They plunged through and fled west, throwing down their armor and their shields.

Inside the camp there was a great buzz of voices. Men packed the west end of the wagon ring. They flung the wagons apart and ran for the gap. Psin stood in his stirrups, looking for the men on the fresh horses, and gestured that they should ride west. Arrows fell into the midst of the fleeing Hungarians, but they hardly seemed to matter. The whole camp was escaping.

Almost casually, a full tuman of Mongols on fresh horses started along after them. The trail was clear, marked with wounded and dead and armor the Hungarians had thrown down. Batu called orders, and the rest of the army swung around to pursue. Psin rode around to wake up Sabotai.

"Have we killed their King?"

Psin shrugged. "I don't know. We'll look, later. I'm going hunting. Your guard is here."

"We'll all meet in front of Pesth. Good luck." Sabotai lay back again and sighed. "I'm not as young as I used to be."

Psin laughed at him. He went to the remount herd and collected three horses on a line and started after the fleeing Hungarians.

He headed toward Pesth, gathering Mongols on the way. They found Hungarians hiding in ditches beside the roads, in forests, in small villages, and they killed them all. The villages they left alone. The plundering would come later. The Hungarians seemed to like hiding in churches, and Psin decided that among them, in their own wars, they never killed anyone in a church.

In the evening, he and forty other men rode into a big village with a church packed with runaways from the battle. The villagers fled from them into the fields. On the steps up to the church door armor lay in piles. A man in black coat sat among the heaps, his chin on his hands, and watched Psin ride up.

"This place is sanctuary," he said, in Latin.

"From me nowhere is sanctuary. Move."

"I will not."

One of the men behind Psin lifted his bow and shot. The man in the black coat fell backward with an arrow through his chest. Psin rode his horse up the steps and into the church. The place was mobbed with Hungarians. All kneeling, they prayed in loud voices. Psin turned his horse sideways and drew his bow. They saw him;

they shuddered. Tamely they waited for the arrows. His men padded into the church and began to shoot. Psin thought, Isn't this also blood fever? He took care with his shots, so that no one would suffer. His hands worked independent of his mind. When all the Hungarians were dead he ordered his men out again. He had to ride a little up the aisle to get room to turn his horse. Above the altar hung the symbol of the Christians. If they fought back, he thought, I might have given them mercy.

All the next day they did the same thing, riding toward Pesth. In one village, the women came to plead for the lives of the men taking refuge there. They knelt before Psin, their earnest faces turned upward, and held up their hands to him. He stood still, uncaring, not listening to their voices that he couldn't understand. When they saw that he was unmoved their voices died away into silence. Their eyes looked like bruises in their white faces. One girl was clinging to his coat. He bent down and loosened her fingers and walked out of their midst. His men had their arrows nocked. He nodded, and they began to shoot down the men before them. The women they left alone. When it was over they rode on.

TSHANT SAID, "IS IT ALL DONE?"

"All but the plundering," Psin answered. "You look saddle-sore."

"I feel as if I've never been out of the saddle." Tshant stretched his legs. "We had some good fighting. Those knights . . ."

Psin nodded. "I know all about the knights. How is Djela?"

"He's coming. I told him to fetch your present." Tshant grinned. "What is it?"

"You'll see. Tell me what's happened." He rose and walked around the yurt, flexing the muscles of his back. When he reached the masterpole he took down the kumiss skin and drank.

"We hold all of Hungary east of the Danube River. The whole of it is broken up into sections. Mine is from Pesth to the Szajo River, where we fought the big battle. Batu's is the stretch south of Pesth. When we've stripped our sections we're to set up some kind of government—waystations, a Mongol officer in each village to collect taxes and keep order, and all the rest of it. The King wasn't killed and Kadan will go hunting him soon. Batu has already struck some copper money."

"Where do I go?"

"You are to stay in my section until you're rested. Kaidu has the section just across the Szajo from me. He's there by now. When you're back in condition, it's up to Sabotai where you go."

"I'm in condition now."

"You aren't. You're tired. Sabotai was very impressed with what Baidar had to say about your command in Poland. So was I."

Tshant turned his face toward him. "I may fall on my face and weep with gratitude."

"I didn't mean to sound patronizing."

"You did." He sat down again.

Psin set his teeth together and frowned at him. "You haven't changed, have you."

"What does that mean?"

"I'd thought maybe you learned how to behave, in Poland."

"I didn't. Not a bit."

"That's—"

Djela burst in the door, and Psin got up. "Grandfather." The boy rushed over and threw his arms around Psin. "I missed you. I heard all about your battles."

Psin held him off, smiling. "You're stronger, you'll crush me. Remember my encroaching senility." He ran his eyes over Djela's face—the strong bones and the brightness of his eyes. "Ah. It's good to have you back."

"I got a new bow, and I escaped from a pack of knights—oh. Here's your present." He turned.

A man had come in after Djela and stood beside the door. Psin straightened, frowning, surprised. "Arnulf," he said.

The knight bowed. In slow Mongol he said, "Psin does me honor to remember me."

Tshant said, "I took him captive at Liegnitz. He fought very well, and he'd mentioned your name." He stood up. "I'm going. We'll talk later. Djela, come along."

The knight stepped aside to let them pass. Psin gestured to him to come farther into the yurt. "You've learned some Mongol."

"Yes. I can't understand much."

"Your accent is terrible. Speak Arabic." Psin lowered himself onto the couch. "Did the German Khan send you to help the Poles? I didn't think he would."

"I was there with my Order. Your army was close to German soil at the time." He looked relieved to be speaking Arabic.

"Oh. You hold small territories here. They fought you only twenty-two days after Sandomir fell."

"How wide are your countries?" the knight said, and smiled. "I can't be a slave. It's against my nature."

"What—oh. Don't worry. All my slaves talk back to me. Get me some kumiss—over there, on the wall. To your left. The cups are in that cabinet."

"Your son is a great fighter."

"My son is peculiar."

The knight took a plain gold cup from the cabinet and looked at it. Across his face a strange look passed. "Do you know what this is?"

"It's a cup." Psin peeled off his socks.

"It's a—" The knight searched for the Arabic word. He held the huge cup as if it were the skull of an ancestor. "Chalice," he said at last.

"Fine. Maybe I have my kumiss now?"

"But this is a holy object. It's used in . . . in our religion. To hold the blood of Christ."

Psin shut his eyes. "Put it away and get another one."

The knight set the cup in the cabinet and bent to look. The lamp-light struck the row of cups, so that a patch of gold reflection shone on his cheek. His hair gleamed. He got out a cup with a handle and filled it with kumiss and brought it over.

"I'm sorry," he said. "I forgot that you are heathen." He laughed. "It's odd that I should have forgotten."

"I shouldn't have told you that all my slaves talk back to me. Dmitri."

Dmitri came out of the back of the yurt. He glanced at the knight and back to Psin. In Mongol, Psin said, "This man is named Arnulf. He'll help you. Teach him Mongol."

"The Khan wishes. Shall I take him with me to the commissary?"

"Yes. He's been wounded, I think, so don't burden him. Arnulf." He dragged his mind back to Arabic. "Don't try to escape. We kill slaves who run away. And we would certainly catch you. I'll probably send you as a gift to your Khan before the end of the winter."

"Why?"

"Why send you?" Psin snapped his fingers at Dmitri and pointed to his boots, and Dmitri knelt to unlace them. "I'd have to feed you if I kept you, and I've got slaves enough. Or will have, when my women get here. I'll find you again, when we take Rome."

Dmitri drew off the boots, and Psin rose, barefoot. "Go on. Dmitri, give him the bay mare."

"The Khan wishes."

All the peasants had fled into the forests and the hills. Psin released the prisoners he had taken from the sacked villages, telling them that any who submitted to the Mongols would have his land back and the protection of the khans. He moved his campgrounds from the open plain to a wood, so that they would have shade in the heat of the summer. Two stone forts held out against his attacks, and he invested them tightly and let them starve. Tshant was not taking orders, as usual; they fought over it halfway through the spring.

Djela said, "Why do you fight?"

"Because he won't admit that I have authority over him."

"Oh." Djela looked at his hands. "Are my fingernails made of hair, like cows' horns?"

"I don't know."

The summer came in, hot and dry. Most of the peasants returned to Psin's section and rebuilt their villages. Psin rode around to see them all, taking Djela with him. Near each village a hundred Mongols made a camp. The village was to supply the camp with grain and hay, and the Mongols gave over a part of their hunting to the village, when they had more than they needed. Much of their plunder was in cattle and horses, which they herded.

Tshant said, "Sabotai says I am to stay here, with you."

Psin grunted. "I'll send him a message. He can put you with Mongke, if he wants."

"Anywhere but here?"

"Exactly."

Tshant leaned back on his elbows. "Suppose I don't want to go?"

Psin's temples throbbed. "You'll go. I can't take too much more of you."

Dmitri and Arnulf were chopping up lamb's meat in the back of the yurt, their eyes fixed on the two Mongols. Psin glanced at them and they looked quickly down. Tshant said, "But it's so dull, Father. And fighting with Mongke hasn't got the zest."

"You've got your own yurt. Get out of mine."

"No."

Psin lunged at him; Tshant bounded up and to one side, his fists cocked. Psin stood up straight and tried to stare down his nose. Tshant was too tall to let the gesture work. "Get out before I call my men."

Tshant whooped. "Gladly, gladly. Just to hear you admit

that—" He dodged Psin's kick and ducked out the door. Psin hunkered and yelled obscenities after him.

From the slaves' quarter came a muffled gasp. He looked back and saw the knight laughing, one hand clamped over his mouth. Dmitri was horrified.

"Arnulf," Psin shouted. "There's nothing funny about a son's lack of respect for his father."

Arnulf collapsed backward, weak with laughter. Psin picked up a bowl and threw it at him. The knight got up, wiping juice from his face.

"I beg your pardon. I wasn't laughing at you. It was what you said. Your swearing was . . . imaginative."

"Oh. Don't Europeans swear?"

"Yes. But not so well."

Psin sat down. "Even the Chinese say we're masters at it. Someday you should teach me your language. German. So that I can talk to your old master when I catch him."

"He speaks Arabic."

All the laughter had drained out of the knight's face; he looked as grave as usual. Psin thought he was wary of being questioned. Psin said, "Tell me about him."

"I . . . would rather not."

"How can it harm him? I'm sending you back to him, aren't I? You can tell him all about us."

The knight nodded and smiled. "That's right."

"It will make no difference. There is nothing that can stop us."

"God can stop you."

The knight used the Mongol word, Tengri, and Psin smiled. "Or God can help us. Without God's help, could we stand one day against you?"

"Nothing is possible without God."

"But now we rule Hungary. And well, too. All the peasants are very happy with us, they've made no rebellion."

"Serfs don't fight. Only knights may fight. Serfs grow food."

"Oh? You don't think if we were unbearable masters they would fight us?"

"Perhaps."

"Rijart, that Englander I had with me when I came to Pesth the first time, he says your Khan is irreligious."

The knight looked down. "So they say. I don't know. He likes to frighten people. Perhaps he only pretends. Or sees God differently than the rest of us."

"You are a priest. How can you follow him?"

"Because I love him. He is a great man. Nothing confuses him."

"Only God?"

The knight looked up quickly, smiling. "I doubt even God confuses Frederick. He may mislead him."

Psin smiled. "You've learned the language well enough to quibble in it. Maybe Europeans are born to that. We have news from the west that all your khans and noyons are asking each other for help, should we attack them. But they haven't attacked us. Are they afraid of us?"

"Who is not? Don't judge them by their words. They are all good fighters. I think sometimes if we had planned our attack better, at Liegnitz, we would have beaten your son and his men."

"He says you should have—he was taking orders from one of the Altun, you know, and the way he talks the orders must have been terrible. He lost almost all his men."

Arnulf shrugged. "It's done and over with. Shall I help Dmitri now?"

"Yes. Go on."

Psin's section contained one of the important roads from Europe to the east, and in the early summer merchants began to move along it. He questioned them carefully and gave them safe conducts throughout the dominion of the Kha-Khan, hoping that they would keep coming back with their information. What they told him didn't please him. There was no steppe to the west, and the forests were thick. Mountains crowded up the countryside. He reported it to Sabotai, who said, "You'll have to do thorough reconnaissance."

"Yes. I'll start in the late fall when the river freezes."

"When are you going to get to that village?"

"Oh. Yes. Pretty soon."

There was a village on an island in the Szajo River that hadn't been plundered, mostly because no one was sure whether it was Psin's or Kaidu's, who held the land on the far bank. In the middle of the summer Kaidu sent to Psin that if Psin would give him some troops he would take the village and they would divide the plunder evenly.

"I want you to go," Psin told Tshant.

"Ask me."

"Will you go?"

Tshant's eyes were opaque. He lifted the hand that held his reins and scratched his cheek, and his horse shifted. "Yes. I'll take Djela and my guard."

Djela was behind Tshant. He said, "Oh, good. I can try my new bow."

Tshant said, "But your share of the plunder is mine, Psin."

Psin took a short breath. "Don't anger me."

"I'm doing the work."

"We'll divide it. It's a rich village."

"I want it all."

Psin swiped at him and knocked him off his horse. Tshant's horse reared out of the way, and Djela caught the rein. Psin made his dun back up so that Tshant couldn't reach him.

"We'll talk about it later," he called. "If you need help, child, Mongke and his men are half a day's ride south of that village."

Tshant said, "Come back here and face me."

Psin laughed at him and rode off. He could hear Tshant's voice, but not the words, which he decided was fortunate. When he looked back, Tshant and Djela were riding off. He would have to go; he had accepted the order. Psin rode quickly home.

The knight was tending the bake oven behind Psin's yurt, and when Psin rode up he came over to hold the dun horse. He saw the expression on Psin's face and looked back the way he had come.

"Is something wrong?"

"Nothing. The world is full of pleasure. Have you milked the mares yet?"

"Dmitri did."

Psin dismounted. The knight went back to the oven and made sure there was enough fuel. He wore a Mongol shirt and boots; the fair skin of his neck was red from the sun. Psin had expected him to refuse to do slave work, but the knight had done everything asked him.

Every time he thought of Tshant his chest grew tight with

anger. Tshant was going to great lengths to provoke him. He thought, He wants to prove that he can beat me. Let him try. This time—

The village surrendered as soon as the Mongols approached. In the summer's heat the river ran so shallow that they could ride straight over to the island. Kaidu and Tshant stayed on the bank. Kaidu said, "We'll burn it."

Tshant looked over at him, surprised. "Why? The Khan's order is that they may live in their villages, as long as they have no weapons."

"They held out against us."

"No one came to attack them."

Kaidu's face darkened and he raised his hand. "I give the order to burn it."

Tshant looked over at the village. His men packed it, while Kaidu's, more numerous, waited half in the water. "I hold it. No. It doesn't burn."

"You Merkit pig—" Kaidu struck him in the face. Tshant rolled with the blow, straightened up in his saddle, and dove at Kaidu. He caught a glimpse of Djela's face, white and amazed, a little way from them. They fell together into the dry grass along the river bank. Kaidu kicked and scratched. Tshant reared back and slugged Kaidu in the jaw, and Kaidu bucked him off. He rolled down the bank into the water. Kaidu's voice rose in a wild shout over his head. He got up and clawed back to dry ground and grabbed Kaidu around the waist.

Djela called out. Horses were coming, and Tshant thrust Kaidu away, not wanting their men to see them fighting. Hands caught him from behind and flung him down. His blood hammered in his veins, and he sprang up, looking for the men who had laid hands on him. They were Kaidu's, and he lunged for them. They backed off.

"Hold him," Kaidu yelled.

Djela said, "Father. This way."

The men around Tshant seized him. He drove his fists and his knees into them. One man whined, and he felt bone break under his knuckles, but they clutched him, they brought him down with his face pressed into a smothering coat and his arms hauled behind him. He flung himself violently to one side, got an arm loose, and wrapped it around the nearest neck. His breath rasped through his teeth. Half a dozen hands pried his arm from around the neck.

Far off, people were shouting. He got both feet under him and stood up, six men hanging on his arms and shoulders. Kaidu was standing in front of him, smiling. Tshant took an awkward step toward him, dragging them all, but a boot caught him in the back of the knee and he fell on his face. They locked his wrists up between his shoulders. He tried to roll over. Boots pressed into his back. He couldn't move.

"Hold him," Kaidu cried, in a voice high as a girl's. "Stand clear."

The weight swung off his back and he started up. A whip slashed across his shoulders. In his rage he howled at the top of his lungs. The whip laced his back. They stretched out his arms and flipped him over, and he saw Kaidu's smiling face and the dark frightened faces all around him, and the whip coming down. He drove his heels against the ground but he couldn't break the hold. The whip tore at his face. He squeezed his eyes shut, ashamed that Djela should see his father whipped like a slave. The whip opened up his cheek, and blood soaked his collar. He threw his weight against the hands wrapped around his arms, but it did no good. The whip caught him right across the eyebrows. He could feel the pain, in spite of his anger. He gathered up his strength and heaved against the men holding him and sagged back, exhausted.

Abruptly they let him go. He lay still, panting. There was fighting, somewhere. Hoofs beat the ground around him. Djela's voice rose, young and sharp. Someone dragged him up and flung him face-down across a saddle. He locked his fingers around the girth, and the horse began to gallop. His fingers were cut; the horse's sweat stung ferociously. Someone was hanging onto his belt. He could not open his eyes; he felt himself losing consciousness.

Djela said, "Is he all right? Let me see him. Arcut—"

"He's cut up," Arcut said. "We have to get him somewhere safe, so he can rest. Look at the blood."

Djela put out one hand toward his father's head. The hair was painted with blood. He looked back toward the river. They had outdistanced Kaidu's men in the first rush, but dust spiraled up along their track; they were still being followed. Ahead was a spur of forest, and he nodded toward it.

"We'll go into the trees."

Arcut said, "Someone should go tell the Khan. Get us help."

"Yes. Ugen, you go, And—Tian, go to the camp of Batu Khan and tell him what has happened." Djela gnawed at his lip. Someone else. Someone else. "Kiak, Mongke Khan is camped down the river a little. Go find him. Tell him that I am his cousin and I beg his protection."

The three turned their horses and galloped off. Kaidu's men were closing in on the rest of them. Djela reined his horse around and headed for the trees at a gallop. Once inside the trees they could hold Kaidu off. His heart danced in his chest when he remembered the beating. Kaidu had enjoyed it. He had watched with a little smile on his face. Djela clenched his teeth. If he dies, he thought. What if he dies?

Tshant heard people talking. At first he thought they were far away, but he realized after a moment that they were only whispering. Feet stamped on a rough floor. He was lying belly-down on a couch, but he couldn't open his eyes, and he felt weaker than he ever had before.

"Wake up, Djela," Arcut's voice said. "Your grandfather is here."

Another couch sighed. "Grandfather—" Djela's light feet ran on the floor. By what Tshant heard he knew the building wasn't big enough for a yurt. He could smell meat simmering, and his mouth watered. He heard his father's footsteps come into the hut.

"Djela. What happened?"

"Kaidu whipped Ada. He's over here." A weight plunked down beside Tshant. "Ada, are you awake?"

"I can't open my eyes."

Psin was swearing in a soft voice. The light cloth covering Tshant's back lifted off. Psin's voice seemed to come from everywhere at once; it was vast, it was terrible. He said, "The blood's clotted his eyelids shut. Arcut. Get out of here."

Arcut left. Psin's voice dropped still lower. Something wet and cool touched Tshant's face, infinitely gentle. Djela said, "Will he be all right?"

"Long before Kaidu will," Psin said softly.

Tshant forced one eye open. Psin's hands were trembling. He began to murmur again, speaking Tshant's name over and over.

"Be quiet, old man. You're saying too much."

"Ingrate. If I didn't honor your mother I'd say she got you from a demon." His voice was dead flat. "How do you feel?"

"Hungry." Tshant opened both eyes. Psin's face was expressionless, but the eyes burnt; he tried to smile and could not, and his mouth twisted monstrously in the effort. He turned and spoke in Magyar, and a woman came over with a bowl of meat. Tshant pushed himself up onto his elbows. They were in a woodcutters' hut, and a small Magyar family huddled in one corner. The woman banged her spoon against the edge of the pot and went to join them. Psin stood back and Tshant gobbled food.

"He'll live." Psin started toward the low door.

"Father," Tshant said. "I fight my own feuds."

Psin turned back. A muscle twitched along his jaw. "I'll leave you enough of him to flay for a saddleblanket." He took the gold chain from around his neck and handed it to the Hungarian woman and left.

Tshant gulped the last of the meat, drank the gravy, and sat up, groaning. The pain raced up and down his back. "Go get Arcut. We have to go after him. How many men did he bring?"

"I don't know." Djela got up. The Hungarian woman was stroking the chain. Tshant put his bowl down and stood, shuddering. He took the rings out of his ears and gave them to her. His shirt and coat lay on the couch Djela had been sleeping on, and he put on the shirt. The lightest touch on his back made him wince. His legs felt weak. Djela came back in.

"Arcut says he has orders not to let you leave until you're well."

"I'm well. Go tell him he's my officer, not Psin's. Tell him we're riding."

"He says—"

Tshant swore. He ducked out the door and looked around for Arcut. The trees grew thick around the hut; a goat and some chickens stood in a pen to the right. Arcut rode up and said, "The Khan—"

"Damn him. How many men does he have?"

"At least two hundred—his home guard."

"Where's my horse? Those are better men than Kaidu's. Does he have remounts?"

"Yes."

Tshant's horse came up, and Arcut took it by the bridle so that Tshant could mount. He looked back over his shoulder. Djela was in the doorway of the hut. A Hungarian child stood beside him, one hand in its mouth. Arcut said, "It was the noyon who called us up to get you out of the fight, and who brought you here."

Tshant tried to grin, but it hurt his face. "He's a good boy."

Djela beamed. He moved away from the Hungarian child; their horses were trotting toward them. Tshant climbed stiffly into his saddle and tied his coat to the pommel. The stripes on his back had opened. He could feel the blood running down his spine. He rode quickly off through the trees, hoping the blood wouldn't soak through his shirt too fast and let the others know.

Kaidu had camped on a point of high ground between a river and a marsh. Fires burnt all around, so that nothing could get close without being seen, and sentries walked thick as a procession just behind the fires. Psin growled in his throat. Kaidu was taking no risks.

"Tajin. Take half the men and go down by the riverbank. I'll lead him down toward you. Go to the other side of the bridge."

Tajin rode off. Psin took his bow out of the case, flexed it, and took the top off his quiver. "The rest of you kill sentries."

"Long shots, Khan."

"Watch your aim. Get as many as you can. He can't stay there forever." He drew his bow and settled on his point of aim. When his target was just passing a fire he shot. The sentry took two more steps and fell.

Inside the ring of fires a man shouted, and others answered. Psin's men were shooting quietly, carefully, and another sentry wobbled off with an arrow in his back. Horses neighed. Psin jerked up his dun's head.

"They're coming out. Keep close to the river and watch me. Keep shooting." Psin trotted around toward the river, keeping low, and looked into the camp. Kaidu's men were saddling their horses. He shook himself: these weren't Poles or Hungarians or Russians, to be cowed. He nocked an arrow and shot, but he missed.

A stream of arrows poured out of the camp. Psin's men leapt back. He rode into their midst and called out orders—forty men drew off away from the river toward the marsh, and the rest waited, shooting at nothing. Between the fires Kaidu's men charged toward them.

"Hold up! Hold up, on the order of the Kha-Khan."

With the shout horses galloped into the space between Psin's and Kaidu's men. Psin thrust one arm out to keep his men back. That was Mongke. Kaidu's men yanked their horses to a halt and called out, and Mongke's voice cried, "This is Mongke Khan. Hold your bows or I'll have you all slain."

Mongke had only two men with him. They trotted back and forth between Psin and Kaidu. Psin cursed. If Mongke had come only a little later—

"Psin Khan. Come forward. Kaidu, come forward." Mongke wasn't shouting, but his voice was clear and crisp and everybody heard him. Psin kicked up his horse. Mongke pulled away from his outriders and waited, looking from Psin to Kaidu, riding up behind him.

"By what right do you use the name of the Kha-Khan?" Kaidu shouted.

"By the right of Yasa," Mongke said. "You might not make war on each other without the Kha-Khan's permission."

Psin turned his horse head to head with Mongke's. "He started it. Kaidu. Tell him what you've done."

"I know," Mongke said. "Nothing's worth breaking the Yasa for."

"My son—"

"Nothing. Give me light."

Kaidu's horse was on the other side of Mongke's from Psin. In the silence while they waited for the torch to be brought Mongke sat still and looked from one to the other. At last a man galloped up with a torch from one of the watchfires; the heavy light spilled over them all.

Kaidu said, "When my grandfather comes—"

"Be quiet," Mongke said. "This is a serious matter. If we were near the Gobi the Kha-Khan himself would deal with you. I take on myself the right and duty to judge."

"You are Psin's friend," Kaidu said.

"Mongke is Psin's friend; the Khan isn't. Each of you give me an arrow."

Psin muttered. His temper was cooling. He said, "You've messed up my night's hunting, Khan." He took an arrow from his quiver and handed it toward Mongke, head first.

Mongke took his arrow and Kaidu's and thrust them into his belt. "Your arrows are your pledges. Go home. I'll send a messenger to each of you to tell you when and where I'll judge you. In the meantime cause no trouble. Now go."

Psin turned his horse. His men were bunched up, waiting, and he called to them to move on south. When they were organized, he stopped his horse and looked back. Kaidu had withdrawn inside his fires. Probably he would camp there until morning. Mongke with his outriders trotted toward Psin.

"You meddle," Psin said.

Mongke laughed. "I saw your trap when I came down the river."

"What advantage do you get from this?"

"None. If I had the choice I would not get mixed up in it. But your grandson sent to me, and the messenger told me in front of witnesses."

"Hunh. Djela is starting to use his head."

"He's a good boy. As long as I have to play judge, I mean to do it properly. Don't expect me to be easy with you; you killed six of Kaidu's sentries and you had it in mind to kill them all, every one. Good-by."

Mongke galloped off. His horse moved with great long strides through the torchlight. Psin swung around and went down to the river to collect the men waiting there. He thought he would almost prefer to be judged by Batu than Mongke.

* * *

Tshant was already in the camp when Psin got back at dawn. Djela had told Dmitri that they had met Mongke halfway to Kaidu's camp and Mongke had sent them straight home. Dmitri looked surprised when he said that.

"He must be sick," Psin said. "To let Mongke shoo him off."

The knight Arnulf came over and helped Psin out of his coat. "We thought he had heard the news, maybe."

"Oh? What news? Dmitri, did the courier come from Kadan?"

"Yes." Dmitri went into the back of the yurt, and Psin sat down, sighing when the weight left his feet.

"What news?"

"Your wives are within a day's ride of here," Arnulf said. "All three of them."

"All—three—what?" Psin stopped pulling off his socks.

"Your ladies and your son's."

"Kerulu? She's come to Hungary? Have you told him?"

Dmitri said, "I sent a man over to his yurt, but he was asleep."

"God. Wait until she sees his face. Help me with these boots, and get me something to eat. I'm not sure whether I'm more tired than hungry or more hungry than tired." He looked at the seals on the message Dmitri handed him and tore it open. They dragged his boots off and he wiggled his toes.

"Here. Read this to me. Arnulf, you should learn Uighar script."

The knight looked up; he was kneeling, brushing the mud from Psin's boots. "I can scarcely read Latin, Khan."

Dmitri said, "In the name of God, Kadan the Drunk to Psin Khan."

"He's blunt, Kadan."

"The King of the Hungarians has gone south over the Danube. I shall have to wait until winter when the ice freezes to give chase. I have heard envoys from a city called Constantinople, who wish to send envoys to Batu Khan my cousin. They are going to Pesth to see him there. Is Sabotai ill, that I am to report to you and not to him? Thus, Kadan, in my father's name and the name of God."

"I'll answer him tomorrow. I'm going to sleep. Wake me when the women are almost here." He got up and pulled back the light cover on the couch. "And you'd better see that we have meat for a feast."

When he woke up, in the afternoon, they brought him news that Tshant was feverish. He went immediately over to his yurt. Djela was there, yawning, his face fuzzy with recent sleep. "Is my mother here yet?"

"No. I'm going to meet them." Psin went over to the couch where Tshant lay and looked down at him. His slashed face shone with fever. One of the two Hungarian women he had taken was washing his face and hands. He twitched in his sleep and mumbled, and she bent to whisper to him. Her eyes when she looked at Psin were wary.

"Can he eat?"

"He eats," she said. Her full lips pressed together. "When the other woman comes, let her feed him."

"Mind how you talk of the daughter of the Kha-Khan's brother." He put the back of his hand against Tshant's forehead. "Keep him warm."

"She shouldn't see him when he's sick. Not if she's not seen him for so long."

"She's seen him sicker than that."

He went out; Djela had gotten his horse and mounted. They rode east. Djela said, "He will get well, won't he? It was just the riding. When we got back his shirt was drenched with blood."

"He's not badly sick."

Yet. They rode at a slow jog. Ahead, they could see the wagons coming, under the dust the slow feet of the oxen raised. It was hard to keep from galloping. Djela began to sing, an old ballad of the Merkits that Psin hadn't known he knew. The wild sad music blended with the sound of the wind in the tall brown grass. A woman waved to them from the seat of the lead wagon.

If it were not for the different profiles of the land he could think he was in his home country. The air was the same, and the soft fall of his horse's hoofs on the steppe. Now he had his women again. But when he lifted his eyes beyond the wagons he saw no forest, no stony mountains.

Djela gave a cry and charged toward the wagons. He had seen his mother. Psin held his horse down. Djela's horse plunged up alongside the third wagon, draped in cloth-of-gold and fluttering with silk ribbons. The boy disappeared inside. Psin let his horse jog up to the lead wagon.

Artai said, "Psin, we come sooner than you might have wished."

"Not soon enough." Her smile sent the old familiar shock through him, as if now he could let go. He stood in his off stirrup so that he could reach her and they embraced.

"We've brought Kerulu," she said. "She came out in the winter from Karakorum."

"I heard. You look well." He stroked her hair. "What's that? He's big for his age."

The slave girl grinned and jiggled the baby. He had red hair and drooled. Artai said, "We thought he was strong enough to come with us. There was no one to leave him with."

"What does she think of him?"

"Not much. Go see Chan."

He pulled his horse away and went on to the next wagon. The curtains were tied back; inside, Chan sat on silk cushions, with two maids combing her hair. She looked at him coolly and said, "How much farther am I to be dragged?"

"Oh, a year's trek." He couldn't help laughing. She surveyed him expressionlessly. Abruptly the corners of her mouth twitched; she fought the smile, but her eyes, resting steadily on his, brimmed full of delight. He touched her cheek and rode on to Kerulu's cart.

Her clothes flashed in the sunlight. Djela was sitting beside her on the cushions, and she had her arm around his shoulders. "My son tells me he's been fighting," she said to Psin. Her cheeks were flushed. "Where is Tshant? Can't he dig himself out of his adulterous bed to come meet me?"

"He's been hurt," Psin said. "Not badly. You're just in time to nurse him lovingly back to health." He climbed into the cart to hug her. Her brocades scratched him. She smiled and let him get back on his horse.

"Karakorum is dull," she said. "Who wants to play games with a flock of other women? Psin, you're scarred." Her nose wrinkled. The flush in her cheeks was receding, and the bright birthmark on her cheekbone faded. "But you look no older. I wish I were a Merkit, to age so well."

"Better an old Yek Mongol than a Merkit in the prime of life."

Her eyes flashed. "That depends on the Merkit."

"And not at all on the Mongol?"

She laughed. One forefinger touched the mark on her cheek. "You forget, Khan, that I was born capable of any man. Or so the shaman said. Get me a horse. If he won't come to me, I'll ride to him. Djela, I'll take your horse."

"Ama—"

"You can stay with your little brother. He's in the front wagon." She scrambled clumsily to the side of the cart and reeled in Djela's horse by the reins. "Psin, help me." Under the brocade coat she wore silk trousers. She flung one leg across the saddle, while Psin held the horse, and undid the coat halfway up from the bottom. The horse shied from the flapping brocade. She took the whip from the saddle pommel and lashed the horse twice. It shot between Psin's horse and the wagon and streaked for the open plain, tail high. Psin trotted up to the lead wagon.

Chan said, "She is unwomanly, that one."

He glanced at her, looked after Kerulu, and said, "Hah." To Artai, he said, "I'll see you in the camp," and sent his horse after Kerulu's.

She was already far ahead. She had seen which way he and Djela had come, and she was following their track, but they had swung wide to make sure of meeting the train. He headed the dun horse straight for the camp and let it stretch out. The sun glinted in her heavy coat. He could see that she was having trouble with her horse, which wanted to get away from the coat. The horse slammed to a halt and spun entirely around. She clung easily. He knew she was laughing. The dun was running flat out. When Djela's black heard him coming, it took off again. Kerulu urged it on.

Psin was much closer now, and with each stride pulling up. She raised her whip, but the little black was already straining, and she didn't beat it. The camp lay ahead of her and to the north. She veered toward it. The dun surged up, its muzzle even with the black's girth. Her face was vivid with excitement. Her hair was coming loose from its bands, and long red strands flew out behind her like banners.

A herd of horses between them and the camp burst into a gallop and ran along beside them. Men called out, and a few slavewomen darted forward to shoo the chickens away. A goat bleated. They charged straight into the middle of the camp and Psin tightened his fist on the reins. His horse sat on its haunches to stop. The black bounced twice, slowing, and each time Kerulu had to snatch for the saddle to stay on. She looked over her shoulder at Psin and laughed.

"I've not ridden in months. Where is he?"

Psin pointed to Tshant's yurt with his chin. Kerulu rode over and dismounted. The knight Arnulf was coming toward them, and Psin sent him after Kerulu's horse. His dun was lathered and snorting. The knight led the black over and held Psin's rein.

"You'll have to walk them out," Psin said.

"I will. Dmitri says that we should put up another yurt."

"Oh. Yes. Naturally."

"She rides well. Do all Mongol women ride so well?"

"No. Only Jagatai's daughter."

Tshant said, "I don't feel sick."

"Liar," she said. She squirmed closer to him and pulled the cover over them both. His arms tightened around her, and the heat from his body scalded her. He nuzzled her hair.

"Kerulu."

"And besides," she said, "while I am gone and pining for you, you get a baby on a magnificent Russian girl with big eyes."

"She had hair like yours. She reminded me of you."

He was so close to her that she couldn't remember how unhappy she had been without him. After more than two years they lay under the same robe, skin against skin, their hands clasping. He was half-asleep again, but he was smiling.

"It's only just you should be sick. Your eyelids are gummy."

"It's your cousin's fault."

If she followed that line she'd only anger him. She stroked his cheeks and murmured to him until he started to fall asleep again. He was uncomfortable and she shifted him, smoothing the covers.

Water stood in a bowl beside the couch; she soaked a rag and washed his face.

"Artai says you and Psin aren't getting along again."

"Depends on the day. When one or the other of us is sick or in trouble, we get along almost like friends."

"This Russian girl must have been wonderful. They tell me he suffered the death ban because he wouldn't leave her."

Talk of the Russian girl made him nervous. She could tell by the way his mouth moved. One of the whipstrokes had caught the corner of his lip and puckered it. She stretched her arm across the couch so that he could put his head on it.

"My heart," she said. "Tell me again how much you missed me."

H OW FAR IS THE RIVER?" ARTAI SAID. SHE PICKED THROUGH THE basket of mushrooms one of her women had brought and nodded. "Yes, they're all good."

"Just over the horizon," the knight said.

"No, don't go. So that's why he won't let us leave the camp without an escort. Poor Chan." She smiled at Arnulf, and he smiled back. It was impossible not to love Artai. He sank down next to her again, and she picked up her sewing. "And across the river is freedom for you, of course."

He nodded. For a moment he thought she was trying to find out if he meant to try and escape, but she wasn't looking at him; she was threading an awl. "Do you miss it?" she said.

"Yes. Of course. No one likes to be a slave."

Her hands paused. "No one like you likes being a slave, no."

"I can't imagine anyone enjoying it."

"What? To be cared for, to be protected?"

"Oh." He thought of the serfs. "Yes, I can see that you're right, in some ways."

The door to the next yurt opened, and Chan came out. She had a cat draped over one shoulder. Artai called to her, but Chan either did not hear or did not care to. She sat down in the sun, threw her hair back, and stared straight ahead.

"Don't watch her," Artai said. "Psin is jealous of her."

"Dmitri told me." He turned back to Artai.

"Did you hear the yowling last night? One of her cats got into a fight with the dogs."

"I had to go out and help the Khan rescue it."

Artai laughed. "You don't have any marks. Psin's hands are all clawed up." She glanced toward Chan. "She's furious. She has him tonight, but I don't think he'll enjoy it."

Arnulf felt himself blushing. At first he had thought these women indecent, from the way they talked. He still wasn't used to it. He watched Artai sew a glove. The river was so close, so close.

Chan said, "This is just like the steppe, here."

"It's the last western steppe." Psin lowered himself onto the couch and lay back, his feet still on the floor. "I'm tired."

"What did you do all day?"

He watched her slaves move around the yurt, dishing out meat for him. In the middle of it all she sat still, her face set and unsmiling. "I talked all morning to a batch of round-eyed merchants, had dinner, and went over to the high pasturage to bring back some cattle."

"Tshant could have brought back the cattle."

"Tshant is still sick." He wasn't. He was up and roaring, and Psin had left the camp mostly to keep from knocking Tshant's front teeth through the back of his head.

"You all act as if he'd been mauled by a leopard." She took the bowl from the slave and brought it to Psin.

"He was very sick for a while." He hitched himself up on one elbow and ate the meat. Her women gathered up the dirty dishes and took them off. "What did you do all day?"

"Nothing. I sat in the sun. If I had a horse I could ride."

"I don't want you riding alone in this country. When I have nothing to do I'll ride with you."

"You are always busy." She was staring at him; her eyes had a fixed look, and her mouth was stubborn. "I'm bored. I want to ride when and where I wish. If I had a slave to carry a bow—"

He choked on a bit of meat. "You mean a man? No. You'd turn a eunuch into a wild stag. I'd have to kill him before the next new moon."

"Kerulu rides alone."

"Kerulu rides with Djela. Go with her, if you want to ride."

"I don't like her. And she doesn't go where I want to. Give me a male slave. I won't . . ." Her mouth twisted. "Betray you."

"The slave would."

"Give me the blond knight."

He started. He opened his mouth to swear at her and clamped it shut again. Her eyes were stony, and while he stared she lifted her gaze so that she looked over his shoulder, dismissing him. He pressed his hands against his thighs, swallowed hard, and rose. She said nothing, and when he left the yurt she did not call after him. At the door he turned and saw her kneeling beside the couch, staring. He went out into the darkness.

Arnulf. But the women had been in the camp only a few days.

His stomach clenched. He saw the knight's fair hair in his mind's eye. Chan and the knight. Chan's slender long legs and smooth arms, and the knight's broad shoulders. His palms were sweating, and he rubbed them mechanically against his coat. For a moment he could not breathe. The knight's long-fingered hands, and Chan's sweet skin. He stopped in the middle of the camp and looked out at the fires glistening all around him. But where he stood it was dark.

Artai and her women were chattering around their fire; when he came in they whirled, and their jaws dropped open. Artai scrambled up. "Khan, what's brought you here?"

"I live here. Sometimes." He went into the back of the yurt, where the slaves were. Arnulf and Dmitri were talking in low voices. He put his hand on his belt near his dagger. He could bring him to her one piece at a time. . . . They leapt up and bowed to him.

He fought to keep all the expression out of his face. Arnulf looked up; his eyes widened, and he glanced at Dmitri and back to Psin. "Have I done something wrong?"

Psin stared at him. The knight seemed to recoil into himself. Wide, blue, his eyes met Psin's. Psin's hand dropped to his side. His muscles loosened a little. "Do you want a woman, Arnulf?"

The knight looked more surprised. "It's not permitted to me, Khan. The rule of my Order forbids it."

"I didn't ask that."

Dmitri murmured, in Russian, "He's mad." Psin glared at him.

"Do you want a woman?"

The knight shrugged. "Sometimes. I'm a man. Yes."

"If I gave you one, would you take her?"

"No, Khan."

Psin tugged at his mustaches. He glanced at Dmitri, who was grinning, and Dmitri said, "If you're giving away women, Khan—"

"Be quiet. Arnulf, come with me."

He led Arnulf out through the front room, under the stares of his wife and her women, and into the twilight. Arnulf said, "Khan, I serve you as well as I can, but I can't do anything forbidden me."

Psin halted. Arnulf took two steps beyond him and turned to face him. Psin said, "Knight, all I want is that you keep your vows." He would know when he saw them together.

He started off again. Arnulf trailed him. Chan's grey and white cat was sitting beside the door when they reached it. It followed them in and leapt effortlessly onto a cabinet. Chan was sitting behind the fire, so that the light flooded over her face, with another cat in her lap. When she saw Arnulf, she smiled. Psin's throat closed. He looked at Arnulf, and his hand rose to his dagger.

The knight bowed to her. "Lady," he said.

Psin looked back at Chan. She was watching him, not Arnulf, and her smile was bright. Her eyes were bright. She said, "Thank you, Khan." Her rare smile deepened. "He may stay in Artai's yurt except when I want to ride."

Inside his ribs Psin's heart gave an absurd little beat. He looked across the fire into her eyes, amazed. The cat climbed softly onto her shoulder and sat there, watching him. He turned suddenly, aware of the long silence, and said to the knight, "Go. When she sends for you, you will attend her." The knight bowed and left the yurt.

He heard the soft plop of the cat on the cabinet leaping down. She wasn't smiling anymore. She lowered her eyes and let her face sink into the stillness she said kept away age lines. He went around the fire and sat down beside her.

"Most women enjoy it if their husbands are jealous of them."

She shrugged, brushing the cat off her shoulder. He put his hand to her cheek. She moved closer to him and rested her head against his chest; she shut her eyes.

Mongke's camp sprawled across both banks of a shallow stream, almost dry after the heat of the summer; dust hung over it like a pavilion. Psin had seen it long before they reached it, because of the dust. He remembered what Mongke had said, that he should not expect him to be easy. Tshant, riding next to him, said that if the judgment didn't please him he would have his revenge against Mongke as well.

"I shouldn't have let him turn me off, that night," he said. "I should have kept on."

"If he doesn't give us justice, we can overthrow it. He'll have me stand surety for you, and my authority is higher than his. If he does judge it properly, you'd better like it."

Tshant shoved him, and Psin shoved him back. Kerulu forced her horse in between theirs. "Don't fight, it makes me nervous. What do you think of my hawk? Isn't he good?"

Psin glanced at the hawk on her saddle pommel. "I like the big eagles better."

Tshant called, "He thinks because you favor him that he can turn a judgment against us. He can oil up Kaidu and Batu without losing us."

Kerulu hoisted up the hawk, so that its wings flapped in Tshant's face. "I'll set him on you if you don't keep quiet."

"Damn woman."

They rode into the camp. The rings were packed with people come to hear the judgment. Batu's men rode everywhere, shouting, already half-drunk. Psin dismissed the fifty men he had brought with him, and they went whooping off to harangue Batu's men.

"This is like a kuriltai," Djela shouted.

They rode toward the center of the camp, past yurts of silk, past crowds of men dressed in their fancy clothes. When they saw Psin and Tshant they cheered and rattled their daggers on anything nearby that was metal. The air was stiff with the smells of food cooking. A woman strode by, leading two white donkeys loaded down with bread, and Djela snatched out a loaf. Kerulu's hawk began to scream, and a pack of black dogs barked at them.

Batu's standard stood on the back of a platform built in the middle of the camp. When they came to it, they saw half a dozen men standing guard around it. Tshant said, "We should have brought our standard."

"It's in my chest at home."

"You should have brought it."

"I mean home by Lake Baikal, damn you."

Tshant glared at him. "We'll look like beggers."

"You'll look like a beggar. You were born a beggar. I've stopped trusting Artai."

Tshant kicked Psin's horse in the belly, and when it reared Psin tried to swing its forehoofs around to hit Tshant. Kerulu screamed and pretended to faint. Losing her balance, she slid out of her saddle, and Tshant had to go back to help her. Psin looked for Batu, did not see him, and turned his back on Tshant.

Mongke walked over, smiling. "Now we can get on with this. Batu is here, you know. In force. And Sabotai."

"Sabotai? Where?"

"In the yurt. When he rode out in the crowds they cheered him so much and blocked his way so heavily he couldn't move. They are cheering you, too. Batu they only saluted."

"Let's start." Psin dismounted and threw his reins to a young Kipchak standing in front of his horse. "I'm interested. I want to see how you handle this."

"So am I. Don't be belligerent. You know it was your grandson who got me into it." Mongke climbed up on the platform and looked around. He stood with his shoulders thrown back and his chin up; his eyes snapped. He signaled to someone beyond the crowd.

Tshant came up beside Psin and gave his horse to a slave. "What did he say?"

"Nothing much."

Two men jumped up beside Mongke and blew great snorting blasts on auroch horns. The shouting cut off immediately into a dense silence. Psin looked to his left and saw Kaidu, with Batu and his brothers behind him. The men with the horns yelled orders, and the crowd shoved back away from the platform, leaving a crescent before it where Tshant and his relatives and Kaidu with his could stand. Kaidu's wife wasn't there, although Psin knew that she had come in from the Volga camp early in the summer.

Mongke backed up two steps and stood under his standard. He cleared his throat. The silence grew tense and the crowd stirred. Somewhere a baby cried angrily. Mongke said, "In the name of the Kha-Khan, for the glory of the Eternal God, the Mongols, and Temujin Genghis Khan, and by the will of God. If there is a man here who doubts I have the right to judge this dispute, let him speak."

Silence. The children were quiet, and not even the dogs yapped.

"If there is a man here who will not abide by my judgment, let him speak."

Psin got one of his mustaches into his mouth and chewed on it.

Mongke, so small, so light, stood like a totem, and they all listened.

"Let it be so, then. You come to see two princes judged. There are two complaints. First, that Kaidu Noyon the son of Targai the son of Batu the son of Juji the son of Temujin attacked and injured Tshant Bahadur the son of Psin Khan the son of Tseyan Khan. And that Kaidu did this unfairly and without just cause, giving Tshant Bahadur no chance to defend himself."

Tshant snarled under his breath. Mongke's eyes flickered toward him. Psin wondered if Mongke could have heard the growl; he thought the wind covered it.

"The second complaint is that Psin Khan attacked the camp of Kaidu Noyon and killed six of his men."

Now Kaidu murmured. Mongke hunkered. "Psin Khan. Will you stand surety for Tshant?"

"I will."

"Batu?"

"I stand surety for my grandson."

Mongke leapt up. He shouted, "Sabotai Bahadur, do you stand surety for Psin and Batu?"

"I do," Sabotai shouted, from behind them all.

The crowd screamed Sabotai's name. Psin couldn't hear Tshant cursing for the noise. He spat the end of his mustache out of his mouth and glared at Mongke. Mongke grinned. No matter what he did now, his decision would stand. Psin swore.

The auroch horns blared again, and the noise crashed into silence. Mongke had sat down again.

"You have both broken the Yasa," he said. "The Yasa says no man may make war on another without the permission of the Kha-Khan. I have spoken with both Tshant and Kaidu, and it seems to me that the situation is thus. In the Polish campaign Tshant several times broke Kaidu's orders, or undertook operations without referring them first to Kaidu for approval. This was entirely within his rights as the commander of the vanguard. But Kaidu is young, and the Polish war was his first important command. He resented Tshant's ignoring him. He also believes he has reason to dislike Psin Khan. None of this came fully into his mind that day, but when Tshant again defied him he lost his temper."

"I had reason," Kaidu yelled.

Batu shook him quiet again. Psin frowned, remembering how Kaidu had looked, back in Russia, when they had mentioned the stigma that lay on Juji and his children. He wondered how Mongke had learned of it.

"In payment for the injury done," Mongke said, "I order that Kaidu give Tshant two herds of young mares with their spring foals."

Tshant and Kaidu bellowed in unison, the one that it was too little, the other that it was too much. Psin got one hand on Tshant's arm and held him back. He could see Batu doing the same thing with Kaidu. Tshant's face turned dark red with anger. Abruptly all the blood left his skin and he went livid white. He swung his head to scowl at Psin.

"Quiet," Mongke said. "Such is my judgment. Now, to the second complaint. It is most severely against the Yasa for any man to seek revenge against another without the word of the Kha-Khan. If it were a green youngster, we might excuse it. For a general it is shocking, especially in a territory where we might be at war within a day. Psin Khan, do you have any defense?"

Psin raised his head. "Blood right."

"Only the Kha-Khan has the blood right. Any other?"

"No."

Kaidu said, "He is a Merkit. One of the men he killed was a Yek Mongol. It was his arrow—let him die for it."

Batu wrestled him silent. Mongke said, "This is my judgment. For the injury done to Kaidu, Psin will pay him two herds of young mares with their spring foals."

Psin clamped his jaws shut. He turned and looked back to where Sabotai stood. Sabotai was smiling.

Kaidu said, "I will give up my mares only after I receive Psin's."

Mongke shrugged. "If neither of you gives the other anything, I shall consider the judgment carried out."

"Oh, no," Tshant roared. "My father owes me two herds of mares."

Psin let go of him and backed off, glaring. "Pig of a child." The people just behind him were leaping up and down with glee.

"Well," Mongke said. "We have another complaint registered.

Psin, will you make a complaint?"

"Yes," Psin shouted. "My son is a greedy—"

Mongke clapped his hands. "Yes. The complaint is that due to actions Psin Khan took on behalf of Tshant, he suffered injuries, namely saddlesores and—"

The people screamed. Psin called, "I've never been saddlesore in my life."

"And stiffness in his string finger. Since it is most grievous for a son to cause his father the slightest injury, let Tshant pay Psin Khan—"

"Two herds," the people yelled. "With spring foals."

"Let it be so," Mongke called. "By the acclamation of the people. This judgment is over." He jumped down from the platform. His red sleeves billowed around his arms. The crowd parted, and he walked through toward his yurt. On the way he passed between the beds of two banked fires. Psin looked over at Kaidu; Batu was speaking to him, in a low voice, his head bent.

"My cousin is much changed," Kerulu said.

Tshant said, "He's a sneaking, scheming . . ."

She laughed at him. The mark on her cheek grew bright and distinct. "I'm glad you're well. You weren't at all amusing when you were sick: you were so gentle. Let's go find my brother."

Tshant looked hard at Psin. "Did you teach him that? Did you tell him to do that?"

"No. I never taught you to try to ruin your old father, either. If you fight with Kaidu, I'll thrash you."

"Try," Tshant snarled. But Kerulu got him by the arm and hauled him off.

Psin turned and went through the crowd toward Sabotai's yurt. Now that the judgment was done the camp was giving itself up to eating, drinking, and playing games. A string of horses trotted by. They would be racing on the open ground west of the stream. Down where the yurts pinched in the corner of the square, two young men were putting up a puppet show. Children and dogs ran through the loosening crowd. Psin stopped before Sabotai's threshold to watch a moment. They were taking down the platform and building a target wall for a shooting contest.

"Come inside, Psin Khan," Mongke said, through the open door.

Psin crouched and went in. Mongke and Sabotai were drinking Hungarian wine beside the low fire. The yurt was stuffy and smelled of cooked meat. Psin sat down.

"Roll up the sides of the yurt. It's stifling in here."

"We can't," Sabotai said. "The people try to crawl in."

"What do you think of it?" Mongke said.

"Oh, it was very clever. Especially the way you justified fining Kaidu half as much as he deserved and Tshant and me twice as much." He reached for the ewer. "Kerulu brought some fine news from Karakorum."

"I know," Sabotai said. "Ogodai was sick again when she left. I've had dispatches. They're keeping him away from the wine and he's recovering."

"Oh?" Psin drank and wiped his mustaches. The end he had chewed was soggy. "She says differently. She says this time he ought to die."

Mongke said, "He's not old yet."

Sabotai only frowned. Psin said, "Why would Kerulu leave? Only if Turakina were ruling the Khanate."

"Why haven't we—oh." Sabotai scratched his jaw. "I see. Turakina tells us only what she wishes us to hear, of course. And if she has control of the dispatches . . ." He had always hated Ogodai's wife.

"The women," Mongke said. "Always the women. My mother wrote to me and said that Jagatai is also not well. She says Oghul Ghaimish has been casting spells again."

"Kerulu wouldn't know. She left Karakorum nine months ago."

"In the meanwhile," Sabotai said, "Batu is courting us all. He gave Kaidu a scolding for attacking Tshant—There's something wrong with that boy."

"Tshant?" Mongke said.

"Kaidu."

"He's malicious," Psin said. "He likes to see people hurt. Do we start raiding over the Danube soon? The Hungarians are getting bold."

"Yes," Sabotai said. "And I want you to start thinking about reconnaissance raids for this winter, too. Now that we've settled into Hungary."

*   *   *

Chan said, "Put it there, Arnulf."

"Yes, Lady." He put the rug on the ground and turned back the corners. The air was rich as wine. Autumn air, he thought. He tried to remember how the summer had smelled—hot, of course, and dusty, sweaty. But he couldn't actually remember. Chan sat down on the rug, arranged her robes to cover her feet, and spread out the thin Chinese parchment on the carpet before her.

Sitting to her left, he studied her. Her skin reminded him of heavy cream. She had told him about her children; he found it impossible that she could have grown sons. Chinese, he thought. How many different peoples there are in the world. How wonderful the variety of God's creation. He crossed himself. Once he had struggled against bitterness that God should have thrust him into the hands of these people, but now he recognized the plan, the reason, or as much as any man could see of the mind of God.

She was sketching, looking up occasionally at the plain before her. He tried to see what she was seeing—exactly how the plain looked to her. Brown and gold, it flowed on farther than he could see. The horizon was faintly purple with distance. A little way from them the river ran almost dry, and horses grazed among the scant trees on either bank, with Mongols keeping watch. They had had some trouble with Hungarians sneaking in to steal Mongol horses. Why a Christian would want such shabby, scrawny little horses Arnulf couldn't understand, except that a Mongol horse would trot until a normal horse would drop, turn around, and trot back again.

He started his afternoon prayers, watching the plain. Dmitri had said that the Mongols believed in one God, whom they called Tengri, and no other; many of them were Christians. "Quyuk, who may be the next Kha-Khan, is Christian. But his wife is a witch." Arnulf thought of the river and how easily it could be crossed. O God, he thought. Thy Will be done.

Chan was staring at him. He smiled at her, and she said, "What are you thinking about that makes you so happy?"

"Did I look happy?"

She nodded. Her face was still, almost set, but he had come to understand that it didn't mean she was angry. He said, "I was pray-ing."

"Oh. I used to pray, when I was little. To the Moon."

She changed brushes and made small red marks on the parch-ment. He went around behind her to see. The river and the trees were only lines, and the horses flecks of color, yellow and brown. She had drawn a herder, and his red coat seemed to fill up the whole slice of paper.

"You see things so much differently than I," he said.

"Of course."

The picture was pleasing to look at. He watched it while he prayed. When he was done, she had already finished and was pack-ing up brushes and inks. He helped her stow them in the pouches on her saddle and lifted her onto the horse. She gathered the reins, looking down at him, and said, "Stay here. Stay with us. Why go back to your own people and be conquered?"

"Lady, they are my people."

"The Chinese were mine. I came with the Mongols."

He brought his horse over and mounted. "They are my people. I have always . . . inclined toward the sin of discontent." He smiled. "You're happy here. I am not."

She looked away, toward the river, and turned her eyes back to him. "He will kill you."

His spine tingled. She had guessed; he had thought before that she was speaking of when the Khan would send him back to Rome. He said nothing. She made a face suddenly, so violent that he laughed, and with a kick started her horse at a canter toward the camp.

Djela ran in, towing a puppy by a rope around its neck, and said, "Batu said to ask you if he could talk to you." He flopped down on the carpet before the door, dragged the puppy into his arms, and began to wrestle with it.

Artai said, "Such courtesy from Batu?" She was combing out Psin's hair. With each stroke of the comb his head drew back.

"Djela," Psin said. "Go tell Batu Khan he may talk to me until they grave me."

Djela bounded up and left. The puppy lay panting on the carpet. Artai laid the comb on Psin's left shoulder. "Do your mustaches."

"All four hairs?"

She laughed. "If you didn't chew them they'd grow. Shall I leave when Batu comes?" She pushed the front section of his hair onto his forehead, so that it hung in his eyes.

"Do you want me to talk to a khan looking like a madman? Stay."

Batu came in, with Djela right behind. The puppy banged its tail on the carpet. Batu sat down. "I was going to see Kadan and I thought I'd stop by and see you. It's been a fine autumn, hasn't it?"

"I think the winter's always late here. Djela, fetch your cousin some kumiss. Or wine, Batu?"

"Kumiss," Batu said. He was smiling; he'd put on weight, so that he made a square solid shape in the middle of the carpet. "I wanted to ask you if there is ill feeling between us, because of what my grandson did."

"On your grandson's part, maybe. Not on mine. Tshant should have been more careful."

"Is he angry?"

"Yes. But I can handle him."

Artai cut his hair off evenly and began to braid it. Batu said, "And I can handle Kaidu. So much for that." He took the cup from Djela. Dmitri came through the yurt with a basket of chips for the fire on his shoulder and bowed.

"Is Kadan having any trouble?" Psin said.

"No. At least he's not said so. But he's been drunk since the middle of the summer. His tuman-commander is ruling for him. That's a cunning man."

"Huduk. Yes."

"You know him?" Batu looked surprised.

"I've heard of him. He's a Kipchak, and for a Kipchak to become a tuman-commander is interesting enough to be news."

"Well. Kadan's district is . . . almost a separate country, you know. Because of the hills. If he can rule it so well, maybe I can make him governor of the whole territory when we move on."

Psin licked his mustache into his mouth, remembered, and spat it out. He began to see what Batu was after.

"Do you think so?" Batu said.

"I doubt Huduk should be without a Mongol to keep watch on him."

"Ah." Batu hadn't touched his kumiss. Now he drank it in three gulps. "Who? Not Kadan. Would you do it?"

Artai's fingers clenched in Psin's hair, so that his scalp ached. His back muscles stiffened. "What do you mean?"

"Would you stay as my deputy in Hungary, when we go on west?" Batu leaned forward. "Sabotai can be talked into it. Tshant is a good general—he's itching to take your place in the army. Let him go on. And when we hold Europe, you can rule it all, in my name."

Psin let out his breath. "In the name of Batu Khan, or Batu Kha-Khan?"

Batu's eyes narrowed, and his mouth slipped into a smile. "That . . . would be . . . according to the will of God."

Artai got up and went into the back of the yurt. She called sharply to Djela, who had been listening rapt. The curtain fell between them and the two men. Batu said, "Well?"

"Let me think about it. You honor me. I'm not sure I'm worth it."

"Who but you could do it?"

"Your brothers."

"No. I know them better than you do." He got up. "Tell me when you decide. Don't be hasty. Talk to your son, if you wish."

Psin's head jerked up, but Batu had already turned his back to go. If Batu had mentioned this to Tshant—Psin got up and went into the back of the yurt.

"What will you do?" Artai said.

"Grandfather—"

"Be quiet. Don't tell Tshant. Artai—Djela, will you go?"

Djela ran off. Artai said, "At least he's not subtle, Batu. A third part of the world?"

"Well, it's not taken yet." He laughed.

"Will you accept it?"

"I don't know. Do you think I should?"

She put her hand on his sleeve. "I don't know. Maybe. Maybe

you should." Her eyes searched his face. "But don't, unless you want to."

"Women. Just don't let Tshant know."

"I won't."

He turned to go. Her women were pretending not to listen; their cheeks glowed. When he went out past the curtain, he heard the sudden bubble of their voices, and Artai's, quick and sharp, quieting them. Djela came in, the puppy in his arms, and looked up at Psin.

"May I tell Ama?"

Psin hunkered before him and put his hands on Djela's elbows. "No. Do you know why?"

"Because Ada will be angry if he knows and you do not accept."

"That, too. Batu told me . . . what he told me in confidence. He wouldn't want it around the camp. You keep quiet about it."

"I will."

Psin smiled at him. "I know." Djela was so much bigger, taller, with more heft to him, than he had been only . . . It had been Djela who had pulled Tshant out of Kaidu's hands, who had sent for Psin and Batu and strangely for Mongke. Psin stood up. "If I did, it would be for your sake."

"No," Djela said. "I wouldn't want it."

He went on into the back of the yurt. Psin sank down on the floor with his back to the couch; lacing his fingers together, he set his thumbs under his jaw and stared at the far wall and thought.

THE DAYS SHORTENED, AND THE COLD WINDS FLATTENED THE grass. Batu said nothing more, even after he came back from Kadan's territory in the south. Tshant and Kerulu went out hunting alone and stayed away for a full day and a night. Artai was scandalized.

"They are too old to act like that."

"They aren't," he said. "Unfortunately, I am. Let them alone."

Artai pressed her lips together and glared at him.

Chan said, later, "You never took me away hunting."

"I never thought you wanted to go."

"I didn't. But you never even suggested it."

"If I had, you would have—"

"You never think of me except as something nice for your bed."

"What are you trying—"

"Do you?"

"I think of you a lot. I do."

"You don't. I'm nothing but a broodmare to you. I wish I were back in China, where at least the men treated me like a woman."

"If there ever was a man in China—"

He broke off. Her eyes were snapping. He muttered under his breath. Her unexpected smile burst over her face, and she dove into his arms. "Keep me warm."

He tightened his arms around her. "Chan. You'll drive me to my death."

She was laughing, the sound muffled against his chest. He lay back, and she curled up against him. Her cats were sprawled all around the couch; they got up and purring started to lick Psin's face and Chan's, until they had to pull the covers over their heads to get away from them.

The next day he spent the whole afternoon talking to Kerulu about Quyuk and his mother and wife. Tshant came home just before sundown and Psin spoke with him a moment and left. When he went back to his own yurts, Artai said, "I'm glad you're finally here. I have work for Arnulf."

Psin stooped to sniff at the cooking pot. "Grouse? What does my coming here have to do with Arnulf?"

"Chicken. I sent him after you." She shook out a robe and folded it, with three of her women holding the other corners. "But I suppose whatever you were doing had—"

"You sent him after me?"

"Yes. He said you'd gone down to the—where is he?"

"I never saw him. Dmitri."

Dmitri looked in the door.

"Where is Arnulf?"

"I've not seen him, Khan."

"Get me a horse. Artai, I was over at Tshant's yurt all day. Where did he say I'd gone?"

"To the river to check on the herds." She sat down heavily. "And he took a horse—I said he could."

"God above." He pointed to the Kipchak woman, who was rolling up felt socks. "Go over to my son's yurt and tell him that Arnulf has run off. Tell him to call up all the men around here." He took his bowcase from the wall and counted his arrows. The Kipchak woman trotted out, holding up the slack in her trousers with one hand.

Artai said, "Be easy with him."

"The Yasa says he must be killed."

He went outside. The dark was filled with an unnatural soft wind. Dmitri ran up with the dun horse and held him while Psin mounted. Dmitri said, "Khan, you were too easy with him. He never understood—"

"Don't criticize me. Get me a torch." The dun pawed at the ground and swung his hindquarters.

Tshant rode up on his dark brown horse. "Where did he go?"

"West. He has the white-footed bay horse, I think. That mare."

Four or five men milled in the darkness before Psin's yurt, getting on their horses. Dmitri came out with the torch and Psin thrust it into the lashings of his saddle.

"What did you do to him to make him run away?" Tshant said.

"Nothing. He's European. They're all crazy."

Dmitri took hold of Psin's stirrup and said, "Khan, don't hurt him. He doesn't know."

"He knows."

They rode out of the camp to the west. Before they'd passed the last yurt six other men had joined them—Kipchaks. Psin told them to spread out and yell if they saw anything. The plain rolled away before them to the river, and under the moonlight everything looked more distinct. They rode at a fast lope. Arnulf would have left the camp as if he went to find Psin—he'd told Artai that Psin was by the river so that he could go that way. Probably he had hidden in the trees on the bank until dark. Everybody around here knew Psin Khan's yellow-haired slave.

The plain looked black as tundra under the full moon. He could smell the pitch on the torch, and far to his left one of the riders carried a torch lit. That had to be a Kipchak. No Mongol would ruin his night vision with a lit torch.

They reached the river and searched quickly through the trees. Psin studied the far bank, looking for hoofprints. He was sure Arnulf had crossed by now. Tshant called out, and he started at a canter toward him, ducking branches; suddenly the dun snuffled the freshening wind and neighed.

Psin reined him to the riverbank, stood in his stirrups, and looked. The grass of the plain beyond the river crawled under the wind. The hills at its far edge were under the horizon. The dun was staring at something, and looking where he looked Psin saw the moving thing, all but lost between the huge sky and the plain.

He turned the dun and started into the river. Tshant called a question and Psin pointed ahead. The others leapt into the shallow water and waded their horses across. Scrambling up the far bank, the dun broke into a gallop, and Psin had to pull him back to a trot.

Arnulf was far ahead. If he reached the hills they'd have to get help to dig him out. The other Mongols had seen him, and they drew closer together and in a single rank trotted after the knight.

The moonlight was hard on Psin's eyes. Sometimes it seemed like a liquid. He stopped watching the knight all the time. The horse's trot relaxed him and made him realize he was hungry. He dropped the rein over the pommel of his saddle and rode with his hands on his thighs, wondering what to do with Arnulf. He was too easy with his slaves; everybody said so, and wondered how he could live so well in households full of people constantly expressing their own opinions. He'd never had a slave run away before.

He looked up. Arnulf was slightly nearer than before. He had to have seen them coming. If he turned back and surrendered himself, or even if he stopped and waited, Psin would only have to flog him.

The horses trotted along almost in a loose rank. He looked over at Tshant. In the moonlight Tshant's face was gaunt, and the bones stuck out like rocks from the earth. Psin called to him, and he veered over.

"What shall I do with him?"

"You know the Yasa. Kill him."

"I don't want to."

"Maybe he wants you to. Maybe he thinks his honor requires him to run away."

"Maybe." Why had he waited so long?

"The Christians believe that when they die they are made birds and taken up into the sky. So they aren't afraid of dying. If he's unhappy with us—"

"I told him I would send him back to Rome. I don't understand him."

"Neither do I. But just because we don't understand doesn't make it impossible."

Psin glanced at him, amused. "You sound like a shaman. Are you learning new things at your age? And trying to teach me, too."

"Kerulu told me that Djela acts older than I do, sometimes. He's stopped. He's waiting. Has he got a weapon?"

"Possibly." Psin looked. The white-footed bay was still, and Arnulf had dismounted. But Arnulf turned and mounted again and rode off. "If he had none when he left he has one now."

"A stone, a stick—"

"He's strong. You saw him fight. Would you like to go up against him, hand to hand?"

"No." Tshant grinned. "Not at all."

They trotted on. The knight had lost ground to them when he stopped, but he wasn't moving his horse out; he seemed content enough with this distance.

"Do you remember Kobe Sechen?" Tshant said.

"Yes."

"Whenever he sent off mounted slaves, he gave them wind-broken horses."

"I hope he never sent them off with urgent messages."

"We'd have caught him by now if that bay were windbroken."

"Am I to herd unsound horses, just in case I've got a restless slave? That mare has a bad hock. She'll go lame sooner or later."

They were catching up with Arnulf. The mare wouldn't have a chance to go lame. The dun horse trotted along, his ears pricked.

Tshant said, "Your horse is hard as rock."

"He'll go all day like this."

"Do you think it's the Ferghana incross?"

"God, no. It's the steppe pony. You remember that black stallion of mine—the one with the bald face and the white patch behind the girth? This horse is linebred back to him. All the black's foals had bottom. I should never have given him to Temujin."

"When the Ancestor asked—"

"He never asked. He told me. I warned him the black would never throw white foals, but he said if necessary he'd paint them white. He rode a colt by that black during the campaign he died on. It was a red bay, bright as blood, with no white hair on him. Beautiful black points. Arnulf's almost within bowshot."

Tshant turned and called to the others, "Don't hurt him. The Khan wants to talk to him."

They spread out again. Arnulf looked back, saw them, and turned his horse. Facing them, he waited. In his hands he carried a long stick, like a lance. Moonlight flashed on the tip. Psin frowned. The stick he must have cut from the trees beside the river; he'd tied his dagger to it. Psin pulled out his bow and an arrow.

"Arnulf," he called. "Surrender to me, and you'll get nothing but a whipping."

Arnulf said nothing. He raised his head. In the silver light his hair gleamed. He sat the bay mare like a knight, not like a Mongol; his stirrup leathers were let down so that his legs were almost straight, and he carried his head and shoulders back. Psin nocked his arrow.

The knight lowered his lance and held it out before him, with the butt clamped between his elbow and his side. Psin heard him click his tongue to the bay horse, and the bay burst into a gallop, headed straight for Psin. Psin threw one hand out to keep Tshant and the others from doing anything. The bay charged down on him. When the horse was so close he could not doubt his aim, he shot Arnulf in the chest.

The knight flew out of the saddle and rolled over once in the crisp grass. Psin rode to him. The knight lay on his back, one knee drawn up. His hands were locked around the arrow shaft.

"You're a fool," Psin said.

The knight muttered something in Latin and smiled. He shut his eyes. The arrow trembled in his chest. His mouth slipped open, and the arrow stood still. Psin dismounted and bent to make sure he was dead. He took the arrow by the shaft, put his foot on the knight's chest, and tore the head out of the wound.

"Go home," Tshant said to the other men.

They rode off. Psin threw the knight's body over the empty saddle and lashed it tight. They started back, more slowly to the others to let them get ahead. Tshant was fretting.

Abruptly, he said, "How can we rule these people?"

"I don't know," Psin said.

A few days before the winter solstice, Sabotai called up six tumans and prepared to cross the Danube; on the other side, there were four or five Hungarian towns still untaken. Psin went up to meet him to talk about reconnaissance. The vicious wind had made ripples in the scarred ice of the river. The whole army shivered around its fires.

On the day Sabotai had meant to cross, it began to snow. The three thousands already on the ice scurried back to the Mongol bank. Sabotai swore and postponed the crossing until the next day, but on the next day the snow continued to fall. Psin, who was not crossing, sat wrapped in his sable cloak and smiling listened to Sabotai's soft cursing.

"Laugh all you want to," Sabotai said. "The word's all over Hungary that you are supporting Batu for the Khanate."

"That's not so. He asked me, and I told him I would think about it."

"What has he offered you?"

"Nothing much."

"What precisely?"

"I won't tell you. He let it out, not I. Ask him."

"I did. He wouldn't say. Tell me."

"I've forgotten."

Sabotai gnawed his thumbnail, and the snow pounded the yurt.

Water dripped in through the smoke hole. Psin lay back. "I'm leaving within five days."

"Where for?"

"On my reconnaissance."

"Oh, yes. Well, do whatever you feel is necessary. Tell me what—"

"No."

"Damn you." The wind howled suddenly, and he ducked, but the yurt only shook a little. "This weather is terrible."

"They say such storms are common, this early in the winter. Later on it gets better."

"All right. Yes. You're going to follow the upper part of the Danube west to some stinking German city."

Psin nodded. "The merchants I've spoken to say there's a plain beyond it we could graze our herds on. I'll scout as far as I can."

"How many men are you taking?"

"Five hundred and Mongke."

"I know Mongke's going. You'll need more men."

Psin shook his head. "I don't think so."

"What's the name of that city?"

"Vienna. Beyond it there are more. I'll try to capture prisoners for information."

Batu crowded in through the door; snow blew after him into a furrow on the carpet. "Someone play chess with me."

"Not I," Sabotai said. "You've beaten me too often."

Psin turned his head toward the back of the yurt and bellowed for Tshant. Batu said, "Ah. I wondered where he was." Tshant came out, yawning as if he had been asleep. Through the tail of his eye he gave Psin a piercing look. Psin pretended not to notice. Batu, talking happily, set up his chess board and men, and Tshant without a word sat down across from him.

It snowed for two days more. Sabotai was entertaining all through—he ranted, beat his fists on the ground, stared gloomily into the swirling grey and white storm, and refused to eat. Djela played chess with Batu and lost only narrowly, while Batu cheered his every good move and explained why the bad ones were bad. He mentioned to Tshant that he had a little granddaughter just Djela's age, and Djela's mouth fell open. Tshant said that while his younger brother was unmarried Djela could not be pledged.

"But don't give her to someone else," he said. "Sidacai has to marry someday."

"We might take care of that," Batu said, smiling.

On the fifth day, at last, the sky cleared. From the door of the yurt the east bank of the river was a series of tiny hills; except for the dark circles around their smoke holes the yurts were covered with snow. A few horses stood in the lee of Sabotai's yurt, eating the hay dumped there. Pale as ice, the sun shone through a double ring, and the wind moaned over the crusted snow.

"It's going to get colder," Mongke said.

They roused their five hundred and pulled off to the north of the main army. Already a full tuman was riding up and down the far banks, bows ready. Occasionally the wind lifted the snow like a veil and hid the army from their sight. Sabotai was crossing his baggage trains.

"Let's go," Psin said. He turned to the standardbearer. "Black banner."

His men shouted. They started off at a jog, forging through the heavy drifts beside the river. From the army crossing came a bellow of a cheer, and Psin's men cheered back. The sun grew stronger, and the rings faded.

"Kadan is chasing the King of the Hungarians," Psin said. "He'll cover our southern flank. In the north . . ."

"After the pounding they took last winter they won't attack us," Mongke said.

"Don't be so sure. These are strange people."

"Yes. I hear you lost your German slave."

"He ran away, and I had to kill him."

Mongke said nothing. Their horses heaved themselves through a drift and came out on a place swept almost clear by the wind. "What are you thinking about?" Psin said.

"That if your German had been a Mongol he wouldn't have been as . . . good." Mongke looked up quickly. "Do you follow me?"

"As good for what?"

Mongke grinned. "I've forgotten what I was thinking about. Never mind."

"Bad habit."

"Not really."

They rode all that day; at sundown they reached the outskirts of Pesth—the rubble buried under the snow, only a remnant of a wall and a wrecked tower to show where the city was. Across the river was another city, far smaller. Lights burnt all around it. Probably they were waiting for the Mongol attack. Psin let his men camp in the lee of the wall. They had to dig the snow away, and the horses had trouble foraging. In the morning they continued on north.

Just after noon, Mongke said, "What has Batu promised you?"

"For what?"

"To help elect him Kha-Khan. He's offering us all something. I'm to have southern China, which is kind of him since we don't hold it yet."

Batu was fond of giving away things he didn't have. Psin said, "He's ready to provide all my children and grandchildren with wives of his own blood."

"Did you agree?"

"I said I'd think about it."

Mongke was staring at his horse's ears. He reached forward and brushed part of its mane over to the right side. "I shouldn't think he'd try to purchase you so cheaply. Indeed, did he try so cheap? If I ever aspire to the Khanate I shall have to draw up a list of the men I need and how much will buy them."

"Do you aspire?"

"Not now. I'm too young. Maybe. But it's locked into Ogodai and his bone, and . . . only drunkards might raise their eyes so far, it would seem."

"Batu is no drunkard."

Mongke grinned. "Batu will never be the Kha-Khan, either. Will he."

Psin looked away.

Just before dark, the river started to cut to the west. Psin knew this stretch of country well, because his section lay just east of it, and he took them to a good campground, where the snow was only a finger deep and the grass was still good. West of this he had never been. He had spoken to Arnulf about it once, but Arnulf had told him very little. He was surprised to find that thinking about Arnulf unsettled him even now. The merchants said that the hills started a few days' ride up the river, and that there were parts—waterfalls— that never froze. They said the hills became mountains. Psin began to worry about ambush and sent out scouts and a small vanguard.

All that day and the next it was bitter cold. Storm clouds flew across the sky into the south, and the damp wind sliced through even Psin's sable cloak. When they camped at night their hands inside their gloves were so cold that they couldn't undo their girths until the fires were lit and their fingers warmed. Several men, chopping wood, cut their hands to shreds and didn't notice until they saw the blood on the snow.

By sunset of the second day after the river had begun to bend, they were within sight of low hills to the west. North lay plain, and to the northeast, in the distance, were mountains with snowcamps. Tshant and Baidar had come south from Poland by this route; they said north of the Carpathians was only a great plain.

Mongke said, "It can't be colder than the Gobi."

"It's not. Just wetter." Psin crouched beside the fire, trying to keep all of himself warm. "Tomorrow, I think, we'll start meeting people."

"How pleasant. Why do you think so?"

"There are villages and forts all through those hills. This used to be a boundary. I don't want any fighting. If we see anything hostile, we'll run."

"I'm good at running," Mongke said. He gnawed on a hard piece of bread.

"I'm glad to hear it."

During the night Psin woke fifteen or twenty times; his nose was cold, and nothing he did kept it warm. If he buried it in his cloak he couldn't breathe. If he cupped his hands over his face, his hands as well as his nose got cold. If he lay close to the fire his mustaches and his hair began to singe. He was so glad to see the eastern sky grow light that he leapt up, put on an extra pair of socks, and walked around the camp to check on the horses.

They were all huddled together, tails to the wind, and marks in the snow showed how hard they'd worked to get grass. He dug

down and plucked some stems of grass and tasted it. It was poor
fodder. When he started through the hills it would be worse. He
squinted toward the west. Pine trees covered the slopes; white
patches, like scars, were scattered through the forest. Those would
be meadows. A hawk was gliding across the sky above the hills. He
went back and got the camp moving.

When they rode out he broke the band into five columns, sent
one under Mongke's commander across the river to ride the far
bank, and told the other three to ride north certain distances and
turn west. Mongke's column crossed the ice before the sun was entirely up and jogged along the far bank, even with Psin's column.
The two white banners floated back with the speed of the standardbearers' horses. Most of the men around Psin smeared their faces
with grease against the cold. The quick jog was warming them all
up. On the leadline the dun horse tried a twisting buck, and the
other three horses shied away from him.

The hills humped up before them, pinching the river. Mongke
sent three men out ahead—one rode slightly south of west. Birds
screamed in the trees when Psin's men rode under them.

The wind was howling out of the north. Psin worked his hands
inside his gloves. One half the sky was cloud, grey and dark grey-
blue, the other half was clear, and the line where the two met was
straight as a bowstring.

As soon as they were into the hills, Mongke's column swerved
away from the river and rode after the scout who had gone southwest. Hills hid them from sight. Psin swung his column around a
great lump of a hill and swerved right back to the river bank. The
ice looked unsafe here.

He saw signs of people living around here—smoke, bent under
the wind, rising two hills to the north, and traps laid out under the
trees. He wondered what they caught—beaver, perhaps, or hares.
Two of his men dashed off into the forest and returned almost at
once, laughing, with two hares each swinging from their saddles.
Psin rode over and looked at them; the hares were big, well-
muscled, and by the softness of their ears only yearlings.

"Take one," the two men said.

"I'm a Mongol. I eat gruel." He made a face and they laughed.

All morning, while they rode, men darted away to rob traps. The thought of meat made Psin's mouth water. He had never liked hare but he was beginning to develop a taste for it.

The river curved around to the north, and he reined in. There was a ford in the deepest part of the curve, smothered with snow, and ahead the ground was too even. Hills crowded down on the far bank and the edge of the flat ground. He rode to it, dismounted, and kicked away the snow. The ground was cut into semi-circles, thousands of them, and he nodded. This was a road. When he looked at the river ahead, he was sure that there was a village or a fort just around the bend.

"Bows up," he shouted. He mounted again. "And we'll go through at a dead gallop, if you can work it out of your horses."

They jeered at him. He put his horse into a lope and pushed it steadily up into a flat run. Where the ground was frozen under the snow it was slippery, and he took hold of the horse to steady it. His remounts strung out behind him, caroming into one another. They veered around a horn of rock and into a meadow, and on the hill behind the meadow stood a tower.

The Mongols yelled; from the tower high-pitched voices answered. Psin threw his leadrope to a passing man and jerked his horse to a stop. His men charged by behind him. He could see people in the tower windows—red and gold banners flew from its peak. The tower was of stone, block on block, without ornament or ledge. Only one gate cut the wall, and that was bound in iron.

Abruptly the gate clanged open, and knights galloped out. Psin's men were already out of sight, riding along the river. He spun his horse and raced after them. The knights shouted in a language he had never heard. He used his whip on his horse. Dropping the rein, he nocked an arrow and shot it, and the lead knight's horse leapt violently to one side. The sun flashed on the armor. Psin's horse leaned into a turn. Its knee drove frantically. Ahead, the other Mongols were waiting beside the river, poised to gallop off again. He gestured to them to keep going, and they whirled and streamed along the riverbank.

The knights pounded after. The ground was rough and rocky, but every few strides the Mongols would turn and shoot back. When the knights shifted up their shields they aimed for the horses. Psin felt the road veer north and shouted ahead, and the column

swung to follow the road. Only a few knights still clung to their
trail, far back, and when the Mongols turned away from the river
the knights stopped and went back home.

Psin called a halt and they let their horses blow. The pine-
covered hills made a fence all around them, with the road clear even
under the snow. South, behind and above the hills, he could see the
indistinct heights of mountains rimmed with snow. His horses
pawed for grass and got only a few mouthfuls, full of thorns.

"Bad graze," someone said.

"Let them eat the pine bark when we stop."

He remembered riding back from Khwaresm with Temujin,
when they had beaten Muhammed Shah; Temujin had wanted to
find a way home through the mountains that lay east of Khwaresm
and southwest of the Chinese. They had ridden through a clear cold
valley and onto a high ridge, and there they had seen the mountains
waiting for them, rock on rock like the knights' tower, but endless,
illimitable, rearing up their sheer faces to the sun, ridged and mor-
tared in snow. Temujin had turned back.

The mountains to the south, the Alps . . .

But ahead there were no mountains, only more of the shaggy
hills. He led his men on and listened to the scouts from the north
report on the whereabouts and condition of other roads.

They camped that night in the pines, made low fires, and banked
them as soon as their dinners were cooked. With the trees to hold
back the wind it wasn't so cold. The horses chewed on the trees,
eating young needles and the bark. Sentries kept watch from the
upper branches. At moonrise, Mongke and six of his men rode in
and reported; they were camped just across the river.

Psin crawled under a tree whose branches grew close to the
ground and wrapped himself in his cloak. The spongy cushion of
needles under him was dry and warm. He thought about what his
scouts had told him—ahead, more hills, flattening out a little, and
the river grew a little wider. A city great as Tver or Vladimir, with
a wall. The scouts had said there was little grassland, but beyond,
the merchants had said, there was a plain.

He rested his chin in his hands. If the Mongols bypassed Vienna
and took the plain beyond, they would have graze, and they could

starve the city out. But these hills were full of stone towers and knights, and the stretch of ground between Hungary and the plain was so hilly and close that the knights would have no trouble cutting the Mongol lines of communication. Rough terrain always bothered him.

On the other hand, if the Polish plain extended on far west of this point—

Mongke crept in under the branches. "You're too clever to live. Ah. It's warm in here. What's the matter?"

"I was worrying about taking Vienna."

Mongke settled down and pulled the hem of his cloak over his feet. "Um. Yes, with a six-day ride through country like this between Hungary and the city—Sabotai will have fun working this out."

"If we could clear the knights out of these hills—"

"We'd have to siege the towers and it would take a while. And you've noticed, I assume, that the towers stand wherever the road is narrow and the slopes alongside steep."

"Let Sabotai worry about it. You said you thought the summers are mild."

Mongke nodded. "There's game, too, even in the winter, although the deer I've seen are undersized and ribby. How do you suppose they fed their horses? Those stallions must eat twice what our horses do."

"Arnulf said that they grain them."

"Ah? What do they eat?"

"They raise enough food for themselves and their horses."

"Are there other roads?"

"There's one a day's ride north of us that seems to come from Poland. And another north of that, but it's through a forest and badly kept up. Windfalls and the like."

Mongke nodded and settled back, with his hands inside his cloak. "Have you ever wondered what we're doing here?"

For a moment Psin said nothing. Mongke lowered his eyes, taking it as a reproof, and Psin said, "Yes. Sometimes. Last summer, after I'd come here with the embassy."

"Did you . . . figure it out?"

"No. Temujin said that we should conquer the world. So we are."

Mongke's eyes rose. "We hold all the ground from here to China. Isn't it enough?"

"You know the reasoning. If we don't attack them, they'll attack us."

"So I've been told." Mongke stretched his arms out. "It says little for us, though, that we keep going just because we started. Sometimes I wonder if we could stop."

"I think we could. If we had to."

"Why should we have to? Why can't we just say, 'This is enough, we don't want any more,' and stop?"

Psin shrugged. "There can be only one overlord on the earth."

"I know. Temujin said so. Is there no compromise?"

Psin said nothing. He could feel the tension in Mongke, although he looked relaxed and even comfortable.

Mongke said, "The black lantern, you know. There are the four colors for the four directions. If you raised a green banner no one would know what you were talking about. But there can be no black light, so we use green lanterns to mean north."

"Why should we stop?"

"I don't know. It's just . . . Your German, you know. He wasn't happy with us. Why should everybody else be like us? And —don't you ever wonder what will happen to us if—when—we forget why we're doing it?"

Psin said, "We'll be beaten. I was beaten once, you know. I was conquered. It's not so terrible. Everything works toward God's ends or fails, and it's not all that important whether the ends of God are amenable to us."

"We have shed blood enough to choke us all, if we had let it in our own name and not God's."

"Yes." Psin looked at his hands. It was so pleasant to come up with smooth, well-modulated answers; why couldn't he think of any for the important questions? In the quiet he heard the horses chewing on pine bark, just outside his shelter.

"My father was a wicked man," Mongke said, finally.

"No."

"How can you deny it? Since I was born I've heard stories of his doings—"

Mongke's voice broke. Psin looked into his troubled eyes. "Did you know that he and I were friends?"

Mongke smiled. "No. I always assumed—you're so different. You're more like Jagatai."

Psin laughed and swatted at him. "That's no compliment. Of them all, Tuli was the most brilliant. I've never known anyone with more energy, except Temujin himself. He had Jagatai's temper, but he wasn't as arrogant."

Mongke looked down. His hands moved restlessly over his coat.

"Had you done what he did, you would be wicked," Psin said. "But in Tuli . . . He was more just than merciful, that's all."

"How can you call it justice, what he did? The massacres and the destroying—"

"What we all did. He and your uncles and your grandfather and Kasar and Sabotai and Jebe and Mukali and I . . ." They are most of them dead now. He put his hand to his forehead. "To us it is sin, this disorder in the world. We had to make it right. How could we know the world is so much larger than it seemed?"

"If God had wished it different, it would have been made different long ago."

But Temujin had not been born. . . . "You know I can't answer you. Talk to Quyuk. Talk to Tshant. How could a man my age answer any of you? You're all much more different from me than I was from my father."

Mongke grinned. "Is that so foul?"

"No. Go away and let me sleep." He dropped his hands in his lap. "Why ask me such questions? Can't your own kind say anything?"

"No. Them I fight with. You I talk to." Mongke crawled out through the branches. "Don't freeze to death. Who would I talk to, then?"

WHEN THEY RODE INTO SIGHT OF VIENNA THE CITY'S BELLS BEGAN to ring. The gates were shut, and the wall was crowded with people. Psin galloped his column down to the riverbank just east of the city. To its south, the hills rose into sharp peaks, like the tops of the towers. He could see children scrambling up onto the red-tiled roofs of the houses inside the wall.

The men on the wall began to throw things and shoot arrows. Psin looked across the river, saw that it was mostly flat, grassy plain until the forest closed in again, and led his men across to it. The plain tilted up into a little hillcrest, and he left his men behind to make a camp and rode to the height and looked west. The river wound like a strip of copper under the sun, down through trees and low hills. Against the hazy sky he could just see the tip of another tower, on this side of the river. In the south the hills rose toward the mountains, heavy with pine forest.

His men were walking their horses back and forth, shouting things at the Germans in the city. He jogged back to them and gave orders to set out sentries. "We'll ride out at sundown," he said. "Make sure the horses rest and eat." While they took the remounts up the slope, he rode west along the river to a place where the ice looked solid and crossed again.

People came running along the ramparts to follow him. He wondered how long it would take them to get some knights together. The wall was as thick as a man was tall, and small bushes grew out of the mortar. On this side there was another gate.

When he was just past it the gate opened, and a dozen men on horseback charged out. They weren't knights—they wore no armor. He lifted his horse into a gallop, not quite flat out, and moved along ahead of them. They did a lot of shouting. He swung back around the east end of the city, toward the river.

The gate there was already open. He grabbed his bow and three arrows. A mass of horses and men, half mounted, half waiting on the ground, filled the wide gate. He shot his three arrows one right after another. Horses collapsed in the road, blocking the way. The men behind him yowled. He whipped his horse into a dead run and leapt it onto the river ice.

The horse landed with all four feet braced and slid over the ice.

Psin clamped his legs around its barrel. The horse bowed its neck and pricked up its ears, coasted to a gentle stop, and took three sliding steps toward the bank. Two short arrows smacked into the snow just to Psin's right. He kicked the horse, and it bounded forward, slipping, went to its knees, heaved up, and flung itself up the bank.

On the city's bank the Germans cheered and shook their fists. He shouted, "Cowardly, soft, whining Germans, come chase me. Water for blood, that's what you have."

Their voices doubled. He made a sign at them and rode up to his camp. When they attacked him here, he would take some prisoners to question. He was beginning to see how Vienna could be taken.

Kerulu said, doubtfully, "He's a cute little baby."

Tulugai gurgled. Artai juggled him, crooned part of a lullaby, and flipped him over so that she could undo his coat. "Djela's very fond of him. Aren't you, Djela."

Djela said, "Oh, he's all right. For a baby. I don't see why I—"

"Couldn't go with your father," Kerulu said. "Because we are only women and must be protected." She pulled his hair playfully. To Artai, she said, "He has a long nose, this baby."

"He's part Russian."

"Here. Let me have him."

Chan said, "I don't like babies."

"I don't see why," Artai said. "Yours were all so good." She turned to Kerulu. "Chan's babies never cried or got sick."

Kerulu rocked Tulugai. "Djela had croup all the time when he was this one's age."

Chan said, "My babies were all good because they knew if they cried or got sick I wouldn't go near them."

"Have you told Tshant yet?" Artai said to Kerulu.

"No. I'm not sure." Kerulu put her hand on her belly. She was sure; she felt pregnant.

"Tell me when I can tell Psin."

"When I tell Tshant, he won't let me ride. He's terrible when I'm pregnant, he thinks I'll break."

"Or lose the baby," Artai said sharply. "I should think after the others died you'd be more careful."

Chan glanced at her. "You said the same thing when I was going to have Malekai, and I hadn't even lost one."

Kerulu remembered the others. Her throat tightened. "I hope this one is a girl." Her first baby had been a girl. Her heart had beat and beat, but she couldn't breathe, and she had died.

Chan said, "Don't worry. You were too young, the other times. That's why. Did you see the rings Psin brought me for my ears?"

"No," Kerulu said. Chan got up and went into the back of her yurt. Artai glanced after her and turned back.

"I'm sorry," she said. "I'm an old woman. I don't mean to make you unhappy."

Kerulu smiled. "You don't." This one she would not lose. Chan came back with the earrings; they were huge gold oblongs made of filigree. Chan put them on, and the other women exclaimed over them. Chan's eyes met Kerulu's, and Kerulu smiled, but Chan's face showed no expression at all, as usual.

Psin woke up with a start. Beyond the tops of the trees, the night sky was full of stars; the wind curled the trees over. His muscles were drawn tight, and he knew that something was wrong. He got up, shook the snow off his cloak, and slung it over his shoulders.

All around the fires, his men were only lumps under their cloaks. He got his standardbearer awake and whispered, "Do you hear anything?"

The standardbearer sat bolt upright. Psin straightened. Down the slope, in the meadow, the dark shapes of the horses stood hipshot, their heads sunk toward their knees. While he watched one horse jerked his head up—the dun. Its ears pricked and it looked east.

"Wake everybody up. Hurry."

By twos and threes, the other horses were lifting their heads; they all looked east. An owl hooted in the trees beside the meadow, and Psin caught a glimpse of the thick wings, the bulk of its body, swooping. He heaved his saddle up onto his shoulder and started down toward the horses.

The Mongols woke up smoothly, getting to their feet without a word. Those who had German prisoners roped to their wrists knelt to check the bindings. The dun horse snuffled and neighed.

Halfway to the horses, Psin whirled and shouted, "Scatter. Go home." He ran awkwardly through the rumpled snow to the dun. The horses were shifting, nickering and kicking at each other. He caught the dun and swung the saddle onto its back.

Now he could hear them. Armor clinked, and they wore spurs, even if they were on foot. Their horses were tethered to the east but the knights were slipping down on the camp from all sides. He wondered what had happened to the sentries. The dun fought the cold bit and he rammed it between its teeth.

"Watch, watch, watch—"

That was a sentry. Two Mongols raced down through the trees from the north, plunged into the midst of the horses, and leapt up bareback. Psin pulled the dun's tail through the crupper and hauled his girths tight. Half of his men were mounted. One dismounted to help another throw a prisoner face-down across a saddleless horse and tie him there.

A trumpet blew. Psin stepped into his saddle, got out his bow, and swept his eyes around. Men on foot were charging down the slopes on three sides. He thought, They want us to run east, right into their charge. Most of his men were mounted—all were—and the loose remounts were bunched in the middle.

"Scatter. Go home."

He spun the dun horse and charged west. A dozen men followed him. The knights, gleaming in their chain armor, faltered and waited, right at the edge of the trees. Horses neighed frantically behind him. He turned the dun and circled back, behind the remounts, and herded them up toward the knights. In a wide line a batch of Mongols burst into the trees to the south, and he heard the ring of iron and the high yelps of his men.

The remounts stretched out. Their tails streamed behind them, and their eyes rolled. Psin cased his bow and called to the men following him, and they moved around to keep the loose horses together and running. Their whips curled over their shoulders. The owl beat its wings heavily in the brush, fighting to get out of the way. Ahead, the knights broke and ran.

They pounded into the trees, and knights dropped on them like snow from the lower branches. Arms wrapped around Psin's neck. He dropped his rein and dragged at the fingers locked under his chin. The knight was breathing heavily in his ear. He could feel him trying to get a grip with one hand so that he could use the dagger in the other. The dun horse was getting ready to buck. Psin kicked away his stirrups and wrapped his legs around the horse's barrel, and the dun slammed to a stop, threw its head down, and bounded twisting into the air.

The knight fell heavily to the left. Psin clung to his saddle with one hand. The knight would not let go; he hung by his arms around Psin's neck, while the dun bucked and whirled and scraped up against trees. Branches flogged them. Psin caught a glimpse of wide pale eyes and a gaping mouth. The dun spun all the way around and smashed the knight into a rock, and the knight fell. Psin was half out of the saddle, and the saddle was slipping sideways. He lurched back. The breastplate was jammed against the dun's neck. With a scream the dun bolted into the deep wood, kicking and changing leads every three strides. Psin got back his right stirrup and drove his weight into it, and the saddle slid back into position. A branch smacked him in the face.

He could hear fighting, to the right and to the left, but behind him. He pulled the dun to a halt and looked around. He was headed northwest, and ahead was a high ridge. He could see horses moving along it—two loose, three ridden. Mongols. He headed the dun toward them, bending so that his nose brushed the dun's mane to duck the branches.

The three Mongols grinned at him. "It's wild down there," one said. "Look." He pointed.

Psin looked over his shoulder. Through the trees he could see the empty meadow, and among the trees the men struggling. Two Mongols broke loose and galloped due east through deep brush. The knights made a close ring around the meadow, but the Mongols were beating their way through to the outer edge and running, and on foot the knights couldn't follow. He could see dead men in clumps under the trees at the edge of the meadow.

"Let's go," he said. "There are more in the east, and mounted."

They started off, single file, east along the ridge. The two loose horses followed without being led. Before they had gone out of earshot of the fighting, four more Mongols joined them, two with prisoners draped in front of their saddles. The ridge tapered off into a low hill, and they rode down its north slope toward the narrow valley beyond. In the trees at the foot of the slope they collected six more loose horses and a wounded Mongol. Psin ordered a halt while the wounded man was tended and with his dagger cut gashes in the bark of six trees, where anyone passing would see.

When they moved on again it was dawn. They followed the valley north until it ended in another ridge, climbed the ridge, and rode east along it, through trees with dead leaves clinging to the branches. When the sun was up they made a fireless camp.

All that morning, more horses and Mongols found them. Several of the horses had saddles but no riders; one was carrying the mangled body of a prisoner, still lashed in place but torn by swords until there seemed to be no blood left in it.

Halfway through the day it began to snow; just before nightfall, when they rode on, the snow turned to ice. They rode all night through the storm, their teeth chattering, their hands frozen to senseless lumps. The ice falling made the whole forest hiss. The horses hated it. One of the wounded Mongols died, and they tied him onto his horse and went on.

The ice storm ended before dawn. When the sun came up the glare nearly blinded them. Every tree, every bush was cased in ice that glittered and changed color in the sun. The wind rattled the branches, and shards of ice fell onto their heads and shoulders. The footing was so slick the horses would not move out of a slow walk.

All that day, and for the three days after it, they stopped only to change horses and drink from streams, never to sleep or eat. Whenever they saw towers shining in the icy trees, they rode wide circles around them; they ran off the cattle from a village near their trail and butchered them and singed the meat and ate it, but they didn't make a camp until they reached the Hungarian steppe.

Tshant came into the yurt, scowling, and Kerulu gestured to one of the slaves to take him kumiss. He sank down on the couch and began to pull off his socks and boots. Djela trotted in, glanced at his father, and without a word circled around him and came over to Kerulu.

"He's angry. Is it because of the horses?"

Kerulu shook her head. Two nights before wolves from the hills had scattered the horse herd, and the men from the camp were still collecting them; the horses had drifted almost as far east as the Danube. Ever since they'd come to this district they'd had trouble with wolves.

She picked up the felt she was cutting and measured it against Djela's back. Whatever was bothering Tshant had nothing to do with loose horses. "Go out and play," she said to Djela.

"Play," he said. "I'm too old to play." He walked, very straight, to the door. Tshant was gulping down kumiss; he dropped the cup onto the carpet and sprawled on the couch with his arms behind his head. She picked up the baby and took it out to the cradle at the head of the couch.

"What's wrong?" she said.

"Psin is back." He stared at the ceiling.

She tied the baby into the cradle. "Oh." Psin hadn't let him go on the big raid into Poland. Maybe that was what it was. "Is he coming here?"

"He'll be here to sleep tonight."

"And you've found out about Batu's offer, haven't you."

"Yes. I have. Everybody knew about it but me."

"Don't cry," she said. "We still love you."

"Do I sound like that?"

She grinned at him over her shoulder. "Yes. If you'd feel better for it, I had to worm it out of Artai."

"Don't you think I ought to know about such things?" He took her by the wrist and laid her hand against his cheek.

"I decided not long after I married you that I'd never take sides between you and your father." She sat down beside him. "I don't plan to now."

"When I see him I'm going to lose my temper."

She frowned. When he spoke so softly, he was more trouble than when he ranted. She put her head down on his chest. "Is it warm out?"

"I didn't notice."

"Have you got all the horses back?"

"I think so."

"Talk to me."

"I am."

She sighed. He was stroking her shoulder, absently, and the silk began to chafe her skin. The baby gurgled. His baby, not hers. Artai had said that Psin never thought about her and Chan on campaign. How did she know? She said that it was good, in a way. They thought of nothing but fighting. Kerulu had heard, in the camp, stories of how Tshant had fought at the siege of the Hungarian city Gran—they said he had driven his men like a wind at their backs, straight into the faces of the defenders.

Djela said, "Grandfather's here."

Tshant's fingers clenched around her shoulder. She wrenched free, and he looked at her, amazed. "I'm sorry. I didn't mean to." He got up and barefoot went out the door.

Kerulu plunged after him. The full sunlight hurt her eyes. Tshant was walking slowly toward the middle of the camp, where Psin sat on his dun horse, talking to three men on foot. He lifted his eyes toward Tshant. The men looked around and backed off, saluting. Psin straightened, and the dun turned its head and scratched its shoulder with its teeth.

"Was it a good raid?" Tshant said. He was only four or five strides away from Psin.

"Good enough." Psin looked toward Kerulu. She pressed her hands into fists against her thighs; she would not warn him. The look on Tshant's face was warning enough. It was cool but she was sweating.

"I heard something of you and Batu," Tshant said pleasantly. He was close to Psin; he put one hand on the dun's nose, and the horse pinned its ears back. "I heard you could make yourself rich, if you wish."

Psin's mouth twisted. He dropped his rein on the dun's thick mane, threw one leg over the pommel of the saddle, and slid down. "I don't want to talk about it." He started toward Kerulu, leading the horse.

Tshant stepped in front of the dun, and the horse stopped dead to keep from treading on him. Psin jerked around at the end of the rein. Tshant said, "You'll talk about it to me."

Psin turned to face him. Kerulu's mouth was dry. She had never noticed how Psin's bulk made Tshant look slender. They faced each other—Psin's back was to her, but she could see Tshant's face settle into hard angles.

"I'm tired," Psin said. "I'm really not up to arguing with you. I'm not going to talk about anything in the open, either."

"Will you accept it?"

"I haven't decided. And it's mine to decide, not yours. Get away from my horse."

Tshant did not move. Psin's huge shoulders hunched, as if he were coiling himself. Kerulu almost heard his temper snap. He flung the rein to Tshant and said, "Tend him, then." He turned and walked toward Kerulu. His eyes were blazing. If he saw her at all he gave no sign of it.

In two leaps Tshant reached him, and his arm swung out to turn Psin around. Psin whirled. He ducked under Tshant's arm; his fist drove across the space between them. Tshant wobbled back. Psin leaned to one side and tripped him.

The men watching gasped. Tshant landed on his back in the mud. The dun horse, reins trailing, stood with its ears pricked watching. Tshant got slowly to his feet. He wasn't hurt, only collecting himself. Kerulu took a deep breath.

Djela said, "Don't worry, Ama. They always fight."

She jerked her eyes around to stare at him. He was sitting on his heels, watching without concern. She looked back at the men. They were circling, their arms loose at their sides. Before her eyes they shrank back to human size, and all the fear left her, and she almost laughed.

They lunged together and struggled, gritting their teeth in each other's faces, and leapt apart. Psin snarled something and turned and went to his horse. Tshant prowled nervously around, eyeing him, and when he was mounted walked stiff-legged toward Kerulu. Psin rode slowly off in the other direction. When they were shouting distance apart, Tshant spun around and yelled an obscenity, and Psin turned and gestured at him. Tshant spat in the dust. He came up past Kerulu and without speaking ducked into the yurt.

"What do you do that for?" she said, following him.

He flopped down on the couch. "I almost killed him once. I don't dare lose my temper. I might do it right, this time."

"That isn't what I meant."

He reached for the kumiss jug standing on the carpet beside him, fumbled, and knocked it over. She yelped, furious. The clear liquor puddled on the floor. One of the slaves charged out of the back with a rag. Kneeling, Kerulu snatched up the jug before it emptied.

"You clumsy ox. I like that carpet."

"I'm sorry. I'll get you another."

She clenched her teeth. "Look when you reach, will you?" She went over to the masterpole and filled the jug again. When she brought it back, his eyes were shut, and his bare, muddy feet were staining the furs on the couch. She put the jug down with a clunk and stamped off; she sat fuming in the back long enough for him to fall asleep before she realized that he'd knocked the jug over on purpose.

"What do you think I should do?" Psin said.

Tshant unwrapped one of the black elephants to his chess set and put it on the board. "You said it wasn't mine to decide."

"It isn't. But I want your opinion."

Kerulu came in from the back of the yurt, looked surprised, and left. Tshant took out the other black elephant and investigated a nick in the onyx. "Every time we move another piece breaks."

"You still have the jade one at home."

"I like this set better. I don't know. Do you want to accept it?"

Psin rubbed his jaw. Tshant dug out another wrapped piece. "No," Psin said finally. "Because I don't like Batu."

"There isn't much to him."

"But it would be . . . I don't know. I would dislike turning it down."

Tshant set the pawn on the board. "Your move."

"Tshant. I can't play chess."

"Pay attention."

"And declining it because I don't like him isn't a good enough reason."

Tshant frowned. "Make up your own mind."

"If I don't ask you you're angry; if I ask you you're angry. Nothing makes you happy." Psin moved a pawn.

"I doubt my happiness was anywhere in your mind."

"No, it wasn't." He moved again. Tshant picked up one of his pawns, smacked it down on the board, and sat back. Psin was a bad player, and at least he'd have the satisfaction of trouncing him at one thing today.

"What did your prisoners tell you?" Sabotai said.

Psin took his feet out of his stirrups and let them dangle. "The plain goes on, in the north, through the German territory beside the sea and down into the country of the French. They say there's grass the year round. It's a long ride."

Sabotai nodded. They rode past the last of the cattle and veered to head them back into the herd. The ground squished under the horses' hoofs. Across the muddy plain to the river, the cattle grazed and chewed their cuds. Their winter coats hung in dull patches on their flanks and shoulders; on the new grass great mats of hair showed where they had rolled to get it off. The first calves were already working their knobby legs.

"Kadan is back," Sabotai said. "He chased the Hungarian King south as far as a city called Ragusa. The King took ship. It's mountainous down there, except very near the coast. Boats, I thought. We could sail to Italy from there."

Psin looked at him and nodded. "Maybe." He reined in. Up from the river a dozen Mongols were riding, rope-poles in their hands. "The west is rich. What we've taken so far is nothing. Gold, furs, slaves, grain—"

"There are obstacles," Sabotai said. "I've heard it all in bits, but it seems . . . Those mountains. The Alps. How would they affect our communications?"

"We couldn't communicate across them. If there were an army in Italy and one in Germany. Maybe around, but through the mountains the odds would be too great that the couriers would be caught. We could send so large an army into Italy that they wouldn't need to be supported from the main army."

"How many men?"

"To take it all?"

Sabotai nodded.

"Twenty-five tumans."

"God above." Sabotai winced dramatically. "Do you know what you're saying?"

"I've thought enough about it. Yes. Twenty-five tumans."

"What if we did this? One army to advance along the plain in the north, another to ride through into the north of Italy, and a third to attack straight through to Vienna? All keeping roughly even."

"We'd have to do it that way. And we would need twenty-five tumans."

"Letting the southern flank operate independently once it was in Italy."

"Yes. You could let them block up the passes out of Italy. Pure defensive fighting."

"Name of God. Twenty-five tumans, with remounts." Sabotai shut his eyes. "When the vanguard reached Vienna the rearguard would still be on this side of the Danube."

Psin nodded.

"We need more reconnaissance. Another season's worth. You have to know that country so well you can tell me exactly which cities to take, which to bypass, how many men to the ten I can use, and the proportion of heavy cavalry to light."

"In a season I can do it. Where is Kadan now?"

"Just south of the Danube. He's crossing his army back into Hungary by boats, since the river's thawed. Batu is holding court just south of Pesth. Tshant is in the west, Batu's brothers are in the east. Mongke is in the north, Baidar is in the center, and we are here."

"Maybe we should hold a kuriltai."

"Not until I decide some things."

The dun horse lifted his head and stared. Psin squinted to see better. The rider was coming up from the southeast; his horse was tired, and stumbled once while Psin watched. Psin could see the glint of silver on the man's belt: courier's bells.

The wind touched his cheek and blew the dun's mane up straight. Small in the great plain, under the great sky, the courier galloped wearily toward them. Sabotai had seen him, but he said nothing. The dun horse shifted uneasily, and Psin thought, What if there's no reason to decide?

When the courier reached the cattle herd he called out, and a herdsman pointed up to Sabotai. The horse staggered toward them. Sabotai shook himself and rode forward. Without a word the courier held out his dispatches. Psin waited where he was. Sabotai pulled the wrappings off the top packet and opened it and read.

Psin knew when he had stopped reading, but Sabotai went on staring at the bit of paper. The courier, panting gently, waited to be dismissed. Sabotai turned his horse back to Psin. His face was slack and aged. He said, "We shall have to call a kuriltai now, I guess," and blindly handed Psin the paper.

Tshant said, "Is everybody here?"

Mongke yawned. "Only us. No thousand-commanders, no tuman-commanders. Just the Altun. I suppose they want advice on something."

"Hunh."

They were the only people in the big yurt, except for two slaves who were dragging in another couch. Tshant sprawled out on the carpet and drank kumiss. "What did you find in Poland?"

"Trouble. I don't like fighting those knights. It makes me nervous."

Kadan came in, and Tshant shouted to him. When Kadan turned his face toward them the words stuck in Tshant's throat. "What's wrong?"

"Nothing. I'm sober, that's all. I hate being sober." Kadan sat down and put his face in his hands.

"Hangover," Tshant said softly.

Mongke twitched. "Did you bring your wife?"

"Yes. I—"

Baidar walked in through the back and sat down beside Kadan. He spoke some soft words to him, looked over at Tshant, and jerked a smile onto his face. Baidar was pale as birch.

Something's wrong, Tshant thought. He stood up. "What is it?"

Kadan lifted his head and stared back. In the silence Tshant heard men approaching the front door. He looked at Mongke, whose eyes were slits, whose mouth was twisted into a bad smile. Suspicion beat at him. The door opened, and his father and Batu and Sabotai came in. Immediately after, Batu's brothers and Kaidu entered; they ranged themselves around the yurt. Kadan had lowered his face to his hands again. Kaidu and Tshant made routine threatening moves at each other.

Batu said, "Let you all know, now, that we are to mourn. The Kha-Khan is dead."

Very softly, Mongke said, "O God."

Nobody said anything. Psin sank down on his heels, staring at the floor. Tshant felt nothing but bewilderment. He looked at Kadan, tore his eyes away, and turned back toward his father. Outside, women began to wail, and men. The walls of the yurt blurred the growing sound of weeping.

Who will take care of us? Tshant thought. His hands were clammy and he rubbed them together. Quyuk—

Mongke said, "Sabotai, is the campaign done?"

"It's done."

Mongke got up and rushed out of the yurt. Noise swept in through the door. Before the flap fell closed they heard him calling in a strong high voice to his men. Baidar rose and helped Kadan get onto his feet, and Kadan took a deep breath. He said, "Batu Khan, thank you for the nice war." He started for the door and with each step grew more steady. Baidar followed him.

Psin got up and spoke to Sabotai. He caught Tshant's eye and bobbed his head toward the door, and Tshant went outside.

The camp was roiled up like a pond. Women sat in clumps before their yurts, sobbing and beating themselves on the breasts with their fists. Their children stared at them; some of the small children were beginning to cry. Three separate strings of horses trotted past Tshant—two of chestnuts, one of sorrels. He ducked around the last and thrust through a swelling crowd to his yurt.

Most kuriltais lasted for days. This one had gone on for two sentences. He looked for Kerulu and could not find her.

Djela ran up. "Is it true? Is it true?"

"Yes. Go find Arcut. And tell him to get horses for twenty men. Go on."

"But—but—"

"Go on!"

Kerulu came out of the back, her eyes sleek with tears. "Am I going?"

"Not with a baby coming."

"But my father—"

Psin came in behind Tshant and drew him aside. "Jagatai is dying too. I'll bring her. One of us should go straight to Karakorum."

"I'll go."

Kerulu sank down. Tshant sat beside her and put his arms around her, and she turned her face against his shoulder and wept. Tshant said, "When did he die?"

"Over three months ago. They kept it secret, damn them."

"Siremon is still under age."

"Yes." Psin chewed his mustaches. "It has to be Quyuk. You know how he is. Don't bargain with him, just tell him that we vote for him."

Kerulu said, "Can't I go? Please?"

Tshant hugged her. "If you could, I wouldn't leave here without you." He shut his eyes and leaned his head against hers. "You know that." When he looked up again Psin was gone. As soon as he could, he left Kerulu and went out.

Psin was on his own doorstep, and Tshant went quickly over to him. Mongke rode up, leading twenty-five men of his guard; his banner, stowed all through the campaign, floated wrinkled over his head. "I'll see you in Karakorum," he said. "Batu is coming this way. Tshant, are you leaving now?"

"As soon as my men are together."

"I can't wait. Try to catch up with me." Mongke galloped away.

"Can we hold Hungary?" Tshant said.

Psin shook his head. "The Altun will pull their tumans back to the Gobi. Without them Batu won't have the men."

Batu trotted up and turned his horse sideways so that he had to twist to face Psin. He looked hard at Tshant, frowned, and said, "Psin Khan, stay here. Stay with me—I'll make you a prince."

Psin shook his head. "I have my own people, Batu."

Batu's face contorted. "Damn you." He whirled his horse and rode off. Tshant shifted from foot to foot.

"We won't be home before the late summer," Psin said. "When I get the clan settled I'll come to Karakorum."

Across the camp a banner streamed, decked with black horse tails, and beneath it rode Kadan. Tshant bellowed to him, and

Kadan waved. He charged away to the east.

"I'm going," Tshant said. "There's Arcut with my horses. I'll see you in Karakorum."

Psin nodded. Tshant rushed off across the dusty, pulsating camp. Baidar cantered by, waved, and called, "Until the Gobi." Psin waved back. He saw his own banner through the dust: Tshant was riding out.

Artai said, "Are we going home?"

"Yes."

"Good." She went back inside.

The camp was almost empty. The dust began to settle into a patina over everything. Across the way from Psin one of Chan's cats clung mewling to the side of a yurt. In his mind's eye Psin saw the deep forests around Lake Baikal, the grass under the wind in the meadows.

Sabotai said, "What are you thinking about?"

"Nothing much."

"We could have taken Europe, you know."

Psin shrugged. "I doubt we could have held it." He wasn't interested anymore. He went across and got Chan's cat off the yurt and started back. Sabotai was smiling at him, and together they went inside.

Cecelia Holland

———————◆———————

Cecelia Holland was born in Nevada on New Year's Eve, 1943. Raised in Metuchen, New Jersey, she now lives in Woodbridge, Connecticut. A graduate of Connecticut College, she is the author of three earlier novels, *The Firedrake* (1966), dealing with the Norman invasion of England, *Rakóssy* (1967), a novel of the Turk-Magyar wars of the early sixteenth century, and *The Kings in Winter* (1968), the scene of which is Ireland in the early part of the eleventh century.